# The RED CONVERTIBLE

*Selected and New Stories*

*1978–2008*

# *The* RED CONVERTIBLE

*selected and new stories*
*1978–2008*

# LOUISE ERDRICH

HarperCollins*Publishers*

Nothing in this book is true of anyone alive or dead.

HarperCollins books may be purchased for educational, business, or sales promotional use. For information, please write: Special Markets Department, HarperCollins Publishers, 10 East 53rd Street, New York, NY 10022.

FIRST EDITION

*Designed by Joy O'Meara*

Printed on acid-free paper

Library of Congress Cataloging-in-Publication Data
is available upon request.

ISBN-13: 978-0-06-153607-6

08 09 10 11 12   OV/RRD   10 9 8 7 6 5   3 2 1

*For my mother and father*

# Contents

# Preface

EVERY TIME I WRITE a short story, I am certain that I have come to the end. There is no more. I'm finished. But the stories are rarely finished with me. They gather force and weight and complexity. Set whirling, they exert some centrifugal influence. I never plan stories as novels, but it seems that the way I often (but not always) write novels is to begin with stories that I have to believe, every time, that I have finished.

Most of the stories in this volume are those germinal ones that would not let go of me. Some waited many years to make their way into books. Some were first published in magazines. Others stayed in my notebooks until I decided to finish them for this collection and are published here for the first time.

I own a bookstore, or rather, as the drink takes the habitual inebriate, the bookstore owns me. Over the years, the remarkable bookseller who manages the store, Brian Baxter, has insisted that I publish the short stories. When I answer that many of the stories are contained in the novels, he is not satisfied. I like stories as stories, too, so I decided to take his advice.

With the help of my admirable friend Lisa Record, who found and cataloged the stories as they were originally published, I have put together this collection. In almost every case I have not changed the stories from their first incarnations. I tried not to tinker around with them and have edited only when I could not help it, or when, as with "Naked Woman Playing Chopin," the story was cut for length.

As for the new and hitherto unpublished ones, I am certain, as always, they are finished and will remain stories.

I would like to thank the original magazine editors who took a chance on me; my editor, Terry Karten, for her omniscient work on this project; Trent Duffy, as ever and always; and, finally, my parents, Rita Gourneau Erdrich and Ralph Erdrich, who told me stories from the very beginning.

# *The* RED CONVERTIBLE

*Selected and New Stories*

*1978–2008*

# The Red Convertible

I WAS THE first one to drive a convertible on my reservation. And of course it was red, a red Olds. I owned that car along with my brother Stephan. We owned it together until his boots filled with water on a windy night and he bought out my share. Now Stephan owns the whole car and his younger brother Marty (that's myself) walks everywhere he goes.

How did I earn enough money to buy my share in the first place? My one talent was I could always make money. I had a touch for it, unusual in a Chippewa and especially in my family. From the first I was different that way and everyone recognized it. I was the only kid they let in the Rolla legion hall to shine shoes, for example, and one Christmas I sold spiritual bouquets for the Mission door-to-door. The nuns let me keep a percentage. Once I started, it seemed the more money I made the easier the money came. Everyone encouraged it. When I was fifteen I got a job washing dishes at the Joliet Café, and that was where my first big break came.

It wasn't long before I was promoted to busing tables, and then the short-order cook quit and I was hired to take her place. No sooner than you know it I was managing the Joliet. The rest is history. I went on managing. I soon became part-owner and of course there was no stopping me then. It wasn't long before the whole thing was mine.

After I'd owned the Joliet one year it burned down. The whole operation. I was only twenty. I had it all and I lost it quick, but before I lost it I had every one of my relatives, and their relatives, to dinner and I also bought that red Olds I mentioned, along with Stephan.

THAT TIME WE first saw it! I'll tell you when we first saw it. We had gotten a ride up to Winnipeg and both of us had money. Don't ask me why because we never mentioned a car or anything, we just had all our money. Mine was cash, a big bankroll. Stephan had two checks—a week's extra pay for being laid off, and his regular check from the Jewel Bearing Plant.

We were walking down Portage anyway, seeing the sights, when we saw it. There it was, parked, large as alive. Really as *if* it was alive. I thought of the word "repose" because the car wasn't simply stopped, parked, or whatever. That car reposed, calm and gleaming, a FOR SALE sign in its left front window. Then before we had thought it over at all, the car belonged to us and our pockets were empty. We had just enough money for gas back home.

We went places in that car, me and Stephan. A little bit of insurance money came through from the fire and we took off driving all one whole summer. I can't tell you all the places we went to. We started off toward the Little Knife River and Mandaree in Fort Berthold and then we found ourselves down in Wakpala somehow and then suddenly we were over in Montana on the Rocky Boys and yet the summer was not even half over. Some people hang on to details when they travel, but we didn't let them bother us and just lived our everyday lives here to there.

I do remember there was this one place with willows; however, I laid under those trees and it was comfortable. So comfortable. The branches bent down all around me like a tent or a stable. And quiet, it was quiet, even though there was a dance close enough so I could see it going on. It was not too still, or too windy either, that day. When the dust rises up and hangs in the air around the dancers like that I feel comfortable. Stephan was asleep. Later on he woke up and we started driving again. We were somewhere in Montana, or maybe on the Blood Reserve, it could have been anywhere. Anyway, it was where we met the girl.

•  •  •

ALL HER HAIR was in buns around her ears, that's the first thing I saw. She was alongside the road with her arm out so we stopped. That girl was short, so short her lumbershirt looked comical on her, like a nightgown. She had jeans on and fancy moccasins and she carried a little suitcase.

"Hop on in," says Stephan. So she climbs in between us.

"We'll take you home," I says, "Where do you live?"

"Chicken," she says.

"Where's that?" I ask her.

"Alaska."

"Okay," Stephan says, and we drive.

We got up there and never wanted to leave. The sun doesn't truly set there in summer and the night is more a soft dusk. You might doze off, sometimes, but before you know it you're up again, like an animal in nature. You never feel like you have to sleep hard or put away the world. And things would grow up there. One day just dirt or moss, the next day flowers and long grass. The girl's family really took to us. They fed us and put us up. We had our own tent to live in by their house and the kids would be in and out of there all day and night.

One night the girl, Susy (she had another, longer name, but they called her Susy for short), came in to visit us. We sat around in the tent talking of this thing and that. It was getting darker by that time and the cold was even getting just a little mean. I told Susy it was time for us to go. She stood up on a chair. "You never seen my hair," she said. That was true. She was standing on a chair, but still, when she unclipped her buns the hair reached all the way to the ground. Our eyes opened. You couldn't tell how much hair she had when it was rolled up so neatly. Then Stephan did something funny. He went up to the chair and said, "Jump on my shoulders." So she did that and her hair reached down past Stephan's waist and he started twirling, this way and that, so her hair was flung out from side to side. "I always wondered what it was like to have long pretty hair," Stephan says! Well, we laughed. It was a funny sight, the way he did it. The next morning we got up and took leave of those people.

ON TO GREENER pastures, as they say. It was down through Spokane and across Idaho then Montana, and very soon we were racing the weather right along under the Canadian border through Columbus, Des Lacs, and then we were in Bottineau County and soon home. We'd made most of the trip, that summer, without putting up the car hood at all. We got home just in time, it turned out, for the Army to remember Stephan had signed up to join it.

I don't wonder that the Army was so glad to get Stephan that they turned him into a Marine. He was built like a brick outhouse anyway. We liked to tease him that they really wanted him for his Indian nose, though. He had a nose big and sharp as a hatchet. He had a nose like the nose on Red Tomahawk, the Indian who killed Sitting Bull, whose profile is on signs all along the North Dakota highways. Stephan went off to training camp, came home once during Christmas, then the next thing you know we got an overseas letter from Stephan. It was 1968, and he was stationed in Khe Sanh. I wrote him back several times. I kept him informed all about the car. Most of the time I had it up on blocks in the yard or half taken apart because that long trip wore out so much of it although, I must say, it gave us a beautiful performance when we needed it.

IT WAS AT least two years before Stephan came home again. They didn't want him back for a while, I guess, so he stayed on after Christmas. In those two years, I'd put his car into almost perfect shape. I always thought of it as his car, while he was gone, though when he left he said, "Now it's yours," and even threw me his key. "Thanks for the extra key," I said, "I'll put it up in your drawer just in case I need it." He laughed.

When he came home, though, Stephan was very different, and I'll say this, the change was no good. You could hardly expect him to change for the better; I know this. But he was quiet, so quiet, and never comfortable sitting still anywhere but always up and moving around. I thought back to times we'd sat still for whole afternoons, never moving, just shifting our weight along the ground, talking to whoever sat with us, watching things. He'd always had a joke then, too, and now you couldn't get him to laugh, or when he did it was more the sound of a man choking, a sound that stopped up the laughter in the throats of other people around him. They got to leaving him alone most of the time and I didn't blame them. It was a fact, Stephan was jumpy and mean.

I'd bought a color TV set for my mother and the kids while Stephan was away. (Money still came very easy.) I was sorry I'd ever bought it, though, because of Stephan, and I was also sorry I'd bought color because with black-and-white the pictures seem older and farther away. But what are you going to do? He sat in front of it, watching it, and that was the only time he was completely still. But it was the kind of stillness that you see in a rabbit when it freezes and before it will bolt. He was not comfortable. He sat in his chair gripping the armrests with all his might as if the chair itself was moving at a high speed, and if he let go at all he would rocket forward and maybe crash right through the set.

Once I was in the same room and I heard his teeth click at something. I looked over and he'd bitten through his lip. Blood was going down his chin. I tell you right then I wanted to smash that tube to pieces. I went over to it but Stephan must have known what I was up to. He rushed from his chair and shoved me out of the way, against the wall. I told myself he didn't know what he was doing.

My mother came in, turned the set off real quiet, and told us she had made something for supper. So we went and sat down. There was still blood going down Stephan's chin but he didn't notice it, and no one said anything even though every time he took a bite of his bread his blood fell onto it until he was eating his own blood mixed in with the food.

WE TALKED, WHILE Stephan was not around, about what was going to happen to him. There were no Indian doctors on the reservation, no medicine people, and my mother was afraid if we brought him to a regular hospital they would keep him. "No way would we get him there in the first place," I said, "so let's just forget about it." Then I thought about the car. Stephan had not even looked at the car since he'd gotten home, though like I said, it was in tip-top condition and ready to drive.

One night Stephan was off somewhere. I took myself a hammer. I went out to that car and I did a number on its underside. Whacked it up. Bent the tailpipe double. Ripped the muffler loose. By the time I was done with the car it looked worse than any typical Indian car that has been driven all its life on reservation roads which they always say are like government promises—full of holes. It just about hurt me, I'll tell you that! I threw dirt in the carburetor and I ripped all the electric tape off the seats. I made it look just as beat up as I could. Then I sat back, and I waited for Stephan to find it.

Still, it took him over a month. That was all right because it was just getting warm enough, not melting but warm enough, to work outside, when he did find it.

"Marty," he says, walking in one day, "that red car looks like shit."

"Well it's old," I says. "You got to expect that."

"No way!" says Stephan. "That car's a classic! But you went and ran the piss right out of it, Marty, and you know it don't deserve that. I kept that car in A-1 shape. You don't remember. You're too young. But when I left, that car was running like a watch. Now I don't even know if I can get it to start again, let alone get it anywhere near its old condition."

"Well, you try," I said, like I was getting mad, "but I say it's a piece of junk."

Then I walked out before he could realize I knew he'd strung together more than six words at once.

AFTER THAT I thought he'd freeze himself to death working on that vehicle. I mean he was out there all day and at night he rigged up a little lamp, ran a cord out the window, and had himself some light to see by while he worked. He was better than he had been before, but that's still not saying much. It was easier for him to do the things the rest of us did. He ate more slowly and didn't jump up and down during the meal to get this or that or look out the window. I put my hand in the back of the TV set, I admit, and fiddled around with it good so that it was almost impossible now to get a clear picture. He didn't look at it very often. He was always out with that car or going off to get parts for it. By the time it was really melting outside, he had it fixed.

I had been feeling down in the dumps about Stephan around this time. We had always been together before. Stephan and Marty. But he was such a loner now I didn't know how to take it. So I jumped at the chance one day when Stephan seemed friendly. It's not that he smiled or anything. He just said, "Let's take that old shitbox for a spin." But just the way he said it made me think he could be coming around.

We went out to the car. It was spring. The sun was shining very bright. My little sister Bonita came out and made us stand together for a picture. He leaned his elbow on the red car's windshield and he took his other arm and put it over my shoulder, very carefully, as though it was heavy for him to lift and he didn't want to bring the weight down all at once. "Smile," Bonita said, and he did.

THAT PICTURE. I never look at it anymore. A few months ago, I don't know why, I got his picture out and tacked it on my wall. I felt good about Stephan at the time, close to him. I felt good having his picture on the wall until one night when I was looking at television. I was a little drunk and stoned. I looked up at the wall and Stephan was staring at me. I don't know what it was but his smile had changed. Or maybe it was gone. All I know is I couldn't stay in the same room with that picture. I was shaking. I had to get up, close the door, and go into the kitchen. A little later my friend Rayman came and we both went back into that room. We put the picture in a bag and folded the bag over and over and put the picture way back in a closet.

I still see that picture now, as if it tugs at me, whenever I pass that closet door. It is very clear in my mind. It was so sunny that day, Stephan had to squint against the glare. Or maybe the camera Bonita held flashed like a mirror, blinding him, before she snapped the picture. My face is right out in the sun, big and round. But he might have drawn back a little because the shadows on his face are deep as holes. There are two shadows curved like little hooks around the ends of his smile as if to frame it and try to keep it there—that one, first smile that looked like it might have hurt his face. He has his field jacket on, and the worn-in clothes he'd come back in and kept wearing ever since. After Bonita took the picture and went into the house, we got into the car. There was a full cooler in the trunk. We started off, east, toward Pembina and the Red River because Stephan said he wanted to see the high water.

THE TRIP OVER there was beautiful. When everything starts changing, drying up, clearing off, you feel so good it is like your whole life is starting. And Stephan felt it too. The top was down and the car hummed like a top. He'd really put it back in shape, even the tape on the seats was very carefully put down and glued back in layers. It's not that he smiled again or even joked or anything while we were driving, but his face looked to me as if it was clear, more peaceful. It looked as though he wasn't thinking of anything in particular except the blank fields and windbreaks and houses we were passing.

The river was high and full of winter trash when we got there. The sun was still out, but it was colder by the river. There were still little clumps of dirty snow here and there on the banks. The water hadn't gone over the banks yet, but it would, you could tell. It was just at its limit, hard, swollen, glossy like an old gray scar. We made ourselves a fire, and we sat down and watched the current go. As I watched it I felt something squeezing inside me and tightening and trying to let go all at the same time. I knew I was not just feeling it myself; I knew I was feeling what Stephan was going through at that moment. Except that Marty couldn't stand it, the feeling. I jumped to my feet. I took Stephan by the shoulders and I started shaking him. "Wake up," I says, "wake up, wake up, wake up!" I didn't know what had come over me. I sat down beside him again. His face was totally white, hard, like a stone. Then it broke, like stones break all of the sudden when water boils up inside them.

"I know it," he says. "I know it. I can't help it. It's no use."

We started talking. He said he knew what I'd done with the car that time. It was obvious it had been whacked out of shape and not just neglected. He said he wanted to give the car to me for good now; it was no use. He said he'd fixed it just to give back and I should take it.

"No," I says, "I don't want it."

"That's okay," he says. "You take it."

"I don't want it though," I says back to him and then to emphasize, just to emphasize you understand, I touch his shoulder. He slaps my hand off.

"Take that car," he says.

"No," I say, "make me," I say, and then he grabs my jacket and rips the arm loose. I get mad and push him backwards, off the log. He jumps up and bowls me over. We go down in a clinch and come up swinging hard, for all we're worth, with our fists. He socks my jaw so hard I feel like it swings loose. Then I'm at his rib cage and land a good one under his chin so his head snaps back. He's dazzled. He looks at me and I look at him and then his eyes are full of tears and blood and he's crying I think at first. But no, he's laughing. "Ha! Ha!" he says. "Ha! Ha! Take good care of it!"

"Okay," I says, "Okay no problem. Ha! Ha!"

I can't help it and I start laughing too. My face feels fat and strange and after a while I get a beer from the cooler in the trunk and when I hand it to Stephan he takes his shirt and wipes my germs off. "Hoof and mouth disease," he says. For some reason this cracks me up and so we're really laughing for a while then, and then we drink all the rest of the beers one by one and throw them in the river and see how far the current takes them, how fast, before they fill up and sink.

"I'm an Indian!" he shouts after a while.

"Whoo I'm on the lovepath! I'm out for loving!"

I think it's the old Stephan. He jumps up then and starts swinging his legs out from the knees like a fancydancer, then he's down doing something between a grouse dance and a bunny hop, no kind of dance I ever saw before but neither has anyone else on all this green growing earth. He's wild. He wants to pitch whoopee! He's up and at 'em and all over. All this time I'm laughing so hard, so hard my belly is getting tied up in a knot.

"Got to cool me off!" he shouts all of the sudden. Then he runs over to the river and jumps in.

There's boards and other things in the current. It's so high. No sound comes from the river after the splash he makes so I run right over. I look around. It's dark. I see he's halfway across the water already and I know he didn't swim there but the current took him. It's far. I hear his voice, though, very clearly across it.

"My boots are filling," he says.

He says this in a normal voice, like he just noticed and he doesn't know what to think of it. Then he's gone. A branch comes by. Another branch. By the time I get out of the river, off the snag I pulled myself onto, the sun is down. I walk back to the car, turn on the high beams, and drive it up the bank. I put it in first gear and then I take my foot off the clutch. I get out, close the door, and watch it plow softly into the water. The headlights reach in as they go down, searching, still lighted even after the water swirls over the back end. I wait. The wires short out. It is all finally dark. And then there's only the water, the sound of it going and running and going and running and running.

# Scales

I WAS SITTING before my third or fourth Jellybean—which is anisette, grain alcohol, a lit match, and a small, wet explosion in the brain. On my left sat Gerry Nanapush of the Chippewa Tribe. On my right sat Dot Adare of the has-been, of the never-was, of the what's-in-front-of-me people. Still in her belly and tensed in its fluids, coiled the child of their union, the child we were waiting for, the child whose name we were making a strenuous and lengthy search for in a cramped and littered bar at the very edge of that Dakota town.

Gerry had been on the wagon for thirteen years. He was drinking a tall glass of tonic water in which a crescent of soiled lemon bobbed, along with a maraschino cherry or two. He was thirty-six years old and had been in prison, or out of prison and on the run, for exactly half of those years. He was not in the clear yet nor would he ever be, that is why the yellow tennis player's visor was pulled down to the rim of his eyeglass frames. The bar was dimly lit and smoky; his glasses were very dark. Poor visibility must have been the reason Officer Lovchik saw him first.

Lovchik started toward us with his hand on his hip, but Gerry was over the backside of the booth and out the door before Lovchik got close enough to make a positive identification.

"Siddown with us," said Dot to Lovchik when he neared our booth. "I'll buy you a drink. It's so dead here. No one's been through all night."

Lovchik sighed, sat, and ordered a blackberry brandy.

"Now tell me," she said, staring at him, "honestly. What do you think of the name Ketchup Face?"

IT WAS THROUGH Gerry that I first met Dot, and in a bar like that one, only denser with striving drinkers, construction crews in town because of the highway. I sat down by Gerry early in the evening and we struck up a conversation, during the long course of which we became friendly enough for Gerry to put his arm around me. Dot entered at exactly the wrong moment. She was quick-tempered anyway and being pregnant (Gerry had gotten her that way on a prison visit five months previous) increased her irritability. It was only natural then, I guess, that she would pull the bar stool out from under me and threaten my life. Only I didn't know she was threatening my life at the time. I didn't know anyone like Dot, so I didn't know she was serious.

"I'm gonna bend you out of shape," she said, flexing her hands over me. Her hands were small, broad, capable, with pointed nails. I used to do the wrong thing sometimes when I was drinking, and that time I did the wrong thing even though I was stretched out on the floor beneath her. I started laughing at her because her hands were so small (though strong and determined looking, I should have been more conscious of that). She was about to dive on top of me, five-month belly and all, but Gerry caught her in midair and carried her, yelling, out the door. The next day I reported for work. It was my first day on the job, and the only other woman on the construction site besides me was Dot Adare.

THE FIRST DAY Dot just glared toward me from a distance. She worked in the weigh shack and I was hired to press buttons on the conveyor belt. All I had to do was adjust the speeds on the belt for sand, rocks, or gravel, and make sure it was aimed toward the right pile. There was a pyramid for each type of material, which was used to make hot-mix and cement. Across the wide yard, I saw Dot emerge from the little white shack from time to time. I couldn't tell whether she recognized me and thought, by the end of the day, that she probably didn't. I found out differently the next morning when I went to the company truck for coffee.

She got me alongside of the truck somehow, away from the men. She didn't say a word, just held a buck knife out where I could see it, blade toward me. She jiggled the handle and the tip waved like the pointy head of a pit viper. Blind. Heat-seeking. I was completely astonished. I had just put the plastic cover on my coffee and it steamed between my hands.

"Well I'm sorry I laughed," I said. She stepped back. I peeled the lid off my coffee, took a sip, and then I said the wrong thing again.

"And I wasn't going after your boyfriend."

"Why not!" she said at once. "What's wrong with him!"

I saw that I was going to lose this argument no matter what I said, so, for once, I did the right thing. I threw my coffee in her face and ran. Later on that day Dot came out of the weigh shack and yelled, "Okay then!" I was close enough to see that she even smiled. I waved. From then on things were better between us, which was lucky, because I turned out to be such a good button presser that within two weeks I was promoted to the weigh shack, to help Dot.

IT WASN'T THAT Dot needed help weighing trucks, it was just a formality for the State Highway Department. I never quite understood, but it seems Dot had been both the truck weigher and the truck-weight inspector for a while, until someone caught wind of this. I was hired to actually weigh the trucks then, for the company, and Dot was hired by the State to make sure I recorded accurate weights. What she really did was sleep, knit, or eat all day. Between truckloads I did the same. I didn't even have to get off my stool to weigh the trucks, because the arm of the scale projected through a rectangular hole and the weights appeared right in front of me. The standard back dumps, belly-dumps, and yellow company trucks eased onto a platform built over the arm next to the shack. I wrote their weight on a little pink slip, clipped the paper in a clothespin attached to a broom handle, and handed it up to the driver. I kept a copy of the pink slip on a yellow slip that I put in a metal filebox—no one ever picked up the filebox, so I never knew what the yellow slips were for. The company paid me very well.

It was early July when Dot and I started working together. At first I sat as far away from her as possible and never took my eyes off her knitting needles, although it made me a little dizzy to watch her work. It wasn't long before we came to an understanding though, and after this I felt perfectly comfortable with Dot. She was nothing but direct, you see, and told me right off that only three things made her angry. Number one was someone flirting with Gerry. Number two was a cigarette leech (someone who was always quitting but smoking yours). Number three was a piss-ant. I asked her what that was. "A piss-ant," she said, "is a man with fat buns who tries to sell you things, a Jaycee, an Elk, a Kiwanis." I always knew where I stood with Dot, so I trusted her. I knew that if I fell out of her favor she would threaten me and give me time to run before she tried anything physical.

By mid-July our shack was unbearable, for it drew heat in from the bare yard and held it. We sat outside most of the time, moving around the shack to catch what shade fell, letting the raw hot wind off the beet fields suck the sweat from our armpits and legs. But the seasons change fast in North Dakota. We spent the last day of August jumping from foot to numb foot before Hadji, the foreman, dragged a little column of bottled gas into the shack. He lit the spoked wheel on its head, it bloomed, and from then on we huddled close to the heater—eating, dozing, or sitting blankly in its small radius of dry warmth.

By that time Dot weighed over two hundred pounds, most of it peanut-butter cups and egg salad sandwiches. She was a short, broad-beamed woman with long yellow eyes and spaces between each of her strong teeth. When we began working together, her hair was cropped close. By the cold months it had grown out in thick quills—brown at the shank, orange at the tip. The orange dye job had not suited her coloring. By that time, too, Dot's belly was round and full, for she was due in October. The child rode high, and she often rested her forearms on it while she knitted. One of Dot's most peculiar feats was transforming that gentle task into something perverse. She knit viciously, jerking the yarn around her thumb until the tip whitened, pulling each stitch so tightly that the little garments she finished stood up by themselves like miniature suits of mail.

But I thought that the child would need those tight stitches when it was born. Although Dot, as expecting mother, lived a fairly calm life, it was clear that she had also moved loosely among dangerous elements. The child, for example, had been conceived in a visiting room at the state prison. Dot had straddled Gerry's lap, in a corner the closed circuit TV did not quite scan. Through a hole ripped in her panty hose and a hole ripped in Gerry's jeans they somehow managed to join and, miraculously, to conceive. When Dot was sure she was pregnant, Gerry escaped from the prison to see her. Not long after my conversation with Gerry in the bar, he was caught. That time he went back peacefully, and didn't put up a fight. He was mainly in the penitentiary for breaking out of it, anyway, since for his crime (assault and battery when he was eighteen) he had received three years and time off for good behavior. He just never managed to serve those three years or behave well. He broke out time after time, and was caught each time he did it, regular as clockwork.

Gerry was talented at getting out, that's a fact. He boasted that no steel or concrete shitbarn could hold a Chippewa, and he had eellike properties in spite of his enormous size. Greased with lard once, he squirmed into a six-foot-thick prison wall and vanished. Some thought he had stuck there, immured forever, and that he would bring luck like the bones of slaves sealed in the wall of China. But Gerry rubbed his own belly for luck and brought luck to no one else for he appeared, suddenly, at Dot's door and she was hard-pressed to hide him.

She managed for nearly a month. Hiding a six-foot-plus two-hundred-and-fifty-pound Indian in the middle of a town that doesn't like Indians in the first place isn't easy. A month was quite an accomplishment, when you know what she was up against. She spent most of her time walking to and from the grocery store, padding along on her swollen feet, astonishing the neighbors with the size of what they thought was her appetite. Stacks of pork chops, whole fryers, thick steaks disappeared overnight and since Gerry couldn't take the garbage out by day sometimes he threw the bones out the windows, where they collected, where dogs soon learned to wait for a handout and fought and squabbled over whatever there was.

The neighbors finally complained and one day, while Dot was at work, Lovchik knocked on the door of the trailer house. Gerry answered, sighed, and walked over to their car. He was so good at getting out of the joint and so terrible at getting caught. It was as if he couldn't stay out of their hands. Dot knew his problem, and told him that he was crazy to think he could walk out of prison, and then live like a normal person. Dot told him that didn't work. She told him to get lost for a while on the reservation, any reservation, to change his name and although he couldn't grow a beard to at least let the straggly hairs above his lip form a kind of mustache that would slightly disguise his face. But Gerry wouldn't do that. He simply knew he did not belong in prison, although he admitted it had done him some good at eighteen, when he hadn't known how to be a criminal and so had taken lessons from professionals. Now that he knew all there was to know, however, he couldn't see the point of staying in a prison and taking the same lessons over and over. "A hate factory," he called it once, and said it manufactured black poisons in his stomach that he couldn't get rid of although he poked a finger down his throat and retched and tried to be a clean and normal person in spite of everything.

Gerry's problem, you see, was he believed in justice, not laws. He felt he had paid for his crime, which was done in a drunk heat and to settle the question with a cowboy of whether a Chippewa was also a nigger. Gerry said that the two had never settled it between them, but that the cowboy at least knew that if a Chippewa was a nigger he was sure also a hell of a mean and low-down fighter. For Gerry did not believe in fighting by any rules but reservation rules, which is to say the first thing Gerry did to the cowboy, after they squared off, was kick his balls.

It hadn't been much of a fight after that, and since there were both white and Indian witnesses Gerry thought it would blow over if it ever reached court. But there is nothing more vengeful and determined in this world than a cowboy with sore balls, and Gerry soon found out. He also found that white people are good witnesses to have on your side since they have names, addresses, social security numbers, and work phones. But they are terrible witnesses to have against you, almost as bad as having Indians witness for you.

Not only did Gerry's friends lack all forms of identification except their band cards, not only did they disappear (out of no malice but simply because Gerry was tried during powwow time), but the few he did manage to get were not interested in looking judge or jury in the eye. They mumbled into their laps. Gerry's friends, you see, had no confidence in the United States judicial system. They did not seem comfortable in the courtroom, and this increased their unreliability in the eyes of judge and jury. If you trust the authorities, they trust you better back, it seems. It looked that way to Gerry anyhow.

A local doctor testified on behalf of the cowboy's testicles, and said his fertility might be impaired. Gerry got a little angry at that, and said right out in court that he could hardly believe he had done that much damage since the cowboy's balls were very small targets, it had been dark, and his aim was off anyway because of three, or maybe it was only two, beers. That made matters worse, of course, and Gerry was socked with a heavy sentence for an eighteen-year-old, but not for an Indian. Some said he got off lucky.

Only one good thing came from the whole experience, said Gerry, and that was maybe the cowboy would not have any little cowboys, although, Gerry also said, he had nightmares sometimes that the cowboy did manage to have little cowboys, all born with full sets of grinning teeth, Stetson hats, and little balls hard as plum pits.

SO YOU SEE, it was difficult for Gerry, as an Indian, to retain the natural good humor of his ancestors in these modern circumstances. He tried though, and since he believed in justice, not laws, Gerry knew where he belonged (out of prison, in the bosom of his new family). And in spite of the fact that he was untrained in the honest life, he wanted it. He was even interested in getting a job. It didn't matter what kind of job. "Anything for a change," Gerry said. He wanted to go right out and apply for one, in fact, the moment he was free. But of course Dot wouldn't let him. And so, because he wanted to be with Dot, he stayed hidden in her trailer house even though they both realized, or must have, that it wouldn't be long before the police came asking around or the neighbors wised up and Gerry Nanapush would be back at square one again. So it happened. Lovchik came for him. And Dot now believed she would have to go through the end of her pregnancy and the delivery all by herself.

Dot was angry about having to go through it alone, and besides that, she loved Gerry with a deep and true love—that was clear. She knit his absence into thick little suits for the child, suits that would have stopped a truck on a dark road with their colors—bazooka pink, bruise blue, the screaming orange flagmen wore.

The child was as restless a prisoner as his father, and grew more anxious and unruly as his time of release neared. As a place to spend a nine-month sentence in, Dot wasn't much. Her body was inhospitable. Her skin was slack, sallow, and draped like upholstery fabric over her short, boardlike bones. Like the shack we spent our days in, she seemed jerry-built, thrown into the world with loosely nailed limbs and lightly puttied joints. Some pregnant women's bellies look like they always have been there. But Dot's stomach was an odd shape, almost square, and had the tacked-on air of a new and unpainted bay window. The child was clearly ready for a break and not interested in earning his parole, for he kept her awake all night by pounding reasonlessly at her inner walls, or beating against her bladder until she swore. "He wants out, bad," poor Dot would groan. "You think he might be premature?" From the outside, anyway, the child looked big enough to stand and walk and maybe even run straight out of the maternity ward the moment he was born.

The sun, at the time, rose around seven and we got to the weigh shack while the frost was still thick on the gravel. Each morning I started the gas heater, turning the nozzle and standing back, flipping the match at it the way you would feed a fanged animal. Then one morning I saw the red bud through the window, lit already. But when I opened the door the shack was empty. There was, however, evidence of an overnight visitor—cigarette stubs, a few beer cans crushed to flat disks. I swept these things out and didn't say a word about them to Dot when she arrived.

She seemed to know something was in the air, however; her face lifted from time to time all that morning. She sniffed, and even I could smell the lingering odor of sweat like sour wheat, the faint reek of slept-in clothes and gasoline. Once, that morning, Dot looked at me and narrowed her long, hooded eyes. "I got pains," she said, "every so often. Like it's going to come sometime soon. Well all I can say is he better drag ass to get here, that Gerry." She closed her eyes then, and went to sleep.

Ed Rafferty, one of the drivers, pulled in with a load. It was overweight, and when I handed him the pink slip he grinned. There were two scales, you see, on the way to the cement plant and if a driver got past the state-run scale early, before the state officials were there, the company would pay for whatever he got away with. But it was not illicit gravel that tipped the wedge past the red mark on the balance. When I walked back inside I saw the weight had gone down to just under the red. Ed drove off, still laughing, and I assumed that he had leaned on the arm of the scale, increasing the weight.

"That Ed," I said, "got me again."

But Dot stared past me, needles poised in her fist like a picador's lances. It gave me a start, to see her frozen in such a menacing pose. It was not the sort of pose to turn your back on, but I did turn, following her gaze to the door that a man's body filled suddenly.

Gerry, of course it was Gerry. He'd tipped the weight up past the red and leapt down, cat-quick for all his mass, and silent. I hadn't heard his step. Gravel crushed, evidently, but did not roll beneath his tight, thin boots.

HE WAS BIGGER than I remembered from the bar, or perhaps it was just that we'd been living in that dollhouse of a weigh shack so long

I saw everything else as huge. He was so big that he had to hunker one shoulder beneath the lintel and back his belly in, pushing the door frame wider with his long, soft hands. It was the hands I watched as Gerry filled the shack. His plump fingers looked so graceful and artistic against his smooth mass. He used them prettily. Revolving agile wrists, he reached across the few inches left between himself and Dot. Then his littlest fingers curled like a woman's at tea, and he disarmed his wife. He drew the needles out of Dot's fists, and examined the little garment that hung like a queer fruit beneath.

"'S very, very nice," he said, scrutinizing the tiny, even stitches. "'S for the kid?"

Dot nodded solemnly and dropped her eyes to her lap. It was an almost tender moment. The silence lasted so long that I got embarrassed and would have left, had I not been wedged firmly behind his hip in one corner.

Gerry stood there, smoothing black hair behind his ears. Again, there was a queer delicacy about the way he did this. So many things Gerry did might remind you of the way that a beautiful woman, standing naked before a mirror, would touch herself—lovingly, conscious of her attractions. He nodded encouragingly. "Let's go then," said Dot.

Suave, grand, gigantic, they moved across the parking lot and then, by mysterious means, slipped their bodies into Dot's compact car. I expected the car to belly down, thought the muffler would scrape the ground behind them. But instead they flew, raising a great spume of dust that hung in the air a long time after they were out of sight.

I went back into the weigh shack when the air behind them had settled. I was bored, dead bored. And since one thing meant about as much to me as another, I picked up her needles and began knitting, as well as I could anyway, jerking the yarn back after each stitch, becoming more and more absorbed in my work until, as it happened, I came suddenly to the end of the garment, snipped the yarn, and worked the loose ends back into the collar of the thick little suit.

•  •  •

I MISSED DOT in the days that followed, days so alike they welded seamlessly to one another and took your mind away. I seemed to exist in a suspension and spent my time sitting blankly at the window, watching nothing until the sun went down, bruising the whole sky as it dropped, clotting my heart. I couldn't name anything I felt anymore, although I knew it was a kind of boredom. I had been living the same life too long. I did jumping jacks and push-ups and stood on my head in the little shack to break the tedium, but too much solitude rots the brain. I wondered how Gerry had stood it. Sometimes I grabbed drivers out of their trucks and talked loudly and quickly and inconsequentially as a madwoman. There were other times I couldn't talk at all because my tongue had rusted to the roof of my mouth.

SOMETIMES I DAYDREAMED about Dot and Gerry. I had many choice daydreams, but theirs was my favorite. I pictured them in Dot's long tan and aqua trailer house, both hungry. Heads swaying, clasped hands swinging between them like hooked trunks, they moved through the kitchen feeding casually from boxes and bags on the counters, like ponderous animals alone in a forest. When they had fed, they moved on to the bedroom and settled themselves upon Dot's king-size and sateen-quilted spread. They rubbed together, locked and unlocked their parts. They set the trailer rocking on its cement block and plywood foundation and the tremors spread, causing cups to fall, plates to shatter in the china hutches of their more established neighbors.

But what of the child there, suspended between them. Did he know how to weather such tropical storms? It was a week past the week he was due, and I expected the good news to come any moment. I was anxious to hear the outcome, but still I was surprised when Gerry rumbled to the weigh shack door on a huge and ancient, rust-pocked, untrustworthy-looking machine that was like no motorcycle I'd ever seen before.

"She asst for you," he hissed. "Quick, get on!"

I hoisted myself up behind him, although there wasn't room on the seat. I clawed his smooth back for a handhold and finally perched, or so it seemed, on the rim of his heavy belt. Flylike, glued to him by suction, we rode as one person, whipping a great wind around us. Cars scattered, the lights blinked and flickered on the main street. Pedestrians swiveled to catch a glimpse of us—a mountain tearing by balanced on a toy, and clinging to the sheer northwest face, a young and scrawny girl howling something that Dopplered across the bridge and faded out, finally, in the parking lot of the Saint Francis Hospital.

IN THE WAITING room we settled on chairs molded of orange plastic. The spike legs splayed beneath Gerry's mass, but managed to support him the four hours we waited. Nurses passed, settling like field gulls among reports and prescriptions, eyeing us with reserved hostility. Gerry hardly spoke. He didn't have to. I watched his ribs and the small of his back darken with sweat, for that well-lighted tunnel, the waiting room, the tin rack of magazines, all were the props and inevitable features of institutions. From time to time Gerry paced in the time-honored manner of the prisoner or expectant father. He made lengthy trips to the bathroom. All the quickness and delicacy of his movements had disappeared, and he was only a poor weary fat man in those hours, a husband worried about his wife, menaced, tired of getting caught.

The gulls emerged finally, and drew Gerry in among them. He visited Dot for perhaps half an hour, and then came out of her room. Again he settled; the plastic chair twitched beneath him. He looked bewildered and silly and a little addled with what he had seen. The shaded lenses of his glasses kept slipping down his nose. Beside him, I felt the aftermath of the shock wave, traveling from the epicenter deep in his flesh, outward from part of him that had shifted along a crevice. The tremors moved in widening rings. When they reached the very surface of him, and when he began trembling, Gerry stood suddenly. "I'm going after cigars," he said, and walked quickly away.

His steps quickened to a near run as he moved down the corridor. Waiting for the elevator, he flexed his nimble fingers. Dot told me she had once sent him to the store for a roll of toilet paper. It was eight months before she saw him again, for he'd met the local constabulary on the way. So I knew, when he flexed his fingers, that he was thinking of pulling the biker's gloves over his knuckles, of running. It was perhaps the very first time in his life he had something to run for.

It seemed to me, at that moment, that I should at least let Gerry know it was all right for him to leave, to run as far and fast as he had to now. Although I felt heavy, my body had gone slack, and my lungs ached with smoke, I jumped up. I signaled him from the end of the corridor. Gerry turned, unwillingly turned. He looked my way just as two of our local police—Officers Lovchik and Harriss—pushed open the fire door that sealed off the staircase behind me. I didn't see them, and was shocked at first that my wave caused such an extreme reaction in Gerry.

His hair stiffened. His body lifted like a hot-air balloon filling suddenly. Behind him there was a wide, tall window. Gerry opened it and sent the screen into thin air with an elegant, chorus-girl kick. Then he followed the screen, squeezing himself unbelievably through the frame like a fat rabbit disappearing down a hole. It was three stories down to the cement and asphalt parking lot.

Officers Lovchik and Harriss gained the window. The nurses followed. I slipped through the fire exit and took the back stairs down into the parking lot, believing I would find him stunned and broken there.

But Gerry had chosen his window with exceptional luck, for the officers had parked their car directly underneath. Gerry landed just over the driver's seat, caving the roof into the steering wheel. He bounced off the hood of the car and then, limping, a bit dazed perhaps, straddled his bike. Out of duty, Lovchik released several rounds into the still trees below him. The reports were still echoing when I reached the front of the building.

I was just in time to sec Gerry Nanapush, emboldened by his godlike leap and recovery, pop a wheelie and disappear between the neat shrubs that marked the entrance to the hospital.

TWO WEEKS LATER Dot and her boy, who was finally named Jason like most boys born that year, came back to work at the scales. Things went on as they had before, except that Jason kept us occupied during the long hours. He was large, of course, and had a sturdy pair of lungs he used often. When he cried, Jason screwed his face into fierce baby wrinkles and would not be placated with sugar tits or pacifiers. Dot unzipped her parka halfway, pulled her blouse up, and let him nurse for what seemed like hours. We could scarcely believe his appetite. Dot was a diligent producer of milk, however. Her breasts, like overfilled inner tubes, strained at her nylon blouses. Sometimes, when she thought no one was looking, Dot rose and carried them in the crooks of her arms, for her shoulders were growing bowed beneath their weight.

The trucks came in on the hour, or half hour. I heard the rush of air brakes, gears grinding only inches from my head. It occurred to me that although I measured many tons every day, I would never know how heavy a ton was unless it fell on me. I wasn't lonely now that Dot had returned. The season would end soon, and we wondered what had happened to Gerry.

THERE WERE ONLY a few weeks left of work when we heard that Gerry was caught again. He'd picked the wrong reservation to hide on—Pine Ridge. At the time it was overrun with federal agents and armored vehicles. Weapons were stashed everywhere and easy to acquire. Gerry got himself a weapon. Two men tried to arrest him. Gerry would not go along and when he started to run and the shooting started Gerry shot and killed a clean-shaven man with dark hair and light eyes, a federal agent, a man whose picture was printed in all the papers.

They sent Gerry to prison in Marion, Illinois. He was placed in the control unit. He receives his visitors in a room where no touching is allowed, where the voice is carried by phone, glances meet through sheets of Plexiglas, and no children will ever be engendered.

DOT AND I continued to work the last weeks together. Once we weighed baby Jason. We unlatched his little knit suit, heavy as armor, and bundled him in a light, crocheted blanket. Dot went into the shack to adjust the weights. I stood there with Jason. He was such a solid child, he seemed heavy as lead in my arms. I placed him on the ramp between the wheel sights and held him steady for a moment, then took my hands slowly away. He stared calmly into the rough, distant sky. He did not flinch when the wind came from every direction, wrapping us tight enough to squeeze the very breath from a stone. He was so dense with life, such a powerful distillation of Dot and Gerry, it seemed he might weigh about as much as any load. But that was only a thought, of course. For as it turned out, he was too light and did not register at all.

# The World's Greatest Fishermen

I

THE MORNING BEFORE Easter Sunday, June Kashpaw was walking down the clogged main street of oil boomtown Williston, North Dakota, killing time before the noon bus arrived that would take her home. She was a long-legged Chippewa woman, aged hard in every way except how she moved. Probably it was the way she moved, easy as a young girl on slim hard legs, that caught the eye of the man who rapped at her from inside the window of the Rigger Bar. He looked familiar like a lot of people looked familiar to her. She had seen so many come and go. He hooked his arm, inviting her to enter, and she did so without hesitation, thinking only that she might tip down one or two with him and then get her bags to meet the bus. She wanted, at least, to see if she actually knew him. Even through the watery glass she could see that he wasn't all that old and his chest was thickly padded in expensive down.

There were cartons of colored eggs on the bar, each glowing like a jewel in its wad of cellophane. He was peeling one, sky blue as a robin's, palming it while he thumbed the peel aside, when she walked through the door. Although the day was overcast, the snow itself reflected such light that she was momentarily blinded. It was like going underwater. What she walked toward more than anything else was that blue egg in the white hand, a beacon in the murky air.

He ordered a beer for her, a Blue Ribbon, saying she deserved a prize for being the best thing he'd seen for days. He peeled an egg for her, a pink one, saying it matched her turtleneck. She told him it was no turtleneck. You called these things shells. He said he would peel that for her too, if she wanted, then he grinned at the bartender and handed her the naked egg.

June's hand was colder, from the outdoors, than the egg and so she had to let it sit in her fingers for a minute before it stopped feeling rubbery warm. Eating it, she found out how hungry she was. The last of the money that the man before this one had given her was spent for the ticket. She didn't know exactly when she'd eaten last. He seemed impressed, when her egg was finished, and peeled her another one just like it. She ate the egg. Then another egg. The bartender looked at her. She shrugged and tapped out a long menthol cigarette from a white plastic case inscribed with her initials in golden letters. She took a breath of smoke, then leaned toward her companion through the broken shells.

"What's happening?" she said without excitement. "Where's the party?"

Her hair was rolled carefully, sprayed for the bus trip, and her eyes were deeply watchful in their sea-blue flumes of shadow. She was deciding.

"I don't got much time until my bus. . . ." she said.

"Forget the bus!" He stood up and grabbed her arm. "We're gonna party. Hear? Who's stopping us? We're having a good time!"

She couldn't help but notice, when he paid up, that he had a good-size wad of money in a red rubber band like the kind that holds bananas together in the supermarket. That roll helped. But what was more important, she had a feeling. The eggs were lucky. And he had a good-natured slowness about him that seemed different. He could be different, she thought. The bus ticket would stay good, maybe forever. They weren't expecting her up home on the reservation. She didn't even have a man there except the one she'd divorced. Gordie. If she got desperate he would still send her money. So she went on to the next bar with this man in the vest. They drove down the street in his Silverado pickup. He was a mud engineer. She didn't tell him she'd known any mud engineers before or about that one she heard was killed by a pressurized hose. The hose had shot up into his stomach from underground.

The thought of that death, although she'd only been half acquainted with the deceased, always put a panicky, dry lump in her throat. It was the hose, she thought, snaking up suddenly from its unseen nest, the idea of that hose striking like a live thing that was fearful. With one blast it had taken out his insides, she'd heard. And that too made her throat ache, although she'd heard of worse things. It was that moment, that one moment, of realizing you were totally empty. He must have felt that. Sometimes, alone in her room in the dark, she thought she knew what it might be like.

LATER ON, THE dark falling around them at a noisy bar, she closed her eyes for a moment against the smoke and saw that hose pop suddenly through black earth with its killing breath.

"Ahhhhh," she said, surprised, almost in pain, "you got to be."

"I got to be what, honeysuckle?" He tightened his arm around her slim shoulder. They were sitting in a booth with a few others, drinking Angel Wings. Her mouth, the lipstick darkly blurred now, tipped unevenly toward his.

"You got to be different." she breathed.

IT WAS LATER on, still, that she felt so fragile. Walking toward the Ladies she was afraid to bump against anything because her skin felt hard and brittle as the shells of those eggs and she knew it was possible, in this condition, to fall apart at the slightest touch. She locked herself in the bathroom stall and remembered his hand, thumbing back the transparent skin and crackling blue peel. Her clothing itched. The pink shell was sweaty and hitched up too far under her arms but she couldn't take off her jacket, the white vinyl her son Delmar had given her, because the pink top was ripped across the stomach. But as she sat there, something happened. All of a sudden she seemed to drift out of the clothes and skin with no help from anyone. Sitting, she leaned down and rested her forehead on the top of the metal toilet-roll dispenser. She felt that under-neath it all her body was pure and naked—only the skins were stiff and old. She would get through this again, even if he was no different.

Her purse dropped out of her hand, spilling. She sat up straight. The doorknob rolled out of her open purse and beneath the stall. She had to take that doorknob with her every time she left her room. There was no other way of locking the battered door. Now she picked up the knob and held it by the metal shank. The round grip was porcelain, smooth and white. Hard as stone. She put it in her pocket and, holding it, walked back to the booth through the gathering crowd. Her room was locked. And she was ready for him now.

IT WAS A relief when they finally stopped, far out of town on a county road. She let him wrestle with her clothing but he worked so clumsily that she had to help him along. She rolled her top up carefully, still hid-ing the rip, and arched her back to let him undo her slacks. They were made of a stretch fabric that crackled with electricity and shed blue sparks when he pushed them down around her ankles. He knocked his hand against the heater's controls. She felt it open at her shoulder like a pair of jaws, blasting heat, and had the momentary and voluptuous sensation that she was lying stretched out before a great wide mouth. The breath swept across her throat, tightening her nipples. Then his vest plunged down against her, so slick and plush that it was like being rubbed by an enormous tongue. She couldn't get a handhold anywhere. And she felt herself slipping along the smooth plastic seat, slipping away, until she wedged the crown of her head against the opposite door.

"Oh God," he was moaning. "Oh God, Mary. Oh God, it's good."

He wasn't doing anything, just wiggling his hips on top of her, and at last his head fell heavily.

"Say there," she said, shaking him. "Andy?" She shook him harder. He didn't move or miss a beat in his deep breathing. She knew there wasn't any rousing him now so she lay still, under the weight of him. She remained quiet until she felt herself getting frail again. Her skin felt smooth and strange. And then she knew that if she lay there any longer she would crack wide open, not in one place but in many pieces that he would crush by moving in his sleep. She thought to pull herself into a piece. So she hooked an arm over her head and brought her elbow down slowly on the handle, releasing it. The door suddenly sprang wide.

June had wedged herself so tight against the door that when she sprang the latch she fell out. Into the cold. It was a shock like being born. But somehow she landed with her pants halfway up, as though she'd hoisted them midair, and then she quickly did her bra, pulled her shell down, and reached back into the truck. Without groping she found her jacket and purse. By now it was unclear to her whether she was more drunk or more sober than she'd ever been in her life. He didn't move or miss a beat of his breath. She left the door open. The heater, set to an automatic temperature, yawned hoarsely behind her and she heard it, or thought she did, for about a half mile down the road. Then she heard nothing but her own boots crunching ice. She concentrated on her feet, on steering them strictly down the packed wheel ruts.

She had walked far enough to see the dull orange glow, the canopy of low, lit clouds over Williston, when she decided to walk home instead of going back there. The wind was mild and wet. A Chinook wind, she thought. She made a right turn off the road, walked up a drift frozen over a snow fence, and began to pick her way through the swirls of dead grass and icy crust of open ranch land. Her boots were thin. So she stepped on dry ground where she could and avoided the slush and rotten gray banks. It was exactly as if she were walking back from a friend's house, or from a fiddle dance in town, a hayride maybe, swinging her purse as she crossed the wide field, stepping carefully to keep her feet dry.

Even when it started to snow she did not lose her sense of direction. Her feet grew numb but she did not worry about the distance. The heavy winds couldn't blow her off course. She continued. Even when her heart clenched and her skin turned crackling cold it didn't matter because the pure and naked part of her went on.

The snow fell deeper that Easter than it had in forty years, but June walked over it like water and came home.

## II

"OH, SHE CERTAINLY *was* good-looking," argued Aurelia, hands buried in a dishpan of potato salad.

"Some people use spoons to mix." Aunt Zelda held out a heavy tin one from the drawer. Her lips were screwed up like a coin purse. "I was only saying she had seen a few hard times and there was bruises. . . ."

"Wasn't either. You never saw her." Aurelia, plump, a "looker," waved Zelda's spoon off with a caked hand. "In fact, did anybody see her? Nobody saw her. Nobody knows for sure what happened so who's to squawk about bruises and so on . . . nobody saw her."

"Well, I heard," said Zelda, "I heard she was with a man and he dumped her off."

"Heard nothing," Aurelia snapped. "Don't trust nothing you don't see with your own eyes. June was all packed up. Ready to come home. They found her bags when they busted in her room. She walked out there because"—Aurelia foundered, then her voice strengthened "—what did she have to come home to after all? Nothing!"

"Nothing!" said Zelda. "Nothing!" She puffed her cheeks out in concentration, patting and crimping the edges of the pies. They were rhubarb, wild Juneberry, apple, and gooseberry, all fruits gathered and preserved by different Kashpaw aunts.

"I suppose you washed your hands before you put them in that salad," she said to Aurelia.

Aurelia squeezed her face into sickle moons of patient exasperation. "Now, Zelda," she said, "Patsy's daughter going to go home and tell her mama you still treat me like your baby sister."

"Well, you are aren't you? Can't change that."

I gave Aurelia my pickles, all diced into little cubes. Since morning I had been following their directions. In this house where I hadn't been for many years I was not sure where I stood now. Old enough to take my place among the aunts, I had still borne no children, had no husband, and so I felt myself strangely counted among the very young. I'd felt the stubborn meekness of the outsider and the comfort of kin all at once. My mother was coming up later in the week, and I already missed the security of having her speak for me.

"Where's those hard-boil eggs?" Aurelia wondered, not to me but to Zelda.

"I suppose you left them cool too slow so they're turning green on the yellows," Zelda pondered critically. "If you threw cold water on them right after boiling them they'd stay nice on the inside."

"But then they peel so hard! That's why I let them cool slow. Only where'd they go?"

"The skin shucks *off*...," Zelda insisted.

"You put them in the wood box," I said. Aurelia had put her eggs in the wood box where nobody would disturb them this late in June. Most of the uncles, aunts, children had driven up to Spirit Lake to fish and camp. They had gone off that morning in pickups with wilderness toppers packed with sleeping bags, full coolers, boxes of lures and tackle. They were camping overnight while we made tomorrow's dinner down here.

"June had those kids and Gordie," Zelda finally thought now. "Not to mention her new grandson, little Delmar. And it's just clear how Gordie loved her, only now he takes it out in liquor. He's always over at Eli's house trying to get Eli to join him for a toot. You know after the way June treated him I don't know why he didn't just let her go to ruin."

"Well, she couldn't get much more ruined than dead," observed Aurelia.

The odd thing I kept noticing about my aunts—the pious Zelda with her careful permanent and pitted gray face, Aurelia with her flat blue-black ponytail, high rounded cheeks, tight jeans, and frilled rodeo shirts—was the differenter they acted the more alike they fundamentally showed themselves. They were like my mother in their rock-bottom opinionation. They were so strong in their beliefs that there came a time when it hardly mattered what exactly those beliefs were; they all fused into a single stubbornness.

Zelda gave up discussing June after Aurelia's observation and began on me.

"So, Little Patsy. Who's this man I hear you're going to marry?" Her flat gray thumbs pursued each other around and around in circles, leaving perfect squeezed scallops. "It sure took you long enough. I guess you're choosy like me."

Aurelia snorted, but contained her remark, which probably would have referred to Zelda's first, disastrous marriage to a Swedish farm boy.

"Patsy met her intended at school," Aurelia answered for me. "He's a real handsome Indian boy. I saw his picture."

"He's grown-up," I let them know. "He used to be my teacher."

"Oh, my," said Zelda, pleased. "Just like your mama, only *she* married her high school teacher. Isn't that something?"

She froze with her hands in the air, seemingly paralyzed by the coincidence.

"I suppose you're going to teach him a few things now," said Aurelia to me, not joking, but serious. "Don't tell your dad but he learnt an awful lot about life from your mother."

I said I agreed with that, and vice versa too.

"But not so *much* vice versa," Zelda stated, and then she wondered if my fiancé went to Mass. I told her he had been born a Catholic, and she was satisfied at least for the present.

"Then he's always going to be one," she said, "whether he knows it or not. Just like you're a Kashpaw." She nicked her head at me, as if to warn.

"Patsy knows she's a Kashpaw," Aurelia said. "Otherwise how come she came here?"

Seeing the eggs I had peeled, Zelda forgot my fiancé and plucked one up in her fingers to point out the dull-green velvet on the yolks. Aurelia bridled. The two were still going back and forth on the fine points of boiling eggs when Delmar and Lynette drove up in their new car with Delmar Junior in the front seat and both Grandma and Grandpa Kashpaw in back.

"There's that white girl," Zelda peeked out the window.

"Oh, for God sakes," Aurelia gave her heady snort again, "what about your Swedish boy!"

"Learnt my lesson." Zelda wiped firmly around the edges of Aurelia's dishpan.

"Oh, Zelda . . . ," the younger aunt murmured sadly and feelingly. She never finished her sentence, but that beginning was enough. Stung by even the remotest hint of pity, Zelda stiffened and walked out.

GRANDMA KASHPAW'S BABY-DOLL anklets and nurse's shoes appeared first, then her head in its iron-gray pageboy. Last of all the entire rest of her squeezed through the door, swathed in acres of tiny purple flowers. When I was young she had always seemed the same size to me as monuments in the park. But every time I saw her now I realized that she wasn't so large, it was just that her figure was weathered and massive as a statue roughed out in rock. She never changed much, at least not so much as Grandpa Kashpaw. Since I'd been away at school, he'd turned into an old man. Age had come on him suddenly, like a storm in autumn shaking colored leaves down overnight, and now his winter—quiet, deep—was upon him. As Grandma shook out her dress and pulled bundles out of the trunk, Grandpa sat quietly in the car. He hadn't noticed that it had stopped.

"Why don't you tell him it stopped," Grandma called to Lynette.

Lynette was changing Delmar Junior's diaper in the backseat. She generally used paper diapers with stick-'em tabs at her home in the Cities, but since she'd been here Zelda had shamed her into using washable cloth diapers and sharp pins. The baby wiggled and fought her hands, soundlessly and happily. He was in a kind of winter too, like Grandpa, only Delmar Junior's was the new, quiet winter of gestation in which life forms and prepares to meet the world.

"You hear?" Big Delmar, already out of the car and nervously examining his tires, stuck his head back in the driver's side window, "She was calling you. My father's mother. She just told you to do something."

Lynette's face, stained and swollen, bloomed over the wheel. She was a dyed blonde with roots black as tar. "Yes, I heard," she hissed through the safety pins in her teeth. "You tell him."

Jerking the baby up, ankles pinned in the forks of her fingers, she repositioned the triangle of cloth under his bottom.

"Grandma told you to tell him," Delmar leaned farther in. He had his mother's long, slim legs and I remembered all at once, seeing him bend all the way into the car, June bending that way too. Me behind her. She had pushed a rowboat off the sharp gravel beach of some lake we'd all gone to visit together. I had jumped into the rowboat with her. She had two sons at the time and, as yet, no daughter, so she spoiled me and told me everything, thinking I did not understand, needing someone to tell it to, I suppose. She told me things you'd only tell another woman, full grown, and I had adored her wildly for these adult confidences, for her wreaths of blue smoke, for the slim hard bright figure she cut. I had adored her into telling me everything she needed to tell and it was true, I hadn't understood the words at the time. But she hadn't counted on my memory. Those words stayed with me.

And even now, Delmar was saying something to Lynette that had such an uncanny dreamlike ring to it I almost heard it in her voice.

June had said: "He used the flat of his hand. He hit me good." And now Delmar was saying: "Flat of my hand . . . but good . . ."

Lynette rolled out the door, shedding cloth and pins, packing the bare-bottomed child on her hip, and I couldn't tell what had happened.

Grandpa hadn't noticed, whatever it was. He turned to the open door and stared at his house.

"This reminds me of something," he said.

"Well, it should. It's your house!" Zelda grabbed both his hands through the opposite door and pulled him through. Lynette fled us all, diaper bag flying.

"You have your granddaughter here, too!" Zelda shrieked carefully into Grandpa's face. "Patsy's daughter. She came all the way up here to visit before she got married."

"Patsy . . . second to the oldest . . . born April fourteenth, nineteen thirty-eight . . ."

"No, Daddy. This here is Patsy's daughter. Your granddaughter."

But it was dates, numbers, figures that stuck with him and not the weary intricacies of his spawn, proliferating beyond those numbers into eternity. He took my hand and went along, accepting me whoever I was.

HE HAD BROUGHT Grandma Vitaline here, to the original allotment, in 1929. Together they had raised six children born between them and four others born to neighbors, feeding them all through the Depression from the biggest truck garden on the reservation. Behind the house a patch of rhubarb still spread, newly uncrumpling its poisonous leaves on red stalks. I walked back there with Grandpa, holding his arm. He had to get reacquainted with the place every time he and Grandma drove in from the retirement home. Uncle Gordie lived on the land now, and he kept only the rhubarb from that original garden. I remembered dipping the stalks in a cup of sugar, eating them on long hot afternoons. Across the stubbly, beaten yard a broad swale of wheat began, swirled down the hill, curled up a moment around a rich green slough and swirled off again until it ran into a horseshoe of birch and trembling aspen. All this was Grandpa's land, rented out now to a wheat farmer.

Grandpa had been born in a bark house on the Apostle Islands of Lake Superior. He grew up wandering with the seasons through different reservations until the missionaries or the truancy people sent him off to government schools. He was twin to Uncle Eli, who never went to those schools but stayed home and learned the woods. Eli's mind was sharply domestic these days, like Grandma's, but Grandpa's had become wary and wild. Sometimes I felt his thoughts were swimming between us, hiding under rocks, disappearing in weeds, and I was fishing for them, dangling my words like baits and lures.

"Remember this . . . remember that . . . what was it like . . . the old schools . . . Washington . . . Leech Lake?"

Elusive, pregnant with history, they finned off and vanished. The same color as water. Grandpa shook his head, remembering dates with no events to go with them, names without faces, occurrences out of place and time. There were moments I could almost envy his winter, for his loss of memory was protective, absolving him of the past, and he lived calmly now without guilt or desolation. When he thought of June, for instance, she was young. She fed him wild plums. That was the way she would always be for him. His great-grandson, Delmar Junior, was happy because he hadn't yet acquired a memory. Grandpa's happiness lay in losing his. I felt more comfortable with Grandpa, this visit, than with anyone else. Since his mind had been absorbed into the world and I was merely a part of his habitat, a piece of furniture, an aspect of landscape, I did not have to fend for myself with him, or even speak.

"HE LIKES THAT busted lawn chair," Grandma hollered now, seeing us together. "Let him set there a while."

I pulled the frayed, woven plastic and aluminum into the shape of a chair and he settled into it, counting something under his breath. Clouds. Trees. All the blades of grass.

In the house Grandma was unwrapping her expensive supermarket ham. She patted it lovingly before putting it in the oven and closed the door carefully so as not to disturb its rest.

"She's not used to buying this much meat," Zelda said. "Remember we used to trade for it?"

"Or slaughter our own." Aurelia blew a round gray cloud of Winston smoke across the table.

"Pew," said Zelda. "Put the top on the butter." She flapped her hand in front of her nose. "You know, Mama, I bet this makes you wish it was like it used to be. All us kids in the kitchen again."

"Oh, I never had no trouble with kids." Grandma wiped each finger on a dishrag. "Except for once in a while."

"Except for when?" said Aurelia.

"Well, now." Grandma lowered herself onto a long-legged stool, waving Zelda's more substantial chair away. Grandma liked to balance on that stool like an oracle on her tripod. "There was that time someone tried to hang their little cousin," she declared and then stopped short.

The sisters gave her quick, unbelieving looks. Then they were both stubbornly silent, neither of them willing to take up the slack and tell the story I knew was about June. I'd heard June and my mother laughing and accusing each other of the hanging in times past when it had been a childhood anecdote and not the private trigger of special guilts. The aunts looked at me, wondering if I knew the story, but neither would open her lips to ask, so I said I'd heard June herself tell it.

"That's right," Aurelia jumped in. "June told it herself. If she minded being hung, well she never let on!"

"Hah!" Zelda said. "If she minded! You were playing cowboys. You had her up on a box with the rope looped over a branch, tied on her neck, very accurate. If she minded! I had to rescue her myself!"

"Oh, I know," Aurelia pouted in dismay. "We saw it in the movies. Kids imitate them, you know. We got notorious after that, me and Gordie. Remember, Zelda? How you came screaming in the house for Mama?"

"Mama! Mama!" Grandma yodeled an imitation of her daughter. "They're hanging June!"

"You came running out there, Mama!" Zelda was swept into the story. "I didn't know you could run so fast."

"We had that rope around her neck and looped over the tree and poor June was bawling, she was so scared. But we *never* would have done it."

"Yes!" asserted Zelda. "You meant to!"

"Oh, I licked you two good," Grandma remembered. "Aurelia, you and Gordie both. Oh, I had to lick you!"

"And then you took little June in the house. . . ." Zelda broke down suddenly.

Aurelia put her hands to her face. Then, behind her fingers, she made a sound with her throat like a stick breaking.

"Oh, Mama, we could have killed her. . . ."

Zelda crushed her mouth behind a fist.

"But then she came in the house. You wiped her face off," Aurelia remembered. "That June. She yelled at us, 'I wasn't scared! You damn rotten eggs, you go to hell!'"

And then Aurelia started giggling behind her hands. Zelda put her fist down on the table with surprising force.

"Rotten eggs!" said Zelda.

"You had to lick her, too . . . ," Aurelia gurgled, wiping her eyes.

"For saying hell and damn. . . ." Grandma nearly lost her balance.

"Then she got madder yet . . . ," I said.

"That's right!" Now Grandma's chin was pulled up to hold her laughter back. "She called me a damn old hen. Right there! A damn old hen for spanking her!"

Then they were laughing out loud in brays and whoops, sopping tears in their aprons and sleeves, waving their hands helplessly.

"Patsy! Your mama cried for sympathy with June. Then she got mad too and yelled. She called June . . ."

"WHAT DID SHE yell?" I asked Grandma. "She never told me that part."

"Something bad . . . ," Grandma thought back. ". . . I don't know where she heard that awful word."

Outside, Delmar's engine revved grandly and a trickle of music started up.

"He's got a tape deck in that car," Zelda said, patting her heart, her hair, composing herself quickly. "I suppose that costed extra money."

The car moved off, wheels crackling in the gravel and cinders. Then it was quiet again. The aunts sniffed, fished Kleenex, from their sleeves, glanced pensively at each other, and put the story to rest.

"I suppose they're going off to find Gordie," Zelda thought out loud. "He at Eli's place? It's way out in the bush."

"He wanted to give his great-uncle Eli a ride in that new car," said Grandma in strictly measured, knowing tones.

"Eli won't ride in it." Aurelia lighted a cigarette. Her head shook back and forth in scarves of smoke. And for once Zelda's head shook too, in agreement, and then Grandma's as well. She rose, pushing her soft wide arms down on the table.

"Why not?" I had to know. "Why won't Eli ride in that car?"

"Patsy don't know about that insurance." Aurelia pointed at me with her chin. So Zelda turned to me and spoke in her low, prim, explaining voice.

"June's heart stopped, see. They had an autopsy and found out. So insurance came through and all of that money went to Delmar. Because he's oldest. Well, Delmar took some insurance and first bought her a big pink gravestone, which was put up on the hill. Mama, we going up there to visit? I didn't see that gravestone yet."

Grandma was at the stove, bending laboriously to check the roast ham, and she ignored us.

"Just recently he bought this new car," Zelda went on, "with the rest of that money. It has a tape deck and all the furnishings. Eli doesn't like it, or so I heard. That car reminds him of his niece. You know Eli raised June like his own daughter when her mother passed away."

"Delmar got that damn old money," said Grandma suddenly and distinctly, "not because he was oldest. June named him for the money because he took after her the most."

SO THE INSURANCE explained the car. More than that it explained why my uncles and aunts treated the car with special care. Because it was a new expensive Firebird, I had thought. Still, nobody seemed that proud of it except for Delmar and Lynette. Nobody leaned against the sleek fenders, rested elbows on the roof, traced the small birds flaming there, or set their paper plates down on the hood. Nobody even wanted to hear Delmar's tapes. It was as if the car was wired up to something. As if it might give off a shock when touched. They brushed the glazed chrome, or gently tapped the mag wheels with their toes. They would not go riding in it, even though Delmar urged them to experience how smooth and powerful it ran.

"Well, where *are* they?" said Zelda. "Joy riding?"

Grandma was dozing in the next room and Aurelia had taken the last pie from the oven. Gordie's yellow Sears dryer was still huffing away in the tacked-on addition that held toilet, laundry, kitchen sink. The plumbing, only two years old, was hooked up to one side of the house. The tops of the washer and dryer were covered with clean towels, and all the pies had been set there to cool their perfect crusts.

"That white girl," said Zelda, "she's built like a truck driver. Lucky you're slim, Patsy. She won't keep Delmar long."

"Oh *Jeez*, Zelda!" Aurelia came in from the next room. "Why can't you just leave it be? So she's white. What about the Swede? And how you think Patsy feels hearing you talk like this?"

"He's different," Zelda argued.

"*He* stayed with his wife," I said.

"Ooooh," said Aurelia. "Burnt you, Zelda! She's learning quick. They didn't name her after Big Patsy for nothing."

BY THE TIME Delmar and Lynette finally came home it was near dusk and we had already moved Grandpa into the house and laid his supper out.

Lynette sat down next to Grandpa, with Delmar Junior in her lap. She began to feed her son ground liver from a little jar. The baby tried to slap his hands together on the spoon each time it was lowered into his mouth. Every time he managed to grasp the spoon, it jerked out of his hands and came down with more liver. Lynette was weary, eyes watery and red. Her yellow hair, caught in a stiff club, looked as though it had been used to drag her here.

"You don't got any children, do you, Patsy?" she said, holding the spoon away, licking it herself, making a disgusted face. "So you wouldn't know how they just can't leave anything alone!"

"She's not married yet," said Zelda, dangling a bright plastic bundle of keys down to the baby. "She thinks she'll wait for her baby until *after* she's married. Oochy koo," she crooned when Delmar focused and, in an effort of intense delight, snatched the keys down to himself.

Lynette bolted up, shook the keys roughly from his grasp, and snatched him into the next room. He gave a short, outraged wail and then fell silent. Lynette emerged, pulling down her blouse. It was a dark-violet bruised color.

"Thought you wanted to see the gravestone," Aurelia quickly remembered, addressing Zelda. "You better get going before it's dark out. Tell Delmar you want him to take you up there."

"I suppose," said Zelda, turning to me, "Aurelia didn't see those two cases of stinking old beer in their backseat. I'm not driving anywhere with a drunk."

"He's not a drunk!" Lynette wailed in sudden passion. "But I'd drink a few beers too if I had to be in this family."

Then she whirled and ran outside.

DELMAR WAS SLUMPED morosely in the front seat of the car, a beer clenched between his thighs. He drummed his knuckles to Johnny Rivers tapes.

"I don't even let her drive it," he said when I asked. He nodded toward Lynette, who was strolling down the driveway ditch, adding to a straggly bunch of prairie roses. I saw her bend over, tearing at a tough branch.

"She's going to hurt her hands."

"Oh, she don't know nothing," said Delmar. "She never been to school. I seen a little of the world when I was in the service. You get my picture?"

He'd sent a picture of himself in the uniform. I'd been surprised when I saw the picture because I'd realized then that my rough boy cousin, same age as me, had developed hard cheekbones and a movie-star gaze. Now, brooding under the bill of his blue hat, he turned that moody stare through the windshield and shook his head at his wife. "She don't fit in," he said.

"She's fine," I surprised myself by saying. "Just give her a chance."

"Chance," Delmar tipped his beer up. "Chance. She took her chance when she married me. She knew which one I took after."

Then, as if on cue, the one whom Delmar did not take after drove into the yard with a squealing flourish, laying hard on his horn.

UNCLE GORDIE KASHPAW was considered good-looking, although not in the same sharp-cut way as his son Delmar. Gordie had a dark, round, eager face, creased and puckered from being stitched up after a car accident. There was always a compelling pleasantness about him. In some curious way all the stitches and folds had contributed to, rather than detracted from, his looks. His face was like something valuable that was broken and put carefully back together. And all the more lovable for the care taken. In the throes of drunken inspiration now, he drove twice around the yard before his old Chevy chugged to a halt. Old Uncle Eli got out.

"Well, it's still standing up," Eli said to the house. "And so am I. But you," he addressed Gordie, "ain't."

It was true, Gordie's feet were giving him trouble. They caught on things as he groped on the hood and pulled himself out. The rubber foot mat, the fenders, then the little ruts and stones as he clambered toward the front steps.

"Zelda's in there," Delmar shouted. "And Grandma, too!"

Gordie sat down on the steps to collect his wits before making his appearance.

Inside, Uncle Eli sat down next to his twin. They didn't look much alike anymore, for Eli had wizened and toughened while Grandpa was larger, softer, even paler than his brother. They happened to be dressed the same though, in work pants and jackets, except that Grandpa's outfit was navy blue and Eli's was olive green. Eli wore a stained, crumpled cap that seemed so much a part of his head not even Zelda thought of asking him to remove it. He grinned and nodded at Grandpa. He had a huge toothless smile that took up his entire face.

"Here's my uncle Eli," Aurelia said, putting down a plate of food for him. "Here's my favorite uncle. See, Daddy? Uncle Eli's here. Your brother."

"Oh, Eli," said Grandpa, extending his hand. Grandpa grinned and nodded at his brother, but said nothing more until Eli started to eat.

"I don't eat very much anymore. I'm getting so old," Eli was telling us.

"You're eating a whole lot," Grandpa pointed out. "Is there going to be anything left?"

"You ate already," said Grandma. "Now sit still and visit with your brother."

"It's too late," said Grandpa. "He's eating everything."

He watched each bite his brother took intently. Eli wasn't bothered in the least. Indeed, he openly enjoyed his food for Grandpa.

"Oh, for heaven's sake," Zelda sighed. "Are we ever getting out of here? Aurelia. Why don't you take Gordie's car and drive us in? It's too late to see that gravestone now anyway, but I'm darned if I'm going to be here once they start on those cases in the back of June's car."

"Put the laundry out," said Grandma. "I'm ready enough. And you, Patsy"—she nodded at me as they walked out the door—"they can eat all they want. Just as long as they save the pies. Them pies are made special for tomorrow."

"Sure you don't want to come along with us now?" said Zelda.

"She's young," said Aurelia, "Besides, she's got to keep those drunken men from eating on those pies."

She bent close to me. Her breath was sweet with cake frosting, stale with cigarettes.

"I'll be back later on," she whispered. "I got to see a friend."

Then she winked at me exactly the way June had winked about her secret friends. One eye shut, the lips pushed into a small self-deprecating question mark.

Grandpa eased himself into the backseat and sat as instructed, arms spread to either side, holding down the piles of folded laundry.

"They can eat!" Grandma yelled once more. "But save them pies for tomorrow!"

She bucked forward when the car lurched into the hole in the drive, and then they shot over the hill.

III

"SAY, PATSY, DID you know your uncle Eli is the last man on the reservation that could snare himself a deer?"

Gordie unlatched a beer, pushed it across the kitchen table to me. We were still at that table, only now the plates, dishpans of salad, and pie shells were cleared away for ashtrays, beer, packs of cigarettes.

"I had to save on my shells," said Eli thoughtfully. "They was dear."

"Only real old-time Indians know deer that good," Gordie said. "Your uncle Eli's a real old-timer."

"You remember the first thing you ever got?" Eli asked Delmar.

Delmar looked down at his beer, then gave me a proud, sly sideways glance. "A gook," he said. "I was in the Marines."

"Skunk." Gordie raised his voice. "Delmar got himself a skunk when he was ten."

"Did you ever eat a skunk?" Eli asked me.

"It's like a piece of cold chicken," I ventured. Eli and Gordie agreed with solemn grins.

"How do you skin your skunk?" Eli asked Delmar.

Delmar tipped his hat down, shading his eyes from the fluorescent kitchen ring. A blue-and-white patch had been stitched on the front of his hat. World's Greatest Fisherman, it said. Delmar put his hands up in winning ignorance.

"How do *you* skin your skunk?" he asked Eli.

"You got to take the glands off first," Eli explained carefully, pointing at different parts of his body. "Here, here, here. Then you skin it just like anything else. You have to boil it in three waters."

"Then you honestly *eat* it?" said Lynette. She had come into the room with a fresh beer and was now biting contentedly on a frayed end-string of a hair.

Eli sat up straight and tilted his little green hat back. "You picky, too? Like Zelda! One time she came over to visit me with her first husband, that Swede Johnson. It was around dinnertime. I had that skunk dressed out and so I fed it to them. Ooooooh, when she found out what she ate she was mad at me, boy. 'Skunk!' she says, 'How disgusting! You old guys will eat anything!' "

"I'd eat it," Lynette proclaimed, flipping her hair back with a chopping motion of her hand. "I'd eat it just like that."

"You'd eat shit," said Delmar.

I stared at his clean profile. He was staring across the table, at nobody. His lip had curled down in some imitation of soap-opera bravado, but his chin trembled. I saw him clench his jaw and then felt a kind of wet-blanket sadness coming down over us all. Lynette shrugged brightly, and brushed away his remark. But it stayed at the table, as if it had opened a door on something. Some sad, ugly scene we could not help but enter. I took a long hard drink, and leaned comfortlessly toward Uncle Eli.

"A fox sleeps hard, eh?" said Eli, after a few moments.

Delmar leaned forward and pulled his hat still lower so it seemed to rest on his nose.

"I've shot a fox sleeping before," he said. "You know that little black hole underneath a fox's tail? I shot right through there. I was using a bow and my arrow went right through that fox. It got stiff. It went straight through the air. Flattened out like a flash and was gone down its hole. I never did get it out."

"Never shot a bow either," said Gordie.

"Hah, you're right. I never shot a bow either," admitted Delmar with a strange, snarling little laugh. "But I heard of this guy once who put his arrow through a fox, then left it thrash around in the bush until he thought it was dead. He went in there after it. You know what he found? That fox had chewed the arrow off either side of its body and it was gone."

"They don't got that name for nothing," Eli said.

"Fox," said Gordie, peering closely at the keyhole in his beer.

"Can you gimme a cigarette, Eli?" Delmar asked.

"When you ask for a cigarette around here," said Gordie, "you don't say, 'Can I have a cigarette?' You say, 'Ciga Swa?'"

"Them Michifs ask like that," Eli said. "You got to ask a real old Cree like me for the right words."

"Tell 'em, Uncle Eli," Lynette said with a quick burst of cheerleader enthusiasm. "They've got to learn their own heritage! When you go it will all be gone!"

"What you saying there, woman. Hey," Delmar shouted, filling the kitchen with the jagged tear of his voice. "When you talk on my relatives have a little respect." He put his arms out and shoved at her breasts.

"You bet your life, Uncle Eli," he said more quietly, leaning back on the table. "You're the greatest hunter. But I'm the world's greatest fisherman."

"No, you ain't," Eli said. His voice was effortless and happy. "I caught a fourteen-inch trout."

Delmar looked at him carefully, focusing less adeptly now than his son. "You're the greatest then," he admitted. "Here."

He reached over and plucked away Eli's greasy olive-drab hat. Eli's head was brown, shiny, bald, with a flat ring of stubbly white crew cut. Delmar took off his blue hat and pushed it down on Eli's head. The hat slipped over Eli's eyes.

"It's too big for him!" Lynette screamed in a tiny outraged voice.

Delmar adjusted the hat's plastic tab.

"I gave you that hat, Delmar! That's your best hat!" Her voice rose sharply in its trill. "You don't give that hat away!"

Eli sat calmly underneath the hat. It fit him perfectly. He seemed oblivious of Delmar's sacrifice and just sat, his old cap perched on his knee, turning the can around and around in his hand without drinking.

Delmar swayed to his feet, clutched the stuffed plastic backrest of the chair. His voice was ripped and swollen.

"Uncle Eli." He bent over the old man. "Uncle Eli, you're my uncle."

"Damn right," Eli agreed.

"I always thought so much of you, my uncle!" cried Delmar in a loud, unhappy wail.

"Damn right."

"We're gonna see you a fucken twenty more years!"

"Damn right," said Eli. He turned to Gordie. "He's drunk on his behind. I got to agree with him."

"I think the fucken world of you, uncle!"

"Damn right. I'm an old man," Eli said in a flat, soft voice.

It was the sound of omniscience to Delmar, and he suddenly put his hands up around his ears and stumbled out the door.

"Fresh air be good for him," said Gordie in high relief. "Say there, Patsy. You ever hear this one joke about the Indian, the Frenchman, and the Norwegian in the French Revolution?"

"Issat a Norwegian joke?" Lynette asked. "Hey. I'm full-blooded

Norwegian. I don't know nothing about my family but I know I'm full-blooded Norwegian."

"No, it's not about the Norwegians really," Gordie went on. "So anyway . . ."

Nevertheless, she followed Delmar out the door.

"There were these three. An Indian. A Frenchman. A Norwegian. They were all in the French Revolution. And they were all set for the guillotine, right? But when they put the Indian in there the blade just came halfway down and got stuck."

"Fucken bitch! Gimme the keys!" Delmar screamed just outside the door. Gordie paused a moment. There was silence. He continued the joke.

"So they said it was the judgment of God. 'You can go,' they said to the Indian. So the Indian got up and went. Then it was the Frenchman's turn. They put his neck in the vise and were all set to execute him! But it happened the same. The blade stuck."

"Fucken bitch! Fucken bitch!" Delmar shrieked again.

The car door slammed. Gordie's eyes darted to the door, back to me with questions. "Should we go out?" I said.

But he continued the story.

"And so the Frenchman went off and he was saved. But when it came to the Norwegian, see, the Norwegian looks up at the guillotine and says: 'You guys are sure dumb. If you put a little grease on it that thing would work fine!' "

"Bitch! Bitch! I'll kill you! Gimme the keys!" We heard a quick shattering sound, glass breaking, and left Eli sitting at the table.

Lynette was locked in the new car, crouched in the passenger's side. Delmar screamed at her and threw his whole body against the door, thudded on the hood with hollow booms, banged his way across the roof, ripped at antennas and side-view mirror with his fists, kicked into the broken sockets of headlights. Finally, he ripped the mirror off the driver's side and began to beat the car rhythmically, gasping. But though he swung the mirror time after time into the windshield and side windows he couldn't smash them.

"Del baby!" Gordie jumped off the steps and hugged Delmar to the ground with the solid drop of his weight. "It's her car. You're June's boy, Del. Don't cry." For as they lay there, welded in shock, Delmar's face was grinding deep into the cinders and his shoulders shook with heavy sobs. He screamed up through dirt at his father.

"It's awful to be dead. Oh my God, she's so cold."

They were up on their feet suddenly. Delmar twisted out of Gordie's arms and balanced in a wrestler's stance. "It's your fault and you wanna take the car," he said wildly. He sprang at his father but Gordie stepped back, bracing himself, and once again he folded Delmar violently into his arms and again Delmar sobbed and sagged against his father. Gordie lowered him back into the cinders. While they were clenched, Lynette slipped from the car and ran in the house. She walked agitatedly through the kitchen, checked the baby, and then pranced around the table making small excited exploding sounds with her hands.

Clap! She walked over to Eli. Clap! Clap!

"You got troubles out there," he stated.

"Yeah!" she said. "His mom gave him the money!" She sneaked a cigarette from Eli's pack, leering politely. "Because she wanted him to have responsibility. He never had responsibility. She wanted him to take care of his family."

Eli nodded and pushed the whole pack toward her when she stubbed out the cigarette half smoked. She lighted another.

"You know, he really must love his uncle," she cried in a small, hard voice. She plumped down next to Eli and steadily smiled at the blue hat. "That fishing hat. It's his number-one hat. I got that patch for him. Delmar. They think the world of him down in the Cities. Everybody knows him. They know him by that hat. It's his number one. You better never take it off."

Eli took the hat off and turned it around in his hands. He squinted at the patch and read it aloud. Then he nodded, as if it had finally dawned on him what she was talking about, and he turned it back around.

"Let me wear it for a while," Lynette cajoled. Then she took it. Put it on her head and adjusted the brim. "There it is."

Uncle Eli took his old cap off his knee and put it back on his head. "This one fits me," he said.

IN THE NEXT room Delmar Junior made a crowing sound.

"Oh, my baby!" Lynette shrieked as if he were in danger, and darted out. I heard her murmuring Delmar's name when the father and the son walked back inside. Delmar sat down at the table and put his head in his folded arms, breathing hoarsely. Gordie got the keys from Lynette and told Eli they were going home now.

"He's okay," he said, nodding at Delmar.

"Just as long as you let him alone."

So they drove off on that clear blue night in June and left Delmar alone. I put a blanket around Lynette's shoulders. We walked past her husband. He was still breathing hopelessly into his crossed arms. She had a pint of white rum and stopped to take long gagging pulls all the way down the hill. Every time she remembered to hand me the bottle I tried to drink, too. And then, when we got to the bottom, finally, we looked up at the sky as we drank and nearly fell over, in amazement, at the drenching beauty.

Northern lights. Something in the cold, wet atmosphere brought them out. We floated into the field and sank down, crushing green wheat. We chewed the sweet kernels and stared up and were lost. Everything seemed to be one piece. The air, our faces—all cool, moist, and dark—and the ghostly sky. Pale-green licks of light pulsed and faded across it. Living lights. Their fires lobbed over the vault of heaven and died out in blackness. At times the whole sky was concentrically ringed in shooting points and puckers of light gathering and falling, pulsing, fading, rhythmical as breathing. All of a piece. As if the sky were a pattern of nerves and our thoughts and memories traveled across it. As if the sky were one gigantic memory for us all. Or a dance hall. And all the world's wandering souls were dancing there. I thought of June. She would be dancing there, if there were a dance hall in space. She would be dancing a two-step for wandering souls. Her long legs lifting and falling. Her laugh an ace. Her sweet perfume the way all grown-up women were supposed to smell. Her amusement at both the bad and the good. Her defeat. Her reckless victory. Her son.

"Did you ever dream you flew through the air?" asked Lynette. "Did you ever dream you landed on a planet or star?"

I didn't answer, because the question surprised me so. As if she were reading my thoughts.

"I dreamed I flew up there once," she said. "But when I landed on the moon I didn't dare take a breath."

"You didn't dare?" I felt crushed when she said that. It seemed so terribly sad.

"No," she said. "No. I was scared to breathe."

I WOKE UP. I had fallen asleep on my back, in the cold wet wheat, under the flashing sky. I heard the clanging sound of struck metal, pots tumbling in the house. Gordie was gone. Eli was gone. Lynette was gone. I ran into the lighted kitchen and saw at once that Delmar was drowning her. He was pushing her face into the sink of cold dishwater. Holding her by the nape and the ears. Her arms were whirling, knocking spoons and knives and bowls out of the drainer. She struggled powerfully, but he had her. I grabbed a block of birch out of the wood box and hit Delmar on the back of the neck. The wood bounced out of my fists. He pushed her lower and her throat caught and gurgled.

I jumped on his back. He hardly noticed. He pushed her lower. So I had no choice then . . . I bit his ear. My teeth met and his blood filled my mouth. He reeled backward, bucking me off, and I flew across the room, hit the refrigerator solidly, and got back on my feet.

His hands were cocked in boxer's fists. He was deciding who to hit first, I thought, and it seemed not much to matter. I stared at him for a moment, then lost interest. I looked past him. And then I suddenly saw what they had done.

All the pies were smashed. Torn open. Black juice bleeding through the crusts. Bits of jagged shells were stuck to the wall and some were turned completely upside down. Chunks of rhubarb were scraped across the floor. Meringue dripped from his elbow.

"The pies!" I shrieked. "You goddamn sonofabitch, you broke the pies!"

His eyes widened. He glanced around at the destruction. Lynette scuttled under the table. He took in what he could and then his fists lowered and a look at least resembling shame, confusion, swept over his face and he rushed past me. He stepped down flat on his fisherman's hat as he ran, and after he was gone I picked it up.

I stuffed the hat under Delmar Junior's mattress. Then I sat for a long time in that dim room, listening to his light and oblivious breathing. A good baby, or more likely a wise soul, he slept through everything he could possibly sleep through. Gordie drove the car up later and fell asleep too, on the couch. The kitchen was dark, so he didn't notice.

Lynette had turned the lights out, leaving the house, and now I heard her outside the window begging Delmar to take her away in the car.

"Let's go off before they all get back," she said. "It's them. You always get so crazy when you're home. We'll get the baby. We'll go off. We'll go back to the Cities . . . it's like I can hardly breathe here, you know?"

And then she cried out once, but clearly it was a cry something like pleasure. I thought I heard their bodies creak together, or perhaps it was just the wood steps beneath them, the old worn boards, bearing their weight.

They got into the car soon after that. Doors slammed. But they traveled just a few yards and stopped. The horn blared softly. I suppose they knocked against it in passion. The heater roared on from time to time. It was a cold, spare dawn.

SOMETIME THAT MORNING I spooned the fillings back into the crusts, married slabs of dough, smoothed over edges with a wetted finger, fit crimps to crimps and even fluff to fluff on top of berries or pudding. I worked carefully. But once they smash there is no way to put them right.

# Saint Marie

SO WHEN I went there I knew the Dark Fish must rise. Plumes of radiance had soldered on me. No reservation girl had ever prayed so hard. There was no use in trying to ignore me any longer. I was going up there on the hill with the black-robe women. They were not any lighter than me. I was going up there to pray as good as they could, because I don't have that much Indian blood. And they never thought they'd have a girl from this reservation as a saint they'd have to kneel to. But they'd have me. And I'd be carved in pure gold. With ruby lips. And my toenails would be little pink ocean shells, which they would have to stoop down off their high horse to kiss.

I was ignorant. I was near age fourteen. The sky is just about the size of my ignorance. And just as pure. And that—the pure wideness of my ignorance—is what got me up the hill to the Sacred Heart Convent and brought me back down alive. For maybe Jesus did not take my bait, but them Sisters tried to cram me right down whole.

You ever see a walleye strike so bad the lure is practically out its back end before you reel it in? That is what they done with me. I don't like to make that low comparison, but I have seen a walleye do that once. And it's the same attempt as Sister Leopolda made to get me in her clutch.

I had the mail-order Catholic soul you get in a girl raised out in the bush, whose only thought is getting into town. Sunday Mass is the only time my father brought his children in except for school, when we were harnessed. Our souls went cheap. We were so anxious to get there we would have walked in on our hands and knees. We just craved going to the store, slinging bottle caps in the dust, making fool eyes at each other. And of course we went to church.

Where they have the convent is on top of the highest hill, so that from its windows the Sisters can be looking into the marrow of the town. Recently a windbreak was planted before the bar "for the purposes of tornado insurance." Don't tell me that. That poplar stand was put up to hide the drinkers as they get the transformation. As they are served into the beast of their burden. While they're drinking, that body comes upon them, and then they stagger or crawl out the bar door, pulling a weight they can't move past the poplars. They don't want no holy witness to their fall.

Anyway, I climbed. That was a long-ago day. A road for wagons wound in ruts to the top of the hill where they had their buildings of brick painted gleaming white. So white the sun glanced off in dazzling display to set forms whirling behind your eyelids. The face of God you could hardly look at. But that day it drizzled, so I could look all I wanted. I saw the homelier side. The cracked whitewash, and swallows nesting in the busted ends of eaves. I saw the boards sawed the size of broken windowpanes and the fruit trees, stripped. Only the tough wild rhubarb flourished. Goldenrod rubbed up their walls. It was a poor convent. I know that now. Compared with others it was humble, ragtag, out in the middle of no place. It was the end of the world to some. Where the maps stopped. Where God had only half a hand in the Creation. Where the Dark One had put in thick bush, liquor, wild dogs, and Indians.

I heard later that the Sacred Heart Convent was a place for nuns that don't get along elsewhere. Nuns that complain too much or lose their mind. I'll always wonder now, after hearing that, where they picked up Sister Leopolda. Perhaps she had scarred someone else, the way she left a mark on me. Perhaps she was just sent around to test her sisters' faith, here and there, like the spot-checker in a factory. For she was a definite hard trial for anyone, even for those who started out with veils of wretched love upon their eyes.

I was that girl who thought the hem of her black garment would help me rise. Veils of love, which was only hate petrified by longing, that was me. I was like those bush Indians who stole the holy black hat of a Jesuit and swallowed little scraps of it to cure their fevers. But the hat itself carried smallpox, and it was killing them with belief. Veils of faith! I had this confidence in Leopolda. She was different. The other Sisters had long ago gone blank and given up on Satan. He slept for them. They never noticed his comings and goings. But Leopolda kept track of him and knew his habits, the minds he burrowed in, the deep spaces where he hid. She knew as much about him as my grandma, who called him by other names and was not afraid.

In her class, Sister Leopolda carried a long oak pole for opening high windows. On one end it had a hook made of iron that could jerk a patch of your hair out or throttle you by the collar—all from a distance. She used this deadly hook-pole for catching Satan by surprise. He could have entered without your knowing it—through your lips or your nose or any one of your seven openings—and gained your mind. But she would see him. That pole would brain you from behind. And he would gasp, dazzled, and take the first thing she offered, which was pain.

She had a string of children who could breathe only if she said the word. I was the worst of them. She always said the Dark One wanted me most of all, and I believed this. I stood out. Evil was a common thing I trusted. Before sleep sometimes he came and whispered conversation in the old language of the bush. I listened. He told me things he never told anyone but Indians. I was privy to both worlds of his knowledge. I listened to him but, still, I had confidence in Leopolda. For she was the only one of the bunch he even noticed.

There came a day, though, when Leopolda turned the tide with her hook-pole.

It was a quiet day, with all of us working at our desks, when I heard him. He had sneaked into the closets in the back of the room. He was scratching around, tasting crumbs in our pockets, stealing buttons, squirting his dark juice in the linings and the boots. I was the only one who heard him, and I got bold. I smiled. I glanced back and smiled, and looked up at her sly to see if she had noticed. My heart jumped. For she was looking straight at me. And she sniffed. She had a big, stark, bony nose stuck to the front of her face, for smelling out brimstone and evil thoughts. She had smelled him on me. She stood up. Tall, pale, a blackness leading into the deeper blackness of the slate wall behind her. Her oak pole had flown into her grip. She had seen me glance at the closet. Oh, she knew. She knew just where he was. I watched her watch him in her mind's eye. The whole class was watching now. She was staring, sizing, following his scuffle. And all of a sudden she tensed down, poised on her bent knee-springs, cocked her arm back. She threw the oak pole singing over my head. It cracked through the thin wood door of the back closet and the heavy pointed hook drove through his heart. I turned. She'd speared her own black rubber overboot where he'd taken refuge, in the tip of her darkest toe.

Something howled in my mind. Loss and darkness. I understood. I was to suffer for my smile.

He rose up hard in my heart. I didn't blink when the pole cracked. My skull was tough. I didn't flinch when she shrieked in my ear. I only shrugged at the flowers of hell. He wanted me. More than anything he craved me. But then she did the worst. She did what broke my mind to her. She grabbed me by the collar and dragged me, feet flying, through the room and threw me in the closet with her dead black overboot. And I was there. The only light was a crack beneath the door. I asked the Dark One to enter into me and alert my mind. I asked him to restrain my tears, for they were pushing behind my eyes. But he was afraid to come back there. He was afraid of her sharp pole. And I was afraid of Leopolda's pole, too, for the first time. I felt the cold hook in my heart. It could crack through the door at any minute and drag me out, like a dead fish on a gaff, drop me on the floor like a gut-shot squirrel.

I was nothing. I edged back to the wall as far as I could. I breathed the chalk dust. The hem of her full black cloak cut against my cheek. He had left me. Her spear could find me any time. Her keen ears would aim the hook into the beat of my heart.

What was that sound?

It filled the closet, filled it up until it spilled over, but I did not recognize the crying wailing voice as mine until the door cracked open, I saw brightness, and she hoisted me to her camphor-smelling lips.

"He *wants* you," she said. "That's the difference. I give you love."

Love. The black hook. The spear singing through the mind. I saw that she had tracked the Dark-One to my heart and flushed him out into the open. So now my heart was an empty nest where she could lurk.

Well, I was weak. I was weak when I let her in but she got a foothold there. Hard to dislodge as the months passed. Sometimes I felt him—the brush of dim wings—but only rarely did his voice compel. It was between Marie and Leopolda now, and the struggle changed. I began to realize I had been on the wrong track with the fruits of hell. The real way to overcome Leopolda was this: I'd get to heaven first. And then, when I saw her coming, I'd shut the gate. She'd be out! That is why, besides the bowing and the scraping I'd be dealt, I wanted to sit on the altar as a saint.

To this end, I went on up the hill. Sister Leopolda was the consecrated nun who had sponsored me to come there.

"You're not vain," she had said. "You're too honest, looking into the mirror, for that. You're not smart. You don't have the ambition to get clear. You have two choices. One, you can marry a no-good Indian, bear his brats, die like a dog. Or two, you can give yourself to God."

"I'll come up there," I said, "but not because of what you think."

I could have had any damn man on the reservation at the time. And I could have made him treat me like his own life. I looked good. And I looked white. But I wanted Sister Leopolda's heart. And here was the thing: Sometimes I wanted her heart in love and admiration. Sometimes. And sometimes I wanted her heart to roast on a black stick.

SHE ANSWERED THE back door, where they had instructed me to call. I stood there with my bundle. She looked me up and down.

"All right," she said finally. "Come in."

She took my hand. Her fingers were like a bundle of broom straws, so thin and dry, but the strength of them was unnatural. I couldn't have tugged loose if she had been leading me into rooms of white-hot coal. Her strength was a kind of perverse miracle, for she got it from fasting herself thin. Because of this hunger practice, her lips were a wounded brown and her skin was deadly pale. Her eye sockets were two deep, lashless hollows. I told you about the nose. It stuck out far and made the place her eyes moved even deeper, as if she stared out of a gun barrel. She took the bundle from my hands and threw it in the comer.

"You'll be sleeping behind the stove, child."

It was immense, like a great furnace. A small cot was close behind it.

"Looks like it could get warm there," I said.

"Hot. It does."

"Do I get a habit?"

I wanted something like the thing she wore. Flowing black cotton. Her face was strapped in white bandages and a sharp crest of starched cardboard hung over her forehead like a glaring beak. If possible, I wanted a bigger, longer, whiter beak than hers.

"No," she said, grinning her great skull grin. "You don't get one yet. Who knows, you might not like us. Or we might not like you."

But she had loved me, or offered me love. And she had tried to hunt the Dark One down. So I had this confidence.

"I'll inherit your keys from you," I said.

She looked at me sharply, and her grin turned strange. She hissed, taking in her breath. Then she turned to the door and took a key from her belt. It was a giant key, and it unlocked the larder, where the food was stored.

Inside were all kinds of good stuff. Things I'd tasted only once or twice in my life. I saw sticks of dried fruit, jars of orange peel, spices like cinnamon. I saw tins of crackers with ships painted on the side. I saw pickles. Jars of herring and the rind of pigs. Cheese, a big brown block of it from the thick milk of goats. And the everyday stuff, in great quantities, the flour and the coffee.

The cheese got to me. When I saw it my stomach hollowed. My

tongue dripped. I loved that goat-milk cheese better than anything I'd ever eaten. I stared at it. The rich curve in the buttery cloth.

"When you inherit my keys," she said sourly, slamming the door in my face, "you can eat all you want of the priest's cheese."

Then she seemed to consider what she'd done. She looked at me. She took the key from her belt and went back, sliced a hunk off, and put it in my hand.

"If you're good you'll taste this cheese again. When I'm dead and gone," she said.

Then she dragged out the big sack of flour. When I finished that heavenly stuff she told me to roll my sleeves up and begin doing God's labor. For a while we worked in silence, mixing up dough and pounding it out on stone slabs.

"God's work," I said after a while. "If this is God's work, then I've done it all my life."

"Well, you've done it with the Devil in your heart, then," she said. "Not God."

"How do you know?" I asked. But I knew she did. And I wished I had not brought up the subject.

"I see right into you like a clear glass," she said. "I always did."

"You don't know it," she continued after a while, "but he's come around here sulking. He's come around here brooding. You brought him in. He knows the smell of me and he's going to make a last-ditch try to get you back. Don't let him." She glared over at me. Her eyes were cold and lighted. "Don't let him touch you. We'll be a long time getting rid of him."

So I was careful. I was careful not to give him an inch. I said a rosary, two rosaries, three, underneath my breath. I said the Creed. I said every scrap of Latin I knew while we punched the dough with our fists. And still, I dropped the cup. It rolled under that monstrous iron stove, which was getting fired up for baking.

And she was on me. She saw he'd entered my distraction.

"Our good cup," she said. "Get it out of there, Marie."

I reached for the poker to snag it out from beneath the stove. But I had a sinking feeling in my stomach as I did this. Sure enough, her long arm darted past me like a whip. The poker landed in her hand.

"Reach," she said. "Reach with your arm for that cup. And when your flesh is hot, remember that the flames you feel are only one fraction of the heat you will feel in his hellish embrace."

She always did things this way, to teach you lessons. So I wasn't surprised. It was playacting anyway, because a stove isn't very hot underneath, right along the floor. They aren't made that way. Otherwise, a wood floor would burn. So I said yes and got down on my stomach and reached under. I meant to grab it quick and jump up again, before she could think up another lesson, but here it happened. Although I groped for the cup, my hand closed on nothing. That cup was nowhere to be found. I heard her step toward me, a slow step, I heard the creak of thick shoe leather, the little *plat* as the folds of her heavy skirts met, a trickle of fine sand sifting somewhere, perhaps in the bowels of her, and I was afraid. I tried to scramble up, but her foot came down lightly behind my ear, and I was lowered. The foot came down more firmly at the base of my neck, and I was held.

"You're like I was," she said. "He wants you very much."

"He doesn't want me no more," I said. "He had his fill. I got the cup!"

I heard the valve opening, the hissed intake of breath, and knew that I should not have spoken.

"You lie," she said. "You're cold. There is a wicked ice forming in your blood. You don't have a shred of devotion for God. Only wild, cold, dark lust. I know it. I know how you feel. I see the beast . . . the beast watches me out of your eyes sometimes. Cold."

The urgent scrape of metal. It took a moment to know from where. Top of the stove. Kettle. She was steadying herself with the iron poker. I could feel it like pure certainty, driving into the wood floor. I would not remind her of pokers. I heard the water as it came, tipped from the spout, cooling as it fell but still scalding as it struck. I must have twitched beneath her foot because she steadied me, and then the poker nudged up beside my arm as if to guide. "To warm your cold-ash heart," she said. I felt how patient she would be. The water came. My mind was dead blank. Again. I could only think the kettle would be cooling slowly in her hand. I could not stand it. I bit my lip so as not to satisfy her with a sound. She gave me more reason to keep still.

"I will boil him from your mind if you make a peep," she said, "by filling up your ear."

Any sensible fool would have run back down the hill the minute Leopolda let them up from under her heel. But I was snared in her black intelligence by then. I could not think straight. I had prayed so hard I think I broke a cog in my mind. I prayed while her foot squeezed my throat. While my skin burst. I prayed even when I heard the wind come through, shrieking in the busted bird nests. I didn't stop when pure light fell, turning slowly behind my eyelids. God's face. Even that did not disrupt my continued praise. Words came. Words came from nowhere and flooded my mind.

Now I could pray much better than any one of them. Than all of them full force. This was proved. I turned to her in a daze when she let me up. My thoughts were gone, and yet I remember how surprised I was. Tears glittered in her eyes, deep down, like the sinking reflection in a well.

"It was so hard, Marie," she gasped. Her hands were shaking. The kettle clattered against the stove. "But I have used all the water up now. I think he is gone."

"I prayed," I said foolishly, "I prayed very hard."

"Yes," she said. "My dear one, I know."

WE SAT TOGETHER quietly because we had no more words. We let the dough rise and punched it down once. She gave me a bowl of mush, unlocked the sausage from a special cupboard, and took that in to the Sisters. They sat down the hall, chewing their sausage, and I could hear them. I could hear their teeth bite through their bread and meat. I couldn't move. My shirt was dry but the cloth stuck to my back and I couldn't think straight. I was losing the sense to understand how her mind worked. She'd gotten past me with her poker and I would never be a saint. I despaired. I felt I had no inside voice, nothing to direct me, no darkness, no Marie. I was about to throw that cornmeal mush out to the birds and make a run for it, when the vision rose up blazing in my mind.

I was rippling gold. My breasts were bare and my nipples flashed and winked. Diamonds tipped them. I could walk through panes of glass. I could walk through windows. She was at my feet, swallowing the glass after each step I took. I broke through another and another. The glass she swallowed ground and cut until her starved insides were only a subtle dust. She coughed. She coughed a cloud of dust. And then she was only a black rag that flapped off, snagged in bobwire, hung there for an age, and finally rotted into the breeze.

I saw this, mouth hanging open, gazing off into the waving trees.

"Get up!" she cried. "Stop dreaming. It is time to bake."

Two other Sisters had come in with her, wide women with hands like paddles. They were smoothing and evening out the firebox beneath the great jaws of the oven.

"Who is this one?" they asked Leopolda. "Is she yours?"

"She is mine," said Leopolda, "A very good girl."

"What is your name?" one asked me.

"Marie."

"Marie. Star of the Sea."

"She will shine," said Leopolda, "when we have burned off the dark corrosion."

The others laughed, but uncertainly. They were slow, heavy French, who did not understand Leopolda's twisted jokes, although they muttered respectfully at things she said. I knew they wouldn't believe what she had done with the kettle. So I kept quiet.

*"Elle est docile,"* they said approvingly as they left to starch the linens.

"Does it pain?" Leopolda asked me as soon as they were out the door.

I did not answer. I felt sick with the hurt.

"Come along," she said.

The building was quiet now. I followed her up the narrow staircase into a hall of little rooms, many doors, like a hotel. Her cell was at the very end. Inside was a rough straw mattress, a tiny bookcase with a picture of Saint Francis hanging over it, a ragged palm, and a crucifix. She told me to remove my shirt and sit down on her mattress. I did so. She took a pot of salve from the bookcase and began to smooth it upon my burns. Her stern hand made slow, wide circles, stopping the pain. I closed my eyes. I expected to see the docile blackness. Peace. But instead the vision reared up again. My chest was still tipped with diamonds. I was walking through windows. She was chewing up the broken litter I left behind.

"I am going," I said. "Let me go."

But she held me down.

"Don't go," she said quickly. "Don't. We have just begun."

I was weakening. My thoughts were whirling pitifully. The pain had kept me strong, and as it left me I began to forget, I couldn't hold on. I began to wonder if she had really scalded me with the kettle. I could not remember. To remember this seemed the most important thing in the world. But I was losing the memory. The scalding. The pouring. It began to vanish. I felt that my mind was coming off its hinge, flapping in the breeze, hanging by the hair of my own pain. I wrenched out of her grip.

"He was always in you," I said. "Even more than in me. He wanted you even more. And now he's got you. Get thee behind me!"

I shouted that, grabbed my shirt, and ran through the door, throwing the shirt on my body. I got down the stairs and into the kitchen, but no matter what I told myself, I couldn't get out the door. It wasn't finished. And she knew I would not leave. Her quiet step was immediately behind me.

"We must take the bread from the oven now," she said.

She was pretending nothing had happened. But for the first time I had gotten through some chink she'd left in her darkness. Touched some doubt. Her voice was so low and brittle it cracked off at the end of her sentence.

"Help me, Marie," she said slowly.

But I was not going to help her even though she calmly buttoned my shirt up and put the big cloth mittens in my hands for taking out the loaves. I could have bolted then. But I didn't. I knew that something was nearing completion. Something was about to happen. My back was a wall of singing flame. I was turning. I watched her take the long fork in one hand, to tap the loaves. In the other hand she gripped the black poker to hook the pans.

"Help me," she said again, and I thought, Yes, this is part of it. I put the mittens on my hands and swung the door open on its hinges. The oven gaped. She stood back a moment, letting the first blast of heat rush by. I moved behind her. I could feel the heat at my front and at my back. Before, behind. My skin was turning to beaten gold. It was coming quicker than I had thought. The oven was like the gate of a personal hell. Just big enough and hot enough for one person, and that was her. One kick and Leopolda would fly in headfirst. And that would be one millionth of the heat she would feel when she finally collapsed in his hellish embrace.

Saints know these numbers.

She bent forward with her fork held out. I kicked her with all my might. She flew in. But the outstretched poker hit the back wall first, so she rebounded. The oven was not as deep as I had thought.

There was a moment when I felt a sort of thin, hot disappointment, as when a fish slips off the line. Only I was the one going to be lost. She was fearfully silent. She whirled. Her veil had cutting edges. She had the poker in one hand. In the other she held that long sharp fork she used to tap the delicate crusts of loaves. Her face turned upside down on her shoulders. Her face turned blue. But saints are used to miracles. I felt no trace of fear.

If I was going to be lost, let the diamonds cut! Let her eat ground glass!

"Bitch of Jesus Christ!" I shouted. "Kneel and beg! Lick the floor!"

That was when she stabbed me through the hand with the fork, then took the poker up alongside my head and knocked me out.

I came around maybe half an hour later. Things were so strange.

So strange I can hardly tell it for delight at the remembrance. For when I came around this was actually taking place. I was being worshipped. I had somehow gained the altar of a saint.

I was lying back on the stiff couch in the Mother Superior's office. I looked around me. It was as though my deepest dream had come to life. The Sisters of the convent were kneeling to me. Sister Bonaventure. Sister Dympna. Sister Cecilia Saint-Claire. The two with hands like paddles. They were down on their knees. Black capes were slung over some of their heads. My name was buzzing up and down the room like a fat autumn fly, lighting on the tips of the tongues between Latin, humming up the heavy, blood-dark curtains, circling their swaddled heads. Marie! Marie! A girl thrown in a closet. Who was afraid of a rubber overboot. Who was half overcome. A girl who came in the back door where they threw their garbage. Marie! Who never found the cup. Who had to eat their cold mush. Marie! Leopolda had her face buried in her knuckles. Saint Marie of the Holy Slops! Saint Marie of the Bread Fork! Saint Marie of the Burnt Back and Scalded Butt!

I broke out and laughed.

They looked up. All holy hell burst loose when they saw I was awake. I still did not understand what was happening. They were watching, talking, but not to me.

"The marks . . ."

"She has her hand closed."

*"Je ne peux pas voir."*

I was not stupid enough to ask what they were talking about. I couldn't tell why I was lying in white sheets. I couldn't tell why they were praying to me. But I'll tell you this. It seemed entirely natural. It was me. I lifted up my hand as in my dream. It was completely limp with sacredness.

"Peace be with you."

My arm was dried blood from the wrist down to the elbow. And it hurt. Their faces turned like fat flowers of adoration to follow that hand's movements. I let it swing through the air, imparting a saint's blessing. I had practiced. I knew exactly how to act.

They murmured. I heaved a sigh and a golden beam of light suddenly broke through the clouded window and flooded down directly on my face. A stroke of perfect luck!

They had to be convinced.

Leopolda still in the back of the room. Her knuckles were crammed halfway down her throat. Let me tell you, a saint has senses honed keen as a wolf's. I knew that she was over my barrel now. How it had happened did not matter. The last thing I remembered was that she flew from the oven and stabbed me. That one thing was most certainly true.

"Come forward, Sister Leopolda." I gestured with my heavenly wound. Oh, it hurt. It bled when I reopened the place where it had begun to heal. "Kneel beside me," I said.

She kneeled, but her voice box evidently did not work, for her mouth opened, shut, opened, but no sound came out. My throat clenched in the noble delight I had read of as befitting a saint. She could not speak. But she was beaten. It was in her eyes. She stared at me now with all the deep hate of the wheel of devilish dust that rolled wild within her emptiness.

"What is it you want to tell me?" I asked. And at last she spoke.

"I have told my sisters of your passion," she managed to choke out. "How the stigmata . . . the marks of the nails . . . appeared in your palm and you swooned at the holy vision. . . ."

"Yes," I said, curious.

And then, after a moment, I understood.

Leopolda had saved herself with her quick brain. She had witnessed a miracle. She had hid the fork and told this to the others. And of course they believed her, because they never knew how Satan came and went or where he took refuge.

"I saw it from the first," said the large one who had put the bread in the oven. "Humility of the spirit. So rare in these girls."

"I saw it too," said the other one with great satisfaction. She sighed quietly. "If only it was me."

Leopolda was kneeling bolt upright, face blazing and twitching, a barely held fountain of blasting poison.

"Christ has marked me," I agreed. I smiled a saint's smirk in her face. And then I looked at her. That was my mistake.

For I saw her kneeling there. Leopolda with her soul like a rubber overboot. With her face of a starved rat. With her desperate eyes drowning in the deep wells of her wrongness. There would be no one else after me. And I would leave. I saw Leopolda kneeling within the shambles of her love.

My heart had been about to surge from my chest with the blackness of my joyous heat. Now it dropped. I pitied her. I pitied her. Pity twisted in my stomach as if that hook-pole were driven through me at last. I was caught. It was a feeling more terrible than any amount of boiling water and worse than being forked. Still, still, I couldn't help what I did. I had already smiled in a saint's mealy forgiveness. I heard myself speaking gently.

"Receive the dispensation of my sacred blood," I whispered.

But there was no heart in it. No joy when she bent to touch the floor. No dark leaping. I fell back onto the white pillows. Blank dust was whirling through the light shafts. My skin was dust. Dust my lips. Dust the dirty spoons on the ends of my feet.

"Rise up!" I thought. "Rise up and walk! There is no limit to this dust!"

# The Plunge of the Brave

I NEVER WANTED much, and I needed even less, but what happened was that I got everything handed to me on a plate. It came from being a Kashpaw, I used to think. Our family was respected as the last hereditary leaders of this tribe. But Kashpaws died around here, people forgot, and I still kept getting offers.

What kind of offers? Just ask . . .

Jobs for one. I got out of Flandreau with my ears rung from playing football, and the first thing they said was "Nector Kashpaw, go West! Hollywood wants *you!*" They made a lot of westerns in those days. I never talk about this often, but they were hiring for a scene in South Dakota and this talent scout picked me out from the graduating class. His company was pulling in extras for the wagon-train scenes. Because of my height, I got hired on for the biggest Indian part. But they didn't know I was a Kashpaw, because right off I had to die.

"Clutch your chest. Fall off that horse," they directed. That was it. Death was the extent of Indian acting in the movie theater.

So I thought it was quite enough to be killed the once you have to die in this life, and I quit. I hopped a train down the wheat belt and threshed. I got offers there too. Jobs came easy. I worked a year. I was thinking of staying on, but then I got a proposition that discouraged me out of Kansas for good.

Down in the city I met this old rich woman. She had her car stopped when she saw me pass by.

"Ask the chief if he'd like to work for me," she said to her man up front. So her man, a buffalo soldier, did.

"Doing what?" I asked.

"I want him to model for my masterpiece. Tell him all he has to do is stand still and let me paint his picture."

"Sounds easy enough," I agreed.

The pay was fifty dollars. I went to her house. They fed me, and later on they sent me over to her barn. I went in. When I saw her dressed in a white coat with a hat like a little black pancake on her head, I felt pity. She was an old wreck of a thing. Snaggle-toothed. She put me on a block of wood and then said to me, "Disrobe."

No one had ever told me to take off my clothes just like that. So I pretended not to understand her. "Dis or dat robe?" I asked.

"Disrobe," she repeated. I stood there and looked confused. Pitiful! I thought. Then she started to demonstrate by clawing at her buttons. I was just about to go and help her when she said in a near holler, "Take off your clothes!"

She wanted to paint me without a stitch on, of course. There were lots of naked pictures in her barn. I wouldn't do it. She offered money, more money, until she offered me so much that I had to forget my dignity. So I was paid by this woman a round two hundred dollars for standing stock-still in a diaper.

I could not believe it, later, when she showed me the picture. *Plunge of the Brave*, was the title of it. Later on, that picture would become famous. It would hang in the Bismarck state capitol. There I was, jumping off a cliff, naked of course, down into a rocky river. Certain death. Remember Custer's saying? The only good Indian is a dead Indian? Well from my dealings with whites I would add to that quote: "The only interesting Indian is dead, or dying by falling backwards off a horse."

When I saw that the greater world was only interested in my doom, I went home on the back of a train. "Riding the rails one night, the moon was in the boxcar." A nip was in the air. I remembered that picture, and I knew that Nector Kashpaw would fool the pitiful rich woman that painted him and survive the raging water. I'd hold my breath when I hit and let the current pull me toward the surface, around jagged rocks. I wouldn't fight it, and in that way I'd get to shore.

Back home, it seemed like that was happening for a while. Things were quiet. I lived with my mother and Eli in the old place, hunting or roaming or chopping a little wood. I kept thinking about the one book I read in high school. For some reason this priest in Flandreau would teach no other book all four years but *Moby Dick*, the story of the great white whale. I knew that book inside and out. I'd even stolen a copy from school and taken it home in my suitcase.

This led to another famous misunderstanding.

"You're always reading that book," my mother said once. "What's in it?"

"The story of the great white whale."

She could not believe it. After a while, she said, "What do they got to wail about, those whites?"

I told her the whale was a fish as big as the church. She did not believe this either. Who would?

"Call me Ishmael," I said sometimes, only to myself. For he survived the great white monster like I got out of the rich lady's picture. He let the water bounce his coffin to the top. In my life so far I'd gone easy and come out on top, like him. But the river wasn't done with me yet. I floated through the calm sweet spots, but somewhere the river branched.

So far I haven't mentioned the other offers I had been getting. These offers were for candy, sweet candy between the bedcovers. There was girls like new taffy, hardened sourballs of married ladies, rich marshmallow widows, and even a man, rock salt and barley sugar in a jungle of weeds. I never did anything to bring these offers on. They just happened. I never thought twice. Then I fell in love for real.

Lulu Nanapush was the one who made me greedy.

At boarding school, as children, I treated her as my sister and shared our peanut-butter-syrup sandwiches on the bus to stop her crying. I let her tag with me to town. At the movies I bought her licorice. Then we grew up apart from each other, I came home, and saw her dancing in the Friday-night crowd. She was doing the butterfly with two other men. For the first time, on seeing her, I knew exactly what I wanted. We sparked each other. We met behind the dance house and kissed. I knew I wanted more of that sweet taste on her mouth. I got selfish. We were flowing easily toward each other's arms.

Then Marie appeared, and here is what I do not understand: how instantly the course of your life can be changed.

I only know that I went up the convent hill intending to sell geese and came down the hill with the geese still on my arm. Beside me walked a young girl with a mouth on her like a flophouse, although she was innocent. She grudged me to hold her hand. And yet I would not drop the hand and let her walk alone.

Her taste was bitter. I craved the difference after all those years of easy sweetness. But I still had a taste for candy. I could never have enough of both, and that was my problem and the reason that long past the branch in my life I continued to think of Lulu.

Not that I had much time to think once married years set in. I liked each of our babies, but sometimes I was juggling them from both arms and losing hold. Both Marie and I lost hold. In one year, two died, a boy and a girl baby. There was a long spell of quiet, awful quiet, before the babies showed up everywhere again. They were all over in the house once they started. In the bottoms of cupboards, in the dresser, in trundles. Lift a blanket and a bundle would howl beneath it. I lost track of which were ours and which Marie had taken in. It had helped her to take them in after our two others were gone. This went on. The youngest slept between us, in the bed of our bliss, so I was crawling over them to make more of them. It seemed like there was no end.

Sometimes I escaped. I had to have relief. I went drinking and caught holy hell from Marie. After a few years the babies started walking around, but that only meant they needed shoes for their feet. I gave in. I put my nose against the wheel. I kept it there for many years and barely looked up to realize the world was going by, full of wonders and creatures, while I was getting old baling hay for white farmers.

So much time went by in that flash it surprises me yet. What they call a lot of water under the bridge. Maybe it was rapids, a swirl that carried me so swift that I could not look to either side but had to keep my eyes trained on what was coming. Seventeen years of married life and come-and-go children.

And then it was like the river pooled.

Maybe I took my eyes off the current too quick. Maybe the fast movement of time had made me dizzy. I was shocked. I remember the day it happened. I was sitting on the steps, wiring a pot of Marie's that had broken, when everything went still. The children stopped shouting. Marie stopped scolding. The babies slept. The cows, too. The dogs stretched full out in the heat. Nothing moved. Not a leaf or a bell or a human. No sound. It was like the air itself had caved in.

In the stillness, I lifted my head and looked around.

What I saw was time passing, each minute collecting behind me before I had squeezed from it any life. It went so fast, is what I'm saying, that I myself sat still in the center of it. Time was rushing around me like water around a big wet rock. The only difference is, I was not so durable as stones. Very quickly I would be smoothed away. It was happening already.

I put my hand to my face. There was less of me. Less muscle, less hair, less of a hard jaw, less of what used to go on below. Fewer offers. It was 1952, and I had done what was expected—fathered babies, served as chairman of the tribe. That was the extent of it. Don't let the last fool you, either. Getting into the big-time local politics was all low pay and no thanks. I never even ran for the office. Someone put my name down on the ballots, and the night I accepted the job I became somebody less, almost instantly. I grew gray hairs in my sleep. The next morning they were hanging in the comb teeth.

Less and less, until I was sitting on my steps in 1952 thinking I should hang on to whatever I still had.

That is the state of mind I was in when I began to think of Lulu. The truth is I had never gotten over her. I thought back to how swiftly we had been moving toward each other's soft embrace before everything got tangled and swept me on past. In my mind's eye I saw her arms stretched out in longing while I shrank into the blue distance of marriage. Although it had happened with no effort on my part, to ever get back I'd have to swim against the movement of time.

I shook my head to clear it. The children started to shout. Marie scolded, the babies blubbered, the cow stamped, and the dogs complained. The moment of stillness was over; it was brief, but the fact is when I got up from the front steps I was changed.

I put the fixed pot on the table, took my hat off the hook, went out and drove my pickup into town. My brain was sending me the kind of low ache that used to signal a lengthy drunk, and yet that was not what I felt like doing.

Anyway, once I got to town and stopped by the tribal offices, a drunk was out of the question. An emergency was happening.

And here is where events loop around the tangle again.

IT IS JULY. The sun is a fierce white ball. Two big semis from the Polar Bear Refrigerated Trucking Company are pulled up in the yard of the agency offices, and what do you think they're loaded with? Butter. That's right. Seventeen tons of surplus butter on the hottest day in '52. That is what it takes to get me together with Lulu.

Coincidence. I am standing there wrangling with the drivers, who want to dump the butter, when Lulu drives by. I see her, riding slow and smooth on the luxury springs of her Nash Ambassador Custom.

"Hey Lulu," I shout, waving her into the bare, hot yard. "Could you spare a couple hours?"

She rolls down her window and says perhaps. She is high and distant ever since the days of our youth. I'm not thinking, I swear, of anything but delivering the butter. And yet when she alights I cannot help notice an interesting feature of her dress. She turns sideways. I see how it is buttoned all the way down the back. The buttons arc small, square, plump, like the mints they serve next to the cashbox in a fancy restaurant.

I have been to the nation's capital. I have learned there that spitting tobacco is frowned on. To cure myself of chewing I've took to rolling my own. So I have the makings in my pocket, and I quick roll one up to distract myself from wondering if those buttons hurt her where she sits.

"Your car's air-cooled?" I ask. She says it is. Then I make a request, polite and natural, for her to help me deliver these fifty-pound boxes of surplus butter, which will surely melt and run if they are left off in the heat.

She sighs. She looks annoyed. The hair is frizzled behind her neck. To her, Nector Kashpaw is a nuisance. She sees nothing of their youth. He's gone dull. Stiff. Hard to believe, she thinks, how he once cut the rug! Even his eyebrows have a little gray in them now. Hard to believe the girls once followed him around!

But he is, after all, in need of her air-conditioning, so what the heck? I read this in the shrug she gives me.

"Load them in," she says.

So the car is loaded up, I slip in the passenger's side, and we begin delivering the butter. There is no set way we do it, since this is an unexpected shipment. She pulls into a yard and I drag out a box, or two, if they've got a place for it. Between deliveries we do not speak.

Each time we drive into the agency yard to reload, less butter is in the semis. People have heard about it and come to pick up the boxes themselves. It seems surprising, but all of that tonnage is going fast, too fast, because there still hasn't been a word exchanged between Lulu and myself in the car. The afternoon is heated up to its worst, where it will stay several hours. The car is soft inside, deep cushioned and cool. I hate getting out when we drive into the yards. Lulu smiles and talks to the people who come out of their houses. As soon as we are alone, though, she clams up and hums some tune she heard on the radio. I try to get through several times.

"I'm sorry about Henry," I say. Her husband was killed on the railroad tracks. I never had a chance to say I was sorry.

"He was a good man." That is all the answer I get.

"How are your boys?" I ask later. I know she has a lot of them, but you would never guess it. She seems so young.

"Fine."

In desperation, I say she has a border of petunias that is the envy of many far-flung neighbors. Marie has often mentioned it.

"My petunias," she tells me in a flat voice, "are none of your business."

I am shut up for a time, then. I understand that this is useless. Whatever I am doing it is not what she wants. And the truth is, I do not know what I want from it either. Perhaps just a mention that I, Nector Kashpaw, middle-aged butter mover, was the young hard-muscled man who thrilled and sparked her so long ago.

As it turns out, however, I receive so much more. Not because of anything I do or say. It's more mysterious than that.

We are driving back to the agency after the last load, with just two boxes left in the backseat, my box and hers. Since the petunias, she has not even hummed to herself. So I am more than surprised when, in a sudden burst, she says how nice it would be to drive up to the lookout and take in the view.

Now I'm the shy one.

"I've got to get home," I say, "with this butter."

But she simply takes the turn up the hill. Her skin is glowing, as if she were brightly golden beneath the brown. Her hair is dry and electric. I heard her tell somebody, where we stopped, that she didn't have time to curl it. The permanent fuzz shorts out here and there above her forehead. On some women this might look strange, but on Lulu it seems stylish, like her tiny crystal earrings and the French rouge on her cheeks.

I do not compare her with Marie. I would not do that. But the way I ache for Lulu, suddenly, is terrible and sad.

"I don't think we should," I say to her when we stop. The shadows are stretching, smooth and blue, out of the trees.

"Should what?"

Turning to me, her mouth a tight gleaming triangle, her cheekbones high and pointed, her chin a little cup, her eyes lit, she watches.

"Sit here," I say, "alone like this."

"For heavensake," she says, "I'm not going to bite. I just wanted to look at the view."

Then she does just that. She settles back. She puts her arm out the window. The air is mild. She looks down on the spread of trees and sloughs. Then she shuts her eyes.

"It's a damn pretty place," she says. Her voice is blurred and contented. She does not seem angry with me anymore, and because of this, I can ask her what I didn't know I wanted to ask all along. It surprises me by falling off my lips.

"Will you forgive me?"

She doesn't answer right away, which is fine, because I have to get used to the fact that I said it.

"Maybe," she says at last, "but I'm not the same girl."

I'm about to say she hasn't changed, and then I realize how much she has changed. She has gotten smarter than I am by a long shot, to understand she is different.

"I'm different now, too," I am able to admit.

She looks at me, and then something wonderful happens to her face. It opens, as if a flower bloomed all at once or the moon rode out from behind a cloud. She is smiling.

"So your butter's going to melt," she says, then she is laughing outright. She reaches into the backseat and grabs a block. It is wrapped in waxed paper, squashed and soft, but still fresh. She smears some on my face. I'm so surprised that I just sit there for a moment, feeling stupid. Then I wipe the butter off my cheek. I take the block from her and I put it on the dash. When we grab each other and kiss there is butter on our hands. It wears off as we touch, then undo, each other's clothes. All those buttons! I make her turn around so I won't rip any off, then I carefully unfasten them.

"You're different," she agrees now, "better."

I do not want her to say anything else. I tell her to lay quiet. Be still. I get the backrest down with levers. I know how to do this because I thought of it, offhand, as we were driving. I did not plan what happened, though. How could I have planned? How could I have known that I would take the butter from the dash? I rub a handful along her collarbone, then circle her breasts, then let it slide down between them and over the rough little tips. I rub the butter in a circle on her stomach.

"You look pretty like that," I say. "All greased up."

She laughs, laying there, and touches the place I should put more. I do. Then she guides me forward into her body with her hands.

MIDNIGHT FOUND ME in my pickup, that night in July. I was surprised, worn out, more than a little frightened of what we'd done, and I felt so good. I felt loose limbed and strong in the dark breeze, roaring home, the cold air sucking the sweat through my clothes and my veins full of warm, sweet water.

As I turned down our road I saw the lamp, still glowing. That meant Marie was probably sitting up to make sure I slept out in the shack if I was drunk.

I walked in, letting the screen whine softly shut behind me.

"Hello," I whispered, hoping to get on into the next dark room and hide myself in bed. She was sitting at the kitchen table, reading an old catalog. She did not look up from the pictures.

"Hungry?"

"No," I said.

Already she knew, from my walk or the sound of my voice, that I had not been drinking. She flipped some pages.

"Look at this washer," she said. I bent close to study it. She said I smelled like a churn. I told her about the seventeen tons of melting butter and how I'd been hauling it since first thing that afternoon.

"Swam in it too," she said, glancing at my clothes. "Where's ours?"

"What?"

"Our butter."

I'd forgotten it in Lulu's car. My tongue was stuck. I was speechless to realize my sudden guilt.

"You forgot."

She slammed down the catalog and doused the lamp.

• • •

I HAD A job as night watchman at a trailer-hitch plant. Five times a week I went and sat in the janitor's office. Half the night I pushed a broom or meddled with odd repairs. The other half I drowsed, wrote my chairman's reports, made occasional rounds. On the sixth night of the week I left home, as usual, but as soon as I got to the road Lulu Lamartine lived on I turned. I hid the truck in a cove of brush. Then I walked up the road to her house in the dark.

On that sixth night it was as though I left my body at the still wheel of the pickup and inhabited another more youthful one. I moved, witching water. I was full of sinkholes, shot with rapids. Climbing in her bedroom window, I rose. I was a flood that strained bridges. Uncontainable. I rushed into Lulu, and the miracle was she could hold me. She could contain me without giving way. Or she could run with me, unfolding in sheets and snaky waves.

I could twist like a rope. I could disappear beneath the surface. I could run to a halt and Lulu would have been there every moment, just her, and no babies to be careful of tangled somewhere in the covers.

And so this continued five years.

How I managed two lives was a feat of drastic proportions. Most of the time I was moving in a dim fog of pure tiredness. I never got one full morning of sleep those years, because there were babies holed up everywhere set to let loose their squawls at the very moment I started to doze. Oh yes, Marie kept taking in babies right along. Like the butter, there was a surplus of babies on the reservation, and we seemed to get unexpected shipments from time to time.

I got nervous, and no wonder, with demands weighing me down. And as for Lulu, what started off carefree and irregular became a clock-work precision of tuning. I had to get there prompt on night number six, leave just before dawn broke, give and take all the pleasure I could muster myself to stand in between. The more I saw of Lulu the more I realized she was not from the secret land of the Nash Ambassador, but real, a woman like Marie, with a long list of things she needed done or said to please her.

I had to run down the lists of both of them, Lulu and Marie. I had much trouble to keep what they each wanted, when, straight.

In that time, one thing that happened was that Lulu gave birth.

It was when she was carrying the child I began to realize this woman was not only earthly, she had a mind like a wedge of iron. For instance, she never did admit that she was carrying.

"I'm putting on the hog." She clicked her tongue, patting her belly, which was high and round while the rest of her stayed slim.

One night, holding Lulu very close, I felt the baby jump. She said nothing, only smiled. Her white teeth glared in the dark. She snapped at me in play like an animal. In that way she frightened me from asking if the baby was mine. I was jealous of Lulu, and she knew this for a fact. I was jealous because I could not control her or count on her where-abouts. I knew what a lively, sweet-fleshed figure she cut.

And yet I couldn't ask her to be true, since I wasn't. I was two-timing Lulu in being married to Marie, and vice versa of course. Lulu held me tight by that string while she spun off on her own. Who she saw, what she did, I have no way to ever know. But I do think the boy looked like a Kashpaw.

EVERY SO OFTEN I would try to stop time again by finding a still place and sitting there. But the moment I was getting the feel of quietness, leaning up a tree, parked in the truck, sitting with the cows, or just smoking on a rock, so many details of love and politics would flood me. It would be like I had dried my mind out only to receive the fresh dous-ing of, say, more tribal news.

Chippewa politics was thorns in my jeans. I never asked for the chairmanship or, for that matter, anything, and yet I was in the thick and boil of policy. I went to Washington about it. I talked to the gov-ernor. I had to fight like a weasel, but I was fighting with one paw tied behind my back because of wrangling over buying a washer for Marie.

For a time there, Marie only wanted one thing that I could give her. Not love, not sex, just a wringer washer. I didn't blame her, with all the diapers and the overalls and shirts. But our little stockpile of money kept getting used up before it came anywhere near a down payment on the price.

This wrangling and tearing went on with no letup. It was worse than before I'd stopped or took the butter from the dash. Lulu aged me while at the same time she brought back my youth. I was living fast and furious, swept so rapidly from job to home to work to Lulu's arms, and back again, that I could hardly keep my mind on straight at any time. I could not fight this, either. I had to speed where I was took. I only trusted that I would be tossed up on land when everyone who wanted something from Nector Kashpaw had wrung him dry.

So I was ready for the two things that happened in '57. They were almost a relief, to tell the truth, because they had to change my course.

Number one was a slick, flat-faced Cree salesman out of Minneapolis that came and parked his car in Lulu's yard. He was Henry's brother, Beverly Lamartine, a made-good, shifty type who would hang Lulu for a dollar. I told her that. She just laughed.

"There's no harm in him," she said.

"I'll kill him if he puts a hand on you."

She gave me a look that said she wouldn't call a bluff that stupid or mention the obvious except to say, blasting holes in me, "If it wasn't for Marie . . ."

"What?" I said.

She bit her lip and eyed me. I went cold. It entered my mind that she was thinking to marry this urban Indian, this grease-haired vet with tattoos up his arms.

"Oh no," I said, "you wouldn't."

I got desperate with the thought, but I was helpless to sway her anvil mind. I laid her down. I pinned her arms back. I pulled her hair so her chin tipped up. Then I tried my best to make her into my own private puppet that I could dance up and down any way I moved her. That's what I did. Her body sweat and twisted.

I made her take my pleasure. But when I fell back there was still no way I could have Lulu but one—to leave Marie—which was not possible.

Or so I thought.

That night I left Lulu right after she fell back in the pillows. I got in my truck and drove to the lake. I parked alone. I turned the lights off. And then, because even in the stillest of hours, by the side of the water, I was not still, I took off my clothes and walked naked to the shore.

I swam until I felt a clean tug in my soul to go home and forget about Lulu. I told myself I had seen her for the last time that night. I gave her up and dived down to the bottom of the lake where it was cold, dark, still, like the pit bottom of a grave. Perhaps I should have stayed there and never fought. Perhaps I should have taken a breath. But I didn't. The water bounced me up into the thick of my life.

THE NEXT DAY, I was glad of my conclusion to leave Lulu forever. The area redevelopment went through. I was glad, because if I hadn't betrayed Lulu before, I had to do it now, over the very land she lived on. It was not hers. Even though she planted petunias and put the birdbath beneath her window, she didn't own the land, because the Lamartines had squatted there. That land had always belonged to the tribe, I was sorry to find, for now the tribal council had decided that Lulu's land was the one perfect place to locate a factory.

Oh, I argued. I did as much as I could. But government money was dangling before their noses. In the end, as tribal chairman, I was presented with a typed letter I should sign that would formally give notice that Lulu was kicked off the land.

My hand descended like in a dream. I wrote my name on the dotted line. The secretary licked it in an envelope and then someone delivered it to Lulu's door. I tried to let things go, but I was trapped behind the wheel. Whether I liked it or not I was steering something out of control.

That night, I tried to visit Lulu's window out of turn. It was not the sixth night of the week, but I know she expected me. I know because she turned me away.

And that is where the suffering and burning set in to me with fierceness beyond myself. No sooner had I given her up than I wanted Lulu back.

It is a hot night in August. I am sitting in the pool of lamplight at my kitchen table. It is night six, but I am home with Marie and the children. They are all around me, breathing deep or mumbling in a dream. Aurelia and Zelda are hunched in the roll-cot beside the stove. Zelda moans in the dim light and says, "Oh, quick!" Her legs move and twitch like she is chasing something. Her head is full of crossed black pins.

I have my brown cowhide briefcase beside me, open, spilling neat-packed folders and brochures and notes. I take out a blue-lined tablet and a pencil that has never been sharpened. I shave the pencil to a point with my pocketknife. Then I clean the knife and close it up and wonder if I'm really going to write what some part of my mind has decided.

I lick my thumb. The pencil strokes. *August 7, 1957.* My hand moves to the left. *Dear Marie.* I skip down two lines as I was taught in the government school. *I am leaving you.* I press so hard the lead snaps on the pencil.

Zelda sits bolt upright, sniffing the air. She was always a restless sleeper. She would walk through the house as a little girl, to come and visit her parents. Often I would wake to find her standing at the end of our bed, holding the post with both hands as if it was dragging her someplace.

Now, almost full-grown, Zelda frowns at something in her dream and then slowly sinks back beneath her covers and disappears but for one smudge of forehead. I give up. I take the pencil in my hand and begin to write.

*Dear Marie,*

*Can't see going on with this when every day I'm going down even worse. Sure I loved you once, but all this time I am seeing Lulu also. Now she pressured me and the day has come I must get up and go. I apologize. I found true love with her. I don't have a choice. But that doesn't mean Nector Kashpaw will ever forget his own.*

After I write this letter, I fold it up very quickly and lay it in the briefcase. Then I tear off a fresh piece of paper and begin another.

*Dear Lulu,*

*You wanted me for so long. Well you've got me now! Here I am for the taking, girl, all one hundred percent yours. This is my official proposal put down in writing.*

*Yours till hell freezes over,*
*Nector*

And then, because maybe I don't mean it, maybe I just need to get it off my mind, I lock the letters in the briefcase, blow out the lamp, and make my way around sleeping children to Marie. I hang my shirt and pants on the bedpost and slip in next to her. She always sleeps on her side, back toward me, curved around the baby, which is next to the wall so it won't tumble off. She sleeps like this ever since I rolled over on one of them. I fit around her and crook my arm at her waist.

She smells of milk and wood ash and sun-dried cloth. Marie has never used a bottle of perfume. Her hands are big, nicked from sharp knives, roughed by bleach. Her back is hard as a plank. Still she warms me. I feel like pleading with her but I don't know what for. I lay behind her, listening to her breath sigh in and out, and the ache gets worse. It fills my throat like a lump of raw metal. I want to clutch her and never let go, to cry to her and tell her what I've done.

I make a sound between my teeth and she moves, still in her dream. She pulls my arm down tighter, mumbles into her pillow. I take a breath with her breath. I take another. And then my body becomes her body. We are breathing as one, and I am falling gently into sleep still not knowing what will happen.

I sleep like I've been clubbed, all night, very hard. When I wake she has already gone into town with Zelda. They were up early, canning apples. The jars are stacked upside down at one end of the table, reddish gold, pretty with the sun shining through them. I brew my morning coffee and chew the cold galette she has left for me. I am still wondering what I am going to do. It seems as though, all my life up till now, I have not had to make a decision. I just did what came along, went wherever I was taken, accepted when I was called on. I never said no. But now it is one or the other, and my mind can't stretch far enough to understand this.

I go outside and for a long time I occupy myself chopping wood. The children know how to take care of themselves. I pitch and strain at the wood, splitting with a wedge and laying hard into the ax, as if, when the pile gets big enough, it will tell me what to do.

As I am working I suddenly think of Lulu. I get a clear mental picture of her sitting on the lap of her brother-in-law. I see Beverly's big ham reach out and wrap around her shoulder. Lulu's head tips to the side, and her eyes gleam like a bird's. He is nodding at her. Then his mouth is falling onto hers.

I throw the ax. The two lovebirds propel me into the house. I am like a wildman, clutching through my briefcase. I find the letter to Marie and I take it out, read it once, then anchor it on the table with the jar of sugar. I cram the letter to Lulu in my pocket, and then I go.

All I can see, as I gallop down the steps and off into the woods, is Lulu's small red tongue moving across her teeth. My mind quivers, but I cannot stop myself from seeing more. I see his big face nuzzle underneath her chin. I see her hands fly up to clutch his head. She rolls her body expertly beneath his, and then I am crashing through the brush, swatting leaves, almost too blind to see the old deerpath that twists through the woods.

I creep up on her house, as though I will catch them together, even though I have heard he is back in the Cities. I crouch behind some bushes up the hill, expecting her dogs to scent me any moment. I watch. Her house is fresh painted, yellow with black trim, cheerful as a bee. Her petunias are set out front in two old tractor tires painted white. After a time, when the dogs don't find me, I realize they have gone off somewhere. And then I see how foolish I am. The house is quiet. No

Beverly. No boys in the yard, either, fixing cars or target practicing. They are gone, leaving Lulu alone.

I put my hands to my forehead. It is burning as if I have a fever. Since the Nash I have never taken off Lulu's clothes in the daylight, and it enters my head, now, that I could do this if I went down to her house. So I make my way out of the dense bush.

For the first time ever, I go up to her front door and knock. This feels so normal, I am almost frightened. Something in me is about to burst. I need Lulu to show me what this fearful thing is. I need her hand to pull me in and lead me back into her bedroom, and her voice to tell me how we were meant for each other by fate. I need her to tell me I am doing right.

But no one comes to the door. There is no sound. It is a hot, still afternoon, and nothing stirs in Lulu's dull grass, though deep in the trees, to all sides, I have the sense now of something moving slowly forward. An animal that is large, dense furred, nameless. These thoughts are crazy, I know, and I try to cast them from my mind. I round the house. The backyard is the one place where Lulu's tidiness has been defeated. The ground is cluttered with car parts, oil pans, pieces of cement block, and other useful junk.

No one answers at the back door either, so I sit down on the porch. I tell myself that no matter how long it takes Lulu to get here, I will wait. I am not good at waiting, like my brother Eli, who can sit without moving a muscle for an hour while deer approach him. I am not good at waiting, but I try. I roll a cigarette and smoke it as slow as possible. I roll another. I try to think of anything but Lulu or Marie or my children. I think back to the mad captain in *Moby Dick* and how his leg was bit off. Perhaps I was wrong, about Ishmael I mean, for now I see signs of the captain in myself. I bend over and pick up a tin can and crush it flat. For no reason! A bit later I bang the side of her house until my fist hurts. I drop my head in my hands. I tell her, out loud, to get back quick. I do not know what I will do if she doesn't.

I am tired. I have started to shake. That is when I take out the letter I have crumpled in my pocket. I decide that I will read it a hundred times, very slow, before I do anything else. So I read it, word by word, until the words make no sense. I go on reading it. I am keeping careful, concentrated count, when suddenly I think of Marie.

I see her finding the other letter now. Sugar spills across the table as she sits, crying out in her shock. A jar of apples explodes. The children shout, frightened. Grease bubbles over on the stove. The dogs howl. She clutches the letter and tears it up.

I lose count. I try reading Lulu's letter once more, but I cannot finish it. I crumple it in a ball, throw it down, then I light up another cigarette and begin to smoke it very quick while I am rolling a second to keep my hands distracted.

This is, in fact, how the terrible thing happens.

I am so eager to smoke the next cigarette that I do not notice I have thrown down my half-smoked one still lit on the end. I throw it right into the ball of Lulu's letter. The letter smokes. I do not notice right off what is happening, and then the paper flares.

Curious and dazed, I watch the letter burn.

I swear that I do nothing to help the fire along.

Weeds scorch in a tiny circle, and then a bundle of greasy rags puffs out in flames. It burns quickly. I leave the steps. An old strip of rug curls and catches onto some hidden oil slick in the grass. The brown blades spurt and crackle until the flame hits a pile of wood chips. Behind that are cans of gasoline that the boys have removed from dead cars. I step back. The sun is setting in the windows, black and red. I duck. The gas cans roar, burst. Blue lights flash on behind my eyelids, and now long oily flames are licking up the side of the house, moving snakelike along the windows of the porch, finding their way into the kitchen where the kerosene is stored and where Lulu keeps her neatly twine-tied bundles of old newspapers.

The fire is unstoppable. The windows are a furnace. They pop out, raining glass, but I merely close my eyes and am untouched.

I have done nothing.

I feel the heat rise up my legs and collect, burning for Lulu, but burning her out of me.

I don't know how long I stand there, moving back inch by inch as fire rolls through the boards, but I have nearly reached the woods before the heat on my face causes me to abandon the sight, finally, and turn.

That is when I see that I have not been alone.

I see Marie standing in the bush. She is fourteen and slim again. I can do nothing but stare, rooted to the ground. She stands tall, straight and stern as an angel. She watches me. Red flames from the burning house glare and flicker in her eyes. Her skin sheds light. We are face-to-face, and then she begins to lift on waves of heat. Her breast is a glowing shield. Her arm is a white-hot spear. When she raises it the bush behind her spreads, blazing open like wings.

I go down on my knees, a man of rags and tinder. I am ready to be burned in the fire too, but she reaches down and lifts me up.

"Daddy," she says, "Let's get out of here. Let's go."

# The Blue Velvet Box

LONG BEFORE THEY planted beets in Argus and built the highways, there was a railroad. Along the track, which crossed the Dakota–Minnesota border and sketched on east to Minneapolis, everything that made the town arrived. All that diminished the town departed by that route too. On a cold spring morning in 1932 the train brought both an addition and a subtraction. They came by freight. By the time they reached Argus their lips were violet and their feet were so numb that, when they jumped out of the boxcar, they stumbled and scraped their palms and knees through the cinders.

The boy was a tall fourteen, hunched with his sudden growth and very pale. His mouth was sweetly curved, his skin fine and girlish. His sister was only eleven years old, but already she was so short and ordinary that it was obvious she would be this way all her life. Her name was as square and practical as the rest of her: Mary. She brushed her coat off and stood in the watery wind. Between the buildings there was only more bare horizon for her to see, and from time to time men crossing it. Wheat was the big crop then, and the topsoil was so newly tilled that it hadn't all blown off yet, the way it had in Kansas. In fact, times were generally much better in eastern North Dakota than in most places, which is why Karl and Mary Lavelle had come there on the train. Their mother's sister, Fritzie, lived on the eastern edge of town. She ran a butcher shop with her husband.

The two Lavelles put their hands up their sleeves and started walking. Once they began to move they felt warmer, although they'd been traveling all night and the chill had reached in deep. They walked east, down the dirt and planking of the broad main street, reading the signs on each false-front clapboard store they passed, even reading the gilt letters in the window of the brick bank. None of these places was a butcher shop. Abruptly, the stores stopped and a string of houses, weathered gray or peeling gray, with dogs tied to their porch railings, began.

Small trees were planted in the yards of a few of these houses and one tree, weak, a scratch of light against the gray of everything else, tossed in a film of blossoms. Mary trudged solidly forward, hardly glancing at it, but Karl stopped. The tree drew him with its delicate perfume. His cheeks went pink, he stretched his arms out like a sleepwalker, and in one long transfixed motion he floated to the tree and buried his face in the white petals.

Turning to look for Karl, Mary was frightened by how far back he had fallen and how still he was, his face pressed in the flowers. She shouted, but he did not seem to hear her and only stood, strange and stock-still, among the branches. He did not move even when the dog in the yard lunged against its rope and bawled. He did not notice when the door to the house opened and a woman scrambled out. She shouted at Karl too, but he paid her no mind and so she untied her dog. Large and anxious, it flew forward in great bounds. And then, either to protect himself or to seize the blooms, Karl reached out and tore a branch from the tree.

It was such a large branch, from such a small tree, that blight would attack the scar where it was pulled off. The leaves would fall away later that summer and the sap would sink into the roots. The next spring, when Mary passed it on some errand, she saw that it bore no blossoms and remembered how, when the dog jumped for Karl, he struck out with the branch and the petals dropped around the dog's fierce outstretched body in a sudden snow. Then he yelled, "Run!" and Mary ran east, toward Aunt Fritzie. But Karl ran back to the boxcar and the train.

• • •

SO THAT'S HOW I came to Argus. I was the girl in the stiff coat. After I ran blind and came to a halt, shocked not to find Karl behind me, I looked up to watch for him and heard the train whistle long and shrill. That was when I realized Karl had jumped back on the same boxcar and was now hunched in straw, watching out the opened door. The only difference would be the fragrant stick blooming in his hand. I saw the train pulled like a string of black beads over the horizon, as I have seen it so many times since. When it was out of sight, I stared down at my feet. I was afraid. It was not that with Karl gone I had no one to protect me; but just the opposite. With no one to protect and look out for, I was weak. Karl was taller than me but spindly, older of course, but fearful. He suffered from fevers that kept him in a stuporous dream state and was sensitive to loud sounds, harsh lights. My mother called him delicate, but I was the opposite. I was the one who begged rotten apples from the grocery store and stole whey from the back stoop of the creamery in Minneapolis, where we were living the winter after my father died.

This story starts then, because before that and without the year 1929, our family would probably have gone on living comfortably and even have prospered on the Minnesota land that Theodor Lavelle broke and plowed and where he brought his bride, Adelaide, to live. But because that farm was lost, bankrupt like so many around it, our family was scattered to chance. After the foreclosure, my father worked as day labor on other farms in Minnesota. I don't even remember where we were living the day that word came. I only remember that my mother's hair was plaited in two red crooked braids and that she fell, full length, across the floor at the news. It was a common grain-loading accident, and Theodor Lavelle had smothered in oats. After that we moved to a rooming house in the Cities, where my mother thought that, with her figure and good looks, she could find work in a fashionable store. She didn't know, when we moved, that she was pregnant. In a surprisingly short amount of time we were desperate.

I didn't know how badly off we were until my mother stole six heavy, elaborately molded silver spoons from our landlady, who was kind or at least harbored no grudge against us, and whom my mother counted as a friend. Adelaide gave no explanation for the spoons, but she probably did not know I had discovered them in her pocket. Days later, they were gone and Karl and I owned thick overcoats. Also, our shelf was loaded with green bananas. For several weeks we drank quarts of buttermilk and ate buttered toast with thick jam. It was not long after that, I believe, that the baby was ready to be born.

One afternoon my mother sent us downstairs to the landlady. This woman was stout and so dull that I've forgotten her name although I recall vivid details of all else that happened at that time. It was a cold late-winter afternoon. We stared into the glass-faced cabinet where the silver stirrup cups and painted plates were locked after the theft. The outlines of our faces stared back at us like ghosts. From time to time Karl and I heard someone groan upstairs. It was our mother, of course, but we never let on as much. Once something heavy hit the floor directly above our heads. Both of us looked up at the ceiling and threw out our arms involuntarily, as if to catch it. I don't know what went through Karl's mind, but I thought it was the baby, born heavy as lead, dropping straight through the clouds and my mother's body. Because Adelaide insisted that the child would come from heaven although it was obviously growing inside of her, I had a confused idea of the process of birth. At any rate, no explanation I could dream up accounted for the groans, or for the long scream that tore through the air, turned Karl's face white, and caused him to slump forward in the chair.

I had given up on reviving Karl each time he fainted. By that time I trusted that he'd come to by himself, and he always did, looking soft and dazed and somehow refreshed. The most I ever did was support his head until his eyes blinked open. "It's born," he said when he came around, "let's go upstairs."

But as if I knew already that our disaster had been accomplished in that cry, I would not budge. Karl argued and made a case for at least going up the stairs, if not through the actual door, but I sat firm and he had all but given up when the landlady came back downstairs and told us, first, that we now had a baby brother, and, second, that she had found one of her grandmother's silver spoons under the mattress and that she wasn't going to ask how it got there, but would only say we had two weeks to get out.

The woman probably had a good enough heart. She fed us before she sent us upstairs. I suppose she wasn't rich herself, could not be bothered with our problems, and besides that, she felt betrayed by Adelaide. Still, I blame the landlady in some measure for what my mother said that night, in her sleep.

I was sitting in a chair beside Adelaide's bed, in lamp light, holding the baby in a light wool blanket. Karl was curled in a spidery ball at Adelaide's feet. She was sleeping hard, her hair spread wild and bright across the pillows. Her face was sallow and ancient with what she had been through, but after she spoke I had no pity.

"We should let it die," she mumbled. Her lips were pale, frozen in a dream. I would have shaken her awake but the baby was nestled hard against me.

She quieted momentarily, then she turned on her side and gave me a long earnest look.

"We could bury it out back in the lot," she whispered, "that weedy place."

"Mama, wake up," I urged, but she kept speaking.

"I won't have any milk. I'm too thin."

I stopped listening. I looked down at the baby. His face was round, bruised blue, and his eyelids were swollen almost shut. He looked frail, but when he stirred I put my little finger in his mouth, as I had seen women do to quiet their babies, and his suck was eager.

"He's hungry," I said urgently, "wake up and feed him."

But Adelaide rolled over and turned her face to the wall.

MILK CAME FLOODING into Adelaide's breasts, more than the baby could drink at first. She had to feed him. Milk leaked out in dark patches on her pale-blue shirtwaists. She moved heavily, burdened by the ache. She did not completely ignore the baby. She cut her skirts up for diapers, sewed a layette from her nightgown, but at the same time she only grudgingly cared for his basic needs, and often left him to howl. Sometimes he cried such a long time that the landlady came puffing upstairs to see what was wrong. I think she was troubled to see us in such desperation, because she silently brought up food left by the boarders who paid for meals. Nevertheless, she did not change her decision. When the two weeks were up, we still had to move.

Spring was faintly in the air the day we went out looking for a new place. The clouds were high and warm. All of the everyday clothes Adelaide owned had been cut up for the baby, so she had nothing but her fine things, lace and silk, good cashmere. She wore a black coat, a pale green dress trimmed in cream lace, and delicate string gloves. Her beautiful hair was pinned back in a strict knot. We walked down the brick sidewalks looking for signs in windows, for rooming houses of the cheapest kind, barracks, or hotels. We found nothing, and finally sat down to rest on a bench bolted to the side of a store. In those times, the streets of towns were much kindlier. No one minded the destitute gathering strength, taking a load off, discussing their downfall in the world.

"We can't go back to Fritzie," Adelaide said, "I couldn't bear to live with Pete."

"We have nowhere else," I sensibly told her, "unless you sell your heirlooms."

Adelaide gave me a warning look and put her hand to the brooch at her throat. I stopped. She was attached to the few precious treasures she often showed us—the complicated garnet necklace, the onyx mourning brooch, the ring with the good yellow diamond. I supposed that she wouldn't sell them even to save us. Out hardship had beaten her and she was weak, but in her weakness she was also stubborn. We sat on the store's bench for perhaps half an hour, then Karl noticed something like music in the air.

"Mama," he begged, "Mama, can we go? It's a fair!"

As always with Karl, she began by saying no, but that was just a formality and both of them knew it. In no time, he had wheedled and charmed her into going.

The Orphan's Picnic, a fair held to benefit the orphans of Saint Jerome's after the long winter, was taking place just a few streets over at the city fairground. We saw the banner blazing cheerful red, stretched across the entrance, bearing the seal of the patron saint of loneliness. Plank booths were set up in the long, brown winter grass. Cowled nuns switched busily between the scapular and holy medal counters, or stood poised behind racks of rosaries, shoeboxes full of holy cards, tiny carved statuettes of saints, and common toys. We swept into the excitement, looked over the grab bags, games of chance, displays of candy and religious wares. Adelaide stopped at a secular booth that sold jingling hardware, and pulled a whole dollar from her purse.

"I'll take that," she said to the vendor, pointing. He lifted a pearl-handled jacknife from his case and Mama gave it to Karl. Then she pointed at a bead necklace, silver and gold.

"I don't want it," I said to Adelaide.

Her face reddened, but after a slight hesitation she bought the necklace anyway. Then she had Karl fasten it around her throat. She put the baby in my arms.

"Here, Miss Damp Blanket," she said.

Karl laughed and took her hand. Meandering from booth to booth, we finally came to the grandstand, and at once Karl began to pull her toward the seats, drawn by the excitement. I had to stumble along behind them. Bills littered the ground. Posters were pasted up the sides of trees and the splintery walls. Adelaide picked up one of the smaller papers.

"The Great Omar," it said, "Aeronaut Extraordinaire. Appearing here at noon." Below the words there was a picture of a man—sleek, mustachioed, yellow scarf whipping in a breeze.

"Please" Karl said, "please!"

And so we joined the gaping crowd.

The plane dipped, rolled, buzzed, glided above us and I was no more impressed than if it had been some sort of insect. I did not crane my neck or gasp, thrilled, like the rest of them. I looked down at the baby and watched his face. He was just emerging from the newborn's endless sleep and from time to time now he stared fathomlessly into my eyes. I stared back. Looking into his face that day, I found a different arrangement of myself—bolder, quick as light, ill-tempered. He frowned at me, unafraid, unaware that he was helpless, only troubled at the loud drone of the biplane as it landed and taxied toward us on the field.

Thinking back now, I can't believe that I had no premonition of what power The Great Omar had over us. I hardly glanced when he jumped from the plane and I did not applaud his sweeping bows and pronouncements. I hardly knew when he offered rides to those who dared. I believe he charged a dollar or two for the privilege. I did not notice. I was hardly prepared for what came next.

"Here!" my mother called, holding her purse up in the sun. Then without a backward look, without a word, with no warning and no hesitation, she elbowed through the crowd collected at the base of the grandstand and stepped into the cleared space around the pilot. That was when I looked at The Great Omar for the first time, but, as I was so astonished at my mother, I can hardly recall any detail of his appearance. The general impression he gave was dashing, like his posters. The yellow scarf whipped out and certainly he had some sort of mustache. I believe he wore a grease-stained white sweater, perhaps a loose coverall. He was slender and dark, much smaller in relation to his plane than the poster showed, and older. After he helped my mother into the passenger's cockpit and jumped in behind the controls, he pulled a pair of green goggles down over his face. And then there was a startling, endless moment, as they prepared for the takeoff.

"Clear prop!"

The propeller made a wind. The plane lurched forward, lifted over the low trees, gained height. The Great Omar circled the field in a low swoop and I saw my mother's long red crinkly hair spring from its tight knot and float free in an arc that seemed to reach out and tangle around his shoulders.

Karl stared in stricken fascination at the sky, and said nothing as The Great Omar began his stunts and droning passes. I did not watch. Again, I fixed my gaze on the face of my little brother and concentrated on his features, blind to the possibilities of Adelaide's sudden liftoff. I only wanted her to come back down before the plane smashed.

The crowd thinned. People drifted away, but I did not notice. By the time I looked into the sky The Great Omar was flying steadily away from the fairgrounds with my mother. Soon the plane was only a white dot, then it blended into the pale blue sky and vanished.

I shook Karl's arm but he pulled away from me and vaulted to the edge of the grandstand. "Take me!" he screamed, leaning over the rail. He stared at the sky, poised as if he'd throw himself into it.

Satisfaction. That was the first thing I felt after Adelaide flew off. For once she had played no favorites between Karl and me, but left us both. So there was some compensation in what she did. Karl threw his head in his hands and began to sob into his heavy wool sleeves. Only then did I feel frightened.

Below the grandstand, the crowd moved in patternless waves. Over us the clouds spread into a thin sheet that covered the sky like muslin. We watched the dusk collect in the corners of the field. Nuns began to pack away their rosaries and prayer books. Colored lights went on in the little nonreligious booths. Karl slapped his arms, stamped his feet, blew on his fingers. He was more sensitive to cold than I. Huddling around the baby kept me warm.

The baby woke, very hungry, and I was helpless to comfort him. He sucked so hard that my finger was white and puckered, and then he screamed. People gathered around us there. Women held out their arms, but I did not give the baby to any of them. I did not trust them. I did not trust the man who sat down beside me, either, and spoke softly. He was a young man with a hard-boned, sad, unshaven face. What I remember most about him was the sadness. He wanted to take the baby back to his wife so she could feed him. She had a new baby of her own, he said, and enough milk for two.

"I am waiting," I said, "for our own mother."

"When is she coming back?" asked the young man.

I could not answer. The sad man waited with open arms. Karl sat mute on one side of me, gazing into the dark sky. Behind and before, large interfering ladies counseled and conferred.

"Give him the baby, dear."

"Don't be stubborn."

"Let him take the baby home."

"No," I said to every order and suggestion. I even kicked hard when one woman tried to take my brother from my arms. They grew discouraged, or simply indifferent after a time, and went off. It was not the ladies who convinced me, finally, but the baby himself. He did not let up screaming. The longer he cried, the longer the sad man sat beside me, the weaker my resistance was, until finally I could barely hold my own tears back.

"I'm coming with you then," I told the young man. "I'll bring the baby back here when he's fed."

"No," cried Karl, coming out of his stupor suddenly, "you can't leave me alone!"

He grabbed my arm so fervently that the baby slipped, and then the young man caught me, as if to help, but instead he scooped the baby to himself.

"I'll take care of him," he said, and turned away.

I tried to wrench from Karl's grip, but like my mother he was strongest when he was weak, and I could not break free. I saw the man walk into the shadows. I heard the baby's wail fade. I finally sat down beside Karl and let the cold sink into me.

One hour passed. Another hour. When the colored lights went out and the moon came up, diffused behind the sheets of clouds, I knew the young man wasn't coming back. And yet, because he looked too sad to do any harm to anyone, I was more afraid for Karl and myself. We were the ones who were thoroughly lost. I stood up. Karl stood with me. Without a word we walked down the empty streets to our old rooming house. We had no key but Karl displayed one unexpected talent. He took the thin-bladed knife that Adelaide had given him, and picked the lock.

Once we stood in the cold room, the sudden presence of our mother's clothing dismayed us. The room was filled with the faint perfume of the dried flowers that she scattered in her trunk, the rich scent of the clove-studded orange she hung in the closet and the lavender oil she rubbed into her skin at night. The sweetness of her breath seemed to linger, the rustle of her silk underskirt, the quick sound of her heels. Our longing buried us. We sank down on her bed and cried, wrapped in her quilt, clutching each other. When that was done, however, I acquired a brain of ice.

I washed my face off in the basin, then I roused Karl and told him we were going to Aunt Fritzie's. He acquiesced, suffering again in a dumb lethargy. We ate all there was to eat in the room, two cold pancakes, and packed what we owned in a small cardboard suitcase. Karl carried that. I carried the quilt. The last thing I did was reach far back in my mother's drawer and pull out her small round keepsake box. It was covered in blue velvet and tightly locked.

"We might need to sell these things," I told Karl. He hesitated but then, with a hard look, he took the box.

We slipped out before sunrise and walked to the train station. In the weedy yards there were men who knew each boxcar's destination. We found the car we wanted and climbed in. There was hay in one corner. We spread the quilt over it and rolled up together, curled tight, with our heads on the suitcase and Adelaide's blue velvet box between us in Karl's breast pocket. We clung to the thought of the treasures inside of it.

We spent a day and a night on that train while it switched and braked and rumbled on an agonizingly complex route to Argus. We did not dare jump off for a drink of water or to scavenge food. The one time we did try this the train started up so quickly that we were hardly able to catch the side rungs again. We lost our suitcase and the quilt because we took the wrong car, farther back, and that night we did not sleep at all for the cold. Karl was too miserable even to argue with me when I told him it was my turn to hold Adelaide's box. I put it in the bodice of my jumper. It did not keep me warm, but even so, the sparkle of the diamond when I shut my eyes, the patterns of garnets that whirled in the dark air, gave me something. My mind hardened, faceted and gleaming like a magic stone, and I saw my mother clearly.

She was still in the plane, flying close to the pulsing stars, when suddenly Omar noticed that the fuel was getting low. He did not love Adelaide at first sight, or even care what happened to her. He had to save himself. Somehow he had to lighten his load. So he set his controls. He stood up in his cockpit. Then in one sudden motion he plucked my mother out of her seat like a doll and dropped her overboard.

All night she fell through the awful cold. Her coat flapped open and her pale green dress wrapped tightly around her legs. Her red hair flowed straight upward like a flame. She was a candle that gave no warmth. My heart froze. I had no love for her. That is why, by morning, I allowed her to hit the earth.

By the time we saw the sign on the brick station, I was dull again, a block of sullen cold. Still, it hurt when I jumped, scraping my cold knees and the heels of my hands. The pain sharpened me enough to read signs in windows and rack my mind for just where Aunt Fritzie's shop was. It had been years since we visited.

Karl was older, and I probably should not hold myself accountable for losing him too. But I didn't call him. I didn't run after him. I couldn't stand how his face glowed in the blossoms' reflected light, pink and radiant, so like the way he sat beneath our mother's stroking hand.

When I stopped running, I realized I was alone and now more truly lost than any of my family, since all I had done from the first was to try and hold them close while death, panic, chance, and ardor each took them their separate ways.

Hot tears came up suddenly behind my eyes and my ears burned. I ached to cry, hard, but I knew that was useless and so I walked. I walked carefully, looking at everything around me, and it was lucky I did this because I'd run past the butcher shop and, suddenly, there it was, set back from the road down a short dirt drive. A white pig was painted on the side, and inside the pig, the lettering "Kozka's Meats." I walked toward it between rows of tiny fir trees. The place looked both shabby and prosperous, as though Fritzie and Pete were too busy with customers to care for outward appearances. I stood on the broad front stoop and noticed everything I could, the way a beggar does. A rack of elk horns was nailed overhead. I walked beneath them.

The entryway was dark, my heart was in my throat. And then, what I saw was quite natural, understandable, although it was not real.

Again, the dog leapt toward Karl and blossoms from his stick fell. Except that they fell around me in the entrance to the store. I smelled the petals melting on my coat, tasted their thin sweetness in my mouth. I had no time to wonder how this could be happening because they disappeared as suddenly as they'd come when I told my name to the man behind the glass counter.

This man, tall and fat with a pale brown mustache and an old blue denim cap on his head, was Uncle Pete. His eyes were round, mild, exactly the same light brown as his hair. His smile was slow, sweet for a butcher, and always hopeful. He did not recognize me even after I told him who I was. Finally his eyes widened and he called out for Fritzie.

"Your sister's girl! She's here!" he shouted down the hall.

I told him I was alone, that I had come in on the boxcar, and he lifted me up in his arms. He carried me back to the kitchen, where Aunt Fritzie was frying a sausage for my cousin, the beautiful Sita, who sat at the table and stared at me with narrowed eyes while I tried to tell Fritzie and Pete just how I'd come to walk into their front door out of nowhere.

They stared at me with friendly suspicion, thinking that I'd run away. But when I told them about The Great Omar, and how Adelaide held up her purse, and how Omar helped her into the plane, their faces turned grim.

"Sita, go polish the glass out front," said Aunt Fritzie. Sita slid unwillingly out of her chair. "Now," Fritzie said. Uncle Pete sat down heavily. The ends of his mustache went into his mouth, he pressed his thumbs together under his chin, and turned to me. "Go on, tell the rest," he said, and so I told all of the rest, and when I had finished I saw that I had also drunk a glass of milk and eaten a sausage. By then I could hardly sit upright. Uncle Pete took me in his strong arms and I remember sagging against him, then nothing. I slept that day and all night and did not wake until the next morning. Sleep robbed me as profoundly as being awake had, for when I finally woke I had no memory of where I was and how I'd got there. I lay still for what seemed like a long while, trying to place the objects in the room.

This was the room where I would sleep for the rest of my childhood, or what passed for childhood anyway, since after that train journey I was not a child. It was a pleasant room, and before me it belonged entirely to cousin Sita. The paneling was warm-stained pine. Most of the space was taken up by a tall oak dresser with fancy curlicues and many drawers. A small sheet of polished tin hung on the door and served as a mirror. Through that door, as I was trying to understand my surroundings, walked Sita herself, tall and perfect with a blond braid that reached to her waist.

"So you're finally awake." She sat down on the edge of my trundle bed and folded her arms over her small new breasts. She was a year older than me. Since I'd seen her last, she had grown suddenly, like Karl, but her growth had not thinned her into an awkward bony creature. She was now a slim female of utter grace.

I realized I was staring too long at her, and then the whole series of events came flooding back and I turned away. Sita grinned. She looked down at me, her strong white teeth shining, and she stroked the blond braid that hung down over one shoulder.

"Where's Auntie Adelaide?" she asked.

I did not answer.

"Where's Auntie Adelaide?" she asked, again. "How come you came here? Where'd she go? Where's Karl?"

"I don't know."

I suppose I thought the misery of my answer would quiet Sita but that was before I knew her. It only fueled more questions.

"How come Auntie left you alone? Where's Karl? What's this?"

She took the blue velvet box from my pile of clothes and shook it casually next to her ear.

"What's in it?"

For the moment at least, I bested her by snatching the box with an angry swiftness she did not expect. I rolled from the bed, bundled my clothes into my arms, and walked out of the room. The one door open in the hallway was the bathroom, a large smoky room of many uses that soon became my haven since it was the only door I could bolt against my cousin.

EVERY DAY FOR weeks after I arrived in Argus, I woke up thinking I was back on the farm with my mother and father and that none of this had happened. I always managed to believe this until I opened my eyes. Then I saw the dark swirls in the pine and Sita's arm hanging off the bed above me. I smelled the air, peppery and warm from the sausage makers. I heard the rhythmical whine of meat saws, slicers, the rippling beat of fans. Aunt Fritzie was smoking her sharp Viceroys in the bathroom. Uncle Pete was outside feeding the big white German shepherd that was kept in the shop at night to guard the canvas bags of money.

Every morning I got up, put on one of Sita's hand-me-down pink dresses, and went out to the kitchen to wait for Uncle Pete. I cooked breakfast. That I made fried eggs and a good cup of coffee at age eleven was a source of wonder to my aunt and uncle, and an outrage to Sita. That's why I did it every morning, with a finesse that got more casual until it became a habit to have me there.

From the first I made myself essential. I did this because I had to, because I had nothing else to offer. The day after I arrived in Argus and woke up to Sita's calculating smile I also tried to offer what I thought was treasure, the blue velvet box that held Adelaide's heirlooms.

I did it in as grand a manner as I could, with Sita for a witness and with Pete and Fritzie sitting at the kitchen table. That morning, I walked in with my hair combed wet and laid the box between the two of them. I looked at Sita as I spoke.

"This should pay my way."

Fritzie looked at me. She had my mother's features sharpened one notch past beauty. Her skin was rough and her short curled hair was yellow, bleached pale, not golden. Fritzie's eyes were a swimming, crazy shade of blue that startled customers. She ate heartily, but her constant smoking kept her string-bean thin and sallow.

"You don't have to pay us," said Fritzie, "Pete, tell her. She doesn't have to pay us. Sit down, shut up, and eat."

Fritzie spoke like that, joking and blunt. Pete was slower. "Come. Sit down and forget about the money," he said. "You never know about your mother . . . ," he added in an earnest voice that trailed away when he looked at Aunt Fritzie. Things had a way of evaporating under her eyes, vanishing, getting sucked up into the blue heat of her stare. Even Sita had nothing to say.

"I want to give you this," I said. "I insist."

"She insists," exclaimed Aunt Fritzie. Her smile had a rakish flourish because one tooth was chipped in front. "Don't insist," she said. "Eat."

But I would not sit down. I took a knife from the butter plate and started to pry the lock up.

"Here now," said Fritzie. "Pete, help her."

So Pete got up slowly and fetched a screwdriver from the top of the icebox and sat down and jammed the end underneath the lock.

"Let her open it," said Fritzie, when the lock popped up. So Pete pushed the little round box across the table.

"I bet it's empty," Sita said. She took a big chance saying that, but it paid off in spades and aces between us growing up, because I lifted the lid a moment later and what she said was true. There was nothing of value in the box.

Stick pins. A few thick metal buttons off a coat. And a ticket describing the necklace of tiny garnets, pawned for practically nothing in Minneapolis.

There was silence. Even Fritzie was at a loss. Sita nearly buzzed off her chair in triumph but held her tongue, that is until later, when she would crow. Pete put his hand on his head in deep vexation. I stood quietly, stunned.

What is dark is light and bad news brings slow gain, I told myself. I could see a pattern to all of what happened, a pattern that suggested completion in years to come. The baby was lifted up while my mother was dashed to earth. Karl rode west and I ran east. It is opposites that finally meet.

# Pounding the Dog

"WE ARE VERY much like the dead," Mary tells me, "except that we have the use of our senses."

She is kneading Polish sausage meat with her bare hands. Clouds of white pepper hang in the air around her head. Her thin hair is the color of a mouse, pinned just over her ears in two pugs. She is being mental again, what I mean is she is going off on flights of fantasy. Since I work for her, I always feel like it is my job to bring her back.

"Sounds like Tol Bayer," I say. "He had all the symptoms of an alcoholic except that he never drank."

Mary Lavelle brings out the worst intimidations of my heart. I can't help myself from pulling her leg. Now she walks over to the salt barrel and stands there, looking quizzical, before she picks up a handful. She walks back, throws it in the meat, and starts kneading again. And for a while that is enough of her boolah about the dead.

MARY TRIES TO get her imagination to mend the holes in her understanding. So I come to see her in the grape arbor the next day. It is Sunday, so the shop is closed down and quiet. She is sitting in a lawn chair picking stems off blue grapes. When she sees me she puts her basket down, reaches underneath her chair, and then hands me a common red brick.

"This flew in my window," she says, "smashed it too."

"I hope you caught the kid," I say.

"There was no kid."

I tell myself not to argue with Mary, but I can't help arguing like I can't help the man in the moon.

"Someone chucked it and ran off," I say.

"Nobody chucked it."

"So what do you suggest did happen?"

"This brick is a sign," she says.

"Of what?"

"Trouble."

That does not surprise me. Mary has never had a sign announcing something good. She goes in to wash casings, and I finish cleaning grapes in the arbor. I don't give her red brick a second thought. I don't want to hear any more of her mysterious claims.

But then, that night, I have a dream.

I dream that Sita Kozka is standing outside in her front yard, underneath the mountain ash. I see the orange berries glowing behind her, the ferny leaves tossing in the air. She is twisting her hands in a blue-checked apron and looking out on the road. She is watching for someone.

"I call and you don't come," she mutters.

"What?" I say.

Her eyes have retreated in bruised pits, and her cheeks are sunken, pale as dough.

"I call and you don't come," she says again.

Maybe it is the brilliance of the berries in the tree, the blue and white of the apron, or Sita's long look of sickness. Whatever it is, the dream is more real than life to me. I awaken, and the sky is the dim gray of predawn. I cannot sleep again. I lay in bed watching the sky gradually lighten, wondering what this dream of Sita Kozka is all about.

In full morning I walk into the shop, and right away I ask Mary to come sit down before we get to work. I put her percolator on the table between us, and then I tell her about my Dream. One thing I know we'll always agree on is Sita. She considers herself high class, above us, ever since she married the state health inspector who was also the mayor of Blue Mound.

"She's got an illness," says Mary.

"She looked half dead to me."

"She's asking for you."

"I don't know what she'd want to see me for."

Yet I was bosom friends with Sita for many years. We grew up together, thick as thieves, fighting and making up. I never got the best of Sita. She is taller than me. She used to sit on my chest and bat me with her long heavy braid. Her hair is short now, fixed by a beauty nook and curly as a poodle. In the dream, it stuck out in spikes, flattened on one side, so I know she has not been to the hairdresser in some time.

"I'll go along with you," says Mary. "After all, she's my cousin. I should go."

So we sit there and wonder what we're going to do with the dog.

In other words, we have decided to motor thirteen miles to Blue Mound and answer Sita's call. She's close, but very far. Blue Mound has a total population of less than 200 so what we say of Sita's husband is big frog, small pond. We will take Highway 189 straight over there like a shot. Just in case we have to stay there long, we pack our nightgowns, a sheet cake, and two summer sausages in the delivery truck. I leave my nephew Adrian in charge of the shop, but he will not care for Mary's dog, Jimmy, so we must visit Uncle Kah on the way out of town.

Uncle Kah still lives down by the river in a little house full of skins and traps that's even shabbier and more broken down than ever. Driving up, it looks like a random pile of boards. And even though I know what it really is, I am surprised to see Uncle Kah emerge. Already, I can see from his grin, he's been at the sour beer. He's full of ginger. There is barely a tooth in his mouth.

"Golly yes," he says, nodding in his excitable way. "I'll take the dog, but if you come back and he's dead, well he's dead."

Mary says that Jimmy is a good little watchdog, and she doesn't care for Kah to pound on him. Sometimes Kah has a wicked mind. So I say thank you anyway, I will take the dog along. There is no hint that the dog will be so much trouble. He yaps at strangers when they come into the house, but there is no harm in him beyond that. I do remember Sita hates dogs, and I ask Mary if she thinks Sita will mind Little Jimmy.

"She'll have to take the bad along with us," says Mary. "After all, it was her that asked you."

"Yes," I say. There is something about this that troubles me. "But she asked in my dream."

"There's no difference," says Mary, and I know there is none to her. She takes out her embroidery yarn, licks a divided thread, and starts sewing. That yarn starts me thinking about Mary's sewing machine and how Sita usurped it, even though it was one of the few things left to Mary by her mother. That machine was a nice cabinet style, antique by now. I think that we could haul it back in our truck, providing that Sita still has it sitting in her garage.

"Maybe we could get your sewing machine, Mary," I say.

"I never wanted it," says Mary. She puts her embroidery away. It is a picture of crows. After a few miles she turns to me and says, "Sita hasn't got long now."

"What makes you think that?"

Mary takes the brick from her pocket and spits on it. The spit will dry in the shape of a calendar date, she says. She stares at the brick like it was suddenly going to talk. I tell her to put it away.

I have worked sorting cookies in a moving trough, and cracking eggs. I have worked doing errands for a bookkeeper who paid me in her old, cast-off dresses. I have wrapped butter and operated a telephone switchboard. But I have never worked with anyone like Mary.

She is an ordinary-looking person, except for her yellow eyes. It's the way she dresses that makes her look odd. For the trip she's wound her head in a black silk scarf with fringes. Her eyes are sharp and bright. She's hunched over like an old turtle, and I can't help wondering, as usual, what's going through her mind. She's got the dog in her lap, and she's eating raisins from a little bag.

SITA LIVES IN the only new house in Blue Mound, a big white house that she calls a colonial, with shutters that do not shut. She is standing there when we turn into the drive. Just like in the dream, her hands are twisted in a stiff blue apron. Just like in the dream, the orange berries glow behind her head. She looks sick. We get out of the car. Unlike in the dream, she puts her hands on her hips and yells.

"Get your damn dog out of my roses!"

Then she reaches into her tree, pulls down a hard clod of those berries, and throws them at Little Jimmy. The dog scampers away.

"He was just watering them for you," says Mary. "Don't get all set back."

I try to smooth the situation over by complimenting Sita. She is usually calmed by compliments, but this time it doesn't work.

"You look good," I tell her.

Her eyes pick me apart.

"So do the leaves before they die," she states.

At that, Mary starts to laugh, which turns Sita's face a greenish white.

"I'm sick," says Sita, glaring nowhere, "sick as a sick cat."

Then she turns on her heel, stamps up the columned entry into her house, and slams the door shut behind her. Mary catches Little Jimmy, and we tie him to the ash tree with a piece of clothesline. We get our bags and our sheet cake from the delivery truck, and Mary follows me up the walk with the summer sausages.

Looking at her, all in black with those sausages wrapped in white paper, I think she reminds me of something. What is it? I pause at Sita's door and look back at Mary. Then I know. She's like the picture of the grim reaper on the month of January. The hem of her black skirt drags. She looks like she's seen it all. And she carries those sausages like they were symbols of her calling.

We usually bring at least one sausage anywhere we go. But now I think it's odd how we decided, without thinking, to bring two. Mary walks up the entry steps light and slow.

"What," she says suspiciously, "are you standing there for?"

I remember the reason we packed the second sausage. For the funeral. For the pallbearers to eat with their beer.

Inside Sita's house everything is neutral. What I mean is Sita doesn't let things pile up, so you don't get any feeling about anyone who lives there. Sita's tables have nothing on them but an ashtray. They are not like my tables. You walk into my house and right away there is a pile of fishing tackle on the table, balls of wool, or a *Fate* magazine to get you over that awkward moment.

Sita is upstairs in the bathroom. We hear the water flushing. So we walk through the living room, hang the sausages in her pantry, and put the sheet cake on her kitchen table. In the kitchen, particularly, we expect to see a few signs of Sita's sickness and neglect. But every pot is washed and put away. The steel sink is scoured. Even the tile floor is freshly waxed.

"I don't know how she does it," I say in a loud voice, thinking she will hear me. But Sita isn't on the stairs, coming down to greet us. The water is still gushing.

I hoped we had got by that awkward moment, but then it comes. We set our traveling bags on the kitchen floor, as that seems the most welcoming room in Sita's house so far. Then we sit down, not knowing what to do with ourselves.

"I suppose she's trying to get fixed up a little," says Mary after several minutes go by. Finally the water stops flowing through the pipes. But then it slaps and gurgles, as if she is bathing.

"At least she can manage that by herself," I say.

Mary is looking, at the pot with a longing expression. "I'll brew some coffee. It'll be nice and hot for her when she gets down here," she says.

"We'll all have a snack," I agree, hungry for the uncut cake.

Mary rifles through the cupboards for the coffee, but of course it's on the counter in the green canister labeled "Coffee."

"I wouldn't think she'd keep it here," says Mary.

"Why not?" I say. "Sita does things by the book."

She is taking her bath by the book now, washing every inch of herself. From the early years we spent close, when I slept over some nights, I know she is using exactly one capful of bath powder. Afterwards she'll dust herself with cornstarch. Then she'll sit down on the edge of her bed, wrapped in a towel, and file her nails into perfect ovals.

"As for me," says Mary, strangely reading my thoughts, "I like to rub a lemon on my face."

"That's why your skin's all puckered up," I blurt. I hate for her to read my thoughts, but now I've hurt her feelings.

"Perhaps I'll stitch," she says after a moment, subdued. She rummages in her strained valise for the picture of the crows and can't seem to find it. I guess I have got touchy. Sita is embarrassing me for her. It is not a hop and a skip to Blue Mound, and we are tired. Outside, Little Jimmy is bawling, probably wound so tight to that tree trunk he cannot move.

"I use my coffee canister for trading stamps," I tell Mary. "It fills up exactly the size of two booklets."

Mary brightens and draws her hand out of her bag.

"The flour bins," she says. "They're too small in those sets. That's where I like to keep my screwdriver and my canning tongs. . . ."

She looks over at Sita's canisters, sharpens her eyes at me, and listens up the stairs to see if Sita is still occupied.

"Go ahead, look," I say. "See if she keeps flour in her canister."

So Mary opens the green canister.

"Wouldn't you know it," she whispers. "Of course she would keep her flour where it belongs." Then, suddenly, she snaps her head down and peers closer. "Mealybugs. Her flour's got the mealybugs," she states.

We feel better immediately. The coffee is boiling. At last, there is a sign that Sita isn't managing for herself, I feel reckless. I can still hear Sita moving around upstairs. She'll die before she hurries down to us.

"Throw it out," I say. "We wouldn't want her to find the bugs in her condition."

"They're having a heyday," says Mary, still watching them. If it were her choice, I think she'd run upstairs and show them to Sita, she seems so reluctant to let them go. "All right," she says at last. "I'll take it out back and dump it in the garden."

In a moment, she brings back the empty canister and puts it in place. We are just pouring the coffee out in three of Sita's matching cups and cutting the cake, when she walks down the stairs.

"We just brewed up some coffee," I say in a pleasant voice.

"There wasn't none made," says Mary in an accusing tone. Then she remembers. "This cake's fresh," she says.

Her black scarf has slipped down over her forehead in a little visor, and when she stares at Sita she looks like she is placing a bet.

I turn to Sita quickly, meaning to compliment her looks now that she's fixed herself up. But Sita looks exactly the same, no fresher than when we first met her in the yard. She hasn't changed her clothes, and her hairdo is still lopsided. I know she sleeps in a roll of pinned toilet paper all week to save her hairdo, and now I find another sign of the strain.

As she turns to the refrigerator to get out the cream, I see that a neat pink square of toilet paper has been left pinned to the back of her head. Yet even this almost seems intentional with her. When she turns back I don't say anything. But Mary is smiling.

"I hope you enjoy this," she says in a sweet, syrupy voice, setting the brown and yellow square of cake before Sita.

Sita opens a drawer and takes out three white paper napkins with scalloped borders. She sets these carefully beside our plates. Then she sits down and takes a bite, and a sip, and another bite. She's about to take a third bite when she looks at her fork.

Mary and I have nearly finished our pieces, and I am thinking how empty this kitchen looks, with no sign of cooking. Does Sita eat from a can or a box?

Sita is gazing with shocked attention at something on the end of her fork. She puts the cake down, and then, prinking her finger, delicately draws a transparent scrap out of the bite of cake and puts it on the edge of her dessert plate.

We crane our necks across the table. We can't help it. We see that the scrap on the edge of Sita's plate is a finely baked amber wing, brittle and threaded with fragile veins.

"That's a wing," Mary observes, putting down her fork.

"It is the wing of an Indian meal moth, to be exact," says Sita. Her voice is acid, her mouth pinched and wry. "They usually don't get to be this size."

Mary gazes at the wing for a moment, interestedly, but not as though it had anything to do with her. She picks up her fork and begins to eat her cake again, relishing it even.

Sita's head slowly turns. The toilet paper on the back of her head flutters like a feather. Her eyes watch the cake moving from plate to fork to mouth of Mary. She looks like an outraged hen sitting there, so boney beaked and peckish.

"How do you know the name of it?" I ask, to divert her attention. Then I remember her husband had something to do with infestations. "Did you learn that from Louis?"

"After he resigned his post as health inspector," she says between her teeth, still intent on the moving bites of cake, "Louis was the county extension entomologist." I try to signal Mary not to take another piece, but already she is lifting the square out of the pan.

"Bugs can't hurt a person when they're cooked," she tells us.

I don't want to look at Sita. I sip my coffee as long as possible. Then I do look at her and see that all the color has left her face; she is fearfully pale. She is so mad that her lips have turned blue. I put the cup down and brace myself, knowing from those early years that her rage must fall.

"You won't bring those loathsome insects in my house!" Sita shrieks, jumping up so suddenly that the piece of toilet paper floats off the back of her head.

Mary looks uncertainly at her fork, but it is too late.

Sita picks up the sheet cake, and without a word or glance, takes it out the back door. I hear her walking down the steps and the garbage pail clanging, and then she slams back in with the empty pan and puts it in the sink. She walks behind Mary, snakes her bony arm around her, and plucks the saucer away from Mary and the fork from her hand.

Now Sita has gone too far. When she walks toward the door again, meaning to shake the cake off the fork and throw the crumbs in the garbage, Mary leaps up. Her head scarf drops over her eyes, so she has to jut her chin in Sita's face to see beneath it.

"You should talk about the bugs!" she shouts. Yellow sparks are spinning from her eyes. "Talk about the bugs in your flour, Miss High Nose! You got the mealybugs. I saw the mealybugs populating in your canister!"

Sita turns. She is rail thin, and her whole face is now blue with wrath. She rushes to the canister, rips the cover off, and sure enough it's empty. She peers into it like Mary did and presently shakes it toward the light. She stands there so long, looking into the bottom of the metal canister, that I wonder if the shock has been too much. Mary looks down at her shoes, ashamed. We just stand there like paralyzed statues.

"There's one now," Sita finally says, "a rust flour beetle." She walks across the kitchen with the canister, kicks open the back screen, and flings the canister out. The can rings when it hits the ground. "I know my beetles," she says, turning. Her face is grim. She sits down with her coffee and begins to drink.

"What's this?"

Lastly, she notices the square of toilet paper that dropped off her head. It has landed precisely in the middle of the table. She looks at us, glancing quickly at each of our faces. She stares back into her cup as though she has seen something terrible. It is as though I can suddenly read minds like Mary, for I believe I hear her thinking a thought.

They have come here to torment me unto the bitter end.

And yet, it was Sita who had called.

POOR LITTLE JIMMY. We have not remembered his food, so in the days that follow we give him scraps or go down to the corner market for expensive emergency cans. A dog living in a butcher shop gets spoiled. But often now Little Jimmy has to fend for himself. He digs holes in Sita's iris borders, looking for a well-cured bone. That first night, he sneaks into the garbage can and gobbles up the sheet cake, bugs and all. We can't keep him on the cord because he bites through it with his strong little teeth whenever he feels like roaming. He's a house dog. But of course we can't keep him in the house.

Sita hates him. You can tell it in her eyes when he begs at the door. I fill the holes up behind him and replant the iris, hoping she will not be too hard on Little Jimmy. If she notices the patched ground, she never says so. We can see now that Sita is as sick as my dream said. The doctor comes. She sleeps afterwards. He says he can't do much and gives me a bottle of pills to smash.

After the strife over the mealybugs, Mary settles in to this visit. It seems to me that she flourishes in the presence of death the way some women perk up around a good-looking man. She removes her black fringed scarf and pins her hair up in soft braids. She wears a dress with purple flowers and hums as she cooks custards and broths to tempt Sita's picky appetite. She shakes her can of brewer's yeast in everything she makes, while I grind the bitter pills that do nothing for Sita except exhaust her with sleep. Everything we eat is flavored with the stale yeast powder, and Sita's with the medicine besides. But Sita hardly notices what she eats anymore.

Indeed, she moves less, says less, as the days go by. In the evenings, we sit on the porch and she wraps herself in her best afghans. A sign. No woman uses the best afghans on herself. But who else is there to save them for? This visit has lengthened from days into weeks, and we are the only people to have visited Sita in all this time. She certainly wouldn't want to save her afghans for us.

One night she is talkative.

"Why did you come here," she asks, "you and my cousin and your damn little dog?"

"Because I knew you were sick," I say.

"You knew I was sick." She rocks in the falling light. Her face is like a carved bone already, and she reads me from dark pits. "Oh yes, you thought you might inherit something that I own."

This gets my goat, "We're good to you because your mother was good to us," I tell her. "We're not here because we want anything of yours."

She sits there, creaking in her chair. I can't tell if it's the ungreased rockers or her weakening bones that make the sound. There is a long silence between us but then I think how mean she has been, and I know I won't be able to help myself from asking what I thought of in the truck.

"But you could will Mary the sewing machine her mother left her," I say.

The creaking stops. Her mouth is open, black and wide as an attic. A bat could swoop in there and perch. Her mouth opens even wider when she starts to laugh. I realize I haven't heard her laugh yet, not since we got here; then all of a sudden she chokes to a halt.

"That hoary old thing broke down twenty years ago, and I gave it to the Stacks."

I know the Stack family. They are the disreputed prodigals of Blue Mound who live mainly off their sales of balled aluminum foil. I know that Stack girl couldn't sew with that machine, wouldn't sew with it, never intended to sew with it in the future, and probably chopped the cabinet up to kindle fires one cold winter.

I have nothing more to say to Sita Kozka. I leave her creaking, her wasted bosom shielded in her arms, and I walk upstairs to see what Mary is doing.

We share Sita's upstairs guest room. Some nights I lay awake for hours, listening to Mary ramble in her sleep. She has long threatening conversations with unknown people. "Hand it over," she says. "We can't wait any longer."

One night, as I am listening, I realize what she is doing in her sleep: she is collecting outstanding bills. She has her foot in the front door of the dream. She shouts when it closes on her foot. "You signed the note," she hollers. "I'll see you in court!" She is good at this, and should be since she's been doing it all her life.

"I'm done," she says when I come in the room.

She has spread out. Her valise unpacked a surprising number of things that are now settled in Sita's bare guest room. The red brick is on the stand beside her bed, wrapped carefully in a washcloth so none of its cosmic powers leak into the air. She is not one to hide her clothes, even underclothes, from view. They are stacked or draped on bureaus or chairs. Only her great white cotton bloomers are neatly hung, clothes-pinned to hangers and swung off the closet doorknobs because Sita will not allow her to dry them out on the line. A chipped green statue of the

Virgin Mary is set up behind the brick. She has stacked her astrology books and embroidery in handy corners. I see now that she has finished her picture of crows swooping down on a field.

She holds it up for me to admire.

The crows are of various sizes. The largest of them is close up in the center of the picture. Its beak is open; its eyes are wild and bright. It looks like it is going to tell us about the end of this farmer's crop.

I am reminded of Mary by this picture, by the crow's sharp eyes.

"The night sky is full of baffling holes," she says. She drops the cloth picture on the arm of the chair. That is not the comment I expected her crow to make. I take the embroidered cloth off the arm of the chair and set it on the footboard. Then I sit down in the chair.

She tells me about holes in space that suck everything into them. They even suck space into space. I cannot picture that. In my mind I see other things, though, drawn away at high speed into the blackness. Just this morning I discovered a pocket of junk in Sita's house. In an old cabinet in the basement I found disorganized clutter, spider nests, real dirt. The shelves hold old bottles and cans: Venetian shoe cream, Moroline, Coconut hair oil, KILL-ALL Rat Tablets. And a book called *The Black Rose,* by Thomas B. Costain.

As I look at these things, a sadness takes hold of me. Sita is the reason all these things are here, and when she goes they will still be here. They will outlast her as they have already outlasted her husband. They will outlast me. Common things, but with a power we cannot match. It makes me sad to see them there, so humble yet indestructible, while Sita, for all her desperation of a lifetime, must die.

I have a strange thought that everything a person ever touched should be buried along with them, because things surviving people does not make sense. As Mary is talking, I see all of us sucked headlong through space. I see us flying in a great wind of our own rubber mats and hairbrushes. Then we are swallowed up with fearful swiftness and disappear.

Everything is getting mixed up. I close my eyes and I don't know if I'm upstairs or downstairs, and it doesn't matter. I'm not even angry when Mary reads my thoughts again and says how the Indian burial mounds this town is named for contain the things that the Indians used in their lives. People have found stone grinders, hunting arrows, and jewelry of colored bones.

So I think it's no use. Even buried, our things survive.

The dog is barking under the window. The dark is growing chill, and I realize that he has bitten his rope and gone digging in the iris beds again. I hear Sita yelling from the porch at Little Jimmy. Her voice is rising and rising until it cracks off. I hear Little Jimmy barking and grunting. Or is it Sita? One of them is groaning. We open the window and Mary leans out to see, but it is too dark. Frail dogwood branches shield Little Jimmy from our view. We hear panting and pounding.

"He found something," says Mary. "Sita's going to kill him if he digs up her border."

"Get out of there! Scat!" she yells.

But the panting and pounding still goes on.

So Mary reaches behind her. Two things are within her grasp: the chipped statue of the Virgin and the special brick. She flings the brick out the window. There is a thud, silence, then Little Jimmy whines.

We run downstairs. The moon isn't up yet. I fumble for the porch light but can't find it, and follow Mary down the front steps. I have to grope my way, holding onto lawn chairs and rose stakes. I cross the grass, and then I see their huddled shapes. Mary's flowered dress patches into the bush, but the white shape on the ground—that is Sita. I know her afghan by touch. It is the pale green pancake-posy stitch that she made when she was young.

I am kneeling, bending close to her. She does not move for many long seconds, and then her body gives a rippling shudder. It flashes into my mind that it's time. Things are being snatched from our grips. The scattered dirt is dry and cold. She whispers in my face.

"You'll eat shit with the chickens someday too."

Her hair is wet where the brick slammed down on her head. I think that she's right. She's right. I'll eat shit with the chickens. We carry her indoors. She is light as toast. We lay her on the long beige couch in the living room. I'm almost afraid to switch on the lamp, but finally Mary does, and then I see how bad Sita looks. Black shadows are in her cheeks.

I sit with her the rest of the night, bathing her forehead and listening to her breath fall and sink. I pack the best afghans around her: the knit strips and whirling clouds, the mouse-and-trap stitch, waving valleys and blue mounds. Mary is sitting in the chair with her head in her hands, not moving, so that sometime in the night I forget she's there.

I forget Little Jimmy too. That dog got pounded anyway. I forget what we have come here for. At some point Mary begins to mumble behind her hands, so I know she is asleep.

"Don't argue with me," she says, "I have checked your account."

Sita smiles at those words and opens her eyes. She looks peacefully around, then focuses at me and frowns. She frowns steadily. I don't know if she's frowning at me or someone else, but I look down into her face.

She takes a deep troubled breath. I don't hear when she lets it out, because I am suddenly remembering how she used to look from beneath, when she sat above me like I am sitting above her. Her pink lips curved. Her teeth were white and square. She swung her long, thick braid over her head. It whipped down, plopped against my cheek, brushed my nose and mouth. I remember, now, that Sita's braid did not hurt. It was only soft and heavy, smelling of Castile soap, but I still yelled as though something terrible was happening. Stop! Get Off! Let Go! Because I could not stand how strong she was, her knees against my chest. I could not stand her holding me down helpless in the dirt.

# Knives

HE IS FINE boned, slick, agreeable, and dressed to kill in his sharp black suit, winy vest, knotted brown tie. His hair is oiled. His lips are fevered and red as two buds. For a long while he stands there, eyeing me, before he opens his mouth.

"You're not pretty," are the first words he speaks.

And I, who have never bit off my words even to a customer, am surprised into a wounded silence, although I don't look in the mirror for pleasure, but only to take stock of the night's damage.

I work for Mary, who learned the butcher's trade and keeps a run-down shop on the edge of Argus, a town in which I've found no hope of marriage. I get along with men. I work right beside them in the cutting room and keep a long tally of the card debts they owe me. But this is not romance. In the novels I read at night, I experience with no satisfaction the veiled look, the guarded approach, the hungers I've come to live with in my thirties. I get heavier each year that no one sweeps me off my feet, so that now I outweigh most men. And perhaps I am too much like them, too strong and imposing when I square my shoulders, and used to taking control.

I am standing on a stool, changing the prices I chalk above the counter each week on a piece of slate. Blutwurst. Swedish sausage. Center-cut chops. Steak. I keep writing and do not give him the satisfaction of an answer. He stands below me, waiting. He has the patience of a cat with women. When I finish, there is nothing left for me to do but climb down.

"But pretty's not the only thing," the man continues smoothly, as though all my silence has not come between.

I cut him off. "Tell me what you want," I say. "I'm closing shop."

"I bet you never thought I'd come back," he says. He steps close to the glass counter full of meats. I can see, through the false, bright glare inside the case, his dumbbell-lifting chest. His sharp, thick hands. Even above the white pepper and sawdust of the shop, I can smell the wild-root, tobacco, penetrating breath mint.

"I never saw you the first time," I tell him. "I'm closing."

"Look here," he says, "Mary—"

"I'm not Mary."

He goes rigid, puts his hand to the back of his skull, pats the hair in place thoughtfully.

"Who are you then?"

"Celestine," I say, "as if it's any of your business."

I have to ring out the register, secure the doors, set the alarm on the safe before I can walk home. Around that time of early evening the light floods through the thick block-glass windows, a golden light that softens the shelves and barrels. Dusk is always my time, that special air of shifting shapes, and it occurs to me that, even though he says I am not pretty, perhaps in the dusk I am impossible to resist. Perhaps there is something about me, like he says.

"Adare. Karl Adare."

He introduces himself without my asking. He crosses his arms on the counter, leans over, and deliberately smiles at my reaction. His teeth are small, shiny, mother-of-pearl.

"This is something," I say. "Mary's brother."

"She ever talk about me?"

"No," I have to answer, "and she's out on a delivery right now. She won't be back for a couple of hours."

"But you're here."

I guess my mouth drops a little. Me knowing who he is has only slightly diverted what seems like his firm intentions, which are what? I can't read him. I turn away from him and make myself busy with the till, but I am fumbling. I turn to look at Karl. His eyes are burning holes and he tries to look right through me if he can. This is, indeed, the way men behave in the world of romance. Except that he is slightly smaller than me, and also Mary's brother. And then there is his irritating refrain.

"Pretty's not everything," he says to me again. "You're built . . ." He stops, trying to hide his confusion. But his neck reddens and I think maybe he is no more experienced at this than I.

"If you curled the ends at least," he says, attempting to recover, "if you cut your hair. Or maybe it's the apron."

I always wear a long white butcher's apron, starched and swaddled around my middle with thick straps. Right now, I take it off, whip it around me, and toss it on the radiator. I decide I will best him at his game, as I have studied it in private, have thought it out.

"All right," I say, walking around the counter, "Here I am." Because of the market visit I am wearing a navy blue dress edged in white. I have a bow at my waist, black shoes, and a silver necklace. I have always thought I looked impressive in this outfit, not to be taken lightly. Sure enough, his eyes widen. He looks stricken and suddenly uncertain of the next move, which I see is mine to make.

"Follow me," I say, "I'll put a pot of coffee on the stove."

It is Mary's stove, of course, but she will not be back for several hours. He does not follow me directly, but lights a cigarette. He smokes the heavy kind, not my brand anymore. The smoke curls from his lips.

"You married?" he asks.

"No," I say. He drops the cigarette on the floor, crushes it out with his foot, and then picks it up and says, "Where shall I put this?"

I point at an ashtray in the hall, and he drops the butt in. Then, as we walk back to Mary's kitchen, I see that he is carrying a black case I have not noticed before. We are at the door of the kitchen. It is dark. I have my hand on the light switch and am going to turn on the fluorescent ring, when he comes up behind me, puts his hands on my shoulders, and kisses the back of my neck.

"Get away from me," I say, not expecting this so soon. First the glances, the adoration, the many conversations must happen.

"How come?" he asks. "This is what you want."

His voice shakes. Neither one of us is in control. I shrug his hands off.

"What I want." I repeat this stupidly. Love stories always end here. I never had a mother to tell me what came next. He steps in front of me and hugs me to himself, draws my face down to his face. I am supposed to taste a burning sweetness on his lips, but his mouth is hard as metal.

I lunge from his grip, but he comes right with me. I lose my balance. He is fighting me for the upper hand, straining down with all his might, but I am more than equal to his weight-lifting arms and thrashing legs. I could throw him to the side, I know, but I grow curious. There is the smell of corn mash, something Mary has dropped that morning. That's what I notice even when it happens and we are together, rolling over, clasped, bumping into the legs of the table. I move by instinct, lurching under him. We're held in my mind as in a glass, and I see my own face, amused, embarrassed, and relieved. It is not so complicated, not even as painful, as I feared, and it doesn't last long either. He sighs when it is over, his breath hot and hollow in my ear.

"I don't believe this happened," he says to himself.

That is, oddly, when I lash out against his presence. He is so heavy that I think I might scream in his face. I push his chest, a dead weight, and then I heave him over so he sprawls in the dark away from me, so I can breathe. We smooth our clothing and hair back so carefully, in the dark, that when we finally turn the light on and blink at the place where we find ourselves, it is as though nothing has happened.

We are standing up, looking anyplace but at each other.

"How about that coffee?" he says.

I turn to the stove.

And then, when I turn around again with the coffeepot, I see that he is unlatching a complicated series of brass fittings that unfold his suitcase into a large stand-up display. He is absorbed, one-minded, not too different from the way he was down on the floor. The case is lined in scarlet velvet. Knives gleam in the plush. Each rests in a fitted compartment, the tips capped so as not to pierce the cloth, the bone handles tied with small strips of pigskin leather.

I sit down. I ask what he is doing but he does not answer, only turns and eyes me significantly. He holds out a knife and a small rectangle of dark wood.

"You can slice." he begins, "through wood, even plaster, with our serrated edge. Or"—he produces a pale dinner roll from his pocket— "the softest bread." He proceeds to demonstrate, sawing the end off the block of balsa wood with little difficulty, then delicately wiggling the knife through the roll so it falls apart in transparent, perfect ovals.

"You could never butter those," I hear myself say, "they'd fall apart."

"It's just as good with soft-skinned vegetables," he says to the air. "Fruits. Fish fillets."

He is testing the edge of the knife. "Feel," he says, holding the blade toward me. I ignore him. One thing I know is knives and his are cheap-john, not worth half the price of the fancy case. He keeps on with his demonstration, slicing bits of cloth, a very ripe tomato, and a box of ice cream from Mary's freezer. He shows each knife, one after the other, explaining its usefulness. He shows me the knife sharpener and sharpens all Mary's knives on its wheels. The last thing he does is take out a pair of utility shears. He snips the air with them as he speaks.

"Got a penny?" he asks.

Mary keeps her small change in a glass jar on the windowsill. I take out a penny and lay it on the table. And then, in the kitchen glare, Karl takes his scissors and cuts the penny into a spiral.

So, I think, this is what happens after the burning kiss, when the music roars. Imagine. The lovers are trapped together in a deserted mansion. His lips descend. She touches his magnificent thews.

"Cut anything," he says, putting the spiral beside my hand. He begins another. I watch the tension in his fingers, the slow frown of enjoyment. He puts another perfect spiral beside the first. And then, since he looks as though he might keep on going, cutting all the pennies in the jar, I decide that I now have seen what love is about.

"Pack up and go," I tell him.

But he only smiles and bites his lip, concentrating on the penny that uncoils in his hands. He will not budge. I can sit here watching the man and his knives, or call the police. But neither of these seems like a suitable ending.

"I'll take it," I say, pointing at the smallest knife.

In one motion he unlatches a vegetable parer from its velvet niche and sets it between us on the table. I dump a dollar in change from the penny-ante jar. He snaps the case shut. I handle my knife. It is razor sharp, good for cutting the eyes from potatoes. But he is gone by the time I have formed the next thought.

IN MY STORIES, they return as a matter of course. So does Karl. There is something about me he has to follow. He doesn't know what it is and I can't tell him either, but not two weeks go by before he breezes back into town, still without ever having seen his sister. I see my brother Russell all the time. I live with him. Russell looks outside one morning and sees Adare straddling the chubstone walk to our house.

"It's a noodle," says Russell. I glance out the window over his shoulder, and see Karl.

"I've got business with him," I say.

"Answer the door then," Russell says. "I'll get lost." He walks out the back door with his tools.

The bell rings twice. I open the front door and lean out.

"I can't use any," I say.

The smile falls off his face. He is confused a moment, then shocked. I see that he has come to my house by accident. Maybe he thought that he would never see me again. His face is what decides me that he has another thing coming. I am standing there in layers of flimsy clothing with a hammer in my hand. I can tell it makes him nervous when I ask him in, but he thinks so much of himself that he can't back down. I pull a chair out, still dangling the hammer, and he sits. I go into the kitchen and fetch him a glass of the lemonade I have been smashing the ice for. I half expect him to sneak out, but when I return he is still sitting there, the suitcase humbly at his feet, an oily black fedora on his knees.

"So, so," I say, taking a chair beside him.

He has no answer to my comment. As he sips on the lemonade, however, he glances around, and seems slowly to recover his salesman's confidence.

"How's the paring knife holding out?" he asks.

I just laugh. "The blade snapped off the handle," I say. "Your knives are duck-bait."

He keeps his composure somehow, and slowly takes in the living room with his stare. When my ceramics, books, typewriter, pillows, and ashtrays are all added up, he turns to the suitcase with a squint.

"You live here by yourself?" he asks.

"With my brother."

"Oh."

I fill his lemonade glass again from my pitcher. It is time, now, for Karl to break down with his confession that I am a slow-burning fuse in his loins. A hair trigger. I am a name he cannot silence. A dream that never burst.

"Oh well . . ." he says.

"What's that supposed to mean?" I ask.

"Nothing."

We sit there for a while collecting dust until the silence and absence of Russell from the house grows very evident. And then, putting down our glasses, we walk up the stairs. At the door to my room, I take the hat from his hand. I hang it on my doorknob and beckon him in. And this time, I have been there before. I've had two weeks to figure out the missing areas of books. He is shocked by what I've learned. It is like his mind darkens. Where before there was shuffling and silence, now there are cries. Where before we were hidden, now the shocking glare. I pull the blinds up. What we do is well worth a second look, even if there are only the squirrels in the box elders. He falls right off the bed once, shaking the whole house. And when he gets up he is spent, in pain because of an aching back. He just lays there.

"You could stay on for supper," I finally offer, because he doesn't seem likely to go.

"I will." And then he is looking at me with his eyes in a different way, as if he cannot figure the sum of me. As if I am too much for him to compass. I get nervous.

"I'll fix the soup now," I say.

"Don't go." His hand is on my arm, the polished fingernails clutching. I cannot help but look down and compare it with my own. I have the hands of a woman who has handled too many knives, deep-nicked and marked with lines, toughened from spice and brine, gouged, even missing a tip and nail.

"I'll go if I want," I say. "Don't I live here?"

And I get up, throwing a housecoat and sweater over myself. I go downstairs and start a dinner on the stove. Presently, I hear him come down, feel him behind me in the doorway, those black eyes in a skin white as veal.

"Pull up a chair," I say. He settles himself heavily and drinks down the highball I give him. When I cook, what goes into my soup is what's there. Expect the unexpected, Russell always says. Butter beans and barley. A bowl of fried rice. Frozen oxtails. All this goes into my pot.

"God almighty," says Russell, stepping through the door. "You still here?" There is never any doubt Russell is my brother. We have the same slanting eyes and wide mouth, the same long head and glaring white teeth. We could be twins, but for his scars and that I am a paler version of him.

"Adare," says the salesman, holding out his perfect hand. "Karl Adare. Representative at large."

"What's that?" Russell ignores the hand and rummages beneath the sink for a beer. He makes it himself from a recipe that he learned in the Army. Whenever he opens that cupboard I stand back, because sometimes the brew explodes on contact with air. Our cellar is also full of beer. In the deepest of summer, on close, hot nights, we sometimes hear the bottles go smashing into the dirt.

"So," says Russell, "you're the one who sold Celestine here the bum knife."

"That's right," Karl says, taking a fast drink.

"You unload many?"

"No."

"I'm not surprised," Russell says.

Karl looks at me, trying to gauge what I've told. But because he doesn't understand the first thing about me, he draws a blank. There is nothing to read on my face. I ladle the soup on his plate and sit down across the table. I say to Russell, "He's got a suitcase full."

"Let's see it then."

Russell always likes to look at tools. So again the case comes out, folding into a display. While we eat Russell keeps up a running examination of every detail a knife could own. He tries them out on bits of paper, on his own pants and fingers. And all the while, whenever Karl can manage to catch my eye, he gives a mournful look of pleading, as if I am forcing this performance with the knives. As if the apple in Russell's fingers is Karl's own heart getting peeled. It is uncomfortable. In the love magazines, when passion holds sway, men don't fall down and roll on the floor and lay there like dead. But Karl does that. Right that very evening, in fact, not long after the dinner when I tell him he must go, he suddenly hits the floor like a toppled statue.

"What's that?" I jump up, clutching Russell's arm, for we are still in the kitchen. Having drunk several bottles in the mellow dusk, Russell isn't clear in the head. Karl has drunk more. We look down. He is slumped beneath the table where he's fallen, passed out, so pale and still I fetch a mirror to his pencil-mustache and am not satisfied until his breath leaves a faint silver cloud.

The next morning, the next morning after that, and still the next morning Karl is here in the house. He pretends to take ill at first, creeping close to me that first night in order to avoid deadly chills. The same the night after, and the night after that, until things begin to get too predictable for my taste.

Sitting at the table in his underwear is something Karl starts doing once he feels at home. He never makes himself useful. He never sells any knives. Every day when I leave for work the last thing I see is him killing time, talking to himself like the leaves in the trees. Every night when I come home there he is, taking up space like one more piece of furniture. Only now, he's got himself clothed. Right away, when I enter the door, he rises like a sleepwalker and comes forward to embrace me and lead me upstairs.

"I don't like what's going on here," says Russell after two weeks of hanging around on the outskirts of this affair. "I'll take off until you get tired of the noodle."

So Russell goes. Whenever things heat up at home he stays up on the reservation with Eli, his half brother, in an old house that is papered with calendars of naked women. They fish for crappies or trap muskrats, and spend their Saturday nights half drunk, paging through the long years on their wall. I don't like to have him go up there, but I'm not ready to say good-bye to Karl.

I GET INTO a habit with Karl and don't look up for two months. Mary tells me what I do with her brother is my business, but I catch her eyeing me, her gaze a sharp yellow. I do not blame her. Karl has gone to her only once for dinner. It was supposed to be their grand reunion, but it fell flat. They blamed each other. They argued. Mary hit him with a can of oysters. She threw it from behind and left a goose egg, or so Karl says. Mary never tells me her side, but after that night things change at work. She talks around me, delivers messages through others. I even hear through one of the men that she says I've turned against her.

Meanwhile, love wears on me. Mary or no Mary, I am tired of coming home to Karl's heavy breathing and even his touch has begun to oppress me.

"Maybe we ought to end this while we're still in love," I say to him one morning.

He just looks at me. "You want me to pop the question?"

"No."

"Yes you do," he says, edging around the table.

I leave the house. The next morning, when I tell him to go away again, he proposes marriage. But this time I have a threat to make.

"I'm calling the state asylum," I say. "You're berserk."

He leans over and spins his finger around his ear.

"Commit me then," he says, "I'm crazy with love."

Something in all this has made me realize that Karl has read as many books as I, that his fantasies always stopped before the woman came home worn out from cutting beef into steaks with an electric saw.

"It's not just you," I tell him. "I don't want to get married. With you around I get no sleep. I'm tired all the time. All day I'm giving wrong change and I don't have any dreams. I'm the kind of person that likes having dreams. Now I have to see you every morning when I wake up and I forget if I dreamed anything or even slept at all, because right away you're on me with your hot breath."

He stands up and pushes his chest, hard, against mine, and runs his hands down my back and puts his mouth on my mouth. I don't have a damn thing to defend myself with. I push him down on the chair and sit, eager, in his lap. But all the while, I am aware that I am living on Karl's borrowed terms.

They might as well cart me off in a wet sheet too, I think.

"I'm like some kind of animal," I say, when it is over.

"What kind?" he asks, lazy. We are laying on the kitchen floor.

"A big stupid heifer."

He doesn't hear what I say though. I get up. I smooth my clothes down and walk off to the shop. But all day, as I wait on customers and tend fire in the smoke room, as I order from suppliers and slice the head-cheese and peg up and down the cribbage board, I am setting my mind hard against the situation.

"I'm going home," I say to Mary, when work is done, "and getting rid of him."

We are standing in the back entry alone; all the men are gone. I know she is going to say something strange.

"I had an insight," she says. "If you do, he'll take his life."

I look at the furnace in the corner, not at her, and I think that I hear a false note in her voice.

"He's not going to kill himself," I tell her. "He's not the type. And you"—I am angry now—"you don't know what you want. At the same time you're jealous of Karl and me, you don't want us apart. You're confused."

She takes her apron off and hangs it on a hook. If she wasn't so proud, so good at hardening her heart, she might have said what kind of time this had been for her alone.

But she turns and sets her teeth.

"Call me up when it's over," she says, "and we'll drive out to the Brunch Bar."

This is a restaurant where we like to go on busy nights when there is no time for cooking. I know her saying this has taken effort, so I feel sorry.

"Give me one hour, then I'll call you," I say.

As usual, when I get home, Karl is sitting at the kitchen table. The first thing I do is fetch his sample case from the couch where he parks it, handy for when the customers start pouring in. I carry it into the kitchen, put it down, and kick it across the linoleum. The leather screeches but the knives make no sound inside their velvet.

"What do you think I'm trying to tell you?" I ask.

He is sitting before the day's dirty dishes, half-full ashtrays, and crumbs of bread. He wears his suit pants, the dark red vest, and a shirt that belongs to Russell. If I have any hesitations, the shirt erases them.

"Get out," I say.

But he only shrugs and smiles.

"I can't go yet," he says. "It's time for the matinee."

I step closer, not close enough so he can grab me, just to where there is no chance he can escape my gaze. He bends down. He lights a match off the sole of his shoe and starts blowing harsh smoke into the air. My mind is shaking from the strain, but my expression is still firm. It isn't until he smokes his Lucky to the nub, and speaks, that I falter.

"Don't chuck me. I'm the father," he says.

I hold my eyes trained on his forehead, not having really heard or understood what he said. He laughs. He puts his hands up like a bank clerk in a holdup and then I give him the once-over, take him in as if he was a stranger. He is better looking than I am, with the dark eyes, red lips, and pale complexion of a movie actor. His drinking has not told on him, not his smoking either. His teeth have stayed pearly and white although his fingers are stained rubbery orange from the curling smoke.

"I give up! You're the stupidest woman I ever met." He puts his arms down, lights another cigarette from the first. "Here you're knocked up," he says suddenly, "and you don't even know it."

I suppose I look stupid, knowing at that instant what he says is true.

"You're going to have my baby," he says in a calmer voice, before I can recover my sense.

"You don't know."

I grab his suitcase and heave it past him through the screen door. It tears right through the rotten mesh and thumps hard on the porch. He is silent for a long time, letting this act sink in.

"You don't love me," he says.

"I don't love you," I answer.

"What about my baby?"

"There's not a baby."

And now he starts moving. He backs away from me toward the door, but he cannot go through it.

"Get going," I say.

"Not yet." His voice is desperate.

"What now?"

"A souvenir. I don't have anything to remember you." If he cries, I know I'll break down, so I grab the object closest to my hand, a book I've had sitting on the top of the refrigerator. I won it somewhere and never opened the cover. I hold it out to him.

"Here," I say.

He takes the book, and then there is no other excuse. He edges down the steps and finally off at a slow walk through the grass, down the road. I stand there a long time, watching him from the door, before

he shrinks into the distance and is gone. And then, once I feel certain
he has walked all the way to Argus, maybe hopped a bus, or hitched
down Highway 30 south, I put my head down on the table and let my
mind go.

The first thing I do once I am better is to dial Mary's number.

"I got rid of him," I say into the phone.

"Give me ten minutes," she says, "I'll come and get you."

"Just wait," I say. "I have to have some time off."

"What for?"

"I went and got myself into the family way."

She says nothing. I listen to the silence on her end before I finally
hear her take the phone from her ear, and put it down.

IN THE LOVE books a baby never comes of it all, so again I am not prepared. I do not expect the weakness or the swelling ankles. The tales of
burning love never mention how I lie awake, alone in the heat of an August night, and panic. I know the child feels me thinking. It turns over
and over, so furiously that I know it must be wound in its cord. I fear
that something has gone wrong with it. The mind is not right, just like
the father's. Or it will look like the sick sheep I had to club. A million
probable, terrible things will go wrong. And then, as I am lying there
worrying into the dark, bottles start going off under the house. Russell's
brew is exploding and all night, with the baby turning, I keep dreaming
and waking to the sound of glass flying through the earth.

# Destiny

"I'M NOT GOING anywhere they put the damn radishes in Jell-O," says my friend and employee, Celestine Duval, when I mention visiting her son, Norris.

Yet that very night my shop catches fire, and she is out of a job until the insurance comes through. It is December. The nearest hydrant was frozen when they put a wrench to it, but I am lucky. Because I have a thick sliding door between the shop and the back room where I live, the only damage to my living quarters was stains from a few gray plumes of smoke blown up the walls.

"They lend an atmosphere," Celestine tells me.

She talks like a restaurant because Norris has opened a steak house in Argus, North Dakota, where he lives among the Swedes. This has led to Celestine's objections to the radishes. She has got a bug up her nose about the Swedes and their customs involving food. She went down to help Norris at the grand opening not so long ago, but she could not stand their habit of slicing odd things into the Jell-O.

Now, since the fire payment won't arrive for a week or so and the workmen won't start on the interior, we decide to close the shop and take a trip. We must get our minds off this disaster. We decide to go to Argus and visit Norris, his wife, Adele, and their daughter with the terrible name.

Wallacette is named after Adele's father, who died in the ninth month of Adele's pregnancy and left his daughter's mind unhinged with grief. Nothing that Norris said could persuade Adele to name their daughter something halfway normal. Wallacette she became.

Like her mother, Wallacette is big and imposing, with a large-jawed grin full of teeth. At eleven years old she towers above the rest of the children in her class, and she is mainly interested in fiercely pursuing love. To get boyfriends, she knocks boys down and grinds their faces in the snowy grit. To get girls, she ties the string waistbands of their dresses to her own dress strings, and drags them around the playground until they promise to write her a note.

The nuns don't know what to do with Wallacette, nor do her parents, for she is strong-willed and determined to get her way. These same traits, however, make her a favorite with Celestine and myself, for we think that she has got spunk, and we always look forward to what surprises each visit with her brings. But to visit Wallacette we must also contend with Norris and, worse, grim Adele, who insists that we help her out in their steak house. The Poopdeck is the name of the place. I can't tell you why, except that this name was Adele's idea too.

The name does have to be an oceangoing kind of name, we admit. To save money on the renovations, Norris put in portholes rather than windows. Then he painted the outside white and blue, like a ship, and built a little captain's steering deck up top. He can't disguise the square shape of the building, though. It certainly doesn't look like it could sail anywhere.

After two hours of driving, we arrive in Argus. The Poopdeck's parking lot is jammed. Furry green plastic branches frame the portholes, decorations for the holidays. Within each porthole glows one red electric candle.

"Celestine," I say, "let's go somewhere else for lunch."

She is wearing a white turban on her head, and earrings that look like tiny red plungers. Christmas plungers. Her slanting eyes are sharp yellow, and the little purple spider veins in her cheeks have darkened like stitches.

"If we help out, they'll feed us afterward. All we can eat," she says.

But it's the helping I can do without.

It is Saturday, however, and we are pleased to see that Wallacette is behind the counter. Her job is to hand out paper boat flags and red and green Life Savers to the children who eat at the Poopdeck. This she does with earnest enjoyment. Sometimes she forces the candy so eagerly on little children that they cry out in fear of her stony jaw and gleaming teeth.

She sees us. She ducks under the counter and hurls herself forward. I can hear the sharp oof! as the air is knocked out of Celestine's lungs. It is hard to think of Celestine as anyone's grandmother. But she seems right as Wallacette's. The girl's pale legs are brawny as a wrestler's. She wears dirty white anklets. A strange light shines in her face. Hunched in her black coat, under the turban with its blazing clip, Celestine looks strange too, and the same light glows within her eyes.

We join the cooks at the steam tables in the back. I am stationed at the deep fryer, with wire baskets and bags of frozen products—fries, shrimp, onion rings, breaded fillets. The fish is always popular because of the boat theme, which is carried on in the menu.

"Old Tar Special," the waitress yells. "Clams Casanova! Fish Waikiki!"

Someone orders a Spinnaker Salad and a Lighthouse malt—a regular malt with a cherry "light."

I lower a basket of fantail shrimp into the popping grease. This is Wallacette's favorite item on the menu. I hear her voice through the cook's window, deep and loud.

"Sure you like candy. You do too. Take these."

A child's thin wail grows and is hushed. I peek out. The boy is hoisted into his mother's arms and carried out, staring over her shoulder, lip hanging. He doesn't know it, but his character has been strengthened by this encounter. Wallacette stands before another child. This time she is poking a striped paper flag through the child's buttonhole. The child stands stiffly, paralyzed, as if the slightest movement would cause the big girl to drive the tiny wooden pole into her heart.

"Don't be a sissy," she booms. "You like candy!"

When the noon rush is over, the three of us sit down in the end booth. The candles blaze in the little round portholes. Nets are draped across the walls. Wallacette has fried twenty-four fantail shrimp to place on a bed of coleslaw for herself. I am having the ham and pineapple rings. Celestine is having a steak and browned onions. She would normally accompany this with a salad, but not here. She won't go near the salad bar, because of Adele. In the cooler, Adele's creative Jell-O salads rest in brilliantly colored sheets. They are filled with walnuts, chopped celery, macaroni, onions, miniature pastel marshmallows, and, worst of all, sliced radishes.

"I'm sure glad you came back," Wallacette says to her grandmother. "Dad was worried that we'd have to come visit you."

The last time Celestine visited Norris and Adele, the nasty confrontation over the Jell-O took place. That is why, so far, Adele has avoided us.

"You're the one I came to see," Celestine tells her granddaughter. "Your mother and father can get along perfectly good without me."

"I guess they can," says Wallacette, who inherited Celestine's honesty. "But not me."

An expression that I've never seen forms on Celestine's face. She is watching Wallacette. It is as though her face is liable to break into pieces, as though the stitching spider veins barely manage to hold her face together. I am confused by this look, and then I realize what it is. Tenderness. The heart of Celestine is cold as clay, something even she'll admit. But she feels a true tenderness for Wallacette.

"You're in time!" Wallacette shouts suddenly. Light breaks over her broad pancake face. Her stony brow lifts. "You'll get to see our Christmas play!"

This is pleasing to both of us.

We enjoy Wallacette's successes and have already seen her in a piano recital, playing "Song of the Volga Boatmen" with tremendous expression. Celestine is chewing her steak eagerly, with pride and enthusiasm, for Wallacette has revealed to us that she will play a leading role.

"I am Joseph, father of the Christ child," she states. Then she grins, long and huge.

At first I think it's awful that they picked a little girl to play the father of Christ. Then I imagine Wallacette wearing a long grizzled beard and a coarse robe. I see the carpenter's maul wielded in her fist. She will be convincing.

"*The Donkey of Destiny* is the name of this play," she tells us. Her face changes suddenly. "I hate the donkey."

The light goes out in the window. I distinctly hear Wallacette's teeth clench together and gnash. I've never heard the sound of gnashing teeth before, only read of it in books. Now I realize why this gnashing of teeth is mentioned so often. It is ominous and frightening to hear.

ADELE AND NORRIS have made their basement over into what they call a recreation center. A Hamm's beer lamp that shows a canoe on an endlessly revolving lake hangs off the side wall. This lamp makes Celestine raise her eyebrows and bend toward me.

"No comment," she whispers. We both dislike the lamp, with its foolish repetition, on sight. But we do not hurt any feelings. We smile and nod at Norris.

At one end of the room is a large cabinet television and a plush couch. In the middle of the room is a pool table that, as Norris now informs us, opens into a bed for guests. Norris seems anxious to demonstrate its double use, and so Celestine and I take our places against the wood-grain paneled walls while he struggles with the pool table. Norris is a small, washed-out, balding man. He is like a version of his mother, left too long in the water. But he is kinder than Celestine, and he wants very much to please us. Hinges creak and springs vibrate as he fiddles with the table. A loose ball rolls through the works. Norris slams his fist to dislodge a hidden latch, and the top springs up like the lid of a box. Then Norris bats a panel loose, and the bed folds into being. Sheets and pillows are secured, and we are ready for the night.

"I'll set the thermostat up for you," Norris says, wiping his brow, looking very much relieved. "Do you think you'll be all right down here?"

"As long as the table doesn't fold up on us," Celestine says. She is eyeing the bed suspiciously. I know that the ball is still loose inside of the pool-table bed, and that makes me a little hesitant. I've never heard this, but I can guess it is unlucky to sleep in a bed with what might be an eight ball folded up in its works. Still, we have no choice. Norris waves from the basement stairs. When he is gone, Celestine removes her shoes and turban and sits down carefully on her side of the bed.

"You want to hear the truth of the matter?" she says. "Wallacette loves the donkey."

I don't understand this at first. I have forgotten about the donkey in the play. But Celestine goes on to explain.

"Wallacette tried to catch the boy who plays the donkey—the head, not the rear end, that is. So far he has outsmarted her. This makes her violent."

"We must tell her to go easy on the boy," I counsel. Celestine seems to agree.

"Say it with flowers," she says abruptly, with a fierce nod.

I wonder, when she says this, if either of us knows enough to say what love is all about. Our husbands are long deceased. At one time we must have loved them. But for me love was not said with flowers, at least not until he died. Every spring now I change the artificial roses on his grave.

FOR THE NEXT several days of our visit Adele continues to elude us, while Norris is always late to get somewhere. We find evidence of Adele in fresh coffee, sweet buns, and little notes pinned or taped on various items in the house.

"Don't touch the color tuner" is taped to the front of their television. "I'm saving the lemon bars for tonight" is taped on the refrigerator door. "Use the striped towels" is pinned to the correct towels in the bathroom. Celestine laughs harshly every time she comes across another bold printed order from Adele.

"Out-and-out gall," she says, crumpling the bits of paper.

I get to wishing that the two of them would settle their account. It would make things much nicer for Norris, myself, and Wallacette. Only those two, Celestine and Adele, halfway enjoy their mortal combat.

When the morning of the play dawns, we are anxious and excited. Even Norris has heightened color. Wallacette's hair is curled with an electric iron, though it will be covered with a wig. She bundles up in a green pile coat and barges down the road. Norris and Adele drive off, leaving us alone in the house.

"There's a potluck dinner after the play," Celestine tells me. "I'm going to make a special secret dish."

Then she whisks herself off into the kitchen and hands me a cup of coffee and a bun through a crack in the door. I feel like a fifth wheel going downstairs to sit alone, first thing in the morning. I switch on the television, but the face of the morning hostess is pulsating blue, and I do not dare disobey Adele's note and adjust the dial.

THE GYMNASIUM THAT night is alive and noisy. The lights blaze in their steel-mesh covers. Folding chairs are lifted from a cart by dads with rolled-up sleeves and are added to the back rows. Mink-collared grandmothers are settled in firmly, ready to enjoy the pageant. The nuns are whispering together in their navy blue veils. The run-down parish gym is also used as a dining hall and for bingo and budget meetings. The purple velveteen curtain is shabby, a castoff from the public school. Celestine insists that we sit far up front. In elbowing through the nuns we lose Adele and Norris.

"Accidentally on purpose," Celestine sniffs. We sit. She has already delivered her secret recipe, a long foil-covered pan, to the school kitchen. During the potluck dinner this dish will be unveiled. Celestine has taped Adele's name where it cannot be missed; she will be known as the author of the great work. For some reason I am uneasy that she has done this. Generosity is not her style.

The noise all around us mounts, and then suddenly it hushes. The lights go down. There is the sound of programs rustling. We have already found and admired the printed presence of Wallacette's name.

When the curtains open, the spotlight shows a boy wearing a knit poncho and a huge sombrero, of the kind that people who have been to Mexico hang on their walls. This boy makes a long sad speech about his friend the donkey, whom he must sell to the glue factory in order to buy food. On a darkened set of bleachers behind him a vague chorus laments the donkey's fate.

The boy pulls the rope he has been twisting in his hands, and the donkey bumbles out of the wings. It is, of course, a makeshift donkey. It is wearing gray pants and tennis shoes. The body is barrel shaped and lopsided, and the papier-mâché head lolls as if the donkey were drunk. The mouth, painted open in a grin, and the slanted, black-rimmed eyes give it a strange expression of cruelty.

Parents ooh and aah, but some look startled. The donkey is an unpleasant creature. Its dyed burlap hide looks moth-eaten. One ear is long and one is short. Celestine must be the only person in the crowd who thinks the donkey is cute. "Oh, look at it prance," she whispers. Her long yellow Tartar eyes gleam softly beneath the flashing buckle of her turban. Her gloves are in a tight ball, like socks. She smiles as the boy and his donkey start out on the long road to the glue factory. Tragedy, her favorite element, is in the air. Her eyes blaze when the chorus wails.

"*Amigos!* We are *amigos!*" the boy shouts from beneath the sombrero. Then they slowly begin to walk across the stage. They are weeping. But before they reach the glue factory, Saint Joseph appears.

Saint Joseph has a long beard of spray-painted cotton, and an old piece of upholstery fabric is tied to her head. She wears a long brown terry-cloth bathrobe that might belong to Norris. Her feet are bare. As in my vision of her, she is carrying a wooden maul. She looks grimmer than the mild church statues, and more powerful. I believe in her. The donkey sidles up to her with its evil, silly grin. She stands before it with her legs spread wide, balancing on the balls of her feet. All I can see of the boy whom, according to Celestine, she loves is a pair of gray corduroy knees and frayed black tennis shoes. Wallacette grabs the donkey around the neck and the gray legs twitch for a moment in the air. Then she sets the donkey down and says her lines to the donkey's *amigo*.

"Young man, where are you going with this donkey?"

"I must sell it to the glue factory, for my family is hungry," the boy says sadly.

"Perhaps I can help you out," Wallacette says. "My wife Mary, myself, and our little boy, Baby Jesus, want to flee King Herod. My wife could ride this donkey if you would sell it."

"I will sell my donkey to help you," the boy shouts. "He will not be killed!"

"Of course not," Wallacette says. "We will only ride him across the desert to Egypt."

She takes some large coins made of crushed aluminum foil from her bathrobe pocket and gives them to the boy.

And so the transaction is accomplished. The donkey of destiny now belongs to Wallacette, who tries to pat its snarling papier-mâché muzzle. But then the episode occurs that we hope will not mar the mind of our favorite granddaughter for life. The donkey balks. Is this in the script? I glance at Celestine, wondering, but her look has narrowed to a flashlight focus of premonitions.

"Come along, little donkey," Saint Joseph says, through gritted teeth. She pulls, perhaps a bit roughly, at the rope on its neck. Suddenly a hand snakes from the front of the donkey's neck flap and rips the rope out of the grasp of a surprised Saint Joseph.

"Give it back!" she shouts in quick rage. "You're mine!"

The audience twitters; a few loud male guffaws are heard. Saint Joseph hears the audience—laughing at her! Fury tightens in her arms and she raises the maul high. I know what will happen. The audience gapes. Then she brings it down clean, like swift judgment, on the cardboard skull of the beast.

The front of the donkey drops. The head flies off, smashed. The last of that scene that we see is Saint Joseph standing in criminal shock, maul gripped tight, over the motionless body of a towhaired boy.

The curtain has closed and the audience is in a rumble of consternation. A fat, blond, hysterical woman, the mother of the donkey's felled front end, flies down the aisle. Adele and Norris are nowhere to be seen.

"Come!" Celestine says, hoisting her handbag on her elbow. "Or the nuns will take it out on her hide!"

We leave the chairs, find the side stage door, and slip behind the curtains. Angels and shepherds are standing in dismayed clumps. The painted wood silhouettes of sheep and cattle look stupidly baffled. We see Adele, wide and flat-rumped in a red suit, and Norris, with his bald man's ring of hair, standing with the principal nun, gesturing and gabbling excitedly. The wounded boy is nowhere to be seen. Wallacette is gone too.

Adele sees us in the wings and strides over to Celestine.

"Mother," she says, "go home."

"Where's Wallacette?" Celestine asks, ignoring her daughter-in-law's order.

"She ran out the back door of the gym," Norris says bleakly, "and that's the last anyone has seen of her."

"Get out a search party, then!" Celestine says. "She's barefoot in the snow!"

But no search party forms at her words.

As it turns out, Wallacette was headed home. When we arrive there, she is sitting on the living room coffee table with her feet by the heat ducts.

"Young lady!" Adele cries out, marching toward her, but Norris gets there first.

"Wait," he says, "I think she's hurt."

Sure enough, the rare tear is in her eye. She sits in a lump, clutching her play beard, shaking with inner sobs. In Norris's bathrobe she looks, oddly, like an ordinary, middle-aged man. Her face is pale, streaked with misery, and her small blue eyes are dull and still. Adele and Norris look awed, watching her, and do not approach and hug her or pat her, as normal parents might. Perhaps they have never seen her cry before.

Celestine, however, kneels down next to her, and then suddenly, fiercely, she lunges and catches the girl full across the chest and neck with a stranglehold. I expect this to be the moment Wallacette breaks down. It will be good for the girl to shed real tears, I think sympathetically. But instead of melting and crying, Wallacette charges suddenly from the room like a bull, running right over her grandmother. Celestine goes tumbling in a black heap on the carpet, and a door down the hall slams. Adele follows, to pound on the door and reason with her daughter. Norris stays, bending apologetically over his mother, who looks perversely delighted with what has happened. She pushes Norris away and lifts herself up.

"Grandma's girl" is all she says, adjusting her turban.


THAT NIGHT, AS we are lying side by side on the fold-out pool-table bed downstairs, I realize that something still bothers me, something that I wonder about. So I ask Celestine about the special secret dish that was to be placed among the others at the potluck dinner after the Christmas play.

"What was it?" I ask. "Was it your special chocolate bran cake?"

"It was not," Celestine says, waking quickly at my question. The sound of joy lights her voice. She crows.

"What?"

"The Jell-O. My special secret dish."

Of course I ask her what it was that made the Jell-O so special.

Bold as a weasel, she turns in the dark and fixes me with her proud, gleaming stare. She stares a long time, to let my anticipation sink in.

"Nuts and bolts," she finally says, "Washers of all types. I raided Norris's toolbox for the special ingredients."

Then she turns on her back to gloat up into the dark. I turn away from her, pretending to sleep.

But from my side of the bed I cannot escape the changing scenery of the beer lamp, still lit. I am forced to watch it revolve. So I watch, and after a while it isn't irritating anymore. In fact, it is almost as soothing as any real scenery you might find, and has the added advantage that you can relax and watch it in a dark room. Again and again I see the canoe leave the Minnesota lakeshore and venture through the water. The pines along the lake stand green-black and crisp. The water shimmers, lit within. The boat travels. I can almost see the fish rise, curious, beneath its shadow.

# The Little Book

IN THE YEAR 1960, my husband Louis and I built a new house on the edge of Blue Mound. It had a huge backyard and while I was recuperating from some trouble with my nerves I used to occupy myself with growing ornamental shrubs, azaleas, and climbing vines. I had no children and had lapsed from the Church because of Louis, who was a scientist.

I was not entirely certain about leaving the Church yet. For many years Saint Catherine's had been important in my life and religion still had some hold. Among other things, the idea of relying only on Louis and myself for answers and assistance was new. I was not sure I liked it. But I tried to be strong, ready for surprises, and perhaps for that reason I was not dismayed when my cousin crawled, sodden, through my trained clematis. I did not recognize him at first. I hadn't seen him in thirty years. He was dragging a heavy suitcase and he carried a little book.

"Hello there, Sita," he said from where he lay. He had got into my backyard by rolling beneath the fence. "I suppose you don't recognize me," he said, scrambling up and then carefully untangling himself from the leaves, "I'm your cousin Karl."

Thirty years is a long time to remember someone I had met only once as a child. I looked closely at him. A wanderer and a salesman is what I'd heard he'd become. He looked well trampled by the adventures of life. He was frayed at the neck and cuff. Hatless. His face was handsome in an overly pretty, disturbing way, but his lips were too red, as if he had a hangover. His eyes hung half shut, pouched, weary and fevered. His oiled black hair flopped down in strands around his ears.

He looked suspicious, even dangerous in his shabby clothes. Yet I wasn't upset, only interested. I knew if he attacked me all I had to do was scream. Louis was in the garage, not ten feet away, feeding his entomological specimens. I gripped my trowel like a weapon while Karl was talking, and decided if he made a fast move I would split his skull. My white canvas gloves would obscure any fingerprints. Louis and I could bury him beneath the dahlias with the murder weapon. In those days, I read boxes of true crime books to soothe my nerves.

"Karl Lavelle," he repeated, "I'm your cousin, remember?"

I nodded and said that I did. His family had mainly died or vanished during the Depression so I was surprised that he even existed, let alone thought I would be interested in seeing him.

"What brings you here?" I asked.

"I was just passing through," he said, "on my way to a sales conference. I decided to look you up."

I supposed it was a compliment to have a long lost cousin visit, even if he crawled in through the flower bed. It certainly would have been news in Blue Mound, if I'd felt like telling it. All the news here is imaginary—cattle mutilations, UFOs, sightings of wanted criminals—or so ordinary it gives me a headache. I put down my trowel.

"How nice to see you," I said, remembering my manners, "after all this time. You'll join us for lunch, I hope?"

He nodded a relieved acceptance, and looked around at the yard. "Not bad," he said. The way his voice squeezed shut I knew he was envious of my banks of rich flowers, the tile patio, the house which I'd heard people call a mansion, the largest house in Blue Mound. Louis had inherited good farmland, which he rented out.

"And tell me about yourself," I said, indicating his suitcase and the thick little book in his hands. The book looked familiar, black with reddish diamonds on the cover, and once he opened it I knew why. It was a Bible, a rather-typical cheap version of the New Testament.

"There's room to record family events," he said, looking into the cover. "Births, deaths, marriages."

"Let's sit down," I said, but he seemed to have read my mind because he didn't snap the book shut or follow me but continued to look morosely into the cover.

He's preparing a pitch, I thought, and I took his arm.

"You must be tired," I said, "on the road so often."

"I am," he agreed, looking at me steadily and gratefully. "I'm awfully glad to see you, Sita, it's been a long time."

"Too long," I said in a warm voice, although the truth was I'd never missed him, hardly thought about him in all those thirty years, and I was beginning to suspect, just slightly, from nothing I could put my finger on really, that he'd looked me up in the hope of an easy sale.

Just at that moment Louis walked out the back door into the yard. He always looked keenly at people but then never seemed to recall the slightest thing about them once they were gone. Now he stared penetratingly at Karl. Karl smiled back, uncertainly. "I'm Sita's cousin," he called to Louis. "Been a long time!" But Louis ignored him and walked over to the compost pile to gather a few more of his specimens.

"What's he doing?" Karl wondered.

"Digging worms."

"What for?"

"To see how they break down organic matter."

Louis kept me abreast of his every thought. He collected data about the area pests and local helpers. Earthworms were helpers, and Louis was experimenting with their habitat. What to put in the ground to attract their help.

"They make humus," I informed Karl in a stern voice, for his attention had wandered. He was taking in the details of our home again, my white cast-iron lawn furniture, the clipped and flowering shrubs. He soon included me in his accounts, giving me a slow, shy look. I was not at my slimmest, but according to Louis contentment fit me best, and I knew that my color was good.

"Have I changed?" I said, and then, embarrassed by the coy note in my voice, I answered my own question. "Of course I have. Who wouldn't?"

"Beautiful as ever," said Karl. I turned away. Louis rarely gave me compliments when he was deep in his abstract thoughts and what Karl said meant more to me than it should have, and so I was unable to keep from saying what I said next.

"Gray hairs, a few lines here and there. The years show."

"Oh no," said Karl, "you're prettier now. Maturity becomes you."

"It does?" I was acting foolish as a peacock.

"Yes," he said.

We had a long silent moment between us, almost intimate, and then more words popped out of my mouth.

"All flesh is grass," I said, hardly believing my own voice, and because of the strangeness, hearing the phrase as entirely new. We stood uncomfortably, looking at the lawn, and I noticed that the whole yard was covered with the same kind of grass that grows in cemeteries— fine, short-cropped grass of a brilliant green color.

"I'll get lunch," I said, to interrupt myself.

I left my cousin watching Louis pull worms from the mulch, and I went in to make us a plateful of sandwiches. Ham salad. I have a grinder that attaches to my sink. I was mixing the ground ham with capers and mayonnaise when Karl stepped up to the screen door and banged on it lightly.

"Could I use your facilities?"

"Of course," I said.

I let him in. He put the suitcase by the door and laid the book on my kitchen counter as he walked past. He did it so casually that I thought he had done it on purpose, to interest me in it. And so, while he was upstairs, I picked up the book. I looked at the dull red diamonds on the cover. Besides being a New Testament, the book still reminded me of something. It took several moments of concentration for me to place where I had seen it before. Then I knew. Three years ago at a raffle for the Saint Catherine's Society we had given away a New Testament like this, and Celestine Duval, an old school friend of mine, had won it.

"This may be a coincidence," I said to Karl when he returned from upstairs, "but a book just like this belonged to a former friend of mine."

He looked at me blankly, then picked up the book and pressed it in my hands.

"You can have it," he said. "Fill it up."

Then he picked up his suitcase, and went out to sit on the lawn furniture with Louis. I was slightly dumbfounded until I remembered about the spaces for family events. That was what he meant by "fill it up." I opened the book.

Saint Catherine's Society was stamped inside the cover, and then the date, May 4, 1957, and the name Celestine Duval.

"Aha!" I said with cheap fervor, just like a detective. Then, obscurely ashamed at my discovery, I snapped the book shut and continued mixing ingredients in the glassine bowl. Having outgrown my acquaintance with Celestine Duval, I wasn't sure how to handle the Bible anyway. For years I'd had nothing to do with her. I spread the mixture on pieces of bread and cut the sandwiches in triangles and went out. Karl had evidently told my husband that lunch was coming, for Louis had washed with the garden hose and now the men were balanced on the little wrought-iron chairs. The table came no higher than their knees. The sight was comical. But I had learned not to laugh at everything that looked absurd. Laughter had been one symptom of my thinning nerves.

"Isn't it lovely," I said, "the sun's so mild."

I put the tray down, with everything on it except the pitcher and glasses, and I went back for those. When I came out again I saw that the men had started eating without me, which annoyed me.

"What bad manners the two of you have!" I exclaimed.

"You're right," said Louis, putting down his sandwich and passing me the plate. My cousin, however, continued to take his food. I watched him pick up a sandwich and bring it to his lips, then bite it with his strong yellow teeth. One, two, and the sandwich was snapped down. I stared, wondering if he'd done something to Celestine, perhaps threatened her, in order to get the book. Or perhaps he knocked her out. And then there was the suitcase. Did he have more of her possessions tucked away inside of that?

Louis cleared his throat and spoke in a jocular, worried manner.

"Sita, you're keeping rather a close eye on our visitor, aren't you?"

I looked down at my plate. I couldn't help myself. I whispered, "The way my cousin eats is very sinister."

"No it's not," said Louis, and looked around for some other topic of conversation. "Hummingbirds are attracted to Sita's trumpet vines," he said. I smiled at Karl, but he had stopped eating, I suppose he had heard my whispered comment.

"Yes," I went on, "they hover with their beaks reaching down into the, what is it . . ."

"The ovary."

"The ovary of the flower."

Karl gulped down a bite of sandwich and nodded faintly at both of us. I noticed suddenly, although it must have been happening all along, that the sharp iron legs of his chair were digging into the damp lawn. The ground beneath him was evidently very soft, perhaps from all the earthworm activity, and he was settling by slow degrees. The table fit over his knees quite easily now. He seemed not to notice however, and gave me a tight smile.

I returned the smile, but as we bit into our sandwiches without speaking, I realized why Karl was here.

He had robbed Celestine and we were next. Why else would he have been hiding in the clematis, spying, learning our habits, if not in order to steal from us with ease? And another thing. He had not gone upstairs to use the facilities, but to loot my jewelry box. It seemed as though I had even seen him do this myself. I saw him snap off the tiny lock, pluck up my silver pin, diamond locket, necklace of old garnets. I saw him drop my treasures in his pocket. My brooches, my rings, my amethyst.

"I'm going inside, fellows," I announced lightly, and rose.

Louis seemed to sense something. He frowned at the heavy lace of the table. But I was certain of Karl's guilt, now, and went indoors to use the phone.

"The largest hummingbird," I heard Louis say as I walked off, "is a whopping nine inches. Lives down in South America." I knew that Louis was keeping my cousin entertained with some marvel and sure enough, when I had made the proper phone call and returned, I saw that he had so entranced Karl that he had sunk noticeably deeper. He was now at chest level with the table. His arms were crossed in front of him.

"It's sad," I said, fixing him with a look, "how some people just can't keep their hands off of other people's property."

"That's true," said my husband in an earnest voice, "remember how all the little scissors used to vanish from the dissecting kits?"

"Louis taught," I informed my cousin. "He taught in a junior college."

"Know where those scissors went?" said Louis.

Karl's eyes widened and he lifted his shoulders. His mouth was full of sandwich, so he couldn't answer.

"Girls stole them to manicure their nails!" said my husband.

Just then Sheriff Pausch came down the flagstones. He was a little man with a sharp doggish face and a deep, surprising voice that boomed godlike from his bullhorn during crises. Before becoming a sheriff, he'd taught high school botany, so he and Louis had much in common. They were members of the Blue Mound Mycological Society, which met in our basement. It seemed odd to have him here on official business, in his tan uniform, with a paper in his hand instead of bread bags full of dried fungus.

Karl's eyes went still wider when he saw the sheriff. His alarm put the last convincing touches on his guilt. He rose halfway, put his hand out, and said to the sheriff, "Please take my seat."

"No thank you," said Sheriff Pausch firmly, motioning Karl to stay seated. "There's been a complaint."

Karl's face turned childish, tipped upward from his low seat, stricken.

"I'll get the evidence," I muttered, rising to go.

"Stay here," said Louis. "What's all of this about?"

"Sita called me," said Sheriff Pausch. "She said something about a theft."

I pointed down at Karl, and gave him a cold glare. "He stole Celestine Duval's New Testament," I said, "then he went through my jewelry box. He took necklaces, pins, whatever he could lay his hands on. Stuffed them in his pocket. Search him!" I urged the two men. "See for yourself!"

"Put your hands in the air," said Sheriff Pausch in his deep voice. He stepped behind Karl and quickly patted him up and down.

"Excuse me," he said, walking back to face Karl, who had gone as pale as a sheet, whose eyes looked blurred. "You can put your hands down now," said the sheriff, flushing down to the opening in his shirt. "There seems to have been a mistake."

There was a long moment of tension. I looked at each of the men carefully. They looked carefully at me.

"It's true," I finally said. "Let me fetch the book."

"I think there has been a mistake," Sheriff Pausch repeated, and just that suddenly, because there was a wary gentleness in his voice, I knew that I had done something very wrong. Worse yet, I knew that something even more wrong was going to happen. I looked down at Karl. The legs of his chair had sunk still deeper.

"Stop . . . that," I slowly commanded.

"Sita, sit down now, please," said Louis.

But I was locked in an upright position by Karl's dark strained stare. I could not take my eyes away although I had to crane across the table to see him clearly, he'd sunk so far. The air was very still. The tiny birds, light as moths, hovered in the trumpet flowers. One note sounded. I meant to ask Louis if he heard it as well. But then my cousin leaned over sideways and pulled the heavy-looking case, the one he'd dragged through the clematis, onto his lap. He sat there with the case clasped in his arms, perhaps intending to open it, perhaps intending to go. Instead, something happened. I saw it with my eyes.

The case was so heavy, resting on his lap and knees, that his feet began to bury themselves in the earth and very swiftly the lawn rose to his knees. I said nothing. I was paralyzed with fear. I had betrayed him and now I could only watch as the man, the chair, continued to sink. The case submerged. The lawn crept up his oxblood vest. The grass brushed his chin. And still he continued to go down.

It is too late, I thought, watching him, unless he says the healing words.

*"Mea culpa,"* I gasped. *"Mea maxima culpa."*

But already his mouth was sealed by earth. His ears were stopped. His mild, sad stare was covered and then there was only the pale strip of his forehead. The earth paused before swallowing him entirely, and then, quite suddenly, the rest of him went under. The last I saw was the careless white cross in his oiled hair. The ground shook slightly to cover him and there was nothing where he had been.

I stared at the dim, peaceful grass for a long while and then looked up. Louis and the sheriff were looking at me. It seemed as though they were waiting for me to tell them what this meant.

"We wake when we die. We are all judged," I said.

Then I went down to the tree where my silver was hung. Bracelets and rings and old coins of it. I put my hands out. The leaves moved over me, gleaming and sharpened, with tarnished edges. They fell off in mounds. The air was a glittering dry rain. While I was down there, I said many things. Louis wrote them all on a pad of paper. I described the tree. It bore the leaves of my betrayal. The roots reached under everything. Everywhere I walked I had to step on the dead who lay tangled and cradled, waiting for the trumpet, for the voice on the bullhorn, for the little book to open that held a million names.

"You are not in the book," I told Louis. "You are down there with your specimens."

# The Dress

IT BEGAN WHEN Celestine was out of money, when she had no one to ask, when the shop was losing out to supermarket business, and the taxes on the land and the house were barely met. Her husband blew through town and hit her for a loan. Her brother, sick and dangerous, needed a suit of clothes. It was a bad time for Celestine's daughter to have a growth spurt and for school to start. But life is just bad timing to begin with, her own mother had once said. Sometimes Celestine agreed with this and sometimes she did not. Her daughter, for instance, was a little of both—good timing and bad luck, or the other way around. Dot was twelve, perfection on the verge of chaos, and growing breasts.

"My god," said her mother in August, "nothing fits."

"So what."

Dot was captain of Radio Cab, one of the two girls' softball teams in Argus. Her uniform, a purple T-shirt and matching cap, decorated with a sizzling orange bolt representing radio frequency, was all the clothing that Dot ever wore, save a change of jeans. Celestine had to wash the T-shirt while she slept. The cap, which had become soft and porous, was a lost cause. Radio Cab's ferocious dozen laughed at rain, and one of their most determined battles against the other girls' team, First National Bank, had actually been conducted in a storm of hail.

However, that was all over now, Dot would begin junior high school and although she didn't know it, she would need clothes, and more.

"So what," she said again, watching Celestine examine the already let-out hems of her skirts. Dot was not worried that the buttons of her blouses strained open, nor that her muscular arms barely fit into sleeves made for daintier types. She'd tear the armholes out, roll up the cuffs. Who cared if boys laughed when she bent over for a drink at the fountain? She had underwear and she wore it, though strings of elastic lace sometimes detached from the legs and trailed her, at recess, rounding third base.

"Please," said Celestine, a large woman, strong, who almost never in her life had found herself upon the verge of actual despair, "please sit down on the bed with me, Dot, and listen. I have to explain something." Behind her eyes and nose Celestine felt a prickling, a surge of heat that she didn't even recognize at first as tears. It had been so long, almost too long to remember, since she had cried. She didn't now, either; it made no sense to start over something as ordinary as the issue of a dress, although that was, Celestine now realized, connected to larger things in life.

Dot stepped over the pile of ironed and unfolded dresses, pastel mint greens and powder blues. All too small. She sat beside her mother on the crumpled bedcover.

"It's time we had a little talk," Celestine said. "You're going to change. You're going to be thirteen soon and maybe before that, even, you're going to notice a . . ."

Here Celestine's jaws stuck open, right at the hinges, as though the bones had suddenly fused. She shut her mouth carefully. She didn't want to open it again.

"A what?" asked Dot, impatient.

Celestine could almost feel her thoughts run this way, run that, in her skull, like mice trapped in a shut cupboard. She'd cornered herself.

Stain, she almost said, but that was wrong. It sounded like sin, an accident. Not right. She resented with a sudden fury the low balance on this morning's bank statement. Money, the lack of it, had got her into this situation. Birds, bees . . .

"Oh, the hell with it. Go get the Sears catalog," said Celestine.

Dot jumped up, uncharacteristically obedient, and thumped down the steps. She wanted a special first-baseman's glove, a top-grade leather pocket with three of the fingers fused on one side and two on the other. The page on which this glove was displayed was marked with checks and stars. All summer, at various stopping stations in the house—the breakfast table, bathroom sink, bedside stand, and propped against the television console—Celestine had found the book, open to the page of gloves. She always shut the catalog and put it aside, knowing it would follow her elsewhere. As Dot ran up the stairs, her mother realized the price of the thing, the look of it, the trademark, had been subtly and effectively burned into her brain, just as Dot had wished.

*Twenty-two ninety-five*, she thought, *too much*, before Dot laid the catalog, open, on the table of her thighs.

"I have a twenty-dollar bill saved for an emergency," Celestine stated. "Your need for clothing is an emergency." She flipped to the section labeled "Juniors." Sitting next to her mother, Dot looked stonily into the pages of fashions. The style that fall was long straight hair, parted in the middle, or cut into bangs that just brushed the model's brow. The girls, whose perfect faces Dot wanted to slap, wore A-line cut and Empire-waisted dresses, patterned knee socks, shoes with strap heels, block heels, cutaway toes. They were hateful, but it also looked like torture to be those girls, some of them in nylons, even, and bras and little girdles.

"I don't think you're ready for those yet," Celestine mused, turning back from the underwear. "A skirt, a couple blouses. You can do what they say here, Mix 'n Match."

But Dot's hand was reaching into the book, turning pages, thick chunks of pages, until she reached the back cover.

"Look," she said. Perhaps she'd thought this out, perhaps she hadn't. What she turned to was the Sale section. What her finger now pointed to were the words GRAB BAG DRESSES. GREAT VALUE FOR A DOLLAR EACH.

And then with desperate passion, thinking on her feet, her mind clicking with intentions she could see come to life, Dot spoke.

"I've got nine dollars saved from my birthday and my bottle refunds.

That plus the twenty makes twenty-nine all together. Get the glove and there's still six dollars left. Six dresses. One for every school day and one left over, just for Sunday Mass."

"Sunday Mass." Celestine turned the thought over, flipped it in her mind like a pancake until it was done. "You'll go to Sunday Mass if I get you the glove?"

Dot reared back, impressed with both the fast chemical action of her idea on her mother's brain and, even more, at how quickly Celestine had managed to further complicate the bargain.

"Mass, Mass . . ." Dot had recently resisted Mass the only way that she knew how. Drama. Stuck in the front row, she had fainted. Spots gloriously covered the air before her and, half overcome, she'd pitched herself sideways into the middle of the center aisle. The moment of dizziness had been quite real, but Dot had seized upon it and, after that, refused to enter the church.

What was Mass, though, compared to the glove—smooth and fragrant and thick, a golden brown, hand sewn, and signed by Roger Maris—close enough to touch.

"Yes."

"Good."

It was one of those rare and precious moments, an agreement reached by which a mother and daughter both got what they wanted. An order form was soon filled out. No return on sale items was agreed to. The money was deposited and a check was written, added to the order, mailed off. One week passed, another. School started. Dot went.

On the first day, Dot wore the only item that even marginally fit her, a blue plaid coverall with grommeted vents. The second day, she managed to destroy it. Fortunately, that afternoon, the package from Sears, Roebuck arrived. That night, Dot slept with her glove, a firm, sweet pillow. On the morning of the third day, she opened the first of six packages, each of which contained a Grab Bag dress. It was a strange dress, but Dot shrugged and put it on without much thought. The drop-waisted skirt was horizontally striped in alternating olive-green and purple bars. The bodice was a tightly knitted zippered bag, embroidered with frantic-looking little animals in hot, fluorescent pink. The sleeves were striped, too, and seemed to bulge and ripple around her biceps. It had a collar or, to be more accurate, a kind of hinged trap that was animated by interior wires and collapsed constrictingly upon Dot's throat when the zipper was snapped closed.

She came downstairs in the dress. The colors, false as a carnival tent, accentuated the stark reddish tinge of Dot's hair. Her face was pale, a smooth lump above the glowing mass of fabric.

"Well?" said Dot, standing in the door of the kitchen, "what do you think?"

Her mother turned, a thick mug of black coffee in one hand, a plate stacked with toast in the other. She froze. The dress was more a disguise than a piece of ordinary clothing—maybe the costume of a harem girl, a clown. The full skin ballooned outward below the hips, and its edges stiffened at the knees so it resembled a parachute held in suspension by rushing winds.

"Wow," Celestine said carefully, moving cautiously toward Dot. "That sure is a lot of dress for just a dollar!"

"Yeah," Dot said. The stitching of the glove, where she slept, was a fading red track on her cheek. She took a piece of toast from the plate her mother held, and ate with her head bent forward as Celestine rummaged at the back of her neck for the tag. She didn't hear her mother mutter: "Made in Hell. Wash separate. You better believe it." She didn't hear, because within her book bag she had the glove, the golden prize.

It was on the fourth day, the day she brought the glove to school and got less admiration than she'd somehow anticipated, that Dot began to suspect that she'd made a mistake. It was on the morning of the fifth day that she knew the mistake was real. On that morning, time collapsed as Dot opened the remaining packages and found, to her surprise, that every one of them contained the exact and perfect replica of dress number one.

Still, this could be seen as a benefit at first. No picking and choosing. No question of what to wear. With her first-baseman's mitt clutched hard and now somewhat defensively, Dot wore a dress (one of them, snatched up from the frantically shredded wrappings; it didn't matter which) to school each day. In the following days that lengthened to weeks, Dot began to understand that the error was serious, in fact it was worse than that. It was in the nature of a terrible misfortune, a dreadful thing, a blight from which, socially, she might not recover in all of the remaining years she was to spend at Argus High School.

In every school, in that year, in the Midwest, there was a girl named Candy, whose blond or dark brown hair was naturally thick and long and curled under at the ends, a girl whose father was rich, whose mother shopped in dress shops that catered to girls of twelve, a girl with cuteness, school spirit. In every school there was a Candy whose bite was perfect, whose legs were shaven and bronzed from the summer sun, whose wrists were slung with expensive chains and tiny golden charms, and whose heart, the real one in her chest, was a small black lump of coal, hormonally ignited and burning hot.

The Candy assigned to Argus High also had a tongue like a new-honed knife, eyes as cold as the pits of olives, and a mind that was both merciless and obsessive. That this Candy was also the captain of First National Bank would not have mattered, not in some schools, in other locations. But because in that summer animosities had built and in-flamed as, led by Dot, Radio Cab had knocked line drives and long flies to left field of First National and triumphed, eventually, in a way that was both just and cruel, there was, in Candy Pantamounty, an unspeak-able venom, which the sight of Dot's dress, on the first day she wore it, tapped. A small trickle of snide whispers widened to a gusher as weeks passed and upon each day Dot wore the same dress, first in carelessness, then in uncertain defensiveness, and then at last, on the day of Candy Pantamounty's triumph, in skulking and self-horrified embarrassment too rich for tears.

The high school study hall was a wide room, rectangular, bound on a side with windows, presided over by Mr. Stanley Feebe, gym coach and hygiene teacher. In the seventh hour of the day, Dot and Candy, as-signed seats in neighboring rows, self-consciously ignored each other as they paged through workbooks and looked up vocabulary words. Mr.

Feebe liked to run what he called a tight ship. He sentenced talkers to various forms of excommunication, forcing them to sit alone in the band room, on the hallway floor, or next to him at his desk of gray metal, where each day he prepared his lesson on topics related to human development. So as not to disturb him, Candy was forced to attack Dot with silent cunning. In her notebook, one fall morning, she carried a lettered sign, WANT TO BET? which she propped up on her desk.

Since the first time Dot had worn the dress and raised some eyebrows, she had become the object of increasing amounts of attention and talk. But the scrutiny of others was not yet general, that is, until the day that the sign went up and every boy and girl who surreptitiously slipped Candy a note, with fifty cents attached, paused a moment to stare thoughtfully at Dot.

Who stared back, until her classmate's eyes dropped and she or he hastily jotted something down in the notebook with a shiny blue cover that Candy was seen to carry everywhere.

Life progressed at a normal rate. How could it not? Time neither stood still nor did the sun refuse to rise just because the wardrobe of Dot Adare consisted of what her classmate perceived as one terrible dress. Meals were eaten, the electric class bells jangled in the halls, bets were taken, the kitty rose to a hundred, then two hundred dollars, then more. Every student from the seventh through the ninth grade bet once twice, or more, as the prize mounted. Every student except for Dot, who was unaware of what her heart's enemy kept hidden in the blue spiral-bound, or why, every morning when she rounded the brown house on the corner across from the main doors to the school, a crowd was waiting. A glance in her direction, and the crowd then dispersed to take up individual concerns. But not until they had made sure that Dot was wearing *the* dress.

In Dot's room, the glove with its scrawled black signature and careful webbing hung open on her bedpost to receive the unpitched ball. The closet yawned, the mirror laughed. In the corner lurked a pile of dresses. Celestine, overcome with fall orders and backed-up work, had grown accustomed to the brilliance of her daughter's dress over morning coffee and hardly even winced at it anymore. Since she had never thought about her clothing up until this occurrence, it took Dot a while to realize the reason why she was unhappy in the morning, why her soul revolted as she walked, and why, upon rounding the corner and proceeding to the curb, she kept her eyes downcast and managed to produce, in her head, a roaring hum that effectively blocked the voices of those around her.

She went through life in a dream, ignoring everything, existing merely in the shell of her body, which was, in turn, encased, like some unfortunate marine creature, in a loathsome concoction of stripes. The dress served as a sort of natural defense, repelling intruders with its poisonous colors, and friends as well. At lunch, Dot edged hopefully toward schools of girls in coordinated outfits, all of whom flipped their hair and whirled away. She ate in haste, at the end of the table closest to the door, a lonely stickleback, a bottom feeder gulping macaroni and creamed corn. And, as no windfall of money had yet come to Celestine's rescue, it looked as though, like hermit crabs, Dot would have no choice but to grow with fearsome rapidity and literally burst out of the dress. To that end, she ate copiously, which further reduced the budget Celestine had set.

Suspended, existing wholly within herself, Dot thumped from class to class, her arms loaded, heaviness within and heaviness without. No telling how long, how endlessly this misery of unacknowledgment would have managed to spin itself out, had it not been for one of those starkly brisk changes of pressure that occur before winter sets in.

The sky was blue, blue and funneling upward. The wind was still for once. The yellow sawtooth leaves of young elms lined gutters, and the sidewalks were drifted over with the sweet bronze dust of crushed ash and box elder. As Dot neared the corner that morning she was stirred by the clarity of weather, into focusing hard upon the crowd that eyed her and then turned away, some to Candy Pantamounty, who stood, clad in a plaid kilt and richly woven cardigan, with the blue notebook. Walking toward Candy Pantamounty, now and for the first time, Dot allowed her open ears to receive and register the whispers and offhand remarks that whirled to every side.

"I'm out of it. My bet was for yesterday."

"I think she'll wear it for another week."

"Shit man, that makes what, two months?"

"I'm placing a long shot on the end of the year."

"It'll wear *out* by then."

"No way. It's polyester. The home-ec teacher says that wears like iron."

"I'll puke if I see her in it another month."

"Shut up, I bet for two weeks from today. If I'm right I could take the whole pot."

"What's it up to now?"

"Four hundred."

Sound gathered and laughter hissed and crashed like pounding surf, leaving Dot stranded, walking down the very center of the sidewalk. Her understanding widened one small fraction with each step she took until, approaching her smartly dressed enemy, the whole of it engulfed her. The moment was blinding. Dot noticed first that her feet were steaming in her shoes. Then the heat spread upward, spiraling through her stomach and flashing along each rib. Her arms fused in molten shock. Her face, steaming pink, bulged and wobbled like something set to boil upon her neck.

"No," she whispered, and then she realized her cheeks were wet. The only times in her life Dot had cried up till now were usually calculated efforts, attempts to convince and get her way with people. This was the first time, standing stock-still in the swirls and crush of students, that Dot had cried from shame. The first and the last, she vowed, later, when the others had moved around her and she stood outside, alone.

She walked away from school. She had a place she liked to go when she had to think—the Peavey Elevator, out of town and abandoned. Up along one side of the silvered tower, a ladder was tacked leading to a small wooden perch. It was here Dot went for comfort, here she had tried to smoke once, here she sat and looked into the flat gray emptiness. In the next field over, a farmer on a huge green Steiger caressed his field in round after round of woven furrows. Dust rose, drifting high in the clear, dry air. The space consumed all sound into it, each small trace of noise and violence. Just thought was left. The farmer's eye was caught, glancing up once, at the strange blob of color on the Peavey Elevator, but the farm report came on the radio and he forgot what he intended to do about it. By the time he happened to glance again, on his way home, the blob was gone and the light was lengthening toward early dusk.

In which Dot, with sharp determination, proceeded to try to turn her humiliation into gain.

The first step in the process, the key, was the Babe Ruth baseball captain.

He was, perhaps, the male equivalent to Candy Pantamounty. Yes, he was sought after, golden as she was dark. He was older. He had the town home-run record. Yet there was one stark difference that gave Dot hope. Whereas Candy was rich, Mike Stolz was not. If lack of wealth did not cause him to feel a certain amount of compassion toward her plight, then, Dot felt certain, an appeal to his greed might cause him to join her anyway. "Look," she meant to put it, on the phone, as she dialed his number. "We need each other." But did they? As her courage failed and choked her, Mike Stolz answered.

"Hello?"

His voice was deep, resonant, and careless.

"Mike? This is Dot Adare."

"Dot who? You want my mother?"

"No, I need to talk to you."

"Okay, well. Who is this again?"

"My name is Dot."

"I'm sorry . . ."

"I'm in school with you, I'm only in the seventh grade, so you probably haven't noticed me, or maybe you have . . . see, I usually wear this dress to school, purple and green stripes?"

"Oh god, yes, you're *the dress*."

They both stopped. Silence yawned in the receiver, and Dot took heart that he had not hung up on her.

"Look," she said, "we need each other. . . ."

That is how the bet was rigged, and how, through Mike Stolz, Dot gained access to the blue notebook and how, between them, they picked a day that no one else had and how, on that day, when Dot rounded the corner wearing a blouse and sweater borrowed from the drawer of Mike Stolz's sister, she was able to bear the pandemonium, and walk right past. Mike Stolz claimed the prize and Candy lowered her gaze demurely, cocked her head.

"Okay if I bring the whole amount tomorrow?"

"I want it in cash," Mike said, as he and Dot had agreed, "in sixth-hour study hall."

"You got it," said Candy. She stowed her notebook and sauntered off. Her kilt swished invitingly above her knees, but Mike Stolz did not take the opportunity to join her. He glanced at Dot. His look was casual and not quite readable, but after all, they could afford no hint of collusion between them until the cash was paid over, and then . . . plans bloomed in Dot's mind, visions. She would not turn her nose up at Mix 'n Match. Shoes. She would have a pair like Candy Pantamounty's, with spirals stitched onto the toes. Her mother's ratty brown coat would turn to cashmere. Hers would lengthen. Fake fur, blue plush, would encircle her face. And equipment. She'd have her own bat, her own set of cleats. The vision lasted through the night, through the next day, upon which she folded the borrowed clothes into a bag and wore her own dress proudly through the long hours until finally the fifth period bell rang and study hall, with all its promise of sweet vengeance, of triumph, was brought to order.

After Mr. Feebe had begun preparing for his class on the human digestive system, silence descended. Books were opened, but no eye regarded them. Money would change hands, student money, a lump sum that, for the luck of Mike Stolz, any one of them could have had.

With slow finesse, her manicured fingers alight with three birth-stone circlets, Candy Pantamounty opened her purse and extracted a pile of twenties. One by one, her fingers touching her tongue from time to time, she counted them onto the Plastiform of her desk. Anyone who followed her hands knew that when she was finished, four hundred and sixty even had been counted and squared into the pile.

It remained only for Mike Stolz to walk by and collect. It remained only for him to, then, stop at the desk of Dot Adare and, by silently counting half the take out to her, proclaim her clever collusion, her out-witting, her outdoing, of Candy Pantamounty.

In one light motion, Mike Stolz rose. He walked the aisle from front to back and then paused just long enough to place his hands around the counted stack and transfer it from desktop to zippered notebook.

Now, *now*, Dot's heart beat. She straightened as he turned, as his steps traversed the few yards between them. Her breath caught fast in her throat, and then she forgot to breathe out as he walked on, past her, back to the head of the aisle, where he shifted his muscular torso into the small desk seat and opened a thick book.

No thought came to Dot. Pages rustled, routine returned to the rows around her. Mr. Feebe smacked a desktop with a ruler and Mike Stolz started. Dot noticed because she hadn't removed her eyes from his back, and wouldn't, as the fifty minutes passed and she decided that out of embarrassment he had not publicly divided up the spoils. He had to pass her on his way out. Then, she knew, he would hang back, stop, and very stealthily give her the bills. There was a reason for it.

But when the final bell rang and the rows of students bolted for the door, Mike Stolz was the first to rise. He made his way down the center of the aisle. His gaze did not flicker when she called his name.

# Snares

IT BEGAN AFTER church with Margaret and her small granddaughter, Lulu, and was not to end until the long days of Lent and a hard-packed snow. There were factions on the reservation, a treaty settlement in the agent's hands. There were Chippewa who signed their names and there were Chippewa who saw the cash offered as a flimsy bait. I was one and Fleur Pillager, Lulu's mother, was another who would not lift her hand to sign. It was said that all the power to witch, harm, or cure lay in Fleur, the lone survivor of the old Pillager clan. But as much as people feared Fleur, they listened to Margaret Kashpaw. She was the ringleader of the holdouts, a fierce, one-minded widow with a vinegar tongue.

Margaret Kashpaw had knots of muscles in her arms. Her braids were thin, gray as iron, and usually tied strictly behind her back so they wouldn't swing. She was plump as a basket below and tough as roots on top. Her face was gnarled around a beautiful sharp nose. Two shell earrings caught the light and flashed whenever she turned her head. She had become increasingly religious in the years after her loss, and finally succeeded in dragging me to the Benediction Mass, where I was greeted by Father Damien, from whom I occasionally won small sums at dice.

"Grandfather Nanapush," he smiled, "at last."

"These benches are a hardship for an old man," I complained. "If you spread them with soft pine-needle cushions I'd have come before."

Father Damien stared thoughtfully at the rough pews, folded his hands inside the sleeves of his robe.

"You must think of their unyielding surfaces as helpful," he offered. "God sometimes enters the soul through the humblest parts of our anatomies, if they are sensitized to suffering."

"A god who enters through the rear door," I countered, "is no better than a thief."

Father Damien was used to me, and smiled as he walked to the altar. I adjusted my old bones, longing for some relief, trying not to rustle for fear of Margaret's jabbing elbow. The time was long. Lulu probed all my pockets with her fingers until she found a piece of hard candy. I felt no great presence in this cold place and decided, as my rear door ached and my shoulders stiffened, that our original gods were better, the Chippewa characters who were not exactly perfect but at least did not require sitting on hard boards.

When Mass was over and the smell of incense was thick in all our clothes, Margaret, Lulu, and I went out into the starry cold, the snow and stubble fields, and began the long walk to our homes. It was dusk. On either side of us the heavy trees stood motionless and blue. Our footsteps squeaked against the dry snow, the only sound to hear. We spoke very little, and even Lulu ceased her singing when the moon rose to half, poised like a balanced cup. We knew the very moment someone else stepped upon the road.

We had turned a bend and the footfalls came unevenly, just out of sight. There were two men, one mixed-blood or white, from the drop of his hard boot soles, and the other one quiet, an Indian. Not long and I heard them talking close behind us. From the rough, quick tension of the Indian's language, I recognized Lazarre. And the mixed-blood must be Clarence Morrissey. The two had signed the treaty and spoke in its favor to anyone they could collar at the store. They even came to people's houses to beg and argue that this was our one chance, our good chance, that the government would withdraw the offer. But wherever Margaret was, she slapped down their words like mosquitoes and said the only thing that lasts life to life is land. Money burns like tinder, flows off like water. And as for government promises, the wind is steadier. It is no wonder that, because she spoke so well, Lazarre and Clarence

Morrissey wished to silence her. I sensed their bad intent as they passed us, an unpleasant edge of excitement in their looks and greetings.

They went on, disappeared in the dark brush.

"Margaret," I said, "we are going to cut back." My house was close, but Margaret kept walking forward as if she hadn't heard.

I took her arm, caught Lulu close, and started to turn us, but Margaret would have none of this and called me a coward. She grabbed the girl to her. Lulu, who did not mind getting tossed between us, laughed, tucked her hand into her grandma's pocket, and never missed a step. Two years ago she had tired of being carried, got up, walked. She had the balance of a little mink. She was slippery and clever, too, which was good because when the men jumped from the darkest area of brush and grappled with us half a mile on, Lulu slipped free and scrambled into the trees.

THEY WERE OCCUPIED with Margaret and me, at any rate. We were old enough to snap in two, our limbs dry as dead branches, but we fought as though our enemies were the Nadouissouix kidnappers of our childhood. Margaret uttered a war cry that had not been heard for fifty years, and bit Lazarre's hand to the bone, giving a wound which would later prove the death of him. As for Clarence, he had all he could do to wrestle me to the ground and knock me half unconscious. When he'd accomplished that, he tied me and tossed me into a wheelbarrow, which was hidden near the road for the purpose of lugging us to the Morrissey barn.

I came to my senses trussed to a manger, sitting on a bale. Margaret was roped to another bale across from me, staring straight forward in a rage, a line of froth caught between her lips. On either side of her, shaggy cows chewed and shifted their thumping hooves. I rose and staggered, the weight of the manger on my back. I planned on Margaret biting through my ropes with her strong teeth, but then the two men entered.

I'm a talker, a fast-mouth who can't keep his thoughts straight, but lets fly with words and marvels at what he hears from his own mouth.

I'm a smart one. I always was a devil for convincing women. And I wasn't too bad a shot, in other ways, at convincing men. But I had never been tied up before.

"Boozhoo," I said. "Children, let us loose, your game is too rough!"

They stood between us, puffed with their secrets.

"Empty old windbag," said Clarence.

"I have a bargain for you," I said, looking for an opening. "Let us go and we won't tell Pukwan." Edgar Pukwan was the tribal police. "Boys get drunk sometimes and don't know what they're doing."

Lazarre laughed once, hard and loud. "We're not drunk," he said. "Just wanting what's coming to us, some justice, money out of it."

"Kill us," said Margaret. "We won't sign."

"Wait," I said. "My cousin Pukwan will find you boys, and have no mercy. Let us go. I'll sign and get it over with, and I'll persuade the old widow."

I signaled Margaret to keep her mouth shut. She blew air into her cheeks. Clarence looked expectantly at Lazarre, as if the show were over, but Lazarre folded his arms and was convinced of nothing.

"You lie when it suits, skinny old dog," he said, wiping at his lips as if in hunger. "It's her we want, anyway. We'll shame her so she shuts her mouth."

"Easy enough," I said, smooth, "now that you've got her tied. She's plump and good-looking. Eyes like a doe! But you forget that we're together, almost man and wife."

This wasn't true at all, and Margaret's face went rigid with tumbling fury and confusion. I kept talking.

"So of course if you do what you're thinking of doing you'll have to kill me afterward, and that will make my cousin Pukwan twice as angry, since I owe him a fat payment for a gun which he lent me and I never returned. All the same," I went on—their heads were spinning— "I'll forget you bad boys ever considered such a crime, something so terrible that Father Damien would nail you on boards just like in the example on the wall in church."

"Quit jabbering." Lazarre stopped me in a deadly voice.

It was throwing pebbles in a dry lake. My words left no ripple. I saw in his eyes that he intended us great harm. I saw his greed. It was like watching an ugly design of bruises come clear for a moment and reconstructing the evil blows that made them.

I played my last card.

"Whatever you do to Margaret you are doing to the Pillager woman!" I dropped my voice. "The witch, Fleur Pillager, is her own son's wife."

Clarence was too young to be frightened, but his mouth hung in interested puzzlement. My words had a different effect on Lazarre, as a sudden light shone, a consequence he hadn't considered.

I cried out, seeing this, "Don't you know she can think about you hard enough to stop your heart?" Lazarre was still deciding. He raised his fist and swung it casually and tapped my face. It was worse not to be hit full on.

"Come near!" crooned Margaret in the old language. "Let me teach you how to die."

But she was trapped like a fox. Her earrings glinted and spun as she hissed her death song over and over, which signaled something to Lazarre, for he shook himself angrily and drew a razor from his jacket. He stropped it with fast, vicious movements while Margaret sang shriller, so full of hate that the ropes should have burned, shriveled, fallen from her body. My struggle set the manger cracking against the barn walls and further confused the cows, who bumped one another and complained. At a sign from Lazarre, Clarence sighed, rose, and smashed me. The last I saw before I blacked out, through the tiny closing pinhole of light, was Lazarre approaching Margaret with the blade.

When I woke, minutes later, it was to worse shock. For Lazarre had sliced Margaret's long braids off and was now, carefully, shaving her scalp. He started almost tenderly at the wide part, and then pulled the edge down each side of her skull. He did a clean job. He shed not one drop of her blood.

And I could not even speak to curse them. For pressing my jaw down, thick above my tongue, her braids, never cut in this life till now, were tied to silence me. Powerless, I tasted their flat, animal perfume.

IT WASN'T MUCH later, or else it was forever, that we walked out into the night again. Speechless, we made our way in fierce pain down the road. I was damaged in spirit, more so than Margaret. For now she tucked her shawl over her naked head and forgot her own bad treatment. She called out in dread each foot of the way, for Lulu. But the smart, bold girl had hidden till all was clear and then run to Margaret's house. We opened the door and found her sitting by the stove in a litter of scorched matches and kindling. She had not the skill to start a fire, but she was dry eyed. Though very cold, she was alert and then captured with wonder when Margaret slipped off her shawl.

"Where is your hair?" she asked.

I took my hand from my pocket. "Here's what's left of it. I grabbed this when they cut me loose." I was shamed by how pitiful I had been, relieved when Margaret snatched the thin gray braids from me and coiled them round her fist.

"I knew you would save them, clever man!" There was satisfaction in her voice.

I set the fire blazing. It was strange how generous this woman was to me, never blaming me or mentioning my failure. Margaret stowed her braids inside a birchbark box and merely instructed me to put it in her grave, when that time occurred. Then she came near the stove with a broken mirror from beside her washstand and looked at her own image.

"My," she pondered, "my." She put the mirror down. "I'll take a knife to them."

And I was thinking too. I was thinking I would have to kill them. But how does an aching and half-starved grandfather attack a young, well-fed Morrissey and a tall, sly Lazarre? Later, I rolled up in blankets in the corner by Margaret's stove, and I put my mind to this question throughout that night until, exhausted, I slept. And I thought of it first thing next morning, too, and still nothing came. It was only after we had some hot galette and walked Lulu back to her mother that an idea began to grow.

Fleur let us in, hugged Lulu into her arms, and looked at Margaret, who took off her scarf and stood bald, face burning again with smoldered fire. She told Fleur all of what happened, sparing no detail. The two women's eyes held, but Fleur said nothing. She put Lulu down, smoothed the front of her calico shirt, flipped her heavy braids over her shoulders, tapped one finger on her perfect lips. And then, calm, she went to the washstand and scraped the edge of her hunting knife keen as glass. Margaret and Lulu and I watched as Fleur cut her braids off, shaved her own head, and folded the hair into a quilled skin pouch. Then she went out, hunting, and didn't bother to wait for night to cover her tracks.

I would have to go out hunting too.

I had no gun, but anyway that was a white man's revenge. I knew how to wound with barbs of words, but had never wielded a skinning knife against a human, much less two young men. Whomever I missed would kill me, and I did not want to die by their lowly hands.

In fact, I didn't think that after Margaret's interesting kindness I wanted to leave this life at all. Her head, smooth as an egg, was ridged delicately with bone, and gleamed as if it had been buffed with a flannel cloth. Maybe it was the strangeness that attracted me. She looked forbidding, but the absence of hair also set off her eyes, so black and full of lights. She reminded me of that queen from England, of a water snake or a shrewd young bird. The earrings, which seemed part of her, mirrored her moods like water, and when they were still rounds of green lights against her throat I seemed, again, to taste her smooth, smoky braids in my mouth.

I had better things to do than fight. So I decided to accomplish revenge as quickly as possible. I was a talker who used my brains as my weapon. When I hunted, I preferred to let my game catch itself.

SNARES DEMAND CLEVER fingers and a scheming mind, and snares had never failed me. Snares are quiet, and best of all snares are slow. I wanted to give Lazarre and Morrissey time to consider why they had to strangle. I thought hard. One- or two-foot deadfalls are required beneath a snare so that a man can't put his hand up and loosen the knot. The snares I had in mind also required something stronger than a cord, which could be broken, and finer than a rope, which even Lazarre might see and avoid. I pondered this closely, yet even so I might never have found the solution had I not gone to Mass with Margaret and grown curious about the workings of Father Damien's pride and joy, the piano in the back of the church, the instrument whose keys he breathed on, polished, then played after services, and sometimes alone. I had noticed that his hands usually stayed near the middle of the keyboard, so I took the wires from either end.

IN THE MEANTIME, I was not the only one concerned with punishing Lazarre and Clarence Morrissey. Fleur was seen in town. Her thick skirts brushed the snow into clouds behind her. Though it was cold she left her head bare so everyone could see the frigid sun glare off her skull. The light reflected in the eyes of Lazarre and Clarence, who were standing at the door of the pool hall. They dropped their cue sticks in the slush and ran back to Morrissey land. Fleur walked the four streets, once in each direction, then followed.

The two men told of her visit, how she passed through the Morrissey house touching here, touching there, sprinkling powders that ignited and stank on the hot stove. How Clarence swayed on his feet, blinked hard, and chewed his fingers. How Fleur stepped up to him, drew her knife. He smiled foolishly and asked her for supper. She reached forward and trimmed off a hank of his hair. Then she stalked from the house, leaving a taste of cold wind, and chased Lazarre to the barn.

She made a black silhouette against the light from the door. Lazarre pressed against the wood of the walls, watching, hypnotized by the sight of Fleur's head and the quiet blade. He did not defend himself when she approached, reached for him, gently and efficiently cut bits of his hair, held his hands, one at a time, and trimmed the nails. She waved the razor-edged knife before his eyes and swept a few eyelashes into a white square of flour sacking that she then carefully folded into her blouse.

For days after, Lazarre babbled and wept. Fleur was murdering him by use of bad medicine, he said. He showed his hand, the bite that Margaret had dealt him, and the dark streak from the wound, along his wrist and inching up his arm. He even used that bound hand to scratch his name from the treaty, but it did no good.

I figured that the two men were doomed at least three ways now. Margaret won the debate with her Catholic training and decided to damn her soul by taking up the ax, since no one else had destroyed her enemies. I begged her to wait for another week, all during which it snowed and thawed and snowed again. It took me that long to arrange the snare to my satisfaction, near Lazarre's shack, on a path both men took to town.

I set it out one morning before anyone stirred, and watched from an old pine twisted along the ground. I waited while the smoke rose in a silky feather from the tiny tin spout on Lazarre's roof. I had to sit half a day before Lazarre came outside, and even then it was just for wood, nowhere near the path. I had a hard time to keep my blood flowing, my stomach still. I ate a handful of dry berries Margaret had given me, and a bit of pounded meat. I doled it out to myself and waited until finally Clarence showed. He walked the trail like a blind ghost and stepped straight into my noose.

It was perfect, or would have been if I had made the deadfall two inches wider, for in falling Clarence somehow managed to spread his legs and straddle the deep hole I'd cut. It had been invisible, covered with snow, and yet in one foot-pedaling instant, the certain knowledge of its construction sprang into Clarence's brain and told his legs to reach for the sides. I don't know how he did it, but there he was poised. I waited, did not show myself. The noose jerked enough to cut slightly into the fool's neck, a too-snug fit. He was spread-eagled and on tiptoe, his arms straight out. If he twitched a finger, lost the least control, even tried to yell, one foot would go, the noose constrict.

But Clarence did not move. I could see from behind my branches that he didn't even dare to change the expression on his face. His mouth stayed frozen in shock. Only his eyes shifted, darted fiercely and wildly, side to side, showing all the agitation he must not release, searching desperately for a means of escape. They focused only when I finally stepped toward him, quiet, from the pine.

We were in full view of Lazarre's house, face-to-face. I stood before the boy. Just a touch, a sudden kick, perhaps no more than a word, was all that it would take. But I looked into his eyes and saw the knowledge of his situation. Pity entered me. Even for Margaret's shame, I couldn't do the thing I might have done.

I turned away and left Morrissey still balanced on the ledge of snow.

WHAT MONEY I did have, I took to the trading store next day. I bought the best bonnet on the reservation. It was black as a coal scuttle, large, and shaped the same. "It sets off my doe eyes," Margaret said and stared me down.

She wore it every day, and always to Mass. Not long before Lent and voices could be heard: "There goes Old Lady Coal Bucket." Nonetheless, she was proud, and softening day by day, I could tell. By the time we got our foreheads crossed with ashes, she consented to be married.

"I hear you're thinking of exchanging the vows," said Father Damien as I shook his hand on our way out the door.

"I'm having relations with Margaret already," I told him, "that's the way we do things."

This had happened to him before, so he was not even stumped as to what remedy he should use.

"Make a confession, at any rate," he said, motioning us back into the church.

So I stepped into the little box and knelt. Father Damien slid aside the shadowy door. I told him what I had been doing with Margaret and he stopped me partway through.

"No more details. Pray to Our Lady."

"There is one more thing."

"Yes?"

"Clarence Morrissey, he wears a scarf to church around his neck each week. I snared him like a rabbit."

Father Damien let the silence fill him.

"And the last thing," I went on. "I stole the wire from your piano."

The silence spilled over into my stall, and I was held in its grip until the priest spoke.

"Discord is hateful to God. You have offended his ear." Almost as an afterthought, Damien added, "And his commandment. The violence among you must cease."

"You can have the wire back," I said. I had used only one long strand. I also agreed that I would never use my snares on humans, an easy promise. Lazarre was already caught.

JUST TWO DAYS later, while Margaret and I stood with Lulu and her mother inside the trading store, Lazarre entered, gesturing, his eyes rolled to the skull. He stretched forth his arm and pointed along its deepest black vein and dropped his jaw wide. Then he stepped backward into a row of traps that the trader had set to show us how they worked. Fleur's eye lit, her white scarf caught the sun as she turned. All the whispers were true. Fleur had scratched Lazarre's figure into a piece of birchbark, drawn his insides, and rubbed a bit of rouge up his arm until the red stain reached his heart. There was no sound as he fell, no cry, no word, and the traps of all types that clattered down around his body jumped and met for a long time, snapping air.

# *Fleur*

THE FIRST TIME she drowned in the cold and glassy waters of Lake Turcot, Fleur Pillager was only a girl. Two men saw the boat tip, saw her struggle in the waves. They rowed over to the place she went down, and jumped in. When they dragged her over the gunwales, she was cold to the touch and stiff, so they slapped her face, shook her by the heels, worked her arms back and forth, and pounded her back until she coughed up lake water. She shivered all over like a dog, then took a breath. But it wasn't long afterward that those two men disappeared. The first wandered off, and the other, Jean Hat, got himself run over by a cart.

It went to show, my grandma said. It figured to her, all right. By saving Fleur Pillager, those two men had lost themselves.

The next time she fell in the lake, Fleur Pillager was twenty years old and no one touched her. She washed on shore, her skin a dull dead gray, but when George Many Women bent to look closer, he saw her chest move. Then her eyes spun open, sharp black agate, and she looked at him. "You'll take my place," she hissed. Everybody scattered and left her there, so no one knows how she dragged herself home. Soon after that we noticed Many Women changed, grew afraid, wouldn't leave his house, and would not be forced to go near water. For his caution, he lived until the day that his sons brought him a new tin bathtub. Then the first time he used the tub he slipped, got knocked out, and breathed water while his wife stood in the other room frying breakfast.

Men stayed clear of Fleur Pillager after the second drowning. Even though she was good-looking, nobody dared to court her because it was clear that Misshepeshu, the water man, the monster, wanted her for himself. He's a devil, that one, love hungry with desire and maddened for the touch of young girls, the strong and daring especially, the ones like Fleur.

Our mothers warn us that we'll think he's handsome, for he appears with green eyes, copper skin, a mouth tender as a child's. But if you fall into his arms, he sprouts horns, fangs, claws, fins. His feet are joined as one and his skin, brass scales, rings to the touch. You're fascinated, cannot move. He casts a shell necklace at your feet, weeps gleaming chips that harden into mica on your breasts. He holds you under. Then he takes the body of a lion or a fat brown worm. He's made of gold. He's made of beach moss. He's a thing of dry foam, a thing of death by drowning, the death a Chippewa cannot survive.

Unless you are Fleur Pillager. We all knew she couldn't swim. After the first time, we thought she'd never go back to Lake Turcot. We thought she'd keep to herself, live quiet, stop killing men off by drowning in the lake. After the first time, we thought she'd keep the good ways. But then, after the second drowning, we knew that we were dealing with something much more serious. She was haywire, out of control. She messed with evil, laughed at the old women's advice, and dressed like a man. She got herself into some half-forgotten medicine, studied ways we shouldn't talk about. Some say she kept the finger of a child in her pocket and a powder of unborn rabbits in a leather thong around her neck. She laid the heart of an owl on her tongue so she could see at night, and went out, hunting, not even in her own body. We know for sure because the next morning, in the snow or dust, we followed the tracks of her bare feet and saw where they changed, where the claws sprang out, the pad broadened and pressed into the dirt. By night we heard her chuffing cough, the bear cough. By day her silence and the wide grin she threw to bring down our guard made us frightened. Some thought that Fleur Pillager should be driven off the reservation, but not a single person who spoke like this had the nerve. And finally, when people were just about to get together and throw her out, she left on her own and didn't come back all summer. That's what this story is about.

During that summer, when she lived a few miles south in Argus, things happened. She almost destroyed that town.

WHEN SHE GOT down to Argus in the year of 1920, it was just a small grid of six streets on either side of the railroad depot. There were two elevators, one central, the other a few miles west. Two stores competed for the trade of the eight hundred citizens, and three churches quarreled with one another for their souls. There was a frame building for Lutherans, a heavy brick one for Episcopalians, and a long narrow shingled Catholic church. This last had a tall slender steeple, twice as high as any building or tree.

No doubt, across the low, flat wheat, watching from the road as she came near Argus on foot, Fleur saw that steeple rise, a shadow thin as a needle. Maybe in that raw space it drew her the way a lone tree draws lightning. Maybe, in the end, the Catholics are to blame. For if she hadn't seen that sign of pride, that slim prayer, that marker, maybe she would have kept walking.

But Fleur Pillager turned, and the first place she went once she came into town was to the back door of the priest's residence attached to the landmark church. She didn't go there for a handout, although she got that, but to ask for work. She got that too, or the town got her. It's hard to tell which came out worse, her or the men or the town, although the upshot of it all was that Fleur lived.

The four men who worked at the butcher's had carved up about a thousand carcasses between them, maybe half of that steers and the other half pigs, sheep, and game animals like deer, elk, and bear. That's not even mentioning the chickens, which were beyond counting. Pete Kozka owned the place, and employed Lily Veddar, Tor Grunewald, and my stepfather, Dutch James, who had brought my mother down from the reservation the year before she disappointed him by dying. Dutch took me out of school to take her place. I kept house half the time and worked the other in the butcher shop, sweeping floors, putting sawdust down, running a hambone across the street to a customer's bean pot or a package of sausage to the corner. I was a good one to have around because until they needed me, I was invisible. I blended into the stained brown walls, a skinny, big-nosed girl with staring eyes. Because I could fade into a corner or squeeze beneath a shelf, I knew everything, what the men said when no one was around, and what they did to Fleur.

Kozka's Meats served farmers for a fifty-mile area, both to slaughter, for it had a stock pen and chute, and to cure the meat by smoking it or spicing it in sausage. The storage locker was a marvel, made of many thicknesses of brick, earth insulation, and Minnesota timber, lined inside with sawdust and vast blocks of ice cut from Lake Turcot, hauled down from home each winter by horse and sledge.

A ramshackle board building, part slaughterhouse, part store, was fixed to the low, thick square of the lockers. That's where Fleur worked. Kozka hired her for her strength. She could lift a haunch or carry a pole of sausages without stumbling, and she soon learned cutting from Pete's wife, a string-thin blonde who chain-smoked and handled the razor-sharp knives with nerveless precision, slicing close to her stained fingers. Fleur and Fritzie Kozka worked afternoons, wrapping their cuts in paper, and Fleur hauled the packages to the lockers. The meat was left outside the heavy oak doors, which were only opened at five each afternoon, before the men ate supper.

Sometimes Dutch, Tor, and Lily ate at the lockers, and when they did I stayed too, cleaned floors, restoked the fires in the front smokehouses, while the men sat around the squat cast-iron stove spearing slats of herring onto hardtack bread. They played long games of poker or cribbage on a board made from the planed end of a salt crate. They talked and I listened, although there wasn't much to hear since almost nothing ever happened in Argus. Tor was married, Dutch had lost my mother, and Lily read circulars. They mainly discussed the auctions to come, equipment, or women.

Every so often, Pete Kozka came out front to make a whist, leaving Fritzie to smoke cigarettes and fry raised doughnuts in the back room.

He sat and played a few rounds but kept his thoughts to himself. Fritzie did not tolerate him talking behind her back, and the one book he read was the New Testament. If he said something, it concerned weather or a surplus of sheep stomachs, a ham that smoked green, or the markets for corn and wheat. He had a good-luck talisman, the opal-white lens of a cow's eye. Playing cards, he rubbed it between his fingers. That soft sound and the slap of cards was about the only conversation.

Fleur finally gave them a subject.

Her cheeks were wide and flat, her hands large, chapped, muscular. Fleur's shoulders were broad as beams, her hips fishlike, slippery, narrow. An old green dress clung to her waist, worn thin where she sat. Her braids were thick like the tails of animals, and swung against her when she moved, deliberately, slowly in her work, held in and half tamed, but only half. I could tell, but the others never saw. They never looked into her sly brown eyes or noticed her teeth, strong and curved and very white. Her legs were bare, and since she padded around in beadwork moccasins they never saw that her fifth toes were missing. They never knew she'd drowned. They were blinded, they were stupid, they only saw her in the flesh.

And yet it wasn't just that she was a Chippewa, or even that she was a woman, it wasn't that she was good-looking or even that she was alone that made their brains hum. It was how she played cards.

Women didn't usually play with men, so the evening that Fleur drew a chair up to the men's table without being asked, there was a shock of surprise.

"What's this," said Lily. He was fat, with a snake's cold pale eyes and precious skin, smooth and lily-white, which is how he got his name. Lily had a dog, a stumpy mean little bull of a thing with a belly drum-tight from eating pork rinds. The dog liked to play cards just like Lily, and straddled his barrel thighs through games of stud, rum poker, *vingt-un*. The dog snapped at Fleur's arm that first night, but cringed back, its snarl frozen, when she took her place.

"I thought," she said, her voice soft and stroking, "you might deal me in."

There was a space between the heavy bin of spiced flour and the wall where I just fit. I hunkered down there, kept my eyes open, saw her black hair swing over the chair, her feet solid on the wood floor. I couldn't see up on the table where the cards slapped down, so after they were deep in their game I raised myself up in the shadows, and crouched on a sill of wood.

I watched Fleur's hands stack and ruffle, divide the cards, spill them to each player in a blur, rake them up and shuffle again. Tor, short and scrappy, shut one eye and squinted the other at Fleur. Dutch screwed his lips around a wet cigar.

"Gotta see a man," he mumbled, getting up to go out back to the privy. The others broke, put their cards down, and Fleur sat alone in the lamplight that glowed in a sheen across the push of her breasts. I watched her closely, then she paid me a beam of notice for the first time. She turned, looked straight at me, and grinned the white wolf grin a Pillager turns on its victims, except that she wasn't after me.

"Pauline there," she said, "how much money you got?"

We'd all been paid for the week that day. Eight cents was in my pocket.

"Stake me," she said, holding out her long fingers. I put the coins in her palm and then I melted back to nothing, part of the walls and tables. It was a long time before I understood that the men would not have seen me no matter what I did, how I moved. I wasn't anything like Fleur. My dress hung loose and my back was already curved, an old woman's. Work had roughened me, reading made my eyes sore, caring for my mother before she died had hardened my face. I was not much to look at, so they never saw me.

When the men came back and sat around the table they had drawn together. They shot one another small glances, stuck their tongues in their cheeks, burst out laughing at odd moments, to rattle Fleur. But she never minded. They played their *vingt-un*, staying even as Fleur slowly gained. Those pennies I had given her drew nickels and attracted dimes until there was a small pile in front of her.

Then she hooked them with five-card draw, nothing wild. She dealt, discarded, drew, and then she sighed and her cards gave a little shiver. Tor's eye gleamed, and Dutch straightened in his seat.

"I'll pay to see that hand," said Lily Veddar.

Fleur showed, and she had nothing there, nothing at all.

Tor's thin smile cracked open, and he threw his hand in too.

"Well, we know one thing," he said, leaning back in his chair, "the squaw can't bluff."

With that I lowered myself into a mound of swept sawdust and slept. I woke up during the night, but none of them had moved yet, so I couldn't either. Still later, the men must have gone out again, or Fritzie come out to break the game, because I was lifted, soothed, cradled in a woman's arms and rocked so quiet that I kept my eyes shut while Fleur rolled me into a closet of grimy ledgers, oiled paper, balls of string, and thick files that fit beneath me like a mattress.

The game went on after work the next evening. I got my eight cents back five times over, and Fleur kept the rest of the dollar she'd won for a stake. This time they didn't play so late, but they played regular, and then kept going at it night after night. They played poker now, or variations, for one week straight, and each time Fleur won exactly one dollar, no more and no less, too consistent for luck.

By this time, Lily and the other men were so lit with suspense that they got Pete to join the game with them. They concentrated, the fat dog sitting tense in Lily Veddar's lap, Tor suspicious, Dutch stroking his huge square brow, Pete steady. It wasn't that Fleur won that hooked them in so, because she lost hands too. It was rather that she never had a freak hand or even anything above a straight. She only took on her low cards, which didn't sit right. By chance, Fleur should have gotten a full or flush by now. The irritating thing was she beat with pairs and never bluffed, because she couldn't, and still she ended up each night with exactly one dollar. Lily couldn't believe, first of all, that a woman could be smart enough to play cards, but even if she was, that she would then be stupid enough to cheat for a dollar a night. By day I watched him turn the problem over, his hard white face dull, small fingers probing at his knuckles, until he finally thought he had Fleur figured out as a bit-time player, caution her game. Raising the stakes would throw her.

More than anything now, he wanted Fleur to come away with something but a dollar. Two bits less or ten more, the sum didn't matter, just so he broke her streak.

Night after night she played, won her dollar, and left to stay in a place that just Fritzie and I knew about. Fleur bathed in the slaughtering tub, then slept in the unused brick smokehouse behind the lockers, a windowless place tarred on the inside with scorched fats. When I brushed against her skin I noticed that she smelled of the walls, rich and woody, slightly burnt. Since that night she put me in the closet I was no longer afraid of her, but followed her close, stayed with her, became her moving shadow that the men never noticed, the shadow that could have saved her.

AUGUST, THE MONTH that bears fruit, closed around the shop, and Pete and Fritzie left for Minnesota to escape the heat. Night by night, running, Fleur had won thirty dollars, and only Pete's presence had kept Lily at bay. But Pete was gone now, and one payday, with the heat so bad no one could move but Fleur, the men sat and played and waited while she finished work. The cards sweat, limp in their fingers, the table was slick with grease, and even the walls were warm to the touch. The air was motionless. Fleur was in the next room boiling heads.

Her green dress, drenched, wrapped her like a transparent sheet. A skin of lakeweed. Black snarls of veining clung to her arms. Her braids were loose, half unraveled, tied behind her neck in a thick loop. She stood in steam, turning skulls through a vat with a wooden paddle. When scraps boiled to the surface, she bent with a round tin sieve and scooped them out. She'd filled two dishpans.

"Ain't that enough now?" called Lily. "We're waiting." The stump of a dog trembled in his lap, alive with rage. It never smelled me or noticed me above Fleur's smoky skin. The air was heavy in my corner, and pressed me down. Fleur sat with them.

"Now what do you say?" Lily asked the dog. It barked. That was the signal for the real game to start.

"Let's up the ante," said Lily, who had been stalking this night all month. He had a roll of money in his pocket. Fleur had five bills in her dress. The men had each saved their full pay.

"Ante a dollar then," said Fleur, and pitched hers in. She lost, but they let her scrape along, cent by cent. And then she won some. She played unevenly, as if chance was all she had. She reeled them in. The game went on. The dog was stiff now, poised on Lily's knees, a ball of vicious muscle with its yellow eyes slit in concentration. It gave advice, seemed to sniff the lay of Fleur's cards, twitched and nudged. Fleur was up, then down, saved by a scratch. Tor dealt seven cards, three down. The pot grew, round by round, until it held all the money. Nobody folded. Then it all rode on one last card and they went silent. Fleur picked hers up and blew a long breath. The heat lowered like a bell. Her card shook, but she stayed in.

Lily smiled and took the dog's head tenderly between his palms.

"Say, Fatso," he said, crooning the words, "you reckon that girl's bluffing?"

The dog whined and Lily laughed. "Me too," he said, "let's show." He swept his bills and coins into the pot and then they turned their cards over.

Lily looked once, looked again, then he squeezed the dog up like a fist of dough and slammed it on the table.

Fleur threw her arms out and drew the money over, grinning that same wolf grin that she'd used on me, the grin that had them. She jammed the bills in her dress, scooped the coins up in waxed white paper that she tied with string.

"Let's go another round," said Lily, his voice choked with burrs. But Fleur opened her mouth and yawned, then walked out back to gather slops for the one big hog that was waiting in the stock pen to be killed.

The men sat still as rocks, their hands spread on the oiled wood table. Dutch had chewed his cigar to damp shreds, Tor's eye was dull. Lily's gaze was the only one to follow Fleur. I didn't move. I felt them gathering, saw my stepfather's veins, the ones in his forehead that stood out in anger. The dog had rolled off the table and curled in a knot below the counter, where none of the men could touch it.

Lily rose and stepped out back to the closet of ledgers where Pete kept his private stock. He brought back a bottle, uncorked and tipped it between his fingers. The lump in his throat moved, then he passed it on. They drank, quickly felt the whiskey's fire, and planned with their eyes things they couldn't say out loud.

When they left, I followed. I hid out back in the clutter of broken boards and chicken crates beside the stock pen, where they waited. Fleur could not be seen at first, and then the moon broke and showed her, slipping cautiously along the rough board chute with a bucket in her hand. Her hair fell, wild and coarse, to her waist, and her dress was a floating patch in the dark. She made a pig-calling sound, rang the tin pail lightly against the wood, froze suspiciously. But too late. In the sound of the ring Lily moved, fat and nimble, stepped right behind Fleur and put out his creamy hands. At his first touch, she whirled and doused him with the bucket of sour slops. He pushed her against the big fence and the package of coins split, went clinking and jumping, winked against the wood. Fleur rolled over once and vanished in the yard.

The moon fell behind a curtain of ragged clouds, and Lily followed into the dark muck. But he tripped, pitched over the huge flank of the pig, who lay mired to the snout, heavily snoring. I sprang out of the weeds and climbed the side of the pen, stuck like glue. I saw the sow rise to her neat, knobby knees, gain her balance, and sway, curious, as Lily stumbled forward. Fleur had backed into the angle of rough wood just beyond, and when Lily tried to jostle past, the sow tipped up on her hind legs and struck, quick and hard as a snake. She plunged her head into Lily's thick side and snatched a mouthful of his shirt. She lunged again, caught him lower, so that he grunted in pained surprise. He seemed to ponder, breathing deep. Then he launched his huge body in a swimmer's dive.

The sow screamed as his body smacked over hers. She rolled, striking out with her knife-sharp hooves, and Lily gathered himself upon her, took her foot-long face by the ears, and scraped her snout and cheeks against the trestles of the pen. He hurled the sow's tight skull against an iron post, but instead of knocking her dead, he merely woke her from her dream.

She reared, shrieked, drew him with her so that they posed standing upright. They bowed jerkily to each other, as if to begin. Then his arms swung and flailed. She sank her black fangs into his shoulder, clasping him, dancing him forward and backward through the pen. Their steps picked up pace, went wild. The two dipped as one, box-stepped, tripped each other. She ran her split foot though his hair. He grabbed her kinked tail. They went down and came up, the same shape and then the same color, until the men couldn't tell one from the other in that light and Fleur was able to launch herself over the gates, swing down, hit gravel.

The men saw, yelled, and chased her at a dead run to the smokehouse. And Lily too, once the sow gave up in disgust and freed him. That is where I should have gone to Fleur, saved her, thrown myself on Dutch. But I went stiff with fear and couldn't unlatch myself from the trestles or move at all. I closed my eyes and put my head in my arms, tried to hide, so there is nothing to describe but what I couldn't block out, Fleur's hoarse breath, so loud it filled me, her cry in the old language, and my name repeated over and over among the words.

THE HEAT WAS still dense the next morning when I came back to work. Fleur was gone but the men were there, slack faced, hungover. Lily was paler and softer than ever, as if his flesh had steamed on his bones. They smoked, took pulls off a bottle. It wasn't noon yet. I worked awhile, waiting shop and sharpening steel. But I was sick, I was smothered, I was sweating so hard that my hands slipped on the knives, and I wiped my fingers clean of the greasy touch of the customers' coins. Lily opened his mouth and roared once, not in anger. There was no meaning to the sound. His little dog, sprawled limp beside his foot, never lifted its head. Nor did the other men.

They didn't notice when I stepped outside, hoping for a clear breath. And then I forgot them because I knew that we were all balanced, ready to tip, to fly, to be crushed as soon as the weather broke. The sky was so low that I felt the weight of it like a yoke. Clouds hung down, witch teats, a tornado's green-brown cones, and as I watched one flicked out and became a delicate probing thumb. Even as I picked up my heels and ran back inside, the wind blew suddenly, cold, and then came rain.

Inside, the men had disappeared already and the whole place was trembling as if a huge hand was pinched at the rafters, shaking it. I ran straight through, screaming for Dutch or for any of them, and then I stopped at the heavy doors of the lockers, where they had surely taken shelter. I stood there a moment. Everything went still. Then I heard a cry building in the wind, faint at first, a whistle and then a shrill scream that tore through the walls and gathered around me, spoke plain so I understood that I should move, put my arms out, and slam down the great iron bar that fit across the hasp and lock.

Outside, the wind was stronger, like a hand held against me. I struggled forward. The bushes tossed, the awnings flapped off storefronts, the rails of porches rattled. The odd cloud became a fat snout that nosed along the earth and sniffled, jabbed, picked at things, sucked them up, blew them apart, rooted around as if it was following a certain scent, then stopped behind me at the butcher shop and bored down like a drill.

I went flying, landed somewhere in a ball. When I opened my eyes and looked, stranger things were happening.

A herd of cattle flew through the air like giant birds, dropping dung, their mouths opened in stunned bellows. A candle, still lighted, blew past, and tables, napkins, garden tools, a whole school of drifting eyeglasses, jackets on hangers, hams, a checkerboard, a lampshade, and at last the sow from behind the lockers, on the run, her hooves a blur, set free, swooping, diving, screaming as everything in Argus fell apart and got turned upside down, smashed, and thoroughly wrecked.

DAYS PASSED BEFORE the town went looking for the men. They were bachelors, after all, except for Tor, whose wife had suffered a blow to the head that made her forgetful. Everyone was occupied with digging out, in high relief because even though the Catholic steeple had been torn off like a peaked cap and sent across five fields, those huddled in the cellar were unhurt. Walls had fallen, windows were demolished, but the stores were intact and so were the bankers and shop owners who had taken refuge in their safes or beneath their cash registers. It was a fair-minded disaster, no one could be said to have suffered much more than the next, at least not until Fritzie and Pete came home.

Of all the businesses in Argus, Kozka's Meats had suffered worst. The boards of the front building had been split to kindling, piled in a huge pyramid, and the shop equipment was blasted far and wide. Pete paced off the distance the iron bathtub had been flung—a hundred feet. The glass candy case went fifty, and landed without so much as a cracked pane. There were other surprises as well, for the back rooms where Fritzie and Pete lived were undisturbed. Fritzie said the dust still coated her china figures, and upon her kitchen table, in the ashtray, perched the last cigarette she'd put out in haste. She lit it up and finished it, looking through the window. From there, she could see that the old smokehouse Fleur had slept in was crushed to a reddish sand and the stock pens were completely torn apart, the rails stacked, helter-skelter. Fritzie asked for Fleur. People shrugged. Then she asked about the others and, suddenly, the town understood that three men were missing.

There was a rally of help, a gathering of shovels and volunteers. We passed boards from hand to hand, stacked them, uncovered what lay beneath the pile of jagged splinters. The lockers, full of the meat that was Pete and Fritzie's investment, slowly came into sight, still intact. When enough room was made for a man to stand on the roof, there were calls, a general urge to hack through and see what lay below. But Fritzie shouted that she wouldn't allow it because the meat would spoil. And so the work continued, board by board, until at last the heavy oak doors of the freezer were revealed and people pressed to the entry. Everyone wanted to be the first, but since it was my stepfather lost, I was let go in when Pete and Fritzie wedged through into the sudden icy air.

Pete scraped a match on his boot, lit the lamp Fritzie held, and then the three of us stood still in its circle. Light glared off the skinned and hanging carcasses, the crates of wrapped sausages, the bright and cloudy blocks of lake ice, pure as winter. The cold bit into us, pleasant at first, then numbing. We must have stood there a couple of minutes before we saw the men, or more rightly, the humps of fur, the iced and shaggy hides they wore, the bearskins they had taken down and wrapped around themselves. We stepped closer and tilted the lantern beneath the flaps of fur into their faces. The dog was there, perched among them, heavy as a doorstop. The three had hunched around a barrel where the game was still laid out, and a dead lantern and an empty bottle, too. But they had thrown down their last hands and hunkered tight, knuckles raw from beating at the door they had also attacked with hooks. Frost stars gleamed off their eyelashes and the stubble of their beards. Their faces were set in concentration, mouths open as if to speak some careful thought, some agreement they'd come to in one another's arms.

POWER TRAVELS IN the bloodlines, handed out before birth. It comes down through the hands, which in the Pillagers were strong and knotted, big, spidery, and rough, with sensitive fingertips good at dealing cards. It comes through the eyes, too, belligerent, darkest brown, the eyes of those in the bear clan, impolite as they gaze directly at a person.

In my dreams, I look straight back at Fleur, at the men. I am no longer the watcher on the dark sill, the skinny girl.

The blood draws us back, as if it runs through a vein of earth. I've come home and, except for talking to my cousins, live a quiet life. Fleur lives quiet too, down on Lake Turcot with her boat. Some say she's married to the water man, Misshepeshu, or that she's living in shame with white men or windigos, or that she's killed them all. I'm about the only one here who ever goes to visit her. Last winter, I went to help out in her cabin when she bore the child, whose green eyes and skin the color of an old penny made more talk, as no one could decide if the child was mixed-blood or what, fathered in a smokehouse, or by a man with brass scales, or by the lake. The girl is bold, smiling in her sleep, as if she knows what people wonder, as if she hears the old men talk, turning the story over. It comes up different every time and has no ending, no beginning. They get the middle wrong too. They only know they don't know anything.

# A Wedge of Shade

EVERY PLACE THAT I could name you, in the whole world around us, has better things about it than Argus. I just happened to grow up there and the soil got to be part of me; the air has something in it that I breathed, Argus water doesn't taste as good as water in the Cities. Still, the first thing I do, walking back into my mother's house, is stand, at the kitchen sink and toss down glass after glass.

"Are you filled up?" My mother stands behind me. "Sit down if you are."

She's tall and board-square, French-Chippewa, with long arms and big knuckles. Her face is rawboned, fierce, and almost masculine in its edges and planes. Several months ago, a beauty operator convinced her that she should feminize her look with curls. Now the permanent, grown out in grizzled streaks, bristles like the coat of a terrier. I don't look like her. Not just the hair, since hers is salt-and-pepper and mine is a reddish brown, but my build. I'm short, boxy, more like my Aunt Mary. Like her, I can't seem to shake this town. I keep coming back here.

"There's jobs at the beet plant," my mother says.

This rumor, probably false, since the plant is in a slump, drops into the dim, close air of the kitchen. We have the shades drawn because it's a hot June, over a hundred degrees, and we're trying to stay cool. Outside, the water has been sucked from everything. The veins in the leaves are hollow, the ditch grass is crackling. The sky has absorbed every drop. It's a thin whitish blue veil stretched from end to end over us, a flat gauze tarp. From the depot, I've walked here beneath it, dragging my suitcase.

We're sweating as if we're in an oven, a big messy one. For a week, it's been too hot to clean much or even move, and the crops are stunted, failing. The farmer next to us just sold his field for a subdivision, but the construction workers aren't doing much. They're wearing wet rags on their heads, sitting near the house sites in the brilliance of noon. The studs of wood stand upright over them, but uselessly—nothing casts shadows. The sun has dried them up, too.

"The beet plant," my mother says again.

"Maybe so," I say, and then, because I've got something bigger on my mind, "Maybe I'll go out there and apply."

"Oh?" She is intrigued now.

"God, this is terrible!" I take the glass of water in my hand and tip some onto my head. I don't feel cooler, though; I just feel the steam rising off me.

"The fan broke down," she states. "Both of them are kaput now. The motors or something. If Mary would get the damn tax refund, we'd run out to Pamida, buy a couple more, set up a breeze. Then we'd be cool out here."

"Your garden must be dead," I say, lifting the edge of the pull shade.

"It's sick, but I watered. And I won't mulch; that draws the damn slugs."

"Nothing could live out there, no bug." My eyes smart from even looking at the yard, which is a clear sheet of sun, almost incandescent.

"You'd be surprised."

I wish I could blurt it out, just tell her. Even now, the words swell in my mouth, the one sentence, but I'm scared, and with good reason. There is this about my mother: it is awful to see her angry. Her lips press together and she stiffens herself within, growing wooden, silent. Her features become fixed and remote; she will not speak. It takes a long time, and until she does you are held in suspense. Nothing that she ever says, in the end, is as bad as that feeling of dread. So I wait, half believing that she'll figure out my secret for herself, or drag it out of me, not that she ever tries. If I'm silent, she hardly notices. She's not like Aunt Mary, who forces me to say more than I know is on my mind.

My mother sighs. "It's too hot to bake. It's too hot to cook. But it's too hot to eat anyway."

She's talking to herself, which makes me reckless. Perhaps she is so preoccupied by the heat that I can slip my announcement past her. I should just say it, but I lose nerve, make an introduction that alerts her. "I have something to tell you."

I've cast my lot; there's no going back unless I think quickly. My thoughts hum.

But she waits, forgetting the heat for a moment.

"Ice," I say. "We have to have ice." I speak intensely, leaning toward her, almost glaring, but she is not fooled.

"Don't make me laugh," she says. "There's not a cube in town. The refrigerators can't keep cold enough." She eyes me the way a hunter eyes an animal about to pop from its den and run.

"Okay." I break down. "I really do have something." I stand, turn my back. In this lightless warmth I'm dizzy, almost sick. Now I've gotten to her and she's frightened to hear, breathless.

"Tell me," she urges. "Go on, get it over with."

And so I say it. "I got married." There is a surge of relief, a wind blowing through the room, but then it's gone. The curtain flaps and we're caught again, stunned in an even denser heat. It's now my turn to wait, and I whirl around and sit right across from her. Now is the time to tell her his name, a Chippewa name that she'll know from the papers, since he's notorious. Now is the time to get it over with. But I can't bear the picture she makes, the shock that parts her lips, the stunned shade of hurt in her eyes. I have to convince her, somehow, that it's all right.

"You hate weddings! Just think, just picture it. Me, white net. On a day like this. You, stuffed in your summer wool, and Aunt Mary, God knows . . . and the tux, the rental, the groom . . ."

Her head lowered as my words fell on her, but now her forehead tips up and her eyes come into view, already hardening. My tongue flies back into my mouth.

She mimics, making it a question, "The groom . . . ? "

I'm caught, my lips half open, a stuttering noise in my throat. How to begin? I have rehearsed this, but my lines melt away, my opening, my casual introductions. I can think of nothing that would convince her of how much more he is than the captions beneath the poster in the post office. There is no picture adequate, no representation that captures him. So I just put my hand across the table and I touch her hand. "Mother," I say, as if we're in a staged drama, "he'll arrive here shortly."

There is something forming in her, some reaction. I am afraid to let it take complete shape. "Let's go out and wait on the steps, Mom. Then you'll see him."

"I do not understand," she says in a frighteningly neutral voice. This is what I mean. Everything is suddenly forced, unnatural—we're reading lines.

"He'll approach from a distance." I can't help speaking like a bad actor. "I told him to give me an hour. He'll wait, then he'll come walking down the road."

We rise and unstick our blouses from our stomachs, our skirts from the backs of our legs. Then we walk out front in single file, me behind, and settle ourselves on the middle step. A scrubby box elder tree on one side casts a light shade, and the dusty lilacs seem to catch a little breeze on the other. It's not so bad out here, still hot, but not so dim, contained. It is worse past the trees. The heat shimmers in a band, rising off the fields, out of the spars and bones of houses that will wreck our view. The horizon and the edge of town show through the gaps in the framing now, and as we sit we watch the workers move, slowly, almost in a practiced recital, back and forth. Their head cloths hang to their shoulders, their hard hats are dabs of yellow, their white T-shirts blend into the fierce air and sky. They don't seem to be doing anything, although we hear faint thuds from their hammers. Otherwise, except for the whistles of a few birds, there is silence. Certainly we don't speak.

It is a longer wait than I anticipated, maybe because he wants to give me time. At last the shadows creep out, hard, hot, charred, and the heat begins to lengthen and settle. We are going into the worst of the afternoon when a dot at the end of the road begins to form.

Mom and I are both watching. We have not moved our eyes around much, and we blink and squint to try and focus. The dot doesn't change, not for a long while. And then it suddenly springs clear in relief—a silhouette, lost for a moment in the shimmer, reappearing. In that shining expanse he is a little wedge of moving shade. He continues, growing imperceptibly, until there are variations in the outline, and it can be seen that he is large. As he passes the construction workers, they turn and stop, all alike in their hats, stock-still.

Growing larger yet, as if he has absorbed their stares, he nears us. Now we can see the details. He is dark, the first thing. His arms are thick, his chest is huge, and the features of his face are wide and open. He carries nothing in his hands. He wears a black T-shirt, the opposite of the construction workers, and soft jogging shoes. His jeans are held under his stomach by a belt with a star beaded on the buckle. His hair is long, in a tail. I am the wrong woman for him. I am paler, shorter, unmagnificent. But I stand up. Mom joins me, and I answer proudly when she asks, "His name?"

"His name is Gerry—" Even now I can't force his last name through my lips. But Mom is distracted by the sight of him anyway.

We descend one step, and stop again. It is here we will receive him. Our hands are folded at our waists. We're balanced, composed. He continues to stroll toward us, his white smile widening, his eyes filling with the sight of me as mine are filling with him. At the end of the road behind him, another dot has appeared. It is fast moving and the sun flares off it twice: a vehicle. Now there are two figures—one approaching in a spume of dust from the rear, and Gerry, unmindful, not slackening or quickening his pace, continuing on. It is like a choreography design. They move at parallel speeds in front of our eyes. Then, at the same moment, at the end of our yard, they conclude the performance; both of them halt.

Gerry stands, looking toward us, his thumbs in his belt. He nods respectfully to Mom, looks calmly at me, and half smiles. He raises his brows, and we're suspended. Officer Lovchik emerges from the police car, stooped and tired. He walks up behind Gerry and I hear the snap of handcuffs, then I jump. I'm stopped by Gerry's gaze, though, as he backs away from me, still smiling tenderly. I am paralyzed halfway down the walk. He kisses the air while Lovchik cautiously prods at him, fitting his prize into the car. And then the doors slam, the engine roars, and they back out and turn around. As they move away there is no siren. I think I've heard Lovchik mention questioning. I'm sure it is lots of fuss for nothing, a mistake, but it cannot be denied—this is terrible timing.

I shake my shoulders, smooth my skirt, and turn to my mother with a look of outrage. "How do you like that?" I try.

She's got her purse in one hand, her car keys out.

"Let's go," she says.

"Okay," I answer. "Fine. Where?"

"Aunt Mary's."

"I'd rather go and bail him out, Mom."

"Bail," she says. *"Bail?"*

She gives me such a look of cold and furious surprise that I sink immediately into the front seat, lean back against the vinyl. I almost welcome the sting of the heated plastic on my back, thighs, shoulders.

AUNT MARY LIVES at the rear of the butcher shop she runs. As we walk toward the House of Meats, her dogs are rugs in the dirt, flattened by the heat of the day. Not one of them barks at us to warn her. We step over them and get no more reaction than a whine, the slow beat of a tail. Inside, we get no answer either, although we call Aunt Mary up and down the hall. We enter the kitchen and sit at the table, which holds a half-ruined watermelon. By the sink, in a tin box, are cigarettes. My mother takes one and carefully puts a match to it, frowning. "I know what," she says. "Go check the lockers."

There are two—a big freezer full of labeled meats and rental space, and another, smaller one that is just a side cooler. I notice, walking past the meat display counter, that the red beacon beside the outside switch of the cooler is glowing. That tells you when the light is on inside.

I pull the long metal handle toward me and the thick door swishes open. I step into the cool, spicy air. Aunt Mary is there, too proud to ever register a hint of surprise. She simply nods and looks away, as though I've just been out for a minute, although we've not seen each other in six months or more. She is relaxing on a big can of pepper labeled "Zanzibar," reading a scientific-magazine article. I sit down on a barrel of alum. With no warning, I drop my bomb: "I'm married." It doesn't matter how I tell it to Aunt Mary, because she won't be, refuses to be, surprised.

"What's he do?" she simply asks, putting aside the sheaf of paper. I thought she'd scold me for fooling my mother. But it's odd, for two women who have lived through boring times and disasters, how rarely one comes to the other's defense, and how often they are each willing to take advantage of the other's absence. But I'm benefiting here. It seems that Aunt Mary is truly interested in Gerry. So I'm honest.

"He's something like a political activist. I mean he's been in jail and all. But not for any crime, you see; it's just because of his convictions."

She gives me a long, shrewd stare. Her skin is too tough to wrinkle, but she doesn't look young. All around us hang loops of sausages, every kind you can imagine, every color, from the purple-black of blutwurst to the pale whitish links that my mother likes best. Blocks of butter and headcheese, a can of raw milk, wrapped parcels, and cured bacons are stuffed onto the shelves around us. My heart has gone still and cool inside me, and I can't stop talking.

"He's the kind of guy it's hard to describe. Very different. People call him a free spirit, but that doesn't say it either, because he's very disciplined in some ways. He learned to be neat in jail." I pause. She says nothing, so I go on. "I know it's sudden, but who likes weddings? I hate them—all that mess with the bridesmaids' gowns, getting material to match. I don't have girlfriends. I mean, how embarrassing, right? Who would sing 'O Perfect Love'? Carry the ring?"

She isn't really listening.

"What's he do?" she asks again.

Maybe she won't let go of it until I discover the right answer, like a game with nouns and synonyms.

"He . . . well, he agitates," I tell her.

"Is that some kind of factory work?"

"Not exactly, no, it's not a nine-to-five job or anything . . ."

She lets the magazine fall, now, cocks her head to one side, and stares at me without blinking her cold yellow eyes. She has the look of a hawk, of a person who can see into the future but won't tell you about it. She's lost business for staring at customers, but she doesn't care.

"Are you telling me that he doesn't . . ." Here she shakes her head twice, slowly, from one side to the other, without removing me from her stare. "That he doesn't have regular work?"

"Oh, what's the matter, anyway?" I say roughly. "I'll work. This is the 1970s."

She jumps to her feet, stands over me—a stocky woman with terse features and short, thin points of gray hair. Her earrings tremble and flash—small fiery opals. Her brown plastic glasses hang crooked on a cord around her neck. I have never seen her become quite so instantly furious, so disturbed. "We're going to fix that," she says.

The cooler immediately feels smaller, the sausages knock at my shoulder, and the harsh light makes me blink. I am as stubborn as Aunt Mary, however, and she knows that I can go head-to-head with her. "We're married and that's final." I manage to stamp my foot.

Aunt Mary throws an arm back, blows air through her cheeks, and waves away my statement vigorously. "You're a little girl. How old is *he*?"

I frown at my lap, trace the threads in my blue cotton skirt, and tell her that age is irrelevant.

"Big word," she says sarcastically. "Let me ask you this. He's old enough to get a job?"

"Of course he is; what do you think? Okay, he's older than me."

"Aha, I knew it."

"Geez! So what? I mean, haven't you ever been in love, hasn't someone ever gotten you *right here*?" I smash my fist on my chest.

We lock eyes, but she doesn't waste a second in feeling hurt. "Sure, sure I've been in love. You think I haven't? I know what it feels like, you smart-ass. You'd be surprised. But he was no lazy son of a bitch. Now, listen . . ." She stops, draws breath, and I let her. "Here's what I mean by 'fix.' I'll teach the sausage-making trade to him—to you, too—and the grocery business. I've about had it anyway, and so's your mother. We'll do the same as my aunt and uncle—leave the shop to you and move to Arizona. I like this place." She looks up at the burning safety bulb, down at me again. Her face drags in the light. "But what the hell. I always wanted to travel."

I'm stunned, a little flattened out, maybe ashamed of myself. "You hate going anywhere," I say, which is true.

The door swings open and Mom comes in with us. She finds a milk can and balances herself on it, sighing at the delicious feeling of the air, absorbing from the silence the fact that we have talked. She hasn't anything to add, I guess, and as the coolness hits, her eyes fall shut. Aunt Mary's, too. I can't help it, either, and my eyelids drop, although my brain is conscious and alert. From the darkness, I can see us in the brilliance. The light rains down on us. We sit the way we have been sitting, on our cans of milk and pepper, upright and still. Our hands are curled loosely in our laps. Our faces are blank as the gods'. We could be statues in a tomb sunk into the side of a mountain. We could be dreaming the world up in our brains.

IT IS LATER, and the weather has no mercy. We are drained of everything but simple thoughts. It's too hot for feelings. Driving home, we see how field after field of beets has gone into shock, and even some of the soybeans. The plants splay, limp, burned into the ground. Only the sunflowers continue to struggle upright, bristling but small.

What drew me in the first place to Gerry was the unexpected. I went to hear him talk just after I enrolled at the university, and then I demonstrated when they came and got him off the stage. He always went so willingly, accommodating everyone. I began to visit him. I sold lunar calendars and posters to raise his bail and eventually free him. One thing led to another, and one night we found ourselves alone in a Howard Johnson's coffee shop downstairs from where they put him up when his speech was finished. There were much more beautiful women after him; he could have had his pick of Swedes or Sisseton or Dakota, or those Turtle Mountain girls, who are the best-looking of all. But I was different, he says. He liked my slant on life. And then there was no going back once it started, no turning, as though it was meant. We had no choice.

I have this intuition as we near the house, in the fateful quality of light, as in the turn of the day the heat continues to press and the blackness, into which the warmth usually lifts, lowers steadily: We must come to the end of something; there must be a close to this day.

As we turn into the yard we see that Gerry is sitting on the porch stairs. Now it is our turn to be received. I throw the car door open and stumble out before the motor even cuts. I run to him and hold him, as my mother, pursuing the order of events, parks carefully. Then she walks over, too, holding her purse by the strap. She stands before him and says no word but simply looks into his face, staring as if he's cardboard, a man behind glass who cannot see her. I think she's rude, but then I realize that he is staring back, that they are the same height. Their eyes are level.

He puts his hand out. "My name is Gerry."

"Gerry what?"

"Nanapush."

She nods, shifts her weight. "You're from that line, the old strain, the ones . . ." She does not finish.

"And my father," Gerry says, "was Old Man Pillager."

"Kashpaws," she says, "are my branch, of course. We're probably related through my mother's brother." They do not move. They are like two opponents from the same divided country, staring across the border. They do not shift or blink, and I see that they are more alike than I am like either one of them—so tall, solid, dark haired. They could be mother and son.

"Well, I guess you should come in," she offers. "You are a distant relative, after all." She looks at me. "Distant enough."

Whole swarms of mosquitoes are whining down, discovering us now, so there is no question of staying where we are. And so we walk into the house, much hotter than outside, with the gathered heat. Instantly the sweat springs from our skin and I can think of nothing else but cooling off. I try to force the windows higher in their sashes, but there's no breeze anyway; nothing stirs, no air.

"Are you sure," I gasp, "about those fans?"

"Oh, they're broke, all right," my mother says, distressed. I rarely hear this in her voice. She switches on the lights, which makes the room seem hotter, and we lower ourselves into the easy chairs. Our words echo, as though the walls have baked and dried hollow.

"Show me those fans," says Gerry.

My mother points toward the kitchen. "They're sitting on the table. I've already tinkered with them. See what you can do."

And so he does. After a while she hoists herself and walks out back to him. Their voices close together now, absorbed, and their tools clank frantically, as if they are fighting a duel. But it is a race with the bell of darkness and their waning energy. I think of ice. I get ice on the brain.

"Be right back," I call out, taking the car keys from my mother's purse. "Do you need anything?"

There is no answer from the kitchen but a furious sputter of metal, the clatter of nuts and bolts spilling to the floor.

I drive out to the Superpumper, a big new gas station complex on the edge of town, where my mother most likely has never been. She doesn't know about convenience stores, has no credit cards for groceries or gas, pays only with small bills and change. She never has used an ice machine. It would grate on her that a bag of frozen water costs eighty cents, but it doesn't bother me. I take the plastic-foam cooler and I fill it for a couple of dollars. I buy two six-packs of Shasta soda and I plunge them in among the uniform coins of ice. I drink two myself on the way home, and I manage to lift the whole heavy cooler out of the trunk, carry it to the door.

The fans are whirring, beating the air. I hear them going in the living room the minute I come in. The only light shines from the kitchen. Gerry and my mother have thrown the pillows from the couch onto the living room floor, and they are sitting in the rippling currents of air. I bring the cooler in and put it near us. I have chosen all dark flavors—black cherry, grape, red berry, cola—so as we drink the darkness swirls inside us with the night air, sweet and sharp, driven by small motors.

I drag more pillows down from the other rooms upstairs. There is no question of attempting the bedrooms, the stifling beds. And so, in the dark, I hold hands with Gerry as he settles down between my mother and me. He is huge as a hill between the two of us, solid in the beating wind.

# The Fat Man's Race

I WAS IN love with a man named Cuthbert, said Grandma Ignatia, and oh that man could really eat. He would sit down to the table with a haunch of venison, a whole chicken, two or three gullet breads or a bucket of bangs, half a dozen ears of corn or a bag of raw carrots. He'd eat the whole lot, then go out and work in the field. He was very big, but he was also stone solid, muscle not fat. He would grab me up and set me on his lap and talk to me in Michif. He would call me his peti'shoo. I was going to marry Cuthbert and had the date of the wedding all picked out, but then his sisters turned him against me. They told him that I was after his money, I wanted his land, and also that I was having sex with the devil.

Only that last part was true.

Our priest had warned that each one of us has two angels; one is a guardian and the other is an angel of perversion. That last angel will attempt to convince you it is the first, and I suppose I fell for it. I was visited at night in my dreams by a man in blue—a blue suit, a blue shirt, a blue tie, blue shoes, but no hat. He had black hair and black eyes, skin the color of a pale, brown egg, very smooth and markless. He would take off all of his blue clothes and lay them at my feet. His instrument of pleasure—don't laugh at me—was blue also, as though dipped in beautiful ink, midnight at the tip. I would admire him, then I would lie with him all night. You know what I'm telling you. In the morning I'd wake up sick over what I'd done. But next night it would be the same thing again. I could not resist him. He said the sweetest things to me, like a good angel, but the things he did were darkly inspired.

Now I ask you, how was it that Cuthbert's sisters knew the shape of my dreams? When he told me that his sisters were telling this story around, all about me and the devil, he laughed. He was more worried about how I might have my eyes on his eighty acres cleared and planted, or the money that the bank kept locked up. He laughed until he shook about the blue suit his sisters spoke of, and did not notice how, when I heard that, I nearly went faint off my feet. I recovered. I thought about it. It did not take me long to realize that the only way that Cuthbert's sisters possibly could know about my devil was if he had told them about me when he visited them too.

I grew furious and plotted out of jealousy to have my revenge. I decided to kill him, though I wasn't sure just how to destroy a man who existed only as a phantom, without physical substance. Then it came to me that I must dream the instrument of his death. I must conceive of a knife honed and sharp and thorough in its detail.

Each night, I dreamed a knife beneath my pillow. I dreamed about its shape and weight. I dreamed its black wooden handle. I dreamed its sharpness. I dreamed the gleam of white light off its point. I dreamed the way it would feel in my hands. I dreamed how it would fit between the dream ribs of my angel of perversion. I dreamed all of this so well that upon the night I reached beneath the pillow and found the perfectly dreamed weapon, it was a memory of a dream I dreamed, a dream within a dream. The death I dealt him was undreamable, however, and horrible. I woke soaked with terror and tears. The nightmare haunted me all morning as I prepared for the feast day of the Assumption. A celebration was supposed to take place at the church, and at Holy Mass the priest was to read the banns preceding my marriage to Cuthbert.

I was shaky that day and my mother said that I was pale. But I made six pies. Three for Cuthbert. He was running in the fat man's race. Every year only the biggest of the big men lined up. Their race, comical and thunderous, was always the feast day's high point. At the end of it, the winner would have his choice of pies and a holy medal for a ribbon—Saint Jude or Saint Christopher or Theresa of the Little Flowers. As we drove our wagon to the church grounds, I was almost giddy with happiness—I'd killed off the devil and would soon marry Cuthbert. His sisters would wonder at the loss of their own blue demon, but they never would know the one who killed him was me.

Then came shock. As the big men lined up at the far end of the field, as we watched, pointing and making little bets of money on this one or the other, there entered into the group a man in a blue suit and blue shirt, blue tie, blue shoes and with black hair and pale brown skin. Only he was much, much bigger than in my dream. He lined up with the rest of them. I don't know if it was me or Cuthbert's sisters whose eyes popped bigger, and whose mouths dropped wider, but it was only me who knew that having killed him in a dream I had brought the devil to life. And here he was, racing Cuthbert for the fat man's prize.

He didn't look well at all, I saw as they began to run. He was bloated and gray as a gorged tick, his skin almost dead green. He ran holding a hand against his ribs and I nearly shrieked as he passed and turned on me the flash of his red, robbed eyes. His mouth was open and I saw that it was filled with black blood. He and Cuthbert were neck and neck, out ahead of the others, and I saw that the devil was taunting and mocking my husband-to-be, who flew into a rage of running and leaped forward like a great stag to surge ahead.

When it was over, two men lay still at the finish line. One was Cuthbert, who died of a burst heart. The other man was dead all along, people said. When they opened the blue jacket they found a knife with a black handle buried to the hilt between his ribs.

So, said Grandma Ignatia, I married instead a man who hadn't an ounce of spare flesh, a man who hated the color blue and never wore it, a man whose sisters liked me. I lived with him for fifty-seven years now, didn't I, and the two of us had eight children. Adopted twenty. Raised every kind of animal that you can think of, didn't we, and grew our corn and oats and every fall dug out hills of potatoes. We picked wild rice and now and then we shot a deer from off the back porch, and yes we fed our children good, now, didn't we?

# The Leap

MY MOTHER IS the surviving half of a blindfold trapeze act, not a fact I think about much even now that she is sightless, the result of encroaching and stubborn cataracts. She walks slowly through our house here in New Hampshire, lightly touching her way along walls and running her hands over shelves, books, the drift of a grown child's belongings and castoffs. She has never upset an object or so much as brushed a magazine onto the floor. She has never lost her balance or bumped into a closet door left carelessly open.

The catlike precision of her movements in old age might be the result of her early training, but she shows so little of the drama or flair one might expect from a performer that I tend to forget the Flying Avalons. She has kept no sequined costume, no photographs, no fliers or posters from that part of her youth. I would, in fact, tend to think that all memory of double somersaults and heart-stopping catches has left her arms and legs, were it not for the fact that sometimes, as I sit sewing in the room of the rebuilt house that I slept in as a child, I hear the crackle, catch a whiff of smoke from the stove downstairs. Suddenly the room goes dark, the stitches burn beneath my fingers, and I am sewing with a needle of hot silver, a thread of fire.

I owe her my existence three times. The first was when she saved herself. In the town square a replica tent pole, cracked and splintered, now stands, cast in concrete. It commemorates the disaster that put the town on the front page of the Boston and New York tabloids. It is from those old newspapers, now historical records, that I get my information, not from Anna of the Flying Avalons, nor from any of her relatives, now dead, or certainly from the other half of her particular act, Harold Avalon, her first husband. In one news account, it says, "The day was mildly overcast but nothing in the air or temperature gave any hint of the sudden force with which the deadly gale would strike."

I have lived in the West, where you can see the weather coming for miles, and it is true that in town we are at something of a disadvantage. When extremes of temperatures collide, a hot and cold front, winds generate instantaneously behind a hill and crash upon you without warning. That, I think, was the likely situation on that day in June. People probably commented on the pleasant air, grateful that no hot sun beat upon the striped tent that stretched over the entire center green. They bought their tickets and surrendered them in anticipation. They sat. They ate caramelized popcorn and roasted peanuts. There was time, before the storm, for three acts. The White Arabians of Ali-Khazar rose on their hind legs and waltzed. The Mysterious Bernie folded himself into a painted cracker tin, and the Lady of the Mists made herself appear and disappear in surprising places. As the clouds gathered outside, unnoticed, the ringmaster cracked his whip, shouted his introduction, and pointed to the ceiling of the tent, where the Flying Avalons were perched.

They loved to drop gracefully from nowhere, like two sparkling birds, and blow kisses as they doffed their glittering, plumed helmets and high-collared capes. They laughed and flirted openly as they beat their way up again on the trapeze bars. In the final vignette of their act, they actually would kiss in midair, pausing, almost hovering as they swooped past each other. On the ground, between bows, Harry Avalon would skip lightly to the front rows and point out the smear of Anna's lipstick, just off the edge of his mouth. They made a romantic pair all right, especially in the blindfold sequence.

That afternoon, as the anticipation increased, as Mr. and Mrs. Avalon tied sparkling strips of cloth onto each other's faces and as they puckered their lips in mock kisses, lips destined "never again to meet" as one long breathless article put it, the wind rose, only miles off, wrapped iself into a cone, and howled. There came a rumble of electrical energy, drowned out by the sudden roll of drums. One detail, not mentioned by the press, perhaps unknown—Anna was pregnant at the time, seven months and hardly showing, her stomach muscles were that strong. It seems incredible that she would work high above the ground, when any fall could be so dangerous, but the explanation—I know from watching her go blind—is that my mother lives comfortably in extreme elements. She is one with the constant dark now, just as the air was her home, familiar to her, safe, before the storm that afternoon.

From opposite ends of the tent they waved, blind and smiling, to the crowd below. The ringmaster removed his hat and called for silence, so that the two above could concentrate. They rubbed their hands in chalky powder, then Harry launched himself and swung, once, twice, in huge calibrated beats across space. He hung from his knees and on the third swing stretched wide his arms, held his hands out to receive his pregnant wife as she dove from her shining bar.

It was while the two were in midair, their hands about to meet, that lightning struck the main pole and sizzled down the guy wires, filling the air with a blue radiance that Harry Avalon must certainly have seen even through the cloth of his blindfold as the tent buckled and the edifice toppled him forward. The swing continued and did not return in its sweep, and Harry went down, down into the crowd with his last thought, perhaps, just a prickle of surprise at his empty hands.

My mother once told me that I'd be amazed at how many things a person can do in the act of falling. Perhaps at the time she was teaching me to dive off a board at the town pool, for I associate the idea with midair somersaults. But I also think she meant that even in that awful doomed second one could think. She certainly did. When her hands did not meet her husband's, my mother tore her blindfold away. As he swept past her on the wrong side she could have grasped his ankle, or the toe-end of his tights, and gone down clutching him. Instead, she changed direction. Her body twisted toward a heavy wire and she managed to hang on to the braided metal, still hot from the lightning strike. Her palms were burned so terribly that once healed they bore no lines, only the blank scar tissue of a quieter future. She was lowered, gently, to the sawdust ring just underneath the dome of the canvas roof, which did not entirely settle but was held up on one end and jabbed through, torn, and even on fire in places from the giant spark, though rain and men's jackets soon put that out.

Three people died, but except for her hands my mother was not seriously harmed until an overeager rescuer broke her arm in extricating her and also, in the process, collapsed a portion of the tent bearing a huge buckle that knocked her unconscious. She was taken to the local hospital, and there she must have hemorrhaged, for they kept her confined to her bed a month and a half before her baby was born without life.

Harry Avalon had always wanted to be buried in the circus cemetery next to the original Avalon, his uncle, and so she sent him back with his brothers. The child, however, is buried around the corner, beyond this house and just down the highway. Sometimes I used to walk there, just to sit. She was a girl, but I never thought of her as a sister, or even as a separate person, really. I suppose you could call it the egocentrism of a child, of all young children, but I always considered her a less finished version of myself.

When the snow falls, throwing shadows among the stones, I could pick hers out easily from the road, for hers is bigger than the others and is the shape of an actual lamb at rest, its legs curled beneath. The carved lamb looms larger in my thoughts as the years pass, though it is probably just my eyes, the vision dimming the way it has for my mother, as what is close to me blurs and distances sharpen. In odd moments, I think it is the edge drawing near, the edge of everything, the horizon we do not really speak of in the eastern woods. And it also seems to me, although this is probably an idle fantasy, that somewhere the statue is growing more sharply etched as if, instead of weathering itself into a porous mass, it is hardening on the hillside with each snowfall, perfecting itself.

It was during her confinement in the hospital that my mother met my father. He was called in to look at the set of her arm, which was complicated. He stayed, sitting at her bedside, for he was something of an armchair traveler, and had spent his war quietly, at an Air Force training grounds, where he became a specialist in arms and legs broken during parachute training exercises. Anna Avalon had been to many of the places he longed to visit—Venice, Rome, Mexico, all through France and Spain. She had no family of her own, and had been taken in by the Avalons, trained to perform from a very young age. They toured Europe before the war, then based themselves in New York. She was illiterate.

It was in the hospital that she learned to read and write, as a way of overcoming the boredom and depression of those months, and it was my father who insisted on teaching her. In return for stories of her adventures, he graded her first exercises. He brought her first book to her, and over her bold letters, which the pale guides of the penmanship pads could not contain, they fell in love

I wonder whether my father calculated the exchange he offered: one form of flight for another. For after that, and for as long as I can remember, my mother was never without a book. Until now, that is, and it remains the greatest difficulty of her blindness. Since my father's recent death, there is no one to read to her, which is why I returned, in fact, from my failed life where the land is flat. I came home to read to my mother, to read out loud, to read long into the dark if I must, to read all night.

Once my father and mother married, they moved onto the old farm he had inherited but didn't care much for. Though he'd been thinking of moving to a larger city, he settled down and broadened his practice in this valley. It still seems odd to me that they chose to stay in the town where the disaster occurred, and which my father in the first place had found so constricting. It was my mother who insisted upon it, after her child did not survive. And then, too, she loved the sagging farmhouse with its scrap of what was left of the vast acreage of woods and hidden hay fields that stretched to the game park.

I owe my existence, the second time then, to the two of them and the hospital that brought them together. That is the debt we take for granted since none of us asks for life. It is only once we have it that we hang on so dearly.

I was seven the year that the house caught fire, probably from standing ash. It can rekindle, and my father, forgetful around the house and perpetually exhausted from night hours on call, often emptied what he thought were ashes from cold stoves into wooden or cardboard containers. The fire could have started from a flaming box. Or perhaps a buildup of creosote inside the chimney was the culprit. It started right around the stove, and the heart of the house was gutted. The babysitter, fallen asleep in my father's den on the first floor, woke to find the stairway to my upstairs room cut off by flames. She used the phone, then ran outside to stand beneath my window.

When my parents arrived, the town volunteers had drawn water from the fire pond and were spraying the outside of the house, preparing to go inside after me, not knowing at the time that there was only one staircase and that it was lost. On the other side of the house, the superannuated extension ladder broke in half. Perhaps the clatter of it falling against the walls woke me, for I'd been asleep up to that point.

As soon as I awakened, I smelled the smoke. I did things by the letter then, was good at memorizing instructions, and so I did exactly what was taught in the second-grade home fire drill. I got up. I touched the back of my door without opening it. Finding it hot, I left it closed and stuffed my rolled-up rug against the crack. I did not hide beneath my bed or crawl into my closet. I put on my flannel robe, and then I sat down to wait.

Outside, my mother stood below my dark window and saw clearly that there was no rescue. Flames had pierced one side wall and the glare of the fire lighted the mammoth limbs and trunk of the vigorous old maple that had probably been planted the year the house was built. No leaf touched the wall, and just one thin limb scraped the roof. From below, it looked as though even a squirrel would have had trouble jumping from the tree onto the house, for the breadth of that small branch was no bigger than my mother's wrist.

Standing there, my mother asked my father to unzip her dress.

When he treated her too gently, as if she'd lost her mind, she made him understand. He couldn't make his hands work, so she finally tore it off and stood there in her pearls and stockings. She directed one of the men to lean the broken half of the extension ladder up against the trunk of the tree. In surprise, he complied. She ascended. She vanished. Then she could be seen easily among the leafless branches of late November as she made her way up and up and, along her stomach, inched the length of a bough that curved above the branch that brushed the roof.

Once there, swaying, she stood and balanced. There were plenty of people in the crowd and many who still remember, or think they do, my mother's leap through the ice-dark air toward that thinnest extension, and how she broke the branch falling so that it cracked in her hands, cracked louder than the flames as she vaulted with it toward the edge of the roof, and how it hurtled down end over end without her, and their eyes went up, again, to see where she had flown.

I didn't see her leap through air, only heard the sudden thump and looked out my window. She was hanging by her heels from the new gutter we had put in that year, and she was smiling. I was not surprised to see her, she was so matter-of-fact. She tapped on the window. I remember how she did it, too; it was the friendliest tap, a bit tentative, as if she were afraid she had arrived too early at a friend's house. Then she gestured at the latch, and when I opened the window she told me to raise it wider, and prop it up with the stick, so it wouldn't crush her fingers. She swung down, caught the ledge, and crawled through the opening. Once she was in my room, I realized she had on only underclothing, a tight bra of the heavy circular-stitched cotton women used to wear and step-in, lace-trimmed drawers. I remember feeling light-headed, of course, terribly relieved and then embarrassed for her, to be seen by the crowd undressed.

I was still embarrassed as we flew out the window, toward earth, me in her lap, her toes pointed as we skimmed toward the painted target of the firefighter's tarp held below.

I know that she's right. I knew it even then. As you fall there is time to think. Curled as I was, against her stomach, I was not startled by the cries of the crowd or the looming faces. The wind roared and beat its hot breath at our back, the flames whistled. I slowly wondered what would happen if we missed the circle or bounced out of it. Then I forgot fear. I wrapped my hands around my mother's hands. I felt the brush of her lips, and I heard the beat of her heart in my ears, loud as thunder, long as the roll of drums.

# The Bingo Van

WHEN I WALKED into bingo that night in early spring, I didn't have a girlfriend, a home or an apartment, a piece of land or a car, and I wasn't tattooed yet, either. Now look at me. I'm walking the reservation road in borrowed pants, toward a place that isn't mine, downhearted because I'm left by a woman. All I have of my temporary riches is this black pony running across the back of my hand—a tattoo I had Lewey's Tattoo Den put there on account of a waking dream. I'm still not paid up. I still owe for the little horse. But if Lewey wants to repossess it, then he'll have to catch me first.

Here's how it is on coming to the bingo hall. It's a long, low quonset barn. Inside, there used to be a pall of smoke, but now the smoke-eater fans in the ceiling have took care of that. So upon first entering you can pick out your friends. On that night in early spring, I saw Eber, Clay, and Robert Morrissey sitting about halfway up toward the curtained stage with their grandmother Lulu. By another marriage, she was my grandma, too. She had five tickets spread in front of her. The boys each had only one. When the numbers rolled, she picked up a dabber in each hand. It was the Early Bird game, a one-hundred-dollar prize, and nobody had got too wound up yet or serious.

"Lipsha, go get us a Coke," said Lulu when someone else bingoed. "Yourself, too."

I went to the concession with Eber, who had finished high school with me. Clay and Robert were younger. We got our soft drinks and came back, set them down, pulled up to the table, and laid out a new set of tickets before us. Like I say, my grandmother, she played five at once, which is how you get the big money. In the long run, much more than breaking even, she was one of those rare Chippewas who actually profited by bingo. But, then again, it was her only way of gambling. No pull-tabs, no blackjack, no slot machines for her. She never went into the back room. She banked all the cash she won. I thought I should learn from Lulu Lamartine, whose other grandsons had stiff new boots while mine were worn down into the soft shape of moccasins. I watched her.

Concentration. Before the numbers even started, she set her mouth, snapped her purse shut. She shook her dabbers so that the foam-rubber tips were thoroughly inked. She looked at the time on her watch. The Coke, she took a drink of that, but no more than a sip. She was a narrow-eyed woman with a round jaw, curled hair. Her eyeglasses, blue plastic, hung from her neck by a gleaming chain. She raised the ovals to her eyes as the caller took the stand. She held her dabbers poised while he plucked the ball from the chute. He read it out: B–7. Then she was absorbed, scanning, dabbing, into the game. She didn't mutter. She had no lucky piece to touch in front of her. And afterward, even if she lost a blackout game by one square, she never sighed or complained.

All business, that was Lulu. And all business paid.

I think I would have been all business too, like her, if it hadn't been for what lay behind the stage curtain to be revealed. I didn't know it, but that was what would change the order of my life. Because of the van, I'd have to get stupid first, then wise. You see, I had been floundering since high school, trying to catch my bearings in the world. It all lay ahead of me, spread out in the sun like a giveaway at a naming ceremony. Only thing was, I could not choose a prize. Something always stopped my hand before it reached.

"Lipsha Morrissey, you got to go for a vocation." That's what I told myself, in a state of nervous worry. I was getting by on almost no money, relying on my job as night watchman in a bar. That earned me a place to sleep, twenty dollars per week, and as much beef jerky, Beer Nuts, and spicy sausage sticks as I could eat.

I was now composed of these three false substances. No food in a bar has a shelf life of less than forty months. If you are what you eat, I would live forever, I thought.

And then they pulled aside the curtain, and I saw that I wouldn't live as long as I had coming unless I owned that van. It had every option you could believe—blue plush on the steering wheel, diamond side windows, and complete carpeted interior. The seats were easy chairs, with little headphones, and it was wired all through the walls. You could walk up close during intermission and touch the sides. The paint was cream, except for the design picked out in blue, which was a Dakota Drum border. In the back there was a small refrigerator and a carpeted platform for sleeping. It was a home, a portable den with front-wheel drive. I could see myself in it right off. I could see I *was* it.

On TV, they say you are what you drive. Let's put it this way: I wanted to be that van.

Now, I know that what I felt was a symptom of the national decline. You'll scoff at me, scorn me, say, What right does that waste Lipsha Morrissey, who makes his living guarding beer, have to comment outside of his own tribal boundary? But I was able to investigate the larger picture, thanks to Grandma Lulu, from whom I learned to be one-minded in my pursuit of a material object.

I went night after night to the bingo. Every hour I spent there, I grew more certain I was close. There was only one game per night at which the van was offered, a blackout game, where you had to fill every slot. The more tickets you bought, the more your chances increased. I tried to play five tickets, like Grandma Lulu did, but they cost five bucks each. To get my van, I had to shake hands with greed. I got unprincipled.

You see, my one talent in this life is a healing power I get passed down through the Pillager branch of my background. It's in my hands. I snap my fingers together so hard they almost spark. Then I blank out my mind, and I put on the touch. I had a reputation up to then for curing sore joints and veins. I could relieve ailments caused in an old person by a half century of grinding stoop-over work. I had a power in myself that flowed out, resistless. I had a richness in my dreams and waking thoughts. But I never realized I would have to give up my healing source once I started charging for my service.

You know how it is about charging. People suddenly think you are worth something. Used to be, I'd go anyplace I was called, take any price or take nothing. Once I let it get around that I charged a twenty for my basic work, however, the phone at the bar rang off the hook.

"Where's that medicine boy?" they asked. "Where's Lipsha?"

I took their money. And it's not like beneath the pressure of a twenty I didn't try, for I did try, even harder than before. I skipped my palms together, snapped my fingers, positioned them where the touch inhabiting them should flow. But when it came to blanking out my mind I consistently failed. For each time, in the center of the cloud that came down into my brain, the van was now parked, in perfect focus.

I suppose I longed for it like for a woman, except I wasn't that bad yet, and, anyway, then I did meet a woman, which set me back in my quest.

Instead of going for the van with everything, saving up to buy as many cards as I could play when they got to the special game, for a few nights I went short term, for variety, with U-Pick-em cards, the kind where you have to choose the numbers for yourself.

First off, I wrote in the shoe and pants sizes of those Morrissey boys. No luck. So much for them. Next I took my birth date and a double of it—still no go. I wrote down the numbers of my grandma's address and her anniversary dates. Nothing. Then one night I realized if my U-Pick-em was going to win it would be more like *revealed*, rather than a forced kind of thing. So I shut my eyes, right there in the middle of the long bingo table, and I let my mind blank out, white and fizzing like the screen of a television, until something formed. The van, as always. But on its tail this time a license plate was officially fixed and numbered. I used that number, wrote it down in the boxes, and then I bingoed.

I GOT TWO hundred dollars from that imaginary license. The money was in my pocket when I left. The next morning, I had fifty cents. But it's not like you think with Serena, and I'll explain that. She didn't want something from me; she didn't care if I had money, and she didn't ask for it. She was seventeen and had a two-year-old boy. That tells you about her life. Her last name was American Horse, an old Dakota name she was proud of even though it was strange to Chippewa country. At her older sister's house Serena's little boy blended in with the younger children, and Serena herself was just one of the teenagers. She was still in high school, a year behind the year she should have been in, and she had ambitions. Her idea was to go into business and sell her clothing designs, of which she had six books.

I don't know how I got a girl so decided in her future to go with me, even that night. Except I told myself, "Lipsha, you're a nice-looking guy. You're a winner." And for the moment I was. I went right up to her at the Coin-Op and said, "Care to dance?," which was a joke—there wasn't anyplace to dance. Yet she liked me. We had a sandwich and then she wanted to take a drive, so we tagged along with some others in the back of their car. They went straight south, toward Hoopdance, off the reservation, where action was taking place.

"Lipsha," she whispered on the way, "I always liked you from a distance."

"Serena," I said, "I liked you from a distance, too."

So then we moved close together on the car seat. My hand was on my knee, and I thought of a couple of different ways I could gesture, casually pretend to let it fall on hers, how maybe if I talked fast she wouldn't notice, in the heat of the moment, her hand in my hand, us holding hands, our lips drawn to one another. But then I decided to boldly take courage, to take her hand as, at the same time, I looked into her eyes. I did this. In the front, the others talked among themselves. Yet we just sat there. After a while she said, "You want to kiss me?"

But I answered, not planning how the words would come out, "Our first kiss has to be a magic moment only we can share."

Her eyes went wide as a deer's, and her big smile bloomed. Her skin was dark, her long hair a burnt-brown color. She wore no jewelry, no rings, just the clothing she had sewed from her designs—a suit jacket and pair of pants that were the tan of eggshells, with symbols picked out in blue thread on the borders, the cuffs, and the hem. I took her in, admiring, for some time on that drive before I realized that the reason Serena's cute outfit nagged me so was on account of she was dressed up to match my bingo van. I could hardly tell her this surprising coincidence, but it did convince me that the time was perfect, the time was right.

They let us off at a certain place just over the reservation line; and we got out, hardly breaking our gaze from each other. You want to know what this place was? I'll tell you. Okay. So it was a motel—a long, low double row of rooms, painted white on the outside, with brown wooden doors. There was a beautiful sign set up, featuring a lake with some fish jumping out of it. We stood beside the painted water.

"I haven't done this since Jason," she said. That was the name of her two-year-old son. "I have to call up my sister first."

There was a phone near the office, inside a plastic shell. She went over there.

"He's sleeping," she said when she returned.

I went into the office, stood before the metal counter. There was a number floating in my mind.

"Is Room 22 available?" I asked.

I suppose, looking at me, I look too much like an Indian. The owner, a big sandy-haired woman in a shiny black blouse, noticed that. You get so you see it cross their face the way wind blows a disturbance on water. There was a period of contemplation, a struggle in this woman's thinking. Behind her the television whispered. Her mouth opened, but I spoke first.

"This here is Andrew Jackson," I said, tenderizing the bill. "Known for setting up our Southern relatives for the Trail of Tears. And to keep him company we got two Mr. Hamiltons."

The woman turned shrewd, and took the bills.

"No parties." She held out a key attached to a square of orange plastic.

"Just sex." I could not help but reassure her. But that was talk, big talk from a person with hardly any experience and nothing that resembled a birth-control device. I wasn't one of those so-called studs who couldn't open up their wallets without dropping a foil-wrapped square. "No, Lipsha Morrissey was deep at heart a romantic, a wild-minded kind of guy," I told myself, a fool with no letup. I went out to Serena, and took her hand in mine. I was shaking inside but my voice was steady and my hands were cool.

"Let's go in." I showed the key. "Let's not think about tomorrow."

"That's how I got Jason," said Serena.

So we stood there.

"I'll go in," she said at last. "Down two blocks, there's an all-night gas station. They sell 'em."

I went. Okay. Life in this day and age might be less romantic in some ways. It seemed so in the hard twenty-four-hour fluorescent light, as I tried to choose what I needed from the rack by the counter. It was quite a display; there were dazzling choices—textures, shapes. I saw I was being watched, and I suddenly grabbed what was near my hand—two boxes, economy size.

"Heavy date?"

I suppose the guy on the late shift was bored, could not resist. His T-shirt said "Big Sky Country." He was grinning in an ugly way. So I answered.

"Not really. Fixing up a bunch of my white buddies from Montana. Trying to keep down the sheep population."

His grin stayed fixed. Maybe he had heard a lot of jokes about Montana blondes, or maybe he was from somewhere else. I looked at the boxes in my hand, put one back.

"Let me help you out," the guy said. "What you need is a bag of these."

He took down a plastic sack of little oblong party balloons, Day-Glo pinks and oranges and blues.

"Too bright," I said. "My girlfriend's a designer. She hates clashing colors." I was breathing hard suddenly, and so was he. Our eyes met and narrowed.

"What does she design?" he said. "Bedsheets?"

"What does yours design?" I said. "Wool sweaters?"

I put money between us. "For your information, my girlfriend's not only beautiful but she and I are the same species."

"Which is?"

"Take the money," I said. "Hand over my change and I'll be out of here. Don't make me do something I'd regret."

"I'd be real threatened." The guy turned from me, ringing up my sale. "I'd be shaking, except I know you Indian guys are chickenshit."

I took my package, took my change.

"Baaaaa," I said, and beat it out of there. It's strange how a bashful kind of person like me gets talkative in some of our less pleasant border-town situations.

I took a roundabout way back to Room 22 and tapped on the door. There was a little window right beside it. Serena peeked through, and let me in.

"Well," I said then, in that awkward interval, "guess we're set."

She took the bag from my hand and didn't say a word, just put it on the little table beside the bed. There were two chairs. Each of us took one. Then we sat down and turned on the television. The romance wasn't in us now for some reason, but there was something invisible that made me hopeful about the room.

It was just a small place, a modest kind of place, clean. You could smell the faint chemical of bug spray the moment you stepped inside. You could look at the television hung on the wall, or examine the picture of golden trees and a waterfall. You could take a shower for a long time in the cement shower stall, standing on your personal shower mat for safety. There was a little tin desk. You could sit down there and write a letter on a sheet of plain paper from the drawer. The lampshade was made of reeds, pressed and laced tight together. The spread on the double mattress was reddish, a rusty cotton material. There was an air conditioner, with a fan we turned on.

"I don't know why we're here," I said at last. "I'm sorry."

Serena took a small brush from her purse.

"Comb my hair?"

I took the brush and sat on the bed, just behind her. I began at the ends, very careful, but there were hardly any tangles to begin with. Her hair was a quiet brown without variation. My hand followed the brush, smoothing after each stroke, until the fall of her hair was a hypnotizing silk. I could lift my hand away from her head and the hair would follow, electric to my touch, in soft strands that hung suspended until I returned to the brushing. She never moved, except to switch off the light and then the television. She sat down again in the total dark and said, "Please, keep on," so I did. The air got thick. Her hair got lighter, full of blue static, charged so that I was held in place by the attraction. A golden spark jumped on the carpet. Serena turned toward me. Her hair floated down around her at that moment like a tent of energy.

WELL, THE MONEY part is not related to that. I gave it all to Serena, that's true. Her intention was to buy material and put together the creations that she drew in her notebooks. It was fashion with a Chippewa flair, as she explained it, and sure to win prizes at the state home-ec contest. She promised to pay me interest when she opened her own shop. The next day, after we had parted, after I had checked out the bar I was supposed to night-watch, I went off to the woods to sit and think. Not about the money, which was Serena's—and good luck to her—but about her and me.

She was two years younger than me, yet she had direction and a child, while I was aimless, lost in hyperspace, using up my talent, which was already fading from my hands. I wondered what our future could hold. One thing was sure: I never knew a man to support his family by playing bingo, and the medicine calls for Lipsha were getting fewer by the week, and fewer, as my touch failed to heal people, fled from me, and lay concealed.

I sat on ground where, years ago, my greats and my great-greats, the Pillagers, had walked. The trees around me were the dense birch and oak of old woods. The lake drifted in, gray waves, white foam in a bobbing lace. Thin gulls lined themselves up on a sandbar. The sky went dark. I closed my eyes, and that is when the little black pony galloped into my mind. It sped across the choppy waves like a skipping stone, its mane a banner, its tail a flag, and vanished on the other side of the shore.

It was luck. Serena's animal. American Horse.

"This is the last night I'm going to try for the van," I told myself. I always kept three twenties stuffed inside the edging of my blanket in back of the bar. Once that stash was gone I'd make a real decision. I'd open the yellow pages at random, and where my finger pointed I would take that kind of job.

Of course, I never counted on winning the van.

I was playing for it on the shaded side of a blackout ticket, which is always hard to get. As usual, I sat with Lulu and her boys. Her vigilance helped me. She let me use her extra dabber and she sat and smoked a filter cigarette, observing the quiet frenzy that was taking place around her. Even though that van had sat on the stage for five months, even though nobody had yet won it and everyone said it was a scam, when it came to playing for it most people bought a couple of tickets. That night, I went all out and purchased eight.

A girl read out the numbers from the hopper. Her voice was clear and light on the microphone. I didn't even notice what was happening— Lulu pointed out one place I had missed on the winning ticket. Then I had just two squares left to make a bingo, and I suddenly sweated, I broke out into a chill, I went cold and hot at once. After all my pursuit, after all my plans, I was N–6 and G–60. I had narrowed myself, shrunk into the spaces on the ticket. Each time the girl read a number and it wasn't that 6 or 60 I sickened, recovered, forgot to breathe.

She must have read twenty numbers out before N–6. Then, right after that, G–60 rolled off her lips.

I screamed. I am ashamed to say how loud I yelled. That girl came over, got the manager, and then he checked out my numbers slow and careful while everyone hushed.

He didn't say a word. He checked them over twice. Then he pursed his lips together and wished he didn't have to say it.

"It's a bingo," he finally told the crowd.

Noise buzzed to the ceiling—talk of how close some others had come, green talk—and every eye was turned and cast on me, which was uncomfortable. I never was the center of looks before, not Lipsha, who everybody took for granted around here. Not all those looks were for the good, either. Some were plain envious and ready to believe the first bad thing a sour tongue could pin on me. It made sense in a way. Of all those who'd stalked that bingo van over the long months, I was now the only one who had not lost money on the hope.

OKAY, SO WHAT kind of man does it make Lipsha Morrissey that the keys did not tarnish his hands one slight degree, and that he beat it out that very night in the van, completing only the basic paperwork? I didn't go after Serena, and I can't tell you why. Yet I was hardly ever happier. In that van, I rode high, but that's the thing. Looking down on others, even if it's only from the seat of a van that a person never really earned, does something to the human mentality. It's hard to say, I changed. After just one evening riding the reservation roads, passing with a swish of my tires, I started smiling at the homemade hot rods, at the clunkers below me, at the old-lady cars nosing carefully up and down the gravel hills.

I started saying to myself that I should visit Serena, and a few nights later I finally did go over there. I pulled into her sister's driveway with a flourish I could not help, as the van slipped into a pothole and I roared the engine. For a moment, I sat in the dark, letting my headlamps blaze alongside the door until Serena's brother-in-law leaned out.

"Cut the lights!" he yelled. "We got a sick child."

I rolled down my window, and asked for Serena.

"It's her boy. She's in here with him." He waited. I did, too, in the dark. A dim light was on behind him and I saw some shadows, a small girl in those pajamas with the feet tacked on, someone pacing back and forth.

"You want to come in?" he called.

But here's the gist of it: I just said to tell Serena hi for me, and then I backed out of there, down the drive, and left her to fend for herself. I could have stayed there. I could have drawn my touch back from wherever it had gone to. I could have offered my van to take Jason to the I.H.S. I could have sat there in silence as a dog guards its mate, its own blood. I could have done something different from what I did, which was to hit the road for Hoopdance and look for a better time.

I cruised until I saw where the party house was located that night. I drove the van over the low curb, into the yard, and I parked there. I watched until I recognized a couple of cars and saw the outlines of Indians and mixed, so I knew that walking in would not involve me in what the newspapers term an episode. The white door, stained and raked by a dog, had a tiny fan-shaped window. I went through and stood inside. There was movement, a kind of low-key swirl of bright hair and dark hair tossing alongside each other. There were about as many Indians as there weren't. This party was what we call around here a hairy buffalo, and most people were grouped around a big brown plastic garbage can that served as the punch bowl for the all-purpose stuff, which was anything that anyone brought, dumped in along with pink Hawaiian Punch. I grew up around a lot of the people, and others I knew by sight. Among those last, there was a young familiar-looking guy.

It bothered me. I recognized him, but I didn't know him. I hadn't been to school with him, or played him in any sport, because I did not play sports. I couldn't think where I'd seen him until later, when the heat went up and he took off his bomber jacket. Then "Big Sky Country" showed, plain letters on a bright-blue background.

I edged around the corner of the room, into the hall, and stood there to argue with myself. Would he recognize me, or was I just another face, a customer? He probably wasn't really from Montana, so he might not even have been insulted by our little conversation, or remember it anymore. I reasoned that he had probably picked up the shirt vacationing, though who would want to go across that border, over to where the world got meaner? I told myself that I should calm my nerves, go back into the room, have fun. What kept me from doing that was the sudden thought of Serena, of our night together and what I had bought and used.

Once I remembered, I was lost to the present moment. One part of me caught up with the other. I realized that I had left Serena to face her crisis, alone, while I took off in my brand-new van.

I have a hard time getting drunk. It's just the way I am. I start thinking and forget to fill the cup, or recall something I have got to do, and just end up walking from a party. I have put down a full can of beer before and walked out to weed my grandma's rhubarb patch, or work on a cousin's car. Now I was putting myself in Serena's place, feeling her feelings.

*What would he want to do that to me for?*

I heard her voice say this out loud, just behind me, where there was nothing but wall. I edged along until I came to a door, and then I went through, into a tiny bedroom full of coats, and so far nobody either making out or unconscious upon the floor. I sat on a pile of parkas and jean jackets in this little room, an alcove in the rising buzz of the party outside. I saw a phone, and I dialed Serena's number. Her sister answered.

"Thanks a lot," she said when I said it was me. "You woke up Jason."

"What's wrong with him?" I asked.

There was a silence, then Serena's voice got on the line. "I'm going to hang up."

"Don't."

"He's crying. His ears hurt so bad he can't stand it."

"I'm coming over there."

"Forget it. Forget you."

She said the money I had loaned her would be in the mail. She reminded me it was a long time since the last time I had called. And then the phone went dead. I held the droning receiver in my hand, and tried to clear my mind. The only thing I saw in it, clear as usual, was the van. I decided this was a sign for me to get in behind the wheel. I should drive straight to Serena's house, put on the touch, help her son out. So I set my drink on the windowsill. Then I slipped out the door and I walked down the porch steps, only to find them waiting.

I guess he had recognized me after all, and I guess he was from Montana. He had friends, too. They stood around the van, and their heads were level with the roof, for they were tall.

"Let's go for a ride," said the one from the all-night gas pump.

He knocked on the window of my van with his knuckles. When I told him no thanks, he started karate-kicking the door. He wore black cowboy boots, pointy-toed, with hard-edged new heels. They left ugly dents every time he landed a blow.

"Thanks anyhow," I repeated. "But the party's not over." I tried to get back into the house, but, like in a bad dream, the door was stuck, or locked. I hollered, pounded, kicked at the very marks that desperate dog had left, but the music rose and nobody heard. So I ended up in the van. They acted very gracious. They urged me to drive. They were so polite that I tried to tell myself they weren't all that bad. And sure enough, after we had drove for a while, these Montana guys said they had chipped in together to buy me a present.

"What is it?" I asked. "Don't keep me in suspense."

"Keep driving," said the pump jockey.

"I don't really go for surprises," I said. "What's your name, anyhow?"

"Marty."

"I got a cousin named Marty," I said.

"Forget it."

The guys in the back exchanged a grumbling kind of laughter, a knowing set of groans. Marty grinned, turned toward me from the passenger seat.

"If you really want to know what we're going to give you, I'll tell. It's a map. A map of Montana."

Their laughter got wild and went on for too long.

"I always liked the state," I said in a serious voice.

"No shit," said Marty. "Then I hope, you like sitting on it." He signaled where I should turn, and all of a sudden I realized that Lewey's lay ahead. Lewey ran his tattoo den from the basement of his house, kept his equipment set up and ready for the weekend.

"Whoa," I said. I stopped the van. "You can't tattoo a person against his will. It's illegal."

"Get your lawyer on it tomorrow." Marty leaned in close for me to see his eyes. I put the van back in gear but just chugged along, desperately thinking. Lewey was a strange kind of guy, an old Dutch sailor who got beached here, about as far as you can get from salt water. I decided that I'd ask Marty, in a polite kind of way, to beat me up instead. If that failed, I would tell him that there were many states I would not mind so much—smaller, rounder ones.

"Are any of you guys from any other state?" I asked, anxious to trade.

"Kansas."

"South Dakota."

It wasn't that I really had a thing against those places, understand; it's just that the straight-edged shape is not a Chippewa preference. You look around you, and everything you see is round, everything in nature. There are no perfect boundaries, no borders. Only human-made things tend toward cubes and squares—the van, for instance. That was an example. Suddenly I realized that I was driving a wheeled version of the state of North Dakota.

"Just beat me up, you guys. Let's get this over with. I'll stop."

But they laughed, and then we were at Lewey's.

THE SIGN ON his basement door said COME IN. I was shoved from behind and strapped together by five pairs of heavy, football-toughened hands. I was the first to see Lewey, I think, the first to notice that he was not just a piece of all the trash and accumulated junk that washed through the concrete-floored cellar but a person, sitting still as any statue, in a corner, on a chair that creaked and sang when he rose and walked over.

He even looked like a statue—not the type you see in history books, I don't mean those, but the kind you see for sale as you drive along the highway. He was a Paul Bunyan, carved with a chain saw. He was rough-looking, finished in big strokes.

"Please," I said, "I don't want—"

Marty squeezed me around the throat and tousled up my hair, friendly like.

"He's just got cold feet. Now remember, Lewey, map of Montana. You know where. And put in a lot of detail."

I tried to scream.

"Like I was thinking," Marty went on, "of those maps we did in grade school showing products from each region. Cows' heads, oil wells, those little sheaves of wheat, and so on."

"Tie him up," said Lewey. His voice was thick, with a commanding formal accent. "Then leave."

They did. They took my pants and the keys to the van. I heard the engine roar and drive away, and I rolled from side to side in my strict bindings.

I felt Lewey's hand on my shoulder.

"Be still." His voice had changed, now that the others were gone, to a low sound that went with his appearance and did not seem at all unkind. I looked up at him. A broke-down God is who he looked like from my worm's-eye view. His beard was pure white, long and patchy, and his big eyes frozen blue. His head was half bald, shining underneath the brilliant fluorescent tubes in the ceiling. You never know where you're going to find your twin in the world, your double. I don't mean in terms of looks—I'm talking about mind-set. You never know where you're going to find the same thoughts in another brain, but when it happens you know it right off, just like the two of you were connected by a small electrical wire that suddenly glows red-hot and sparks. That's what happened when I met Lewey Koep.

"I don't have a pattern for Montana," he told me. He untied my ropes with a few quick jerks, sneering at the clumsiness of the knots. Then he sat in his desk chair again, and watched me get my bearings.

"I don't want anything tattooed on me, Mr. Koep," I said. "It's a kind of revenge plot."

He sat in silence, in a waiting quiet, hands folded and face composed. By now I knew I was safe, but I had nowhere to go, and so I sat down on a pile of magazines. He asked, "What revenge?" and I told him the story, the whole thing right from the beginning, when I walked into the bingo hall. I left out the personal details about Serena and me, but he got the picture. I told him about the van.

"That's an unusual piece of good fortune."

"Have you ever had any? Good fortune?"

"All the time. Those guys paid plenty, for instance, though I suppose they'll want it back. You pick out a design. You can owe me."

He opened a book he had on the table, a notebook with plastic pages that clipped in and out, and handed it over to me. I didn't want a tattoo, but I didn't want to disappoint this man, either. I leafed through the dragons and the hearts, thinking how to refuse, and then suddenly I saw the horse. It was the same picture that had come into my head as I sat in the woods. Now here it was. The pony skimmed, legs outstretched, reaching for the edge of the page. I got a thought in my head, clear and vital, that this little horse would convince Serena I was serious about her.

"This one."

Lewey nodded, and heated his tools.

THAT'S WHY I got it put on, that little horse, and suffered pain. Now my hand won't let me rest. It throbs and aches as if it was coming alive again after a hard frost had made it numb. I know I'm going somewhere, taking this hand to Serena. Even walking down the road in a pair of big-waisted green pants belonging to Lewey Koep, toward the So Long Bar, where I keep everything I own in life, I'm going forward. My hand is a ball of pins, but when I look down I see the little black horse running hard, fast, and serious.

I'm ready for what will come next. That's why I don't fall on the ground, and I don't yell, when I come across the van in a field. At first, I think it is the dream van, the way I always see it in my vision. Then I look, and it's the real vehicle. Totaled.

My bingo van is smashed on the sides, kicked and scratched, and the insides are scattered. Stereo wires, glass, and ripped pieces of carpet are spread here and there among the new sprouts of wheat. I force open a door that is bent inward. I wedge myself behind the wheel, which is tipped over at a crazy angle, and I look out. The windshield is shattered in a sunlight burst, through which the world is cut to bits.

I've been up all night, and the day stretches long before me, so I decide to sleep where I am. Part of the seat is still wonderfully upholstered, thick and plush, and it reclines now—permanently, but so what? I relax into the small comfort, my body as warm as an animal, my thoughts drifting. I know I'll wake to nothing, but at this moment I feel rich. Sinking away, I feel like everything worth having is within my grasp. All I have to do is put my hand into the emptiness.

# Fuck with Kayla and You Die

ROMAN BAKER STOOD in the bright and crackling current of light that zipped around in patterned waves underneath the oval canopy entrance to the casino. He wasn't a gambler. The skittering brilliance didn't draw him in and he was already irritated with the piped-out carol music. A twenty, smoothly folded in his pocket, didn't itch him or burn his ass one bit. He had come to the casino because it was just a few days before Christmas and he didn't know how to celebrate. Maybe the electronic-bell strum of slot machines would soothe him, or watching the cards spreading from the dealer's hands in arcs and waves. He took a step to the left, toward the cliffs of glass doors.

As he opened his hand to push at the door's brass plate and enter, a white man of medium height and wearing a green leather coat pressed his car keys into Roman's palm. Without waiting for a claim ticket, without even looking at Roman beyond the moment it took to ascertain that he was brown and stood before the doors of an Indian casino, the man walked off and was swallowed into the jingling gloom.

Roman waited before the doors, holding the keys. All of the valets were occupied. He held up the keys. A few seconds later, he put down his hand and clutched the keys in his fist. No one had seen this happen. Roman turned away from the doors, opened his hand, and saw that one shining key among the other keys belonged to a Jeep Cherokee. Immediately, he spotted the white Cherokee parked idling just beyond the lights of the canopy. An amused little voice in his head said *go for it*. He didn't think it out, just walked over to the car, got in, and drove away.

*You couldn't call this stealing, since the guy gave me the keys*, Roman told himself, *but we are on a slippery slope*. He checked the lighted gauge of the Cherokee, and saw that the tank was nearly empty. There was a Superstop handy, just down the road. Roman drove up to the bank of pumps and inserted the hose into the Cherokee's gas tank. *Eight dollars worth should do it*, he thought, and then he wondered. *Do what?* In the store, he decided he should be methodical, buy something to eat or drink. Afterward, he would know what to do. The complicated bar of coffee machines drew him, and he stepped up to the grooved aluminum counter, chose a tall white insulated cup, and placed it under a machine's hose labeled "French Vanilla." He held the button until the cup was three-quarters full, and let the nozzle keep drizzling sweet foam on top. Then he figured out which plastic travel lid matched his cup and pressed it on, over the froth. So as not to burn his hand, he fitted the cup into a little cardboard sleeve. He paid for everything out of his twenty, and walked outside. It was a warm winter night in the middle of a thaw. Bits of moisture hung glittering in the gas-smelling air. There was a very light dust of sparkling fresh snow sinking into the day's brown slush.

"A white Christmas, huh?" said a woman's voice, just to the left.

"Yes, it will be enchanting," Roman answered.

He was the kind of person people spoke to in situations that could easily stay completely impersonal. His face was round, his nose pleasantly blunt, his eyes wide and friendly. His smile was genuine, he had been told. Yet women never stayed with him. Perhaps he was too comfortable, too nurturing, and reminded them of their mothers. Desperate mothers who wanted their children home before dark or wouldn't let them out of sight. Now, in addition to being motherly, plus the kind of person people spoke to on the streets or while pumping their gas, he was the type into whose comfortable palm strange white men trustingly pressed their car keys.

And house keys, too, and other keys. Roman jingled the set before his eyes and then fit the correct car key into the lock. He got into the car and carefully set the cappuccino into the cup holder before he drove to the edge of the parking lot. There, he turned on the dome light and opened the glove compartment. He found the car's registration, folded in a clear plastic sleeve, and the proof of insurance, too, with numbers to call. The owner's name was Torvil J. Morson and his address was 2272 West 195th Street, in the closest suburb. Roman took another drink of the milky, sweet, deadly-tasting cappuccino. Then he put the cup back into the holder and drove carefully out of the lot.

The casino was prosperous because it was just far enough from the city to be considered a Destination Resort, and yet close enough so only an hour's quickly diminishing farmland, pine woods, and snowy fields stood between the reservation boundaries and the long stretch of little towns that had blended via strip malls and housing developments into the biggest population center in that part of the Midwest. Roman knew approximately how far he was from 195th Street, and it took him exactly the forty-five minutes he'd imagined to get there, find the house, and pull into the driveway, which he wouldn't have done unless he'd seen already that the windows were dark. The house was a small one-story ranch-style painted the same drab green as the jacket of the man who had given Roman the car keys.

Roman got out of the car, walked up to the front door, used the key. Just like that, he entered. Once in, he shut the door behind him and wiped his feet on a rough little welcome mat. The house had its own friendly smell—slightly stale smoke, cinnamon buns, wet dried sour wool. A powerful streetlight cast a silvery glow through the front picture window. As his eyes adjusted, Roman stepped onto grayish wall-to-wall carpet and padded silently across the living room. His heart slowed. The carpeting soothed him. He went straight across the room to the kitchen, divided off by only a counter, and opened the freezer section of the refrigerator. He'd heard that people often kept their jewelry and cash there in case of a burglary or fire. There was a coffee can in the freezer, but it only held ground coffee. A few promising Tupperware containers held nothing but old stew, alas. Roman shut the insulated door and rubbed his hands together to strike the chill from his fingers. Then he walked down the hall. He stepped into a bedroom, turned on the light. Posters of pop stars, stuffed animals, pencil drawings, and dried flowers were taped to the walls. A teenage girl's room. Nothing. He turned out the light and found the master bedroom, the one closest to the bathroom. He was just about to turn on the light when the sound of breathing, or the sense of it, anyway, in the room, stopped his hand.

Then it didn't sound like breathing, but something else, sighing and watery. A fish tank, Roman thought. He listened a bit longer, then switched on the light and saw, on a table next to a window, a small plug-in fountain. The water coursed endlessly over an arrangement of smooth, black stones. Roman thought this must belong to the man's wife. He frowned at himself in the dressing room mirror, and adjusted the lapel of his jacket. The wife, or the teen, or another member of the family might return while he was standing in the lighted bedroom. Yet Roman had no prickles up his back, no darts of fear, no sense of apprehension. In fact, he felt as much at home as if he lived in this house himself. He was even tempted to lie down on the big queen-size bed neatly made up with a purple quilt and pillows arranged upon pillows. Where had he read about this? Goldilocks! This bed looked comfortable. He thought of the three bears. There was a Mrs. Morson for sure, thought Roman. He pictured a bear meditating by the fountain. A meditator probably wasn't the type who would own gold and diamond jewelry, but he still had to check. There was not a safe on the closet floor, or even a velvety box on the top of the dresser or in the drawer that held underwear. No, there was only underwear, and it was decent, fresh cotton. *What am I doing*, thought Roman, *with my hands in Mrs. Morson's underwear?*

He shut the drawer firmly and sat on the edge of the bed.

*I'm not going to find any cash*, he decided. *Mr. Morson has taken it to the casino.* Treading down the hall and back across the soft carpet, he felt cheated. What had happened with the car keys was a once-in-a-lifetime thing. Roman had never before done anything that was strictly criminal. But this break-in, where he hadn't had to actually break in, this was given to him. It was as though Mr. Morson had invited him to travel to his house and look for valuables. And nothing there! The house was very still now, the street outside utterly deserted, the neighboring houses dim and shut. Roman sat down on the couch, wishing that he had the rest of his cappuccino, but he'd left the cup in the car. There was a tremendous energy to the quiet, it seemed to him, a seething quality. He felt that he should do something bold, or important, with this piece of fate that he'd been handed. As he was thinking of what he might do, someone knocked on the door. Roman's first instinct was not to answer. But the expectant quality of the silence was too much for him. He went to the door and opened it. There stood a woman and a man, both in coats but wearing no scarves or hats. The woman held a wrapped gift. The man carried a crockpot out of which there issued a faint and delicious, smoky, bean-soup scent.

"Oh, thank God!"

The woman stepped into the entryway, the man also, both exuding an air of conspiratorial excitement.

"Very clever, keeping the lights off," said the man. "But isn't that his car?"

"He gave me the keys and I just drove it here," Roman told him. The man gave a scratchy laugh that turned into a cough.

"Where should I put this?" He lifted the crockpot slightly.

"In the kitchen?" said Roman.

"Let's put his presents in there, too," said the woman. "You must work with T.J. Have we met?"

"I'm Roman Baker."

"You look like an Indian," said the woman.

"People tell me that," said Roman.

"Okay, and I'm Willa and that's Buzz with the seven-bean soup. It's his specialty. Just the countertop lights! No overhead!"

"Right!" Buzz sounded gleeful. "Is Zola back yet? Did she get the cake?"

"I think so," said Roman. His skull suddenly felt tight, his eyes scratchy and shifty in their sockets. "I feel bad," he mumbled. "I don't have a gift. Maybe I should go out for sodas or beer."

"Oh, T.J. won't notice. T.J. will have a shit fit. I think we should all hide behind the counters and the couch. Will you get the door, Roman?"

"Come on in," said Roman, as he opened the door. "Wipe your

feet." Two young men and an older woman stood on the steps. One man carried a neatly foil-covered bowl. The other held a large, pale, tissue-wrapped gift.

"We brought Mom," one of the young men squealed. "She's drunk. She's such a hoot!"

"I drank a strawberry wine cooler. I'm loaded," said the elderly lady in a prim and sober voice. "Let me in so I can ditch these two idiots. Does he suspect?" She eyed Roman with a flare of exasperation, her scarlet mouth down-twisted.

"Not in the slightest," Roman told her. He helped her out of her coat while the two young men settled their things in the kitchen.

"Very clever, all the lights out," the lady muttered, "Zola says he'll pee his pants."

"That's pretty much what Willa says, too," Roman told the lady. Steering her toward the couch, he decided he'd better leave.

"They're sending me out for more strawberry wine coolers," he said. He patted the woman's hand.

"You're an Indian," she said, severely and as if imparting information to him.

"A big one," said Roman.

The others in the kitchen were whooping with secretive anticipation. Roman touched the keys in his pocket, walked out the door. As he neared the white Cherokee two more people stepped into the driveway, asked him in low and enthralled voices if anybody else was there.

"Go on in," Roman told them. "Willa and Buzz are organizing everybody."

"Oh god!" said the woman. "I saw his car! I thought he'd got home already. Zola's following us. She'll be here any minute with the cake."

ROMAN JUMPED INTO the car, backed down the driveway, and drove the opposite way down the street from the way he guessed Zola would arrive.

●  ●  ●

BACK ON THE turnoff to the highway, he thought, *right or left?* But it was inevitable. He headed toward the casino. The cappuccino was still warm and on the way there he finished it. He started to feel good. Yes, he had been given the Morsons' keys, the keys to their life, and he'd visited that life. Enough. Nothing had happened after all. He hadn't taken anything except this car—for a drive. As he neared the vast casino parking lot he slowed and carefully reconnoitered, watching for extra security or flashing lights in case the Cherokee had been reported stolen. But all was bright and calm. Gamblers were walking to and fro, those who had self-parked. Others were waiting with their claim tickets on the swirl patterned carpet in the lobby underneath the lighted canopy. Roman eased the car into a marked space cautiously, far from the activity, and took his empty cappuccino cup with him before he locked the car's door.

*That was your little adventure*, he told himself. *Now what?* But he knew what. He walked back to the casino entrance and walked through, into the icy bells and plucking, continual ring that did predictable and pleasurable things to his central nervous system. He breathed faster in excitement. Possibly, the sound depressed left brain action. He felt connected to an irrational and urgent universe of lucky chance. His fingers twitched. First things first. He scanned the seated players looking for the green leather jacket, which was all he remembered about Morson. He decided to make a sweep, starting at the far end of the casino, checking the men's room first. He went up each row and down each row, passed behind each glazed, ghostly player. It took so long that he thought of giving up and simply turning the keys in at the lost and found. But then, there was T.J. Morson, green jacket slung behind him, staring into the lighted tumble of little pirate cove symbols on his machine's curved torso.

Roman tapped his shoulder and Morson waved him off, not to be bothered. Roman watched the man shove in three more quarters and hold his breath. Then sit back, dazed, rub his hand over his face.

Roman touched his shoulder again. "Happy Birthday."

"What?"

Morson turned and focused on him. His face was clean cut and perfectly square, a solid Norwegian jawline, pale eyes, hair already white and thin, a little tousled. He was falling into heaviness around the neck and then below, like Roman, it was pretty close to a lost cause. Roman dangled the keys. "You dropped these, I think?"

Morson slapped the pockets of his pants.

"For god sakes, thought I had it parked!"

Roman gave him the keys and turned to go, but he couldn't, not quite. He took a last look at Mr. Morson and saw that something was very wrong with him. T.J. Morson was sitting there with his mouth open, staring at the car keys. Not moving.

"Hey," Roman bent toward him, then waved his hand before the man's eyes, "you okay?"

"No," said Mr. Morson. He shut his mouth and then slowly, like a very old man, stood and shrugged on his jacket. He dropped the keys, picked them up. Sat back down and stared once more at the machine. Slowly, from his pants pocket, he drew a bit of change. Held it out questingly to Roman, who rummaged in his own pocket and exchanged what Mr. Morson offered for a quarter. Morson held it a moment, then played it. Nothing.

"You okay?" Roman asked again.

But Morson was staring vacantly before him. His mouth was open and his hands were shaking.

"Not all right, not all right," he muttered.

"Hey," said Roman, "come on. Get up. Let's go sit in the café. I'll buy you a coffee."

"What I need is a drink."

"Yeah, well, maybe." Roman helped steady Mr. Morson. They walked down the aisle of light and sound, along a short hallway, and into a small interior restaurant where the waitress gave them a booth for two and poured their coffee.

"Cream. Lots of it. Thanks," Roman told her. She left the pot and a bowl of tiny plastic servings of flavored half-and-half.

"Thank you," said T.J. Morson, staring at the brown pottery cup.

"And thank you for returning my car keys." His voice was heavy as a pour of concrete. The syllables seemed to harden as they fell from his mouth. "Well," he looked up, scanned the country-themed room, "this is it."

"What are you talking about?" asked Roman.

Morson put his face in his hands and then slowly pushed his hands up his face and over his hair. "That was it," he said again.

"Listen." Roman was beginning to feel alarmed. "It's your birthday. You should be heading home." He thought of all the excited people waiting in the living room of the Morson house, crouched behind the sofa and chairs and kitchen counters, the lights off.

"Weren't you supposed to be home a while ago?"

Mr. Morson looked at Roman, frowning now, momentarily distracted. "Who are you?"

"I'm a friend of Buzz and Willa," Roman told him. "Look, I'm going to let you in on something that's going to cheer you up. You've got to go home now. I'm not supposed to say a thing about it, but they're planning a surprise party in your honor. Zola's got the cake. Even as we speak, they are in your house, waiting for you. They have presents."

Telling this to Morson was surprisingly difficult. Roman felt the bleeding sensation of envy when he imagined stepping onto the warm, thick carpet. The blast of noise from friends. The bean soup. Beer. Cake.

Mr. Morson said nothing.

"You can't just leave them waiting there." Roman heard a note of accusing desperation in his voice.

Morson shook his head now, as though his misery was a fall of water washing over him. His brilliant white hair lifted in the staticky air. Roman felt like reaching over and patting it down, but he kept his hand curled around his coffee cup.

"Fuck's sake, I can't go back there," said Morson wearily. "They don't know. Zola has no idea about this. . . ." He waved his hand toward the casino through the glass doors of the restaurant. "I play when she's at work, when I'm supposed to be at work, except I don't have a job, see.

That's over. She doesn't know I put a second mortgage on our house, a line of credit, then topped it. Cleaned out every one of our accounts." He stared fiercely, disconnectedly, at Roman. "There's nothing," he said. His mouth was suddenly and frighteningly sharklike, an impersonal black hungry V. A bubble of spit formed at either corner. "They'll take the house and then my car. They'll take her car. And Kayla . . . oh god."

MORSON DROPPED HIS face into the bowl of his hands. Roman thought he might either break down and sob or leap up and rake his fingers down the wallpaper. Which would it be? He was feeling oddly disconnected. Maybe this was the way a shrink felt, listening to the woes of a client from behind a clear shield of therapeutic immunity.

With a thick, jerky movement, T.J. Morson struck his hands together.

"I don't even smoke," he said as though appealing to Roman, "I don't drink. But . . ." Again he waved at the lights and bells outside the door. "I think, I know, I had the vision or whatever, that because it was my birthday I could turn it all around if I had just, say, a couple hundred. And I knew where to get it. So today after Zola went to work and Kayla was at school, I sneaked back to the house and I searched Kayla's room. She has this little passbook savings account with me as her cosigner. But where does she keep the passbook? So I dug through the stuff in her drawers, her closets. Can you imagine this?"

Roman's mouth opened. *Better than you know*, he thought. But Morson went on quickly, "I found her secret things. They were under the bed, in this cigar box she had covered on top with a piece of paper. You wouldn't believe this knowing how sweet Kayla is, what a good girl. The box was labeled with a purple marker 'Fuck with Kayla and You Die.' Here she's a good little student, all A's or B's, never given anybody whatsoever any trouble in her life before. So this tough little message . . . I mean . . ."

Morson stopped and drank some coffee.

"It got to you," said Roman.

"Yeah," said Morson. "Anyway, I took the passbook. Withdrew two hundred and eighteen dollars worth of babysitting money."

Roman nodded, poured another coffee for himself and stirred in three creamers. And yet, he thought. *Here is a man for whom people will give a surprise party.* Roman tapped the sugar packets, drank the rest of the coffee, put the money down on top of the check.

"I have to get out of here," he said to Morson, who stared at him for a moment, then widened his eyes and broke the look off with a cunning little grin.

T.J. Morson followed Roman out the door of the café. On the way past the banks of moving lights and bells and trilling knockers, he said, "C'mon. I hit, we'll split."

Roman kept walking. Morson grabbed the sleeve of his jacket. "Please," he said. Roman started at the sight of him. Morson's eyes were rolled back so the whites showed. His lips were drawn away from his gums in a guilty snarl. Roman felt in his pocket, flipped out a quarter. Morson opened the hand that held the car keys. Roman took the keys and gave the quarter to Morson, who played it. The two men watched the rolling tabs of symbols spin over and over, whirling, clicking into place in a disparate row.

"Okay, you satisfied?" said Roman.

Morson wiped his hands slowly on his hips and then followed Roman out the doors, across the gleaming, wet parking lot, over to the Cherokee. Roman still had the keys. He opened the doors and got into the driver's side. Passive, concentrating on something invisible just before him, Morson got into the passenger's seat and shut his eyes. But suddenly, as Roman pulled out of the parking space onto the highway, Morson mumbled, "Thanks anyway," and opened his door to jump out. Roman managed to hook his hand in the collar of Morson's slippery jacket, and as he brought the car to a halt on the shoulder, he yanked the man back toward him with such surprising force that Morson's face smashed into the side of the steering wheel. There was an instant and surprising amount of blood.

"Don't worry," said Morson, his nose behind his hands, "I get these things real bad." There was a girl's striped knit stocking cap in his door's side pocket. Morson grabbed it and put it to his face. Then he said, "Look, I'll just go clean up." He jumped out the door with the cap on his face, and was gone.

Roman pulled ahead about thirty feet into a blind driveway and shut off the engine. He found the lever next to the seat that dropped it backward a few inches. He rested. A peaceful energy flowed through him. He nearly slept. Fifteen minutes, then half an hour passed. Traffic flowed by, snarled behind him, flowed again. A few people crossed before him at the far edge of an overflow lot. They swiftly entered their cars and drove away. Roman dozed another ten minutes and then he suddenly snapped to. He started the car and drove off.

As he pulled back onto the highway a screeching ambulance barreled past. The casino was filled with senior citizens and Roman imagined a whole scenario—a big payout, an old man elated, then clutching at his heart. This fantasy gave him the idea, as he drove toward Morson's house, of something he could say to get Morson off the hook. It wasn't that he liked Morson, but his friends were so eager, so well-meaning.

ROMAN ARRIVED AT the house and parked in the driveway—still empty in order to fool Morson into thinking that the house was deserted. Yet all the lights were on. The little house was blazing. Roman walked up the steps and then tentatively eased the door open and poked his head around the side. He nearly jumped back out. All of the people he'd met before were standing or sitting at attention in the living room. They returned his look with identical stares.

"We know already," said the terse old lady who'd been drinking strawberry wine coolers. "He had his ID right on him, phone number. Kyle took Zola to the emergency room. Zola just called two seconds ago."

"Come on in," said Buzz. "Take a load off. I'll get you a beer. In fact," he said, "let's eat. It's some kind of custom that we all should eat together at a time like this."

• • •

ROMAN SAT DOWN on one end of the couch, leaned back into a stiff pillow. He looked down at his knees, then accepted a bowl of bean soup when it appeared in his line of vision. The bowl was warm and pleasant in his hands.

"They told Zola that he'd crossed the casino's main intersection, running. What is that, two lanes? Not so far, really."

"Four lanes," said Roman.

"Oh," said someone, "then."

The phone rang. Buzz picked up and listened. "Okay," he said. He took a deep breath before he put the phone down. Then he frowned at the phone before he spoke, addressing everyone. "Zola said he was not quite DOA," said Buzz, "but next thing to it. There just wasn't a thing they could do."

There was silence. Eventually, things picked up again. Soon everyone had bowls of soup, and bread, and were busily arranging themselves, patting napkins onto their knees, balancing coffee cups, offering butter around the group.

"We shouldn't eat the cake."

"I agree," said Willa. "We should have his cake at the funeral dinner."

"Are you going to go?" She addressed Roman.

He looked at her. "It can't be true!"

Willa apologized. "I've never been much for denial. I go straight to acceptance. That's just me."

"You don't need to think that far ahead," said Buzz. He touched Roman's arm. "In fact, don't think ahead at all." Buzz put down his bowl of soup and sank forward, elbows on his knees. He cupped his hands over his head and leaned over like someone about to be sick. He stayed that way, motionless. Willa put her hand on his back and patted him with slow, regular beats. She looked over at Roman.

"Go on, eat your soup," she whispered. "It's okay."

Roman placed a spoonful of the soup in his mouth. A moment passed before he realized that the taste was unusually good. Something gave depth to the taste. Roman looked at Buzz, still hunched over. His specialty, he remembered. Maybe Buzz simmered his beans with garlic, or wine, or some kind of herb. Maybe it was the sorrow, or the strangeness. Perhaps Buzz had added a few drops from a vial of Liquid Smoke. Then again a ham bone. Or the fact that these beans were all different types. Roman finished the bowl and put it down.

"You want another?" said Willa.

"It's good," Roman nodded.

She got up to refill the bowl and Roman took over patting Buzz on the back, slow and regular, two or three pats to each of his sighing breaths. He kept feeling the wrench when he'd pulled Morson toward him, in the car, the way Morson had twisted, striking the bridge of his nose. There was the weight of Morson off balance, in his arms, the smell of his hair tonic, aftershave, and the smoke of the casino and the coffee on his breath.

NOW HERE HE was eating Morson's bean soup with Morson's friends and no doubt in two or three days he would be tasting Morson's cake. Roman shut his eyes. His thoughts flickered.

"I'll be right back."

He set the beer down, got up, walked down the hall just like an old friend who knew the place. He opened the door to Kayla's room, walked in, shut the door behind him and knelt on the floor beside her bed. Reaching underneath, he groped for and found the box that he could see, once he turned on her little homework lamp, was indeed labeled "Fuck with Kayla and You Die." He handled it carefully. *You shouldn't have fucked with Kayla.* Psychic time bomb for the girl, though, wasn't it? Morson had replaced her little passbook. Roman flipped to the last page, then tore out a deposit slip. Same bank as his. Anyone could make a transfer, he supposed. He put the passbook back, lay the cigar box on the floor and slid it back underneath the bed. He walked to the living room, passed behind an intense discussion of who should go now to the hospital, who was needed, what arrangements. In the kitchen, he paused at the sink for a drink of warmish, chemical-tasting suburb water. He set the keys to the Cherokee on the counter. Then slipped out the back door.

# The Crest

JACK'S HANDS WERE deep in the oiled workings of his uncle's planting attachment, a piece of farm equipment they were fixing together, as they always fixed things, with bread ties and duct tape and spit and sometimes the right bolt or screw. It was August, not the dog days of heat, but clear and cool. Jack was now on his third wife and although he was losing Candice—at that very moment probably, she was with a lawyer, his lawyer, he didn't tend to think about her at all. *She thinks enough about herself for the two of us,* he'd told his uncle Chuck, weary. Soon, she'd be gone. He couldn't seem to keep a woman.

"The hell!" Chuck delicately fiddled with some flattened threads he'd forced. "I don't think this is gonna work."

The two men were lying on purple plastic toboggans from Kmart, sliding themselves up and down underneath the bellies of various machines in a hot orange quonset garage. Sweat and grease coated Jack's neck, plus a dusting of grit, but it all felt good. He had always liked the fixing and the tinkering, but not the winter paperwork, the sowing, frantic harvesting, the dependence on weather. He hadn't liked the money, either. Lousy once the payments on the big equipment were made. Farming made him think of getting away from it. He thought he should return to the construction site. Just wanted to see his uncle. As usual he'd come to visit and got caught up in a small endless job the way he always did with Chuck.

Chuck stared at him with a pulled-long expression, but then sighed and said so long. *Get the hell out of here. Go play trucks.* Jack wanted to tell him that moment, right there, about the development and the land, but he just couldn't. A few years back when dirt was still cheap and Chuck had got in over his means, Jack had bought out his quarter section just west of Fargo. He'd leased it back, and Chuck Mauser had put all that acreage into flowers. Sunflowers. They were now in bloom. Tomorrow, Jack would draw his first payment on the line of credit he'd been finessing and politicking and begging after for so many years. The bank had come through. He would have to tell Chuck that those fields would soon be a subdivision—a good one, *unique and high quality*, he thought of saying, as though that would matter.

THE NEXT MORNING, early, Jack accepted the bank check, stiff and clean in its plain white envelope. He pinched it in his fingers, lifted it to his face, and inhaled the sharp odor of the ink and paper. But then— and this offhand decision was the one that affected his life for the next two years—he did not deposit the check. No, instead of securing it immediately, Jack kept the envelope in his hands and walked out the doors of heavy glass and polished steel. He went to his car. He put the envelope on the dashboard and laid his fingers on the cool paper.

JACK DROVE BACK out to Chuck's place with the white rectangle of the envelope reflecting into the windshield. As he drove along, houses popping up to either side, new ones, his beliefs were easy, his thoughts simple: *I am the luckiest of lucky sons of bitches.* He had formed an idea, a plan, and he saw now that it was going to work. Jack Mauser was going to put something big into operation.

MAUSER & MAUSER, Construction. Jack twice. He had doubled his name because he thought it looked more stable, as though there were generations involved. But there was no other Mauser, no partner, just him. Over the years, he had built up the cash, crews, and equipment, by himself, from nothing, from a secondhand Cat and a couple of boys who couldn't get their high school diplomas. He'd had luck, but his main secret was he worked everybody just as brutally as he worked himself. Plus, he could crawl and connive with the best and worst. Jack had patched together his own company by scraping money off the cash edifice, the limestone façades of banks. He knew how to wear a suit jacket and a tie, how to shake hands and look a banker in the eye and promise on a schedule he had no hope of meeting, but did anyway, or almost, by killing his crews. And the very last secret of his success—he always paid his best subcontractors just enough of what he owed to keep them working for him on the next job. Keep them hooked in, keep them working alongside him, but never let them get too far away. He never paid anyone entirely, never evened up his accounts. Contractors didn't do that sort of thing, Jack's thought was, while they were alive at least. He kept a keen balance of debt and walked the knife's edge. Of course, he was running low now. Some, the best, wouldn't work with him. Still there were always others to take their places, always would be.

Jack had barged through doors of black glass, through the tinted lobbies, over wheat rich carpet, over sugar-beet wealth and desks of polished oak bought off the interest on loans to sunflower farmers like Chuck. He went in with the grit of digging septic systems under his nails and he came out, time after time, with that dirt turned miraculously paper crisp and green. Every day was a ground-floor day for Jack. The local boom was just beginning. There was an interstate to build. Local crews got hired on by the government. Jack didn't bid too high and didn't bid too low, and he held where proper, a knack he had learned at the keno tables.

All that hustling, and now he had this. Too much, almost. In the middle of his biggest road construction project to date, a highway bypass, his loan came through. Huge draw, first draw on the biggest sum of money he'd ever landed. The check. More zeros in a string than he'd ever seen. *And here he was*, Jack faltered. *Here I am.* He was about to think *in Fargo*, but instead he thought an *Indian*. That part of his background was like a secret joke he had on everyone. His crews. His banker. Asshole clients. Even his own wives. He'd thought, strangely sometimes, when walking through those bank lobby doors, *the hell with all of you. Your doors would swing the other way if you knew who I was!* But who did? He was a mixed-blood with dark eyes and dark hair and a big father and a crazy mother. He never thought of her. Or him, either. Both eaten up by time.

Jack turned down a dirt road between two of his fields, parked, opened the car's windows, and let in the day of perfect sunflowers. Their leaves brushed in the still air, dollar bills in a vault of blue sky. Their fat chock-full faces, surrounded by petals, reminded Jack of legions of rich women in fancy hats. He sank back in the warm seat, let the sun shine hard, stretched, and yawned until his nerves hummed. Cannons popped, set to go off on small timers so the ravenous swirls of blackbirds wouldn't land. Chuck Mauser had tied balloons to his fences, too, and painted them with eyes to look like owls. The fields looked jolly, circus bright, and of course the blackbirds weren't the least afraid. Jack could hear them pecking, flapping, talking, feeding noisily and full of joy.

Chuck Mauser happened by, stopped his truck when he saw Jack. Jack stepped out of the car, walked with his uncle into the field, and then the two men stood together moving clods of dirt back and forth with the toes of their boots. Jack was uncomfortable. His face burned. There was a buzzing in his ears. He thought about getting underneath the seeder again, trying to fix that fuel pump in the old John Deere or goof with the new Steiger, figure it out a little, but more than that he wanted a drink. So Jack and his uncle talked about the crop, the value, weather, and then Jack told Chuck that his first draw was through, showed him the check.

Chuck did not look pleased. He did not in fact look at Jack at all. He just stared over the bright blank flowers. Jack hadn't thought exactly what his good fortune meant for his uncle, but now he grew irritated at Chuck's lack of interest. The truth was, Chuck Mauser only had those fields on a lease which was up four months ago. Chuck knew and had agreed on what was coming. Naturally, Jack intended to let him work the fields until he broke ground next month. A farmer had to obtain his yield, of course. But those fields were the first open land past the last mall, between the DollarSave and Nowhere. Any fool could have figured.

Jack's uncle narrowed his gaze and screwed his mouth sour, scratched his chin. He had a bad shave, all nicked. But he had the guts to bring up the subject.

"So, you're putting in what, a new development?"

Jack nodded. Chuck nodded. The two men stood at the edge of the field nodding with the nodding heads of sunflowers. They were posed in a vast surround of serene and unthinking agreement, but each harbored different thoughts. The farmer looked keenly into his own distance and said:

"These are good fields. Rich dirt. Too bad."

Jack took a step back, swayed, put his thumbs in his belt.

"Location, location, location," he mumbled.

Looking down at the ground, they both saw money. But Chuck thought of rain, too. He looked up the way a farmer looks into the sky—not to see the weekend ahead but to see his whole future. Just a slow rain, a soaking rain, a careful rain, no hail. Please no hail to beat the flowers flat. All right? Just water. Jack thought of water, too. Well water, for instance. However, it did not occur to Jack that just to drill his wells through that lush crust of black dirt, to suck the sinking aquifer into his faucets and underground sprinkling systems and to pipe it through his showerheads and into his dishwashers, was a temporary luxury that would last only as long as the water down there did. Water dries up. Topsoil blows off. Trees topple. Land lasts, but of the two only the farmer knew how easily it can turn against you. Since the Ojibwe part of Jack was inaccessible, he was a German with a trapdoor in his soul, an inner life still hidden to him. Both men saw money when they looked at land. It was just that they saw the fields delivering the wealth in different ways. As dead, as alive, as more and as less autonomous or powerful.

"You'll get a lot of money from this crop," Jack went on, "it's a bumper. You'll buy a big damn house right at the end of this cul-de-sac." He smashed his foot against a chunk of topsoil. "We'll build it here. Every one of your grandkids will have their own room. Your wife will have a dream kitchen."

"I don't have a wife," Chuck reminded Jack. "Your aunt won't come back. Women ditch us."

There was an underlying implication. *They ditch us the way you ditched me, Jack.* But Jack felt no guilt toward his uncle. Only irritation. He never said he'd be a dirt farmer, had he? Never so much as hinted!

"Your grandkids will cook, then," Jack laughed, shrugging off Chuck's malice and loss. "We'll make everything the right height, their bathrooms, the dish sink, whatever, so they won't have to always stand on stools."

"Kids grow," Chuck said.

"Bless 'em," Jack agreed, but there was a note in his voice, a mean little edge, and Chuck stopped talking, shifted nervously. They stood in silence and then Chuck Mauser, the dirt farmer, gathered himself. His voice grated, almost shaking in low rage at the sky, at the horizon, at the creeping façades of the edge of Fargo.

"The more you fill it up the emptier it gets."

Jack stepped back another foot or so.

"People have to live somewhere," Jack said, and he managed to keep his voice mild enough, but inside he was setting to boil. He and his uncle were too much alike, maybe. Candice, deep into the pop psychology she used on her patients, had counseled Jack to memorize a trick that would help him keep his temper when he was in that no-man's-land between feeling normal and letting go. She told Jack to mentally image a wire cage, to visualize himself putting up the chain-link, and then to get right inside the damn thing like an animal. She told him that he could pace inside the cage, he could go wild, he could let off his steam as though he had just been captured in a jungle. The only thing was he had to stay in the cage, not jump the fence, not ever let himself out.

Jack was not ready to do that. He got into his car, backed out and drove away without saying good-bye. His stomach was turning over with the frustration of it all, because he wanted to celebrate, to raise the roof with someone, not deal with a farmer's problems, a farm boy's mistakes. He tried to step back, unheat, look at life through his uncle's glasses. The man probably needed those fields to get himself over the edge, he probably felt like shit when he thought of a new house that he never could afford in this life anyway, in this world, and Jack had pushed it in his face. He didn't look back. He drove to town and wished he could get Candy and go to their favorite bar, which was called The Library, but Candy had probably by now left the lawyer's office and was in a real library. She was back in school taking another class on some new dental technique that she said would stop pain with little electric jolts.

*I want some of those*, thought Jack, *or maybe that drink*.

Jack drove past the bar, then doubled back, pulled into the lot, went in, and sat down. The room was dim and calm, the talk quiet. No music played, no pool balls clicked, the television was a muted natter. It was only eleven o'clock.

He ordered and drank two beers. Ate a hamburger. Two beers more. He considered what next—go back to the office, the bank, or the current work site. There was plenty of work pending, pressure, hordes of details, but he felt that this day should be experienced differently, out of time, out of his regular life's routine. The more he thought about it in the quiet of the morning tavern the more it seemed unfair. He recalled the hard work he'd done and anticipated all of the work that was in store, and with that in mind he felt righteous about enjoying the zeros on the first draw check he held against his chest within his inside pocket. He thought of driving to the lakes, fishing, eating out, taking simple enjoyment in the cash, the fat roll he'd taken out of his account against the big deposit he would feed it later on.

"I should I should," he muttered to himself, tapping the ashtray with the plastic rapier that had held his hamburger together. "I should go back to work," he said decisively, and then instead, as the waitress approached, he ordered his fifth beer.

The fifth was the one that always sent Jack. He weighed 210. He could handle four and then he'd skate in the sky. He promised, as he poured the Blue Ribbon, that this was his last little gesture.

ONE AFTERNOON PASSED. An evening. He slept. He woke. Needed a jump start. Raw egg in a glass of cold Pilsener. More of latter. Morning flowed into another afternoon. A night. The winnowing sky, wild dark and some girl, too young. A long trip to South Dakota. He was as good as divorced. Morning fell. Again the need clamped down but Jack was broke and stank and couldn't find his check.

He decided to go home.

HE'D HAD HIS car keys all along, but couldn't recall where the car was parked. Now he walked over to The Library lot to see if it was there. It was. Plus Candy, sitting in the front seat, reading a book. She had figured Jack would have to come back there before he came home.

Jack leaned over beside her, at the open window.

"I'm sorry," he said.

She waved his breath away.

"Get in."

"Where are you going?" he asked. His voice was so small, so unnoticeable, so guilty, that she was able to brush it away the same as she had his apology.

"I'm driving you out to the construction site," she said. "Your stuff is already out there in the accounts trailer."

"Oh come on, Candy," he was hurting. "It was just a onetime thing." Or was it? He was lost, could not remember.

She turned on him, her face fierce.

"So is this," she answered. "This is the one time I'm getting rid of you."

He needed her right now, addled and in awe of his stupidity, but still he could understand the reasoning. Her self-assurance suddenly made him desperate.

"Tell me, just tell me! I'd do anything for you, baby!"

For some reason this just made her laugh, and her laugh was surprising, free, as though she enjoyed his wit. She hummed a little tune to herself, and it occurred to Jack to tell her it bothered him, to stop, but he didn't. He fantasized that if he kept his mouth shut she'd turn the car around and bring him home, make some lunch. She pulled up into the construction yard. Her car was already parked there alongside the bulldozer and a couple of tractors, so he guessed she had a friend in on this scheme. He felt it coming on then, as she indicated with a neutral wave that he should go. He felt the hot place in his stomach, the empty place that sent the anger up his arms like cold jelly, the rage into his head. The sudden feeling was so blinding and futile that it scared even Jack. He tried to stop it from happening, and he put himself into the cage like Candy herself had always advised. As soon as he was in the wire enclosure, in his mind, Candy walked away and got into her car. Before he could jump out of the cage and catch her, he was alone in the dirt lot. Her car was already raising dust on the road to town.

And she took his car keys. Maybe by mistake, but they weren't there in the ignition.

He stumbled out of the car, wheeled around, went looking in the windows of the other cars, the equipment, finally climbed up on the bulldozer. He was in luck. The silver key was in the ignition, he turned it, started the thing up and went bouncing after Candy at full throttle thinking he would catch her somehow, cut her off before she took the turn to town. He would yell at her, reason with her, weep, pull his hair, and throw himself down at her feet or beneath the black treads of the dozer. He'd humble himself and start all over just as soon as he stopped being mad, which he was as he moved, as the thing got going. It was as though the power of the machine, the throb and heft of it, the things he could do with a lever and a switch, were part of his anger then.

It got too big for him, too big for the wire net he put up to contain it, too big for anything. It roared over him and he grappled with it weakly for one moment and then he was out of the cage, bigger than life, rattling iron on iron down the road with his blade in the air and looking for he didn't know what, until he saw it—fields.

His fields. The flowers looked at Jack, all fat and frowsy, full of light.

"Harvest time," he shouted, sweeping in with the blade lowered, and he kept on shouting, he didn't know what, as he cleared swathe after swathe, as the air above him filled with swirling petals and excited birds, as the seeds rang down on the hot metal, as the seeds poured down his neck and shirt, as the heads of sunflowers bounced off the

fenders and rolled under the cleated treads and the dust flew everywhere, a great cloud that hung around him in the air of a cool and dry
September.

*I'm not a truly destructive man. I've built about anything that you could
name. You look around Fargo—banks, half the hospital complex, the highway, Vistawood Views, the nursing home, most of the mall, house upon
house—you'll see it's set up and hooked in and put there to stay by Jack
Mauser. I do things from plans. I make them real. I could do it for myself
if I could get a guy that could design me. But since that's not possible, I've
always relied on women. Somewhere inside I think—they're women, they
should know. Like if they make kids then by god they should be able to make
me too.*

*And that's how trouble starts—you plant all your hopes in another heart.*

JACK STRIPPED MOST of a field down before that cold strength stopped
flowing through his arms. He was breathing hard and his eyes were
fixed upon the gauges and dials of the machine's control panel. He
couldn't hear anything around him, anything outside himself, and then
gradually his heart slowed and the adrenaline that had flooded him
turned so mellow he lay back in his seat limp with self pity. He surveyed
the crushed welter of stalks and plants on which the birds were already
lighting with starved cries. In the distance, he could see people, his construction crew, coming at him. Candy's car wasn't in sight.

The heat of noon lifted off the fields like a gleaming veil. He'd
always intended to build the best house in the whole development for
Candice. She wouldn't want one, now, he thought. But as he sat there,
he saw them rising anyway. He saw stone trim with clerestory windows, the Gothic look, or colonial homes with shutters, plantationlike
spreads with columns to either side of the front door. He would set
the mailboxes into little brick hutches that could not be knocked over
by a teenager with a baseball bat. He would sod in big lawns, plant
seven-year-old maples. The garages would be double, triple, some with
arches, and all would open automatically to accept their owners. Ex-
ecutives would buy these places, school principals, the owners of local

businesses, wealthy farmers who wanted a town home in the winter. He would name the place The Crest. Just The Crest. Not Crest Park, Crest Acres, Crest Ridge, Crest Wood, or Crest Go Fuck Yourself. His development would speak class through simplicity, like it just meant the top of something, the place we all want to get.

# Best Western

I WAS A straight-A high school English student working my way through community college when I ditched it all and ran away with Ricky Zachs, the lead tenor in the Flathead Valley choir. My voice was adequate, that's all, but I was a fair piano accompanist. Ricky and I formed a duo, the Midnite Specials, and through an agency we booked ourselves to play hotel lounges, wedding dances, and live-music bars from Oregon to the sad, black, forest towns of upper peninsula Michigan. I was a clear alto. My voice had no range, no upstairs, but I knew just how to dress for the spotlight and for my weight. I wore zircons on my fingers so my hands, on the keyboard, glittered. Home Ec had taught me where to vertical-stripe and where to drape, showed me accent points, the tricks of choosing jewelry pieces to draw attention toward good anatomical features and divert the eye from others. I was the visual asset, but Ricky's voice carried us. An Irish lilt, a touch of Hungarian soul, even moments of clear falsetto, it had everything, the whole of Europe I used to think, a world about which Ricky didn't know any more than I did, except he was it, a blend that gave him a haunted, wavy-haired look. When he sang "Volare," he was passionate. At the same time he was darkly wholesome with his big square face and preacher-clean smile.

I had always been the kind of girl that people called attractive, never pretty; the kind who worked for every bit of notice that she got, who never took appreciation for granted. I was the kind of girl who'd go on a date that consisted of six rounds of miniature golf. I fell in love all the time. I couldn't help it. Movie stars, rock stars, even faces in commercials. Football captains, all the assistant coaches, civics teachers, then professors. I nursed unrequited affection until Ricky Zachs. He'd been one of those I'd worshipped from afar, not that he was always handsome.

The thing about Ricky was he had an ugly childhood. All through grade school he was the one the others herded out, the skinny boy who'd give up without a fight, cry, tattle, eat dirt. Then he blossomed into a hunk. In eighth grade, he joined the football team and paid people back. He had no friends exactly, yet everyone was awed by him. By the time we were out of high school, he'd run the gamut of available girlfriends down to the little swaybacked sophomores. He was at loose ends after graduation, working resort clubs here and there, when he noticed my thick blond hair.

"How come we never got together back in high school?" he wondered. "Where were you?"

I was about the only girl left he'd *never* taken on a date, but I said nothing. I never told him how I'd watched him, just wishing. It was luck. I was the last one left and maybe that helped. He talked of eloping, not putting up with church and community bullshit, a wedding, all that. And though I'd already planned a Princess Di dress in white satin, with a tiny sophisticated diamond of a hat and a long lace train, I figured running off might be my best chance to keep him. So we got married in Vermillion, South Dakota, by a justice of the peace with thongs on her feet, whose house smelled of just-canned pickles.

REQUITED FOR THE first time, I threw sparks. I felt it. When I left home we hid out for a month at the Garden Court in Eugene, where Ricky had gone to college. We used my savings, holed up in a room with a narrow balcony and pictures of pots of flowers on the rough tan walls. The double glass-door windows looked out on a parking lot. We didn't care. One afternoon we got in, exhausted, from a live audition, and sitting in our twin captain's chairs, we poured ourselves iced

Cokes to cool down. We were silent. Actually, the day had not gone well. In Ricky's casual refusal to meet my eyes I thought I could detect repressed blame. I'd hit a few bad notes. He'd had to sing over my mistakes. He stared moodily down at the side of the fish restaurant next door. Suddenly, around the corner, came a young long-legged blond girl in shorts, tanned and tall, carrying a violin case in one hand, a large soft drink in the other.

"That's sweet," said Ricky. I could tell he was wondering if she would practice. He was mortally sensitive to noise.

Behind her, a boy, also carrying a violin, popped over a hedge. Then a dozen, some with cellos, and then more girls with all sorts of instruments in cases of molded leather. French horns, trumpets, tubas, and most ominous of all, drums.

"It must be some sort of convention," Ricky said uneasily. We watched as they came toward us across the lot, laughing, swaggering, shrieking, showing off for one another. They streamed toward the Garden Court. We heard them on the stairs. They plunged up, down, thundered. In their rooms. Doors slamming. Out of their rooms. Doors again.

"No, no," Ricky's voice rose, an edge to it, hysterical. "I *need my sleep.*"

Sleep was not mere routine to Ricky but something much more vital and elusive. I'd never thought much about sleep before I shared it with him. Love was the thing he took for granted, adoration. Sleep was the thing he had to court. At the desk, he had asked for the quietest room. Walking into it he put the bags down and turned his face intently, from side to side, checking for the roar of traffic, cries of pleasure from the outdoor pool, thumps overhead, or the whine of television from next door. Even in the deepest quiet of the night, however, it is true that sleep for him was an attainment.

I sensed him beside me those first weeks, till I got used to it. He'd hum to himself a little, trying out new arrangements in his head, or replay the day's tensions, the fights he often had with bar managers, arguments that I smoothed over. As I dropped off, I'd feel him flexing and relaxing each part of his body in a kind of yoga exercise that he had learned from Tarzan books. Sometimes he screwed in foam ear stops and some mornings, when I woke, I saw that he'd won his battle only by donning a black silk eye mask. He claimed that lack of sleep destroyed the timbre of his voice, and whether that was true or not, it sure wrecked his disposition. I began, very early on, to try and ensure a full eight hours. And so that afternoon in Eugene, when he turned to me, his sleek brows wild, his mouth stuck half open, I was already thinking.

As always, we were in the No Smoking wing. He hated smoke. Breathing cigarette smoke, he said, was our only occupational hazard.

"Let's move to a smoking room," I said. "They're teens. They're not supposed to smoke, right?"

I could see him weighing the noxious alternative. He gave in and that night, in the blessed and stale-odored quiet, his nerves soothed by the white noise of a blank station on the radio, Ricky fell asleep in my arms. It was such a rare thing, sleep overcoming him with his neck crooked at an uncomfortable angle, that I didn't dare move although his head on my chest was a weight I had to lift with every breath.

THAT NIGHT AT the Garden Court was a high point. I should have known we were heading for a low. The only nature I got to see in those days of marriage was landscaping. It comes back to me so clear sometimes. Moments. Places. There we were at the Knight's Inn, Detroit. I was looking at the boulevard, at the plantings around the parking lot and pool, at the way the flat yew bushes grew between the clumps of candy-striped petunias and yellow snapdragons. I was looking at the soft shapes of pines, when I suddenly wanted so badly to just lie down. It was midday, the parking lot quiet, but Ricky was in our room, in the bed underneath the crossed spears on the wall. He was catching up on sleep. I needed sleep, too, but I didn't dare go back in the room for fear of waking him.

The pines were six feet tall, maybe more. Their lowest branches touched, forming caves. The cedar bark and shredded wood spread

across the ground beneath looked springy and cool. It looked so inviting that I decided, *why not?* I could choose a lawn chair beside the
pool and fall asleep in it. No one would bother me. Why not the little
shadow, the cave underneath a tree? I stepped carefully around the
bright flowers, and I stretched out right there. And it *was* comfortable.
Outside the greenery, it didn't seem there was a breeze at all. Under the
tree, though, I felt the sigh of needles, heard the singing of some tiny
unfamiliar insect, native to Detroit I guess. There could have been a
bird, a sparrow or something. There was the smell of earth, the thick
white odor of petunias. I closed my eyes.

In my bones, as I lay there, I felt the traffic beyond the boulevard,
the shudder of life. Voices passed, but I felt safe. All around me, leaves
ticked and flowers hummed and took in light. The world was drunk
with light. I was sliding deep into the dark. Underneath the chipped
bark, below the plastic set down so the weeds could not poke through,
under the layer of broken glass and topsoil and clay gumbo, I pictured a
darkness so total it was a fabric of air.

I fell heavily asleep and did not wake up until the sprinklers came
on and soaked the ground. Then, as I stumbled out, back into normal
life, I realized that Ricky would have been absolutely furious if he had
seen me, and I was glad he had not. It didn't occur to me how strange
it was that I was sleeping outdoors, while inside the motel my husband
had two queen-size beds to himself, with royal blue velveteen spreads
on them.

No, the situation did not strike me as odd at all. It had become normal for me to guard Ricky from the world.

The facts only began to clarify in Minneapolis–St. Paul, at the
Thunderbird. I do believe that that motel is cursed by Indians. There's
a thirty-foot chief constructed out of fiberglass in front. That's for start-
ers. Inside, the place is littered with designs. The rubber mats to wipe
your feet on, the carpets, the cocktail napkins, all full of squares and
diamonds, Indian-looking. Strange. There were a bunch of tired plaster
Indians dressed up, enclosed in glass. The animals these people lived
off were stuffed and hiding in the rafters, poised to leap down and attack. Foxes, wolves, raccoons, squirrels, and wild goats. The night we

played at the Thunderbird, the lounge was full of families bumped off a canceled Northwest flight. You can imagine the mood they were in already. Our show did nothing but give them a target, a focus for their irritations.

It was wild, though, the things Ricky tried. He had always told me that patter with the audience was his strong suit. He started out with a few remarks, talking about his family. "My uncle was a deep-sea diver, but he was too polite to last. Met a mermaid and tipped his hat to her. I had an aunt, too, an old maid. She let the dust accumulate beneath the bed. How come? She heard man is made of dust." He got to me, his wife. "She wouldn't kiss me last night. Said, 'Honey, my lips are chapped.' 'Well,' I said, 'one more chap won't hurt 'em!'

"You people come here in an airplane? I hate 'em. I stay on terra firma. The firma the grounda the lessa the terra . . .

"Now, seriously, folks . . ."

Soon after that, we swung into "Raindrops Keep Fallin' on My Head," "Let's Fall in Love," and "I Fall to Pieces." Then Ricky asked the crowd if there were any requests.

"Harmonize," a voice called from a back booth. There was laughter. Ricky shot me a foul look and retorted, "You want to hum a few bars?"

Then it was like we had started some kind of trend, or maybe our airline passengers had got a fright that day and, you know, the way you wake up in the morning and a song is going in your head and you realize it is a comment on your life, they asked for "Falling Rain," "I Fall to Pieces" again, "When Autumn Leaves Start to Fall." We kept singing for them, taking requests for Falling numbers. I think the emphasis on getting dashed to the ground set some kind of tone. Morbid. And when we sat down to take our break a weird thing happened. Of course, Ricky hadn't slept well and I was walking on pins anyway, but he looked at me, all critical.

"Your lipstick's off-center," he said.

"Oh?" I had my purse. I took out a little lipstick tube with a mirror attached. I looked at my lips, applied a touch-up.

"Okay now?" I asked.

But he didn't say yes. He looked over my head, studying a stuffed hawk, and spoke in a dreamy voice. "It's your mouth, to be honest, your mouth is set crooked on your face."

I was astonished, then hollow with hurt.

"Oh?" I said. "Oh, really? Is it?"

Ricky tipped the strong line of his jaw away from me.

"Goes with the rest." He grabbed my arm, hauled me up. I had no time to react, or maybe I was numb. Before I even took in his remark properly, I was in front of the crowd drawing out the opening to "Snowbird." And then, that night, after we had played until the lounge closed and we went upstairs to bed, after I hung up our clothes, turned the covers down, and loosened the tight, clean sheets, Ricky slid in and closed his eyes to block out my face. I turned the lights off. The night, the air, all was still and very black around us. The room's drapes shut out the lights from the parking lot. From time to time, we heard other people in the outside hallway. Doors closed with hollow, watery booms. Voices dropped like stones into the hush.

"Please," I said. I held my breath as he turned in his slumber.

The silence deepened. I didn't dare speak or make any noise at all. Even the sound of my breathing, the ragged need of it, even the rustle of the bed sheets, seemed much too loud.

SINCE THE DAY I turned thirteen and my mother let me put on makeup, I have never begun my morning without the ritual of eyeliner, mascara, blush, and lipstick. The next morning was a first. I forgot about it, didn't even check my face and hair in the mirror. Ricky was downstairs, eating breakfast. He must have slept real good, that meant. After long sleeps he always ordered the specials that included minute steaks, hash browns, three eggs instead of two.

After a good night's sleep, after making love, I'd usually go downstairs fresh and put together, perfect as I could make myself. Ricky and I would sit across the table from each other. Everything around us would seem interesting and intense. We'd read our place mats out loud, flip through the packets of sugar. Even the words on the menu would make us laugh. But that morning, as I stood in the doorway by the

Please Wait to Be Seated sign, I caught sight of Ricky from behind. He sat alone at the counter. Clearly, he did not want company. His back was hunched over his food and his elbows were moving, up and down, up and down, pumping at his work. He ate like a mechanical horse, everything about him given over to the one task.

I turned and walked out. Drumbeats, a wailing kind of faraway sound, Indian-theme music came from the loudspeakers. It was a music so foreign to me that I could not tell whether it was meant to be sad, happy, or something more complicated. I sat down in the lobby, next to a shallow pool laid with blue tiles. Under the ripple of the spotlighted water, coins glinted, a hundred of them, two hundred, each one representing a person's wish. It was just me and a hundred dollars' worth of small desires. I couldn't stand my thoughts. I took out a quarter. I wanted to get my wish all right.

"I hope lightning strikes and burns this place down," I said.

When I threw in my coin the ripple from the little splash spread and continued, moving outward, widening all day.

I'D SEEN RICKY mad. In his anger once, he'd loomed toward me and I was afraid that he was going to hit me, but his hands stayed at his sides. I never thought he would hurt me, not really. But I was wrong. We stopped on the way to Billings, in one of those wayside parks. I made Ricky a sandwich of meat, cheese, and bread. I was cutting it in half with a little paring knife I'd bought when Ricky came up behind me and grabbed my arm and twisted it so the knife went springing across the table, cartwheeled off onto its point.

I heard myself yell, scream really, and I watched the knife as it fell. I watched very closely because the pain in my arm, the wrench, electrified me. The wooden boards stood out in focus. The texture of the bread.

"Surprise!" said Ricky, letting go. "I read your mind just now."

I turned, cradling my elbow.

"Wha'dya mean?"

"Wha'dya mean?" He mimicked a high-pitched whine. I had never been struck, hurt, or touched wrong before. I was like a baby. I could not connect Ricky with the wrench of pain I felt. At the next table over a woman watched us. She looked shocked, her mouth open to say something, so I shrugged at her and shook my head. I was first and foremost terribly embarrassed for Ricky Zachs. But he just bit into his sandwich, chewed, and then that big clean football captain smile spread across his face, all white keys. I held my arm and looked into his eyes, and I don't know. I smiled back at him. I didn't know what else to do.

I KEPT SMILING as we got into the car, as we drove. What *had* I been thinking, I wondered. What had he seen? My smile was easy to hold now. I felt cheerful. The grin was painted there. Then just before Billings, in one of those big gas station stores that sell everything, words began to stick to my feelings. I had gone into the ladies' room. When I came out of the stall, I stood before a padlocked dispenser of condoms. "Placed in this establishment for your convenience," said the lettering on its front. "Savage love. 50 cents. 2 quarters only."

"Too much," I thought.

I went out the door and stood beside Ricky. He was putting some money in the slot of a plastic box full of small soft animals, plush rhinos and pink elephants and candy-striped bears. Over them a little tin crane's arm swung loose. Ricky worked it from a lever.

"Which one do you want?" he said.

"None of them."

"Tough," said Ricky.

The tin claw hovered, touching down. He was going for a small blue bear with shoe-button eyes. The back of the box was mirrored, reflecting the scene somehow from another mirror, one of the infinite-dimension tricks from movies. The pointed tips of the pincers touched the little animal's fur. Ricky had good small motor coordination, that's what he said! He always won prizes at the carnival stands pitching softballs at wooden milk bottles, shooting lead ducks. Part of me admired his delicate touch with the loaded controls, and part of me watched this all happen in the mirror.

I grabbed his arm, as if in excitement.

The crane swung and clinked against the side of the box, the claw bounced and Ricky went dark with anger.

"Get in the car," he ordered.

I walked past him. I was glad. I couldn't stand that fur toy's little stitched-on mouth, its shocked black eyes.

THAT NIGHT, I took a long time getting my hair perfect, setting it to ripple down my shoulders in a golden mane. I chose my red V-neck chiffon and a piece of jewelry with real drama—a large filigreed arrowhead hanging from a wire neckband. I stayed in the little tile bathroom, at the vanity sink, surrounded by my beauty equipment. Blow-dryer. Electric rollers. Sprays. A pronged curling iron. These things were like defensive weaponry. They bristled, hot and female.

Ricky did not come near me. He sat right outside the door, on the balcony, in a webbed vinyl chair. He sipped from a plastic cup and contemplated what was happening below him in the courtyard around the pool. It was after dinner and the sun's rays were long and cool. The water spread out like a gleaming sheet. People sat around on the deck, in white plastic chairs, also drinking out of cups. I heard one of them shout, "You wanna party?"

"No thanks," I heard Ricky answer. I knew that as he watched them he worried that later this evening, maybe as late as after the show, the party would still be going on underneath our room. I knew it too. I could hear it—their voices rising, their laughter, loud and drunken. He would be stuck, listening.

RAIN FILLS RICKY'S tracks. Luck runs out the holes. He leaves his wallet with our money on the bed, and I stuff almost all our cash into my bra. And then when I do not return from fetching ice for his drink, he finds himself stranded at the Billings Best Western with ten dollars, a suitcase, and no ice bucket. I can see it. He does not believe the truth at first. He continues sitting in the same spot.

He never meant to stay here. That was never his intent. This was a

stopping place, a way station on the road to somewhere else, a temporary shelter where he could wait while his luck changed and the damage
collected behind him.

In the sheet of chlorinated water below, reflecting nothing, the sky
goes darker and voices bounce off the tiny ripples. Courtyard beach
umbrellas topple as folks dance to a portable tape deck. A woman
passes, bringing ice, and she isn't me. The night deepens all around
Ricky Zachs. He watches the closing of many numbered doors and finally goes inside our room, crams the pillow to his head.

He is thinking of the time in second grade when girls held him down
and filled his mouth with bark. He is thinking of the time the teacher
wouldn't let him use the bathroom. He is thinking of me, how I'm
supposed to take care of him, and he is planning how he'll throw me
down when I come back. He thinks I will come back, but then he sees a
cracked bell made of frosting, white and glittering. He sees blond hair,
a bunch of tin cans tied to a fender, bouncing, rattling, behind a hot red
car that speeds away and disappears. He tosses and turns but he is unable to sleep. As more people and more people join the party below he
grows furious. Their voices are sodden and raucous while his is beautiful, or was, for as the night wears on he feels the rich sound rusting.

# Anna

THERE IS A kind of woman who, though she had been lovely all her life, attains a burst of reckless glory in her late forties. A golden fish surfacing through deep green waves. That was Anna. Lazily waving her scarves of tail. And she had knowledge. A sureness of sexual purpose made men weak. Her skin was an even water, her black hair waved and tousled. Her cold lake-brown eyes moved with restless interest, lighting on, discarding, or saving men as if she ruffled through a poker hand. A short nose, thrilling cheekbones, extravagant white smile.

Calculation, too. That was the thing. If Anna decided she needed you, wanted you, she'd take your heart and gnaw on it for a while.

I'd seen it happen many times because I am her friend—a shade paler, a degree less attractive, quieter, not anywhere as noticeable. I set her off, in other words, like the neutral background in a studio photograph. No matter what we were doing—circling the drum at a pow-wow, eating lunch, even walking together with our Discmans around the high school track, the slide of men's eyes from me to her was predictable. They would glance in surprise at Anna, check me out quickly as if for reference, and then bounce right back to her.

So I was in a position to marvel from the outside and sympathize, from an intimate standpoint, with Anna when she started living with the two we called the Shypoke brothers—Arnold and Whitey. The brothers were the most notoriously uncaptured bachelors of their era. They had grown up along with Anna, in a time when the seventies collided with the eighties, producing an implosion of sex and drugs that hit the Cities hard and, via increased ease of transport, the reservations. They grew up traveling back and forth. The men were known to have burned themselves out on crack and women, and they had retreated, shell-shocked, into a small government-built house at the edge of a weedy lake. They were steady now. Sober AA-goers and good jobholders. Arnold taught at the community high school—math, sometimes ado-lescent life skills. Whitey made his living off a variety of pursuits. He split ash, collected sinew, and created birchbark baskets, little canoes, coasters, picture frames, and he quilled fancy baskets when he hap-pened on a road-killed porcupine and plucked it. He had enough artistic talent to get by, and a little trader's sense. In the summer he followed the powwow trail in his rattling one-eye Ford pickup with the camper top on back. He sold his baskets or traded for beadwork, CDs of his favorite Native music, or antler carvings. Sold those too. Somehow, one way or another, he managed to contribute as much to the household as his brother Arnold. He made a point of telling that to people because his brother appeared to be so substantial and steady. Whitey wanted people to know that his brother wasn't picking up the tab for his life, I guess. Other than that, there was no competitiveness between the two, as far as I could tell. I saw Arnold from time to time because I work in educa-tional administration, and everybody saw Whitey; he was ubiquitous, he was everywhere. Then Anna lost her job and moved in with them.

Actually, it was more that the job lost her. Shuffling papers in the tribal enrollment office had always bored her, but when her boss moved on and she wasn't promoted to replace him, when instead another woman got the job, she quit for lack of respect. It was a dangerous time in other ways, too. Anna had her children young and her baby, Tito, had just left for the university.

"Why should I keep up a house just for myself? Pay rent? I'm free for the first time, ever," she said.

We were having dinner together in a booth at Beyond's China Buf-fet. We always met there on Sundays. It was our girls' night out, a way to debrief. We'd rehash all that happened over the previous week and weekend, sort of like decluttering the front doorway of shoes and coats, another weekly process. After we talked, we'd be prepared to proceed directly into Monday's work. But since Anna had quit her job and hadn't yet got another, and so was not working a typical week, I wondered whether the usual trajectory of our conversation might change. Usually our talk brought us up to the next week, which we anticipated together and even planned out. But this time things might be different, I imagined. And they were. With Anna's remark about the house, the routine of our comfortable talk went off course.

"Give up your house?" Impossible. Anna was obsessively tidy. She was a very house-oriented person. She loved to clean and, even more, to arrange and rearrange her possessions to the best effect.

"Where would you live?"

"Wherever the Creator wants me to live. I'm serious. Who do I have to keep up a house for? I think I'm gonna put all my stuff in a storage locker."

She grinned at my expression.

"Once and for all, I'm gonna find out. Now's my chance."

"Find out what?"

"Everything I never found out because I married young. You know, like the deep stuff."

"Wait a minute," I told her. "It's not as if like either marriage or kids stood in your way. You had two husbands, I can't even count how many lovers, and you dragged your kids off to every ceremony I ever heard of, chased down every sundance, every powwow. It's not as if you ever let commitment cramp your style."

"BUT IT DID," said Anna. "I've always wanted to just live."

"Live doing what?"

"Think out of the box," she urged, and I frowned. I hate that phrase. Half the time people use it to justify something weird or illegal. Sure enough. "I might as well let you know I've already done it. Tomorrow I'm getting the Shypokes to help me store things. We'll use Whitey's pickup. After that, I'm moving in."

I stared at her, shaking my head slowly in the negative. She looked back at me and shook her head up and down, laughing.

"You're not going to live with Arnold and Whitey." My statement was dead flat. At different times, years apart, she'd hooked up with one and then the other of them. She'd broken their hearts, flamboyantly, at least six times each. Moving in, even as a neutral party, I assumed, paying rent and nothing more, was bound to be awkward. But it turned out Anna had something way past awkwardness in mind.

"Yes, I am. They're a known quantity and so am I. No one man is going to do it for me. That's obvious by now. And with the three of us taking care of the house, I'll have time to explore my spiritual boundaries."

"You're not gonna . . . wait, are you talking about having a relationship?"

"All night, every night," she blinked her eyes rapidly.

"So now you're kidding me." I was suspicious. Disoriented. Anna moving into a house with the Shypoke Brothers wasn't just hard to accept personally. There was something about it that made me anxious on a whole other level. It was as if by doing this she upset something basic in the always tentative order of appearances on our reservation. Perhaps it was the somewhat tattered conviction that only the young were supposed to overturn things and we, who have lived long enough to know better, were supposed to set them right. She was practically an elder. Did not age count anymore? Experience? It was as if a question had been set loose as an open-ended query. And though Anna was my best friend, I was in the dark as much as anybody.

THIS WHOLE IDEA of Anna living with the two brothers just about undid me. I knew what "all night, every night" meant. They'd always taken turns, those two brothers, so they were used to one stepping aside for the other and vice versa since they'd started toddling. But Anna was not a toy, though sometimes she might have thought so. She was not a bike or car or motorcycle, all these things that the brothers had owned together. Anna was not a house. They could not divide her aspects up like rooms and decide who would inhabit which. I foresaw things would mix up, walls disintegrate, personalities become confused, boundaries overlap. Anna already had done her best to burn out the brothers, what now? The disarrangement would go internal. Rage might become involved, or worse, a relapse, alcohol or drugs. All of these fears whirled around in my brain, but nothing prepared me for what actually took place. The most unexpected outcome of all—nothing.

I PICKED UP the telephone many times that first week and even dialed, but hung up before anyone could answer. I guess I was embarrassed, if the truth be told, worried lest any halt of nervousness in my voice betray my discomfort with the situation. Then one day it was Anna, asking why haven't you called me? I wasn't quick enough to engage her in a conversation about my true feelings, and I mumbled some excuse.

"So come on over," she said. "Whitey's got the grill out." And so it was. I arrived with potato salad and found myself the fourth wheel in a happy threesome.

I HAVE A twelve-year-old daughter and a fourteen-year-old son. We live alone. No man. I have simply had enough in the way of emotional excitement and risk taking with my heart. Love will always start out sweet. There will be a sparkle on the other person, a fragile paint. That will wear off and what's beneath become apparent, over time. The father of my children comes around and I get a pain in my chest right over my heart. They are so eager to see him, and I see right through him. I see the crumbling plaster that was just held together by the sparkling paint, that shell, romance. He makes a promise and I know he won't keep to his intentions. He pretends he can stay in one place, attend their school plays, their sports games. I sit in the next room. So far, all of what I describe is typical, and it would stay that way, sad but ordinary, if I did not become so angry that the world shrinks sometimes to his one remark, one look, and I must leave to walk the miles on the new snowmobile path through the woods. I have to walk to calm the surge of my heart, the black wheel of my thoughts.

Myself, Carleen Thunder, so damaged with fury I can't speak straight sometimes, what do I have to say about any situation that is not colored by my own shortcomings and by my baleful, green, aching heart? That is why I just bring my potato salad to the Shypoke house and plunk it down on the picnic table. Although Anna and her lovers are tempting pure chaos I am not much better, me with the spikes I've grown, the prickers.

"Tasty looking," says Whitey.

"Like Mama's," says Arnold, stealing a spoonful.

Anna slaps his hands and he says, "ouchy-o-weh."

"Go tenderize," she orders. Arnold obeys and walks over to the grill, which is just about ready. He carefully begins to sprinkle the steaks with Adolf's powder, coating them evenly and precisely. Patting each one with the back of a knife. In the meantime, Whitey is setting out the paper plates and plastic knives and forks. He weights down a stack of white napkins with a rock. There is pop in a cooler, no beer. When he rips a bag of ice open in front of his chest it is like he is challenging somebody. But all the coins of ice just spill out. Arnold is now dreamily pulling pickles and yellow peppers from their State Fair jars and setting them upon a glass plate.

"This is some fancy barbecue," I notice.

"Pickle?" says Arnold.

There is no tension between them whatsoever, that I can detect, but yet there is something in the background. A power glitch. By the end of the meal I realize that something in them, in each one of them, is buzzing. But muted, like an alarm clock going off in a suitcase. Oh, they talk, even laugh, move normally, make jokes. But there is a vacant suspension here and there in the action. Whitey will shake his head and say, "Where was I?" And Arnold will not know. And Anna will try to laugh, but halfway through the laugh she'll forget. She'll stare at one of the men for a moment, then go on with a whole new subject of conversation. I intended to be skeptical, outraged, worried, but at worst I am only confused. And a little sad about them. They seem suddenly to have aged quickly in their active thoughts. That, or they're drugged with sex.

• • •

IN ONE WAY at least, as it turns out, Anna has aged less than either of us imagine. One month goes by. Another and another without memorable incident, although it seems to me that Anna looks a little wearier, a bit washed-out. The hems of her dresses sag and she does not resew them. She stops her habit of dyeing her hair in bits to alter the gray. She also stops her manicures. In fact, her fingernails now go naked and she bites them short. They're dull as ragged scales. That worries me and I tell her so.

"But I don't care," she says, "what I look like so much anymore."

With other women that might be a good sign, but with her it is not. Especially, curiously, since both Arnold and Whitey grow alert, taller, more muscular even. They may be competing with each other by getting haircuts and lifting weights, but the better they look, the better my friend Anna does not. She loses her radiant, goddessy, arrogant way of walking into a room. She slumps, angry, and on one of our Sunday nights, which we have resumed, I find out why.

"I'm knocked up." Her voice is sour as she pushes away a plate of lo mein.

"How can you be?"

We both thought that we were through with baby having, in fact not capable, and had joked about looking forward to the time in life when women surge ahead and accomplish and make sense of everything around them. That was our plan.

"I just am." She looks critically at her awful nails. She's put her mascara on without powdering her eyelashes first and it has smudged beneath her eyes. Her lips are over lipsticked, comically plump. She looks like a cartoon goldfish.

"How do you feel?" I don't know what else to say.

"I feel like a fucking mess."

I want to say to her, *Clean yourself up! This isn't you! Get moving!* and *You'll be okay!* I want to say to her all the things that two women who have been the best of friends for many years might say to each other.

I want to start that sort of tough and supportive conversation. But the other thing about knowing each other so well is we know when the other person is being insincere. And if I said those things to Anna in her present mood she'd just look at me and narrow her eyes and say, *Like hell.* She'd know that any positive way of looking at her situation would be bullshit. She was the talk of the reservation anyway. Now she'll be hilarious. She'll have a brand-new baby when she should be a grandmother, and nobody, least of all Arnold or Whitey, will know which of the brothers is the father. But then, all of a sudden, Anna does something that lets me know that even in this dire strait she will come out all right. She lets tears fall. I mean it just that way. She doesn't weep or sob or get her nose stuffed up. She never was like that. She pumps big, picturesque tears out of her eyes like a waterfall and says, "I just wanted one chance, one chance to be Anna, one chance I never got in my life."

It's the way she cries, maybe, that gets to me. The irritating truth is that even when she neglects herself and looks like she just got up she still looks like the sort of woman a man wants to drag back into bed. I'm just Carleen, the one who always listens when Anna starts in on her life saga of reasons why in spite of her looks she's still got low self-esteem. As I sit across from her in the booth at Beyond's, watching her number the awful things other people have done to her on one hand, then the next, I begin to feel sorry not for Anna but for this creature that will turn into a baby and then a child who will have her for a mother. I know that somehow Anna will find a way to do just what she wants to do, whether or not it's any good for the baby. It also occurs to me that the only reason Anna stays friendly with me is that I have never gotten in her way. Others who were friends with her were pushed aside if they had something that she wanted—a job, a man, even money. The people she likes the least in the world are the people she owes the most. As I've never had money, man, or enviable job, I've kept my place in her life. Which is what? As I sit there watching her mouth move I understand that I do have a place, or a purpose, and it is this: I am supposed to see Anna as she really is. She doesn't know it, but that's my job. And there will be a use for it some day.

• • •

AFTER HER FIRST three miserable months, Anna adjusts to the wash of conflicting hormones and grows into a magnified version of herself. She is a sleek and exquisite creature. Her hair washes down her back thicker than before, and both Arnold and Whitey pamper her. Drive her to the hairdresser. Buy her fresh fruits and new clothes. Accomplish her whims. She disappears for the last month into an underwater calm and beads obsessively, not on a cradle-board cover for her baby, but on a traditional outfit for herself, for she has imagined, or had a dream of, herself in a long-fringed buckskin dress with an eagle tail-feather fan and a belt with a skinning knife in a beaded sheath. She is having a great many mystical dreams now and, instead of laughing at her, people are saying how strong she is and how it is a sign that she is having a baby at her age.

A sign of what? I wonder. But that is soon answered when she goes into labor, when things go terribly wrong, and when she has to be helicoptered out into the big wide world, where her baby is dramatically saved. A sign of hope. Anna, too, comes through the whole experience with flair and style. People shake their heads over the now open secret of Anna's arrangement, but once a baby arrives, somehow even the most unlikely alliances between people are accepted. So it is with the three new parents. They show up at council meetings, school plays, powwows, and ceremonies. Anna asks an elder to give the baby an old time name. The baby is a girl, by the way, and over the six months that Anna stays with her, it becomes apparent that she is a bigger than average baby with a coarse, loud cry and hair that goes every which way. She isn't cute.

I remember that six-month period of grace. The amount of time when those nursing hormones keep your immunity up and your hair that stayed thick through pregnancy hasn't yet shed. It is the time when the baby has the pull of all helpless and adoring creatures. The time when people look out for you, and coo, and peep into the little bundle you carry. Once those six months are up and the baby begins to develop a personality, you are an ordinary mother with an ordinary baby. To some people, you and your baby are even an annoyance. The magic wears off. Your hair thins out. Blotches show up on your skin and the weariness begins to tell. This all happened to Anna, plus her baby was not adorable. Her baby was belligerent and got her teeth early and developed a skin rash across her cheeks and forehead. With three good-looking sets of genes, she'd surely grow out of it. But right now she was in an awkward stage. Anna's time was spent on visits to the IHS doctors and she began, more and more, to leave the baby in the care of its fathers. She hadn't done that at first—they'd had no experience with babies, after all. But one day she came over to my house and her baby was not with her.

"Oh, they're great with her now," she said. She'd come to talk. "I just got this job offer in the Cities."

She waited for my reaction. I didn't really know how to react, except to ask a lot of questions. It was a good job, solid, in the urban tribal office. Sounded just right for Anna. There was even an apartment, the whole setup. Plus she was the boss of someone else. She had an assistant.

"The only thing is . . ." She eyed me significantly, but I really didn't want to finish her sentence for her. Didn't want to talk about how difficult it might, or might not, be to leave her two husbands. Who knew what she'd set loose in their house, and what time bombs she'd leave behind when she departed? How would they take it? Would they be able to go back to simply being the odd bachelor Shypoke Brothers?

But as always, it was more than that.

". . . I can't take the baby with me, of course. I would have to put her in a day-care program, and I vowed"—her voice took on a noble, ringing quality—"that I would never put her into day care!" Anna shook her head vigorously. "Too many germs. And they still know nothing about day care's effect on a child's overall development."

"So you're leaving her with Arnold and Whitey?"

"Do you think I should?"

I knew the question was the sort of question that was already answered if you asked it. Besides, it is my job as her friend to see Anna for what she really is. So I answered her.

"Definitely."

• • •

ANNA HAS NOT returned, of course; she's been promoted to a job in Washington. She'll lobby for casinos. Things are quieter here but much less interesting. The baby's rash cleared up, her hair grew back, and with her two fathers to adore her she has lost her edge and become a contented, questing toddler who is always riding somewhere on their shoulders. They have gone back to being the bachelors, but they are much less odd now. They are part of things. They have to be. The child will grow into the world and take them with her. After all, she struck her existence and growth from the two of them. She even drove Anna from these men. And while so many of the children around here have no visible father, she has two. Two good ones. When she gets old enough to seriously wonder, and ask, and want to know about her mother and who she is and why she left her, I'll be there to tell.

ONE DAY AS I am having lunch down by the lake, I look up and see a shypoke standing in the water, shielded by a scrap of young willow. A shypoke is a bittern, an awkward and elegant type of heron. Eating my boiled egg, I watch that bird as it pretends not to hunt. It flattens its snaky neck and weaves with the shadow of the willow. It appears to be listening to the water, then goes still. Suddenly, a small fish is flapping in its beak. You never see those birds actually get the fish, they move so quick. Then they return to their painted silhouette. Of course, I always think of the Shypoke Brothers when I see their namesake bird, but this time something outrageous hits me and I start to laugh.

Carleen, I say, Carleen, you never saw it, did you. You never understood until you watched the shypoke pretend not to hunt.

In my mind, the shypoke appears with a bundle tied to its beak like a stork. A pink bundle. A proud bird. I crumple the eggshells in my hands. I can't stop laughing. Anna did not use either Arnold or Whitey, it was the other way around. She did not mess up their lives or screw with their emotions. She'd done that way before. And now they'd managed to have Anna's baby, and then get rid of Anna, too. Oh, they were quiet and you never saw them get their fish. Those shypokes, those brothers. They'd waited years.

# Tales of Burning Love

YOU COULD SAY that I literally put myself into my work. My reproductive system financed my medical future. I wasn't with anyone, not serious, but I dated all the time. So I was fitted with a Dalkon shield in the midseventies. The thing nearly killed me—perforated uterus, quick infection, hysterectomy. I felt fortunate, at first, that I only ended up sterile. I pooh-poohed it. I hadn't wanted children in the first place, I reasoned, otherwise why would I have used the thing? It took me six months to become furious, and by then, there was a class action lawsuit. I got the materials from a friend in Baltimore and joined the other plaintiffs. Two years passed, I graduated from college and went straight to dental school. By the time I got out, I had both my D.D.S. and my settlement from A. H. Robins, a check in my hands that I used to put a down payment on a house and office space. I made do, turned calamity into opportunity. That's who I am—I don't get beaten; I keep going. I have never stopped—not for loss or tragedy or sickness or embarrassment, not for Jack, not for anyone.

I talk about survival like it's easy just to do it, but of course it's the world's toughest assignment. Sometimes you need an angel, just a little bit of grace, a visitor from another dimension.

Sometimes you need a dog.

I was dealing with the aftermath of the shock of understanding, really getting to the heart of what it meant, that I could never bear a child. I was working it out in all sorts of subtle ways, like overbooking myself with an impossible patient load, then swimming a mile in the tiny health club pool, lifting weights, reading every self-help book in the Fargo, North Dakota, library, sleeping four hours, and then back to the first appointment of a long day that started at seven and ran until eight. That's the Norwegian way to get through tough times—denial, hard work, and more denial. Then straight bourbon got involved. Seeing Dr. Hakula, a therapist, I went into a twelve-step program and got in touch with my higher power. Then my higher power fizzled on me and my lower power came back strong. I drank but less than before. I started concentrating on my patients. I got obsessive about their well-being. I traveled, saw the fjords, Stockholm, Copenhagen. Then I came home. I count my life as before the shield (BS) and after the shield (AS). One day, I read my horoscope. "Get outside," it said. I sat in my cozy, newly built, carpeted house and looked around. Out there, the grass was growing. The grass was so tall, it had flopped over. Time to mow!

This huge lawn that went with the two-bedroom house had a riding lawn mower to take care of it, and that's what I used. I rode for two acres, great therapy, and then got off the thing and bagged the grass. I put the bags in the back of the car and drove to the dump in the smell of fresh clippings. There was this compost area. I brought the grass there, stopped my car, and was hauling the bags from the backseat and trunk when my eye was caught by a man getting out of a pickup truck. He was a big nondescript sort of guy, it struck me at first, dressed neutral. Out jumped a dog, a rather plain sort of dog too, but with an alert rakish air I liked. Nose up, the dog sprang around, testing his surroundings. He trotted over to the edge of the pit, glanced down, pleased as anything. Looked back at his master, who was loading a gun.

The sight of the dog, the man loading up the pistol, didn't register, except that I was shocked they let people in here to shoot rats. I mean, that's what I originally thought. Such practices were dangerous. I wasn't about to interfere, but then I didn't know Jack was Jack yet, of course. He spoke sharply, commanded the dog. The dog gave him a disdainful look, walked over, and lifted its leg against Jack's knee. When he kicked the dog, it sat down in front of him and looked up, expectant.

"Fine," said Jack. "Fine. You SOB. Just sit still doggy boy." Jack gave the dog a biscuit from his pocket, and then, while the dog was eating it, he crooked his elbow and steadied the pistol on his forearm. He took a step backward and sighted.

I leaned into my car window and honked. Jack looked around until he saw me, and I waved at him to wait. I got into my car, drove the sixty feet over to him. Keep the car around you during possible tense moments is my theory—a metal skin, a quick getaway. I parked beside him but I didn't get out, just opened my window. That's when I recognized Jack as the Jack I'd gone out with in high school. I called him over. He seemed astounded, distracted, awkward—the way you are after so many years—but not the least embarrassed about what he was about to do.

I asked him what he was up to, pleasantly, and he told me, just as pleasantly, that he was about to shoot his dog when I'd interrupted, and how was I these days?

"Did the dog do something wrong?" I asked.

Jack came over, rolled up his pants leg, and showed me the long gauze wrap.

"Fifteen stitches."

The dog looked damn proud of itself. It had a kind of grin, a curious unsettled expression.

"Tell you what. Instead of shooting it, why don't you sell that dog to me?" I proposed.

Jack just laughed. "That dog is vicious." His voice was like a pat on the head. "You don't want it."

I dug in my purse and held out ten dollars.

"No way," he said. "I can just see the size of the lawsuit."

"Try this: ASPCA."

"What's that?"

"Old times' sake?"

He stepped closer.

"Forget it," I said. "I see I'm going to have to get tough."

I always kept a hundred-dollar bill tucked into the photo section of my wallet—something I learned when traveling—and now I pulled it out and waved it with the ten.

"You're going to sell me that dog."

Jack eyed the money but shook his head, grinned.

When he showed his teeth, I saw decay invading the very top left corner of his right incisor.

"Open your mouth," I said, dropping the charm and putting away my purse.

"Wha—"

"When'd you brush last?"

"—the hell?"

"I mean it. I'm a dentist now."

Meekly, only halfway mocking, Jack bent next to the car, the gun dangling from his grip. He stretched his jaws wide. I examined what I could see with the naked eye, the dog watching us.

"I've got a deal for you," I said.

He shut his mouth, stood, asked if it was what he thought it was. I shrugged.

"There's no telling what's going through your brain, but what I'm offering is this: You give me the dog; I fix your teeth. I'm painless. I swear if I hurt you, then you can just walk out. I feel sorry for you, Jack, I really do!"

He finally nodded. "You bought yourself trouble," he warned.

"It usually comes cheaper." I looked down at his leg again. "Fifteen stitches?"

"And this."

He held up his hand to take my business card, the sleeve fell away from his forearm—scarred with chew marks.

I took the dog home, and it's true he was a fear-biter. He tried to get his teeth into you before you got yours into him. I understood that. We had some go-arounds. At times, I would be gripping an ear in each fist and he'd have his fangs bared and ready to go for me, but he'd have to lose his ears first. Or I'd just step down hard on the choke chain if he lunged. I had that dog's number right from the beginning, and when he finally got mine, it was a perfect relationship. Pepperboy was made to give unspeakable devotion. I was made to get it. But then, of course, life got more complicated.

JACK MADE HIS appointment, came in one morning, late. Opened up his mouth and my hygienist, Andrea, tried not to react and just took the X rays. We took about twenty. Six teeth needed root canals. He had a threshold like you wouldn't believe and had treated what he did feel with rage, I guess, and Jack Daniel's. Said he couldn't tell where the sensations were coming from, felt them on all sides. Said he hadn't slept in months, that the trouble dated way back, years and years. When he laid his head on the pillow, it was like his head made an electrical connection—like all his teeth clamped onto his nervous system, pulsed on, wouldn't quit.

I got Jack to sit down, had him stretch out in the big chair, got him all numbed up. When the pain in his teeth turned off, tears filled his eyes. I felt so sorry for him, this big guy, former boyfriend of mine and all that, whipped. A puppy. I treated him with extra care and then told him we'd be seeing quite a bit of each other during the next few months.

During those visits, between the X rays, while we waited for the Novocain to kick in, we talked. I heard about his life since high school. Once he told me he'd recently gone through a divorce, the teeth made sense. Divorcing people usually neglect their teeth. After his first wife, Eleanor, Jack spent one year, two, pursuing and netting every woman who came near him. During that time, of course, he let his dental hygiene lapse. Not to mention he'd always had a sweet tooth, handed down from his father.

We had a date, my first one with Jack since I was a junior. It was just a lunch date. I'd put the last crown on the last tooth—it was supposed to be a sort of celebration of Jack's mouth, right? In fact, it was a celebration of Jack's other favorite part of himself. The first thing he said to me?

"I have screwed *everything* in Fargo."

He told this to me in a tragic tone as we studied menus in a pseudo-antique booth decorated with brass railings and frosted glass. Old Broadway had large salads, which was why I ate there. I watch my weight.

"That statement is the main problem with you. Jack, if you'd just take a minute to analyze it."

When he had started coming to me, it was just teeth, and over the course of the visits, he had begun to ask for more serious assistance in his private life. At first, I had responded to him with deep suspicion. I knew who he was and what he was, as you only know men you've shared with girlfriends in high school. Jack was worse than transparent to me, he was invisible, a kind of child-man. I watched him eat; no, I X-rayed the rest of him I hadn't yet looked through—I almost saw the progress of his meal like in a science diagram. It made me dizzy. Jack ate a big, solid club sandwich that came in a basket with french-fried potatoes. He had one or two drinks, Bloody Mary, a beer, and a creamy dessert. He was big but not at all fat, just tough and heavy and muscular, and his energy those days was depressed but endless. He said he could go for nights with only an hour or two of sleep, working round the clock, exhorting and screaming at his crew, and bullying the workers on his building projects into mad efforts that sometimes nearly killed them with nervous exhaustion. He was known, already, for completing work on time and within estimates. In construction, you only had to do that once to become a legend.

I suppose, too, I saw him in those days as a man who'd make a lot of money—not that cash swayed me emotionally, you understand, I just sensed the crisp feel of it sliding off him when he cranked his shoulders. New ink. Paper. But his smile was a counterfeiter's press.

"Jack, dear," I said that first time, trying not to sound as though I had any personal interest in the matter of his love life, which I honestly didn't want to touch with a thirty-foot pole. "Maybe it's time you realized that you're a sexual Neanderthal."

I let that remark dangle for a moment, but Jack had turned his sad, dark gaze out of the booth, and now it rested with gloomy clarity on a solid-hipped waitress who flipped her middle finger at him.

"You're right," said Jack decisively, biting hugely into his triple-decker sandwich. "I have made an enemy of everyone I've ever touched, except you. Let's get engaged or something, Candy."

I put down my fork.

"Look at me."

Jack obeyed, stopped eating, and opened his face to me across the table. I know what I can look like, how good, especially having kicked the sauce. I'm a sturdy woman with straight, short hair and a freckle-dusted face. People call me sweet. Fine. I'm glad I give that impression. I'm not, although I've got a farm face, a trustworthy face. I have excellent circulation. I'm always rosy, warm. Underneath it all, I'm tough bone.

"I am the sort of woman who will immediately let you down," I informed Jack. "Treat me right and I'll make you miserable."

Jack held out his hands. "I don't get it!"

"Let me put it simply. I'm not interested, Jack. You're just desperate. But you do need someone stable and strong and, most of all, forgiving."

Jack started eating again, pushing the food steadily and carefully into himself.

"You're probably right," he said. "I'm sure you are. But the thing is, I don't want the kind of woman that I should love."

"Take my advice, don't take it. No skin off my nose."

Jack took the bite of coconut cream pie away from his mouth, lowered his fork carefully, focused on me clearly for the first time, and frowned.

"I'm sure it's not," he said gently. "But what about you? I've been through the mill, and maybe I have actually learned something about my limitations. Maybe you can't give me credit because you knew me when. I take young love seriously. I think about it. Did you ever wonder that maybe we were meant to be? Has it ever occurred to you that maybe you know me so well that you're completely blind to how I've changed? Of course you don't know me entirely, not anymore."

"I've forgotten all about that."

"No, you haven't."

We stared across the ruins of our lunch, all the littered plates and clouded glasses. I watched him very carefully for any sign his speech was sly or underhanded, but he did not meet my eyes. He did not gauge me, watch any longer for my reaction, but devoted his attention to the varnished grain of the tabletop. As I waited him out, I felt that tiny shift, that gear grinding, and suddenly there was something that had not been there before, a hint of speculation, a scent of the unknown, curiosity, that essential component of sexual sympathy.

"Don't mess with me." I think my voice faltered, just a little.

THEN, RIGHT THERE in the booth, with people wheeling around us, not even noticing, Jack reached over calmly and pulled the throat sash, the tie of my red silk blouse. I had something black and intricately lacy underneath it, and when the neckline fell open, I felt Jack register the fact of the garment. I let him look, my face cold, then retied the collar.

"That's as far as you'll get," I said. But I was shaken.

It was the way he smiled at me, both penitently, after the bow was perfect, and unabashedly, knowing we would have to know more. It was the way he dug back into the cream on the top of his pie, the way he eyed me above the crust. It was his hand square on the fork, the shadow at the base of his throat, the pure inch of worry between his eyebrows. What convinced me was nothing that I could name or that truly had a rational basis in understanding, and yet, suddenly, there was no rescue. With each of my relationships, I have experienced something similar to this moment of clarity. Everything seemed much too real. My apprehension of the future pressed in on me with all its weight. My hands shook and my clothes seemed too small and tight. I could feel the lines in my face, a burning sensation in my temples, a pressure on my skull. I couldn't breathe, couldn't fill my lungs. Annoyance covered me, and desperation, and then finally, sheer love, a mantle of amnesia and of hope.

# The Antelope Wife

I USED TO make the circuit as a trader at the western powwows, though I am an urban Indian myself, a teacher in the city schools. I'd hit Montana—Arlee, Elmo, Missoula, swing over to Rocky Boy, and then head on down to Crow Fair. I liked it out there in all that dry space; at first that is, and up until last year. It was restful, a comfort to let my brain wander across the horizontal mystery where sky meets earth.

Now, that line disturbs me with its lie.

Earth and sky touch everywhere and nowhere, like sex between two strangers. There is no definition and no union for sure. If you chase that line, it will retreat from you at the same pace you set. Heart pounding, air burning in your chest, you'll pursue. Only humans see horizon as an actual place. But like love, you'll never get there. You'll never catch it. You'll never know.

Open space plays such tricks on the brain. There and gone. I suppose it is no surprise that it was on the plains that I met my wife, my sweetheart rose, Ninimoshe, kissing cousin, lover girl, the only one I'll ever call my own. I take no credit for what happened, nor blame, nor do I care what people presently think of me—avoiding my eyes, trying not to step in the tracks I've left.

I only want to be with her, or be dead.

You wouldn't think a man as ordinary as myself could win a woman who turns the heads of others in the streets. Yet there are circumstances and daughters that do prevail and certain ways. And, too, maybe I have some talents.

• • •

I WAS SITTING underneath my striped awning there in Elmo—selling carved turtles. You never know what will be the ticket or the score. Sometimes they're buying baby moccasins, little beaded ones the size of your big toe. Or the fad is cheap neckerchiefs, bolo slides, jingles. I can sell out before noon if I misjudge my stock, while someone else set up next to me who took on a truckload is raking the money in with both hands. At those times, all I can do is watch. But that day, I had the turtles. And those people were crazy for turtles. One lady bought three—a jade, a malachite, a turquoise. One went for seven—small. Another bought the turtle ring. It was the women who bought turtles—the women who bought anything.

I had traded for macaw feathers also, and I got a good price on those. I had a case of beautiful old Navajo pawn which I got blessed, because the people who wore that turquoise seem to haunt the jewelry, so I believe. A piece gets sold on a sad drunk for gas money, or it's outright stolen—what I mean is that it comes into the hands of traders in bad ways and should be watched close. I have a rare piece I never did sell, an old cast-silver bracelet with a glacier-green turquoise the shape of a wing. I have to tell you, I can hold that piece only a moment, for when I polish the pattern on some days it seems to start in my hands with a secret life, a secret pain.

I am just putting that old piece away when they pass. Four women eating snow cones as they stroll the powwow grounds.

Who wouldn't notice them? They float above everyone else on springy, tireless legs. It's hard to tell what tribe people are anymore, we're so mixed—I've got a Buffalo Soldier in my own blood, I'm sure, and on the other side I am all Ojibwe. All Nanapush, a story in itself. These ladies are definitely not from anywhere that I can place. Their dance clothes are simple—tanned-hide dresses, bone jewelry, white doeskin down the front and two white doeskin panels behind. Classy, elegant, they set a new standard of simplicity. They make everyone else around them look gaudy or bold, a little foolish in their attempts to catch the eyes of the judges.

I watch these women put their mouths on ice. They tip their faces down, half smiling, and delicately kiss the frozen grains. As they sip the sweet lime and blueberry juice, their black, melting eyes never leave the crowd, and still they move along. Effortless. Easy. The lack of trying is what makes them lovely. We all try too hard. Striving wears down our edges, dulls the best of us.

I take those women in like air. I breathe hard. My heart is squeezing shut. Something about them is like the bracelets of old turquoise. In spite of the secrets of those stones, there are times that I cannot stop touching and stroking their light. I must be near those women and know more. I cannot let them alone. I look at my setup—van, tent, awning, beads, chairs, scarves, jewelry, folding tables, a cashbox, a turtle or two—and I sit as calmly as I can at my trading booth among these things. I wait. But when they don't notice me, I decide I must act bold. I trade store minding with my neighbor, a family from Saskatoon, and then I follow the women.

Tiptoeing just behind at first, then trotting faster, I almost lose them, but I am afraid to get too close and be noticed. They finish circling the arbor, enter during the middle of an intertribal song, and dance out into the circle together. I lean against a pole to watch. Some dancers, you see them sweating, hear their feet pound the sawdust or grass or the Astroturf or gym floor, what have you. Some dancers swelter and their faces darken with the effort. Others, you never understand how they are moving, where it comes from. They're at one with their effort. Those, you lose your heart to and that's what happens to me—I sink down on a bench to watch these women and where usually I begin to drift off in my thoughts, and my scars where my father beat me nag and ache, this morning I am made of smoothest wood. They dance together in a line, murmuring in swift, low voices, smiling carefully as they are too proud to give away their beauty. They are light steppers with a gravity of sure grace.

Their hair is fixed in different ways. The oldest daughter pulls hers back in a simple braid. The next one ties hers in a fancy woven French knot. The hair of the youngest is fastened into a smooth tail with a round shell hairpiece. Their mother—for I can tell she is their mother mainly by the way she moves with a sense of all their consolidated grace—her hair hangs long and free.

Dark as heaven, with roan highlights and arroyos of brown, waves deep as currents, a river of scented nightfall. In her right hand she holds a fan of the feathers of a red-tailed hawk. Those birds follow the antelope to fall on field mice the moving herd stirs up. Suddenly, as she raises the fan high, my throat chills. I hear in the distance and in my own mind and heart the high keer of the stooping hawk—a lonely sound wild as wild hearts.

BACK AT MY tables, later, I place every item enticingly just so. I get provisions of iced tea and soda and I sit down to wait. To scout. Attract, too, if I can manage, but there isn't much I can do about my looks. I'm broad from sitting in my foldable chair, and too cheerful to be considered dangerously handsome. My hair, I'm proud of that—it's curly and dark and I wear it in a tail or braid. But my hands are thick and clumsy. Their only exercise is taking in and counting money. My eyes are too lonesome, my lips too eager to stretch and smile, my heart too hot to please.

No matter. The women come walking across the trampled grass and again they never notice me, anyway. They go by the other booths and ponder some tapes and point at beaded belt buckles and Harley T-shirts. They order a soft drink, eat Indian tacos, order huckleberry muffins at a lunch stand. They come by again to stand and watch the Indian gambling, the stick games. They disappear and suddenly appear. The mother is examining her daughter's foot. Is she hurt? No, it's just a piece of chewing gum that's stuck. All day I follow them with my eyes. All day I have no success, but I do decide which one I want.

Some might go for the sprig, the sprout, the lovely offshoot, the younger and flashier, the darker-hooded eyes. Me, I'm strong enough, or so I think, to go for the source: the mother. She is all of them rolled up in one person, I figure. She is the undiluted vision of their separate loveliness. The mother is the one I will try for. As I am falling into sleep

I imagine holding her, the delicate power. My eyes shut, but that night I am troubled in my dreams.

I'm running, running, and still must run—I'm jolted awake, breathing hard. The camp is dark. All I've got is easily packed and I think maybe I should take the omen. Break camp right this minute. Leave. Go home. Back to the city, Minneapolis, Gakaabikaang we call it, where everything is set out clear in lines and neatly labeled, where you can hide from the horizon, forget. I consider it and then I hear the sounds of one lonely passionate stick game song still rising, an old man's voice pouring out merciless irony, no catch in his throat.

I walk to the edge of the rising moon.

I stand listening to the song until I feel better and am ready to settle myself and rest. Making my way through the sleeping camp, however, I see the four women walking again—straight past me, very quickly and softly now, laughing. They move like a wave, dressed in pale folds of calico. Their pace quickens, quickens some more. I break into a jog and then I find that I am running after them, at a normal speed at first, and then straining, putting my heart into the chase, my whole body pedaling forward, although they do not seem to have broken into a run themselves. Their supple gait takes them to the edge of the camp, all brush and sage, weeds and grazed-down pastures, and from there to alive hills. A plan forms in my mind. I'll find their camping place and mark it! Go by with coffees in the morning, take them off gaurd. But they pass the margin of the camp, the last tent. I pass too. We keep looping into the moonlighted spaces, faster, faster, but it's no use. They outdistance me. They pass into the darkness, into the night.

My heart is squeezing, racing, crowded with longing, and I need help. It must be near the hour that will gray to dawn. Summer nights in high country are so short that the birds hardly stop singing. Still, at dawn the air goes light and fresh. Now the old man whose high, cracked voice was joyfully gathering in money at the gambling tent finally stops. I know him, Jimmy Badger, or know *of* him anyway as an old medicine person spoken about with hushed respect. I can tell his side has won, because the others are folding their chairs with clangs and leaving with soft grumbles. Jimmy is leaning on a grandson. The boy supports him as he walks along. Jimmy's body is twisted with arthritis and age. He's panting for breath. They pause, I come up to him, shake hands, and tell him I need advice.

He motions to his tired grandson to go to bed. I take the medicine man's arm and lead him over tough ground to where my van is parked. I pull out a lawn chair, set it up, lower him into it. Reaching into my stores, I find an old-time twist of tobacco, and I give it to him. Then I add some hanks of cut beads and about eight feet of licorice for his grandkids. A blanket, too, I give him that. I take out another blanket and settle it around his back, and I pour a thermos cap of coffee, still warm. He drinks, looking at me with shrewd care. He's a small man with waiting intrigue in his eyes, and his gambler's hands are gnarled to clever shapes. He has a poker-playing mouth, a head of handsome iron-gray hair that stretches down behind. He wears a beat-up bead-trimmed fedora with a silver headband and a brand-new denim jacket he's probably won in the blackjack tents.

I'm an Ojibwe, I say to him, so I don't know about the plains much. I am more a woods Indian, a city-bred guy. I tell Jimmy Badger that I've got a hunting lottery permit and I'm going to get me an antelope. I need some antelope medicine, I say. Their habits confuse me. I need advice on how to catch them. He listens with close attention, then smiles a little crack-toothed pleasant smile.

"You're talking the old days," he says. "There's some who still hunt the antelope, but of course the antelope don't jump fences. They're easy to catch now. Just follow until they reach a fence. They don't jump over high, see, they only know how to jump wide."

"They'll get the better of me then," I say, "I'm going to hunt them in an open spot."

"Oh, then," he says. "Then, that's different."

At that point, he gets out his pipe, lets me light it, and for a long time after that he sits and smokes.

"See here." He slowly untwists his crushed body. "The antelope are a curious kind of people. They'll come to check anything that they don't understand. You flick a piece of cloth into the air where you're hiding, a flag. But only every once in a while, not regular. They're curious, they'll stop, they'll notice. Pretty soon they'll investigate."

NEXT DAY, THEN, I set up my booth just exactly the same as the day before, except I keep out a piece of sweetheart calico, white with little pink roses. When the women come near, circling the stands again, I flicker the cloth out. Just once. It catches the eye of the youngest and she glances back at me. They pass by. They pass by again. I think I've failed. I wave the cloth. The older daughter, she turns. She looks at me once over her shoulders for the longest time. I flick the cloth. Her eyes are deep and watchful. Then she leans back, laughing to her mother, and she tugs on her sleeve.

In a flash, they're with me.

They browse my store. I'm invisible at first, but not for long. Once I get near enough I begin to fence them with my trader's talk—it's a thing I'm good at, the chatter that encourages a customer's interest. My goods are all top-quality. My stories have stories. My beadwork is made by relatives and friends whose tales branch off in an ever more complicated set of barriers. I talk to each of the women, make pleasant comments, set up a series of fences and gates. They're very modest and polite women, shy, stiff maybe. The girls talk just a little and the mother not at all. When they don't get a joke they lower their lashes and glance at one another with a secret understanding. When they do laugh they cover their lovely calm mouths with their hands. Their eyes light with wonder when I give them each a few tubes of glittering cut beads, some horn buttons, a round-dance tape.

They try to melt away. I keep talking. I ask them if they've eaten, tell them I've got food and show them my stash of baked beans, corn, fry bread, molasses cookies. I make them up heaped plates and I play a little music on the car radio. I keep on talking and smiling and telling my jokes until the girls yawn once. I catch them yawning, and so I open my tent, pitched right near, so nice and inviting. I tell them they are welcome to lie down on the soft heap of blankets and sleeping bags.

Their dark eyes flare, they look toward their mother, wary, but I fend off their worry and wave them inside, smiling the trader's smile.

Alone together. Me and her. Their mother listens to me nice and gentle. I let my look linger just a little, closer, until I find her eyes. And when our eyes do meet, we stare, we stare, we cannot stop looking. Hers are so black, full of steep light and wary. Mine are brown, searching, anxious, I am sure. But we hold on and I can only say that for what happens next I have no adequate excuse.

We get into the van while she is still caught by the talk, the look. I think she is confused by the way I want her, which is like nobody else. I know this deep down. I want her in a new way, a way she's never been told about, a way that wasn't the way of the girls' father. Sure, maybe desperate. Maybe even wrong, but she doesn't know how to resist. Like I say, I get her in my van. I start to play a soft music she acts like she never heard before. She smiles a little, nervous, and although she doesn't speak, uses no words anyway, I understand her looks and gestures. I put back the seat so it's pleasant to recline and watch the stars and then I pamper her.

"You're tired, sleep." I give her a cup of hot tea. "Everything's all right with your daughters. They'll be fine."

She sips the tea and looks at me with dreaming apprehension, as though I'm a new thing on earth. Her eyes soften, her lips part. Suddenly, she leans back and falls hard asleep. Another thing that I forgot to tell—us Ojibwe have a few teas we brew for very special occasions. This is one. A sleep tea, a love tea. Oh yes, there's more. There's more that Jimmy Badger told me.

"YOU'RE SHIFTY LIKE all those woods Indians," Jimmy Badger said. "I see that trader's deception. If you're thinking about those women, don't do it," he said. "Long time ago, we had a man like you followed the antelope, lured one close, and wrestled her down. He made love to her. In the spring she brought human daughters to the camp. They could not keep up with her people as they moved on to better pastures, scattering across the plains. Don't go near them if that is what you're thinking of doing. Few men can handle their love ways. Besides, they're ours. We need them and we take care of these women. Descendants."

"They might be," I said. "Or they might just be different."

"Oh, different," agreed Jimmy. "For sure."

He looked at me keenly, grabbed me with his eyes, kept talking. His voice was remote and commanding.

"Our old women say they appear and disappear. Some men follow the antelope and lose their minds."

I was stubborn. "Or maybe they're just a family that's a little unusual, or wild."

"Leave," said Jimmy Badger. "Leave now."

BUT IN MY heart, I knew I was already caught. The best hunter allows his prey to lead, not the other way around. That hunter doesn't force himself to figure and track, just lets himself be drawn to the meeting. That's what I did.

Suddenly I have her there with me in the van, and she is fast asleep. I sit and watch her for a long time. I am witched. Her eyelashes are so long that in the light from the outdoor flood lamps they cast faint shadows on her cheeks. Her breath has the scent of grass and her hair of sage. I want to kiss her forever. My heart's a panic on my sleeve.

I drive off. Yes, I do. I drive off with this woman while her daughters are breathing softly, there in the tent, unconscious. I leave the girls all of my trade beads and fancy pawn and jewelry, everything that was stored in the corner of the tent. The miles go by, the roads empty. The Missions rear before us, throwing fire off sheer rock faces. Then we're past those mountains into more open country. My sweetheart wakes up, confused and tired. I tell her jokes and stories and funny things that my children did in the classroom. By winter I'm a grade-school teacher, like I said in the beginning. She reacts so little that I wonder if she's been to school. I drive through the day. I drive through the night. Only when I am so exhausted that I'm seeing double, do I finally stop.

Bismarck, North Dakota, center of the universe. Locus of space and time for me and my Ninimoshe. We turn in, take a room at the motel's end. I lead her in first and I close the door behind and then she turns to me—suddenly, she knows she is caught. *Where are my girls*, her eyes say, their fear sharp as bone, *I want my girls!* When she lunges, I'm ready, but she's so fast I cannot keep her from running at the window, falling back. She twists, strong and lithe, for the door, but I block and try to ease her down. She pounds at me with hard fists and launches straight into the bathroom, pulling down the mirror, breaking a tooth on the tub's edge.

What can I do? I have those yards of sweetheart calico. I go back. I tear them carefully and with great gentleness I bandage her cuts. I don't know what else to do—I tie her up. I pull one strip gently through her bleeding mouth. Lastly, I tie our wrists together and then, beside her, in an agony of feeling, I sleep.

I ADORE HER. I'll do anything for her. Anything except let her go. Once I get her to my city, things are better anyway. She seems to forget her daughters, their wanting eyes, the grand space, the air. And besides, I tell her that we'll send for her daughters by airplane. They can come and live with me and go to school right here.

She nods, but there is something hopeless in her look. She dials and dials long-distance numbers, there are phone calls all over the whole state of Montana, all of these 406 numbers are on the bill. She never speaks, though sometimes I imagine I hear her whispering. I try the numbers, but every time I dial one that she's used I get the Indian answering machine. This number's out of service. Does she even understand the phone? And anyway, one night she smiles into my face— we're just the same height. I look deep and full into her eyes. She loves me the way I love her, I can tell. I want to hold her and hold her—for good, for bad. After that, our nights are something I can't address in the day, as though we're wearing other bodies, other people's flaming skins, as though we're from another time and place. Our love is a hurting delicacy, an old killer whiskey, a curse, and too beautiful for words.

I get so I don't want to leave her to go to work. In the morning she sits at her spot before the television, watching in still fascination, jumping a little at the car chases, sympathizing with the love scenes. I catch her looking into the mirror I've hung in the living room and she is mimicking the faces of the women on the soap operas, their love looks, their pouting expressions. Their clothes. She opens my wallet, takes all my money. I'd give her anything. "Here," I say, "take my checkbook too." But she just throws it on the floor. She leaves off her old skins and buys new, tight and covered with bold designs. She laughs harder, but her laugh is silent, shaking her like a tree in a storm. She drinks wine. In a pair of black jeans in a bar she is approached by men whenever I turn aside, so I don't turn aside. I stick to her, cleave to her, won't let her go and in the nights sometimes I still tie her to me with sweetheart calico.

Weeping, weeping, she cries the whole day away. Sometimes I find her in the corner, drunk, marvelous in frothy negligees, laughing and lip-synching love scenes to the mirror again. I think I'll do something, things cannot go on. She's crazy. But if they lock her up, they'll have to lock me up too. She'll rage at me for days with her eyes, bare her teeth, stamp on my feet with her heeled boot if I get near enough to try for a kiss. Then just as suddenly, she'll change. She'll turn herself into the most loving companion. We'll sit at night watching television, touching our knees together while I make up the next day's lessons. Her eyes speak. Her long complicated looks tell me stories—of the old days, of her people. The antelope are the only creatures swift enough to catch the horizon, her sweeping looks say. *We live there. We live there in the place where sky meets earth.*

I bring her sweet grass, tie it into her hair, and then we make love and we don't stop until we're sleeping on each other's pillows.

Winter, and the daylight dwindles. She starts to eat and eat and puffs up before my eyes devouring potato chips and drinking wine until I swear at her, say she's ugly, tell her to get a job, to lose weight, to be the person she was when I first met her. Those teeth are still cracked off, and when she smiles her smile is jagged with hatred but her eyes are still dark with love, with amusement. She lifts into the air in a dance and spins, spins away so I can't catch her and once again she is in my arms and we're moving, moving together. She's so fantastically plump I can't bear it all, her breasts round and pointed and that night I drown, I go down in the depth of her. I'm lost as I never was and next morning, next afternoon, she drags me back into bed. I can't stop although I'm exhausted. She keeps on and she keeps on. Day after day. Until I know she is trying to kill me.

That night, while she's asleep, I sneak into the kitchen. I call Jimmy Badger, get his phone through a series of other people.

"It's her or me," I say.

"Well, finally."

"What should I do?"

"Send her back to us, you fool."

HIS WORDS BURN behind my eyes. If you see one you are lost forever. They appear and disappear like shadows on the plains, say the old women. Some men follow them and do not return. Even if you do return, you will never be right in the head. Her daughters are pouting mad. They don't have much patience, Jimmy says. He keeps talking, talking. They never did, that family. Our luck is changing. Our houses caved in with the winter's snow and our work is going for grabs. Nobody's stopping at the gas pump. Bring her back to us! says Jimmy. There's misery in the air. The fish are mushy inside—some disease. Her girls are mad at us.

Bring her back, you fool!

I'm just a city boy, I answer him, slow, stark, confused. I don't know what you people do, out there, living on the plains where there are no trees, no woods, no place to hide except the distances. You can see too much.

You fool, bring her back to us!

But how can I? Her lying next to me in deepest night, breathing quiet in love, in trust. Her hand in mine, her wicked hoof.

# Father's Milk

## Scranton Fox

DEEP IN THE past during a spectacular cruel raid upon an isolate
Ojibwe village mistaken for hostile during the scare over the starving
Sioux, a dog bearing upon its back a frame-board tikinaagan enclosing
a child in moss, velvet, embroideries of beads, was frightened into the
vast carcass of the world west of the Ottertail river. A cavalry soldier,
spurred to human response by the sight of the dog, the strapped-on
child, both vanishing into the distance, followed and did not return.

What happened to him lives on, though fading in the larger memory,
and I relate it here in order that it not be lost.

Private Scranton Teodorus Fox was the youngest son of a Quaker
father and a reclusive poet mother who established a small Pennsylvania
community based on intelligent conversation. One day into his view a
member of a traveling drama troupe appeared. Unmasked, the woman's
stage glance broke across Fox's brow like fire. She was tall, stunningly
slender, pale, and paler haired, resolute in her character and simple in
her amused scorn of Fox—so young, bright-faced, obedient. To prove
himself, he made a rendezvous promise and then took his way west following her backward glare. An icicle, it drove into his heart and melted
there, leaving a trail of ice and blood. The way was long. She glided like
a snake beneath his footsteps in fevered dreams. When he finally got to

the place she was to meet him, she was not there, of course. Angry and at odds he went against the radiant ways of his father, enlisted in the U.S. Cavalry, and was sent to Fort Snelling on the banks of the Mississippi in St. Paul, Minnesota.

There, he was trained to the rifle, learned to darn his socks using a wooden egg, ate many an ill-cooked bean, and polished his officers' harness leather until one day, in a state of uneasy resignation, he put on the dark blue uniform, fixed his bayonet, set off marching due west.

The village his company encountered was peaceful, then not.

In chaos of groaning horses, dogs screaming, rifle and pistol reports and the smoke of errant cooking fires, Scranton Fox was most disturbed not by the death yells of old men and the few warriors shocked naked from their robes, but the feral quiet of the children. And the sudden contempt he felt for them. Unexpected, the frigid hate. The pleasure in raising, aiming, firing. They ran fleet as their mothers, heading for a bush-thick gully and a slough of grass beyond. Two fell. Fox whirled, not knowing whom to shoot next. Eager, he bayoneted an old woman who set upon him with no other weapon but a stone picked from the ground.

SHE WAS BUILT like the broken bales of hay they'd used for practice, but her body closed fast around the instrument. He braced himself against her to pull free, set his boot between her legs to pull the blade from her stomach, and as he did so tried to avoid her eyes but did not manage. His gaze was drawn into hers and sank into the dark unaccompanied moment before his birth. There was a word she uttered in her language. A groan of heat and blood. He saw his mother, yanked the bayonet out with a huge cry, and began to run.

That was when he saw the dog, a loping dirt-brown cur, circle the camp twice with the child on its back and set off not into cover but into open space. It was as much to escape the evil confusion of this village and his own dark acts as any sympathy for the baby, though he glimpsed its face—mystified and calm—that Scranton Fox started running after the two. Within moments, the ruckus of death was behind him. The farther away the village got the farther behind he wanted it, and he kept on, running, walking, managing to keep the dog in view only because it was spring and the new grass, after a burn of lightning, was just beginning its thrust, which would take it to well over a full-grown man's height.

From time to time, as the day went on, the dog paused to rest, stretched patient beneath its burden. Grinning and panting, she allowed Fox to approach, but just so far. A necklace of blue beads hung from the brow guard of the cradle board. It swayed, clattered lightly. The child's hands were bound in the wrappings. She could not reach for the beads but stared at them as though mesmerized. The sun grew razor-hot. Tiny blackflies settled at the corners of her eyes. Sipped moisture from along her lids until, toward late afternoon, the heat died. A cold wind boomed against Scranton Fox in a steady rush. Still, into the emptiness, the three infinitesimally pushed.

The world darkened. Afraid of losing the trail, Fox gave his utmost. As night fixed upon them, man and dog were close enough to hear each other breathing and so, in that rhythm, both slept. Next morning, the dog stayed near grinning for scraps. Afraid to frighten him with a rifle shot, Fox hadn't brought down game although he'd seen plenty. He managed to snare a rabbit and then, with his tinderbox and fire steel, he started a fire and began to roast it, at which smell the dog dragged itself belly-down through the dirt, edging close. The baby made its first sound, a vague murmuring whimper. Accepting tidbits and bones, the dog was alert, suspicious. Fox could not touch it until the next day when he'd thought to wash himself all over and approach naked to diminish his whiteman's scent.

So he was able at last to remove the child from its wrappings and bathe it, a girl, and to hold her. He'd never done such a thing before. First he tried to feed her a tiny piece of the rabbit. She was too young to manage. He dripped water into her mouth, made sure it trickled down, but was perplexed at what else he might feed her, then alarmed when after a night of deprivation, her tiny face crumpled in need. She peered at him in expectation and, at last, violently squalled. Amazingly, her cries filled the vastness which nothing else could. They resounded, took over everything, and brought his heart clean to the surface. Scranton Fox cradled the baby, sang lewd camp tunes, then stalwart hymns, and at last remembered his own mother's lullabies. Nothing helped. It seemed, when he held her close upon his heart as women did, that the child grew angry with longing and desperately clung, rooted with its mouth, roared in frustration, until at last, moved to near insanity, Fox opened his shirt and put her to his nipple.

She seized him. Inhaled him. Her suck was fierce. His whole body was astonished, most of all the inoffensive nipple he'd never noticed or appreciated until, in spite of the pain, it served to gain him peace. As he sat there, the child holding part of him in its mouth, he looked around just in case there should be any witness to this act which seemed to him strange as anything that had happened in this sky-filled land. Of course, there was only the dog. Contented, freed, it lolled appreciatively near. So the evening passed and then the night. Scranton Fox was obliged to change nipples, the first one hurt so, and he fell asleep with the baby tucked beside him still on his useless teat.

She was still there in the morning, stuck, though he pulled her off to slingshot a partridge, roasted that too, and smeared its grease on his two sore spots. That made her wild for him. He couldn't remove her then and commenced to walk, holding her, still attached, toward a huge stand of cottonwood he could just see in the distance. A river. A place to camp. He'd settle there for a day or two, he thought, and try to teach the baby to eat something, for he feared she'd starve to death although she seemed, except for the times he removed her from his chest, surprisingly contented.

He slung the blue beads around the baby's neck. Tied the cradle board onto his own back. Then the man, child, and dog struck farther into the wilderness. They reached hills of sand, oak covered, shelter. Nearby, sod he cut painstakingly with the length of his bayonet and piled into a square, lightless but secure, and warm. Hoarding his shots, he managed to bring down a buffalo bull fat-loaded with summer grass. He fleshed the hide, dried the meat, seared the brains, stored the pounded fat and berries in the gut, made use of every bone and scrap of flesh even to the horns, which he carved spoons of, and the eyeballs, tossed to the dog. The tongue, cooked tender and mashed in his own mouth, he coaxed the baby to accept. She still much preferred him. As he was now past civilized judgment, her loyalty filled him with a foolish, tender joy.

He bathed each morning at the river. Once, he killed a beaver and greased himself all over against mosquitoes with the fat from its tail. The baby continued to nurse and he made a sling for her from his shirt. He lounged in the doorway of his sod cave, exhausted, fearing that a fever was coming upon him. The situation was confusing. He did not know what course to take, how to start back, wondered if there'd be a party sent to search for him and realized if they did find him he'd be court-martialed. The baby kept nursing and refused to stop. His nipples toughened. Pity scorched him, she sucked so blindly, so forcefully, and with such immense faith. It occurred to him one slow dusk as he looked down at her, upon his breast, that she was teaching him something.

This notion seemed absurd when he first considered it, and then as insights do when we have the solitude to absorb them, he eventually grew used to the idea and paid attention to the lesson. The word "faith" hooked him. She had it in such pure supply. She nursed with utter simplicity and trust, as though the act itself would produce her wish. Half asleep one early morning, her beside him, he felt a slight warmth, then a rush in one side of his chest, a pleasurable burning. He thought it was an odd dream and fell asleep again only to wake to a huge burp from the baby, whose lips curled back from her dark gums in bliss, whose tiny fists were unclenched in sleep for the first time, who looked, impossibly, well fed.

*Ask and ye shall receive. Ask and ye shall receive.* The words ran through him like a clear stream. He put his hand to his chest and then tasted a thin blue drop of his own watery, appalling, God-given milk.

## MISS PEACE MCKNIGHT

FAMILY DUTY WAS deeply planted in Miss Peace McKnight, also the knowledge that if she did not nobody else would—do the duty, that is, of seeing to the future of the McKnights. Her father's Aberdeen street button-cart business failed after he ran out of dead sheep—his own, whose bones he cleverly thought to use after a spring disaster. He sawed buttons with an instrument devised of soldered steel, ground them to a luster with a polisher of fine sand glued to cloth, made holes with a bore and punch which he had self-invented. It was the absence, then, of sheep carcasses that forced his daughter to do battle with the spirit of ignorance.

Peace McKnight. She was sturdily made as a captain's chair, yet drew water with graceful wrists and ran dancing across the rut road on curved white ankles. Hale, Scots, full-breasted as a pouter pigeon, and dusted all over like an egg with freckles, wavy brown-black hair secured with her father's gift—three pins of carved bone—she came to the Great Plains with enough education to apply for and win a teaching certificate.

Her class was piddling at first, all near grown, too. Three consumptive Swedish sisters not long for life, one boy abrupt and full of anger. A German. Even though she spoke plainly and slowly as humanly possible, her class fixed her with stares of tongueless suspicion and were incapable of following a single direction. She had to start from the beginning, teach the alphabet, the numbers, and had just reached the letter *v*, the word *cat*, subtraction, which they were naturally better at than addition, when she noticed someone standing at the back of her classroom. Quietly alert, observant, she had been there for some time. The girl stepped forward from the darkness.

She had roan coppery skin and wore a necklace of bright indigo beads. She was slender, with a pliable long waist, graceful neck, and she was about ten years old.

Miss McKnight blushed pink-gold with interest. She was charmed, first by the confidence of the child's smile and next by her immediate assumption of a place to sit, study, organize herself, and at last by her listening intelligence. The girl, though silent, had a hungry, curious quality. Miss McKnight had a teaching gift to match it. Although they were eight years apart they became, inevitably, friends.

Then sisters. Until late fall, Miss McKnight slept in the school cloakroom and bathed in the river nearby. Once the river froze over, however, an argument developed among the few and far-between homesteads as to which had enough room and who could afford her. No one. Coral Fox stepped in and pestered her father, known as a strange and reclusive fellow, until he gave in and agreed that the new teacher could share the small trunk bed he had made for his daughter, so long as she helped Coral with the poultry.

Mainly, they raised guinea fowl from keets that Scranton Fox had bought from a Polish widow. The speckled purple-black vulturines were half wild, clever. Coral's task was to spy on, hunt down, and follow the hens to their hidden nests. The girls, for Peace McKnight was half girl still while Coral Fox was just growing into womanhood, spent the tag ends of their childhood laughing at the birds' tricks and lying in wait to catch them. Fat, speckled, furious with shrill guinea pride, they acted as house watchdogs and scolded in the oak trees. In lard from a neighbor's pig, Scranton Fox fried strips of late squash, dried sand-dune morels, inky caps, field and oyster mushrooms, crushed acorns, the guinea eggs. He baked sweet bannock, dribbled on it wild aster honey aged in the bole of an oak, dark and pungent as mead.

The sod and plank house was whitewashed inside and the deep sills of small bold windows held geraniums and started seeds. At night, the kerosene lamplight in trembling rings and halos, Miss Peace McKnight felt the eyes of Scranton Fox carve her in space. His gaze was a heat running up and down her throat, pausing elsewhere with the effect of a soft blow.

## SCRANTON FOX

HE IS PECULIAR the way his mother was peculiar—writing poetry on the margins of bits of newspaper, tatters of cloth, even bark. His mother burned her life work, however, and died soon after comforted by the ashes of her words but still in grief for her son, who never did make his survival known but named his daughter for her. Coral. One poem survives. A fragment. It goes like this. *Come to me, thou dark inviolate.* Scranton Fox prays to an unparticular god, communes with the spirit headlong each morning in a rush of ardor that carries him through each difficult day. He is lithe, nearly brown as his daughter, bearded, strong, and serene. He owns over one dozen books and subscribes to periodicals that he lends to Miss McKnight.

He wants to be delivered of the burden of his solitude. A wife would help.

Peace tosses her sandy hair, feels the eyes of Scranton Fox upon her, appreciates their fire, and smiles into the eyes of his daughter, so close to her age they could be sisters, though they end up not. Technically, Miss McKnight becomes a stepmother. Whatever the term, the two young women behave like best girlfriends, holding hands now as they walk to school and tickling each other's necks with long stems of grama grass, cooking for Scranton Fox but also rolling their eyes from time to time at him and breaking into fits of suppressed and impolite laughter.

## CORAL FOX

EMOTIONS UNREEL IN her like spools of cotton.

When he rocks her, Coral remembers the taste of his milk—hot and bitter as dandelion juice. Once, he holds her foot in the palm of his hand and with the adept point of a hunting knife painlessly delivers a splinter, long, pale, and bloody. Teaches her to round her *c*'s and put tiny teakettle handles on her *a*'s. Crooks stray hairs behind her ears. Washes her face with the rough palm of his hand, but gently, scrubbing at her smooth chin with his callus.

He is a man, though he nourished her. Sometimes across the room, at night, in his sleep, her father gasps as though stabbed, dies into himself. She is jolted awake, frightened, and thinks to check his breath with her hand, but then his ragged snore lulls her. In the fresh daylight, staring up at the patches of mildew on the ceiling, Coral watches him proudly from the corners of her eyes as he cracks the ice in the washing pail, feeds a spurt of hidden stove flame, talks to himself. She loves him like nothing else. He is her father, her human. Still, sometimes, afflicted by an anxious sorrow, she holds her breath to see what will happen, if he will save her. Heat flows up the sides of her face and she opens her lips but before her mouth can form a word she sees yellow, passes out, and is flooded by blueness, sheer blueness, intimate and strange, the color of her necklace of beads.

HAVE YOU EVER fallen from a severe height and had your wind knocked forth so that, in the strict jolt's sway, you did experience stopped time? Coral Fox did when she saw her father kiss the teacher. The world halted. There sounded a great gong made of sky. A gasp. Silence. Then the leaves ticked again, the guineas scornfully gossiped, the burly black hound that had replaced the Indian dog pawed a cool ditch in the sand for itself. Sliding back from the casual window to the bench behind the house where she sat afternoons to shell peas, shuck corn, peel dinner's potatoes, pluck guinea hens, and dream, Coral Fox looked at the gold-brown skin on her arms, turned her arms over, turned them back, flexed her pretty, agile hands.

The kiss had been long, slow, and of growing interest and intensity, more educational than any lesson yet given her by Miss Peace Mc-Knight. Coral shut her eyes. Within herself at all times a silent darkness sifted up and down. A pure emptiness fizzing and gliding. Now, along with the puzzling development between her friend and father, something else. It took a long concentration of stillness to grasp the elusive new sensation of freedom, of relief.

# Ozhaawashkwamashkodeykway

## Blue Prairie Woman

THE CHILD LOST in the raid was still nameless, still a half spirit, yet her mother mourned her for a solid year's time and nearly died of the sorrow. A haunting uncertainty dragged the time out. Ozhaawashkwa-mashkodeykway might be picking Juneberries and she feared she would come across her daughter's bones. In the wind at night, a pakuk, she heard it wailing, a white twig skeleton. Stirring the fire, a cleft of flame reminded her of the evil day itself, the massed piles of meat put to the torch, their robes and blankets smoldering, the stinking singe of hair and the hot iron of the rifle barrels. At night, for the first month after that day, her breasts grew pale and hard and her milk impacted, spoiling in her, leaking out under her burnt clothes so that she smelled of sour milk and fire.

An old midwife gave her a puppy and she put it to her breasts. Holding to her nipple the tiny wet muzzle, cradling the needy bit of fur, she cried. All that night the tiny dog mercifully drew off the shooting pains in her breasts and at dawn, drowsy and comfortable, she finally cradled the sweet-fleshed puppy to her, breathed its salty odor, and slept.

Wet ash when the puppy weaned itself. Blood. Her moons began and nothing she pressed between her legs could stop the rush of life. She ate white clay, scratched herself with bull thorns for relief, cut her hair, grew it long, cut it short again, scored her arms to the bone, tied the skull of a buffalo around her neck and for six moons ate nothing but dirt and leaves. It must have been a rich dirt, said her grandmother, for although she slept little and looked tired, Blue Prairie Woman was healthy as a buffalo cow and when her husband returned from his family's wild rice beds, she gave him such a night of sexual pleasure that his eyes followed her constantly after that, narrow and hot. He grew molten when she passed near other men and at night they made their own shaking tent. They got teased too much and moved farther off, to the edge of an island, into the nesting ground of shy and holy loons. There, no one could hear them. In solitude they made love until they became gaunt and hungry, pale wiindigoog with aching eyes, tongues of flame. Still, no child came of their union.

By the time her husband left again with his sled of traps she was calm. During that winter life turned more brutal. The tribe's stores had been burned by order and many times in starving sleep Blue Prairie Woman dreamed the memory of buffalo fat running in rivulets across the ground, soaking into the earth, fat gold from piles of burning meat. She still dreamed, too, with wide-eyed clarity of the young, fleet brown dog, the cradle board bound to its body. She dreamed of her baby bewildered, then howling, then at last riding black as leather, mouth stretched wide underneath a waterless sky. She dreamed its bones rattled in the careful stitching of black velvet, clacked in the moss padding, grown thin. She heard their rhythm, saw the dog, felt the small pakuk flying. She howled and scratched herself half blind and at last so viciously took leave of her mind that the old ones got together and decided to change her name.

On a cool day in spring in the bud-popping moon they held a pitiful feast—only nothing seems pitiful to survivors. In weak sunlight they chewed mud-turtle meat, roasted coot, gopher, their remaining sweet grains of manoomin, acorns and puckoons from a squirrel's cache, and the fresh spears of dandelion. Blue Prairie Woman's name was covered with blood, burned with fire. Her name was old and exquisite and had belonged to many powerful mothers. Yet the woman who had fit inside of it had walked off. She couldn't stop following the child and the dog. Someone else had taken her place. Who, as yet, was unclear. But the old ones did know, agreed between them, that the wrong name would kill what was in there and it had to go—like a husk dried off and scattered. Like a shell to a nut. Hair grown long and sacrificed to sorrow. They had to give her another name if they wanted her to return to the living.

The name they gave her had to be unused. New. Oshke. They asked the strongest of the namers, the one who dreamed original names. This namer was nameless and was neither a man nor a woman, and so took power from the in-between. This namer had long, thick braids and a sweet shy smile, charming ways but arms tough with roped muscle. The namer walked like a woman, spoke in a man's deep voice. Hid coy behind a fan and yet agreed to dream a name to fit the new thing inside Blue Prairie Woman. But what name would help a woman who could be calmed only by gazing into the arrowing distance? The namer went away, starved and sang and dreamed, until it was clear that the only name that made any sense at all was the name of the place where the old Blue Prairie Woman had gone to fetch back her child.

## OTHER SIDE OF THE EARTH

ONCE SHE WAS named for the place toward which she traveled, she was able to be in both places at once—she was following her child into the sun and also pounding the weyass between rocks to dried scruffs of pemmican. She was searching the thick underbrush of her own mind and also punching holes to sew tough new soles on old moccasins. She starved and wandered, tracking the faint marks the dog left as he passed into the blue distance. At the same time, she knocked rice. She parched and stored grain. Sugared. Killed birds. Tamed horses. Her mind was present because she was always gone. Her hands were filled because they grasped the meaning of empty. Life was simple. Her husband returned and she served him with indifferent patience this time. When he asked what had happened to her heat for him, she gestured to the west.

The sun was setting. The sky was a body of fire.

As yet, however, no one had asked. What would happen to the woman called Other Side of the Earth when Blue Prairie Woman found Coral Fox?

## A DOG NAMED SORROW

THE DOG NURSED on human milk grew up coyote gray and clever, a light-boned loping bitch who followed Blue Prairie Woman everywhere. Became her second thought, lay outside the door when she slept, just within the outer flap when it rained, though not in. Never actually inside a human dwelling. Huge with pups or thin from feeding them, teats dragging, the dog followed Blue Prairie Woman. Close and quiet as her shadow, it lived within touch of her, although they never did touch after the dog drew from Blue Prairie Woman's soaked and swollen nipples the heat, the night milk, the overpowering sorrow.

Always there, looking up alert at the approach of a stranger, guarding her in the dusk, waiting for a handout, living patiently on bits of hide, guts, offal, the dog waited. And was ready when Blue Prairie Woman started walking west, following at long last the endless invisible trail of her daughter's flight.

She walked for hours. She walked for years. She walked until she heard about them. The man. The young girl and the blue beads she wore. Where they were living. When she reached the place, she settled on a nearby rise, the dog near. From that distance, the two watched the house—small, immaculate, scent of the hearth fire made of crackling oak twigs. Birth. There was birth in the house, and illness too. She could sense it. Silence, then flurries of motion. Rags hung out. Water splashed from basins or hauled. One shrill cry. Silence again. All day in thin grass, the dog, the woman, sunlight brave on them, their eyes narrowing, breathed each other's air, slept by turns, waited halfway in each other's bodies, the woman, the dog, and then the daughter.

## CORAL FOX

SHE HEARD THE gentle approach that night, the scrawl of leaves, the sighing resonance of discovery. She sat up in her crazy quilt, knowing. Across the room, held in the hot vise of fever, Peace muttered endlessly of buttons and sheep bones. Sounds—a slight tap. The clatter of her beads. In the morning, there was no Coral Fox in the trunk bed. There was only a note, folded twice, penned in the same exquisite, though feminized, handwriting of her father.

*She came for me. I went with her.*

## SCRANTON FOX

PEACE MCKNIGHT WAS never devout, so there was no intimacy of prayer between the newlyweds. Their physical passion suffered, as well, because of the shortness of his bed. There was, after all, very little space inside the sod house and Scranton Fox had slept in a tiny berth on one side of the room, his daughter on the other. Both slept curled like snails, like babies in the wombs of their mothers. More difficult with two in the bedding, however, and it wasn't long before in order to get any rest at all, Peace crawled into Coral's abandoned trunk bed and took up nightly residence apart from her husband.

Still, there were nights when Scranton was inflicted with ardor and arranged himself and his wife in the cramped and absurd postures of love. If only he had thought to use the armless rocking chair before the fire! Peace's mind flashed on the possibility, but she was too Presbyterian to mention it. Even the floor, packed dirt covered with skins, would have been preferable, though cold. But again, she didn't dare introduce that possibility into his mind. Anyway, as it turned out she had every right to turn her back after six months of marriage and the tiny knock of new life began in the cradle of her hipbones. And he retreated, listened to the rasp of her breath, wondered about Coral and imagined the new life to come all at once. Prayed. Wrote poems in his head. *Come to me, thou dark inviolate.*

After her deliverance from the mottled skin sickness, the gasping and fever that made her bones ache, Peace was in her weakness even warier of her husband. For the rest of her pregnancy, she made him sleep alone. Her labor began on a snowy morning. Scranton Fox set out for the Swedish housewife's in a swallowing blizzard that would have cost him his life but for the good sense of his dog, who smelled through driving snow the way back to the door. Reached the door. Smote, rattled, fell into the heat of a bloody scene in which Peace McKnight implored her neglected God in begging futility. For three days her labor shook her in its jaws. Her howls were louder than the wind. Hoarser. Then her voice was lost, a scrape of bone. A whisper. Her face bloated, dark red, then white, then gray. Her eyes rolled back to the whites so she stared mystified with agony into her own thoughts when at last the child tore its way from her. A boy, plump and dead blue. There was no pulse in the birth cord but Scranton Fox thought to puff his own air into the baby's lungs. It answered with a startled bawl.

Scranton wrapped the baby in the skin of a dog and kissed Peace and pressed down her eyelids thinking with tender horror of his own mother, and of all mothers, and of the unfair limitations of our bodies, of the hopeless settlement of our life tasks, and, finally, of the boundless iniquity of God to whom she had so uselessly shrieked. *Look at her*, he called the unseen witness. And perhaps God did or Peace McKnight's mind, pitilessly wracked, finally came out of hiding and told her heart to beat twice more. A weak and fainting gold heeled through a scrap of window, though the snow still blew opaque. Peace saw the wanton gleam, breathed out, gazed out. And then, as she stepped from her ripped body into the utter calm of her new soul, Peace McKnight saw her husband put their son to his breast.

## BLUE PRAIRIE WOMAN

ALL THAT'S IN a name is a puff of sound, a lungful of wind, and yet it is an airy enclosure. How is it that the gist, the spirit, the complicated web of bone, hair, brain, gets stuffed into a syllable or two? How can you shrink the genie of human complexity? How the personality? Unless, that is, your mother gives you her name, Other Side of the Earth.

Who came from nowhere and from lucky chance. Whose mother bore her in shit and fire. She is huge as half the sky. She has tasted in the milk from her father's breasts the disconcerting hatred of her kind, and also protection, so when she falls into the fever she doesn't suffer from it the way Peace did. Although they stop, make camp, and Blue Prairie Woman speaks to her in worried susurrations, the child is in no real danger.

The two camp on the trail of a river cart. The sky opens brilliantly and the grass is hemmed, rife with berries. Blue Prairie Woman picks with swift grace and fills a new-made makak. She dries the berries on sheaves of bark, in the sun, so they will be easy to carry. Lying with her head on her mother's lap, before the fire, Coral asks what her name was as a little baby. The two talk on and on, mainly by signs.

Does the older woman understand the question? Her face burns. As she sinks dizzily into the earth beside her daughter, she feels compelled to give her the name that brought her back. Other Side of the Earth, she says, teeth tapping. Hotter, hotter, confused at first and then dreadfully clear when she sees, opening before her, the western door.

The clouds are pure stratus. The sky a raft of milk. The coyote-gray dog sits patiently there.

Blue Prairie Woman, sick to death and knowing it, reaches swiftly to her left and sets her grip without looking on the nape of the dog's neck. She drags the dog to her. First time she has touched the dog since it drank from her the milk of sorrow. Soft bones, soft muzzle then. Tough old thing now. Blue Prairie Woman holds the dog close underneath one arm and then, knife in hand, draws the clever blade across the beating throat. Slices its stiff moan in half. Collects its dark blood. Blue Prairie Woman then stretches the dog out, skins and guts her, cuts off her head and lowers the chopped carcass into a deep birchbark container. Suspended over flames, just right, adding hot stones, she knows how to heat water the old way in that makak. Tending the fire carefully, weakening, she boils the dog.

When it is done, the meat softened, shredding off the bones, she tips the gray meat, brown meat, onto a birch tray. Steam rises, the fragrance of the meat is faintly sweet. Quietly, she gestures to her daughter. Prods the cracked oval pads off the cooked paws. Offers them to her.

It takes sixteen hours for Blue Prairie woman to contract the fever and only eight more to die of it. All that time, as she is dying, she sings. Her song is wistful, peculiar, soft, questing. It doesn't sound like a death song; rather, there is in it the tenderness and intimacy of seduction addressed to the blue distance.

Never exposed, healthy, defenseless, her body is an eager receptacle for the virus. She seizes, her skin goes purple, she vomits a brilliant flash of blood. Passionate, surprised, she dies when her chest fills, kicking and drumming her heels on the hollow earth. At last she is still, gazing west. That is the direction her daughter sits facing all the next day and the next. She sings her mother's song, holding her mother's hand in one hand and seriously, absently, eating the dog with the other hand—until in the spinning cloud light and across rich level earth, pale reddish creatures, slashed with white on the chest and face, deep-eyed, curious, pause in passing.

The antelope emerge from the band of light at the world's edge.

A small herd of sixteen or twenty flickers into view. Fascinated, they poise to watch the girl's hand in its white sleeve dip. Feed herself. Dip. They step closer. Hooves of polished metal. Ears like tuning forks. Black prongs and velvet. They watch Coral Fox. Blue Prairie Woman's daughter. Other Side of the Earth. Nameless.

She is ten years old, tough from chasing poultry and lean from the fever. She doesn't know what they are, the beings, dreamlike, summoned by her mother's song, her dipping hand. They come closer, closer, grazing near, folding their legs under them to warily rest. The young nurse their mothers on the run or stare at the girl in rapt hilarity, springing off if she catches their wheeling flirtations. In the morning when she wakens, still holding her mother's hand, they are standing all around. They bend to her, huff in excitement when she rises among them quiet and wondering. Easy with their dainty precision, she wanders along in their company. Always on the move. At night she makes herself a nest of willow. Sleeps there. Moves on. Eats bird's eggs. A snared rabbit. Roots. She remembers fire and cooks a handful of grouse chicks. The herd flows in steps and spurting gallops deeper into the west. When they walk, she walks, following, dried berries in a sack made of her dress. When they run, she runs with them. Naked, graceful, the blue beads around her neck.

# The Gravitron

SOME DAYS, I feel the earth's pull more than others. It's only August, but already leaves are drifting to the ground. Bright, then blackening. A low wind rides, trembling in the stiff grass, unwinding and slowing my steps. The gravity tugs harder. Lead instinct. Grave soul. And then I break into a short run, startled. What if? What if just as sure as we are pulled toward earth and destined to go down into it at last, we are also at the same rate pulled toward heaven?

No wonder we are stretched top to bottom from both ends of our being. No wonder the soul can't decide where to wedge itself. And if there are those who aren't troubled by these things, for instance my mother, a checker in a big discount food warehouse who knows that prices change constantly and yet are precisely fixed, well there are others like myself—her daughter, at forty. After a childless marriage that never took, I walk the lake in startling peace, held equally by sky and earth so that some days I feel the perfect suspension, the balance.

OF COURSE, IT only takes one man to throw you off.

There he was one sudden eight P.M. when I went to pick up my mother from work. He was trim, a runner, maybe a Dakota, with braids, glasses, a crooked smile above the six cantaloupe he carried in a red plastic basket.

Cantaloupe that my mother refused to check.

"Go put those back." Her sleek late-fifties face stretched bleak, annoyed and planar, alive with irritation at the man. "I'll wait. Those aren't ripe. You've got to smell them for the test."

He startled us both, then, with his direct line. His love pitch, although at first he was so bold we didn't get it.

"I need a woman."

"My daughter here can help you. She knows how to pick a melon."

"I mean, I *need* a woman."

"Get out of here," my mother advised. "And stay away from my daughter, you!"

Almost with admiration, for certain with respect, he backed away from the cash register. Light on his feet, he turned. Walked down the aisle bearing the cantaloupe. He wasn't old, he wasn't young. Between the two of us, the balance. I picked him out. Right then, I decided what to do with him.

Or decided what to try to do. Given gravity, given earth.

"You keep the line moving. I'll go help him choose a melon," I said to Mom, who helplessly gestured at me not to go.

She was glaring and snapping her eyes in bar-code messages as she dragged cat food and cheeses across her scanner. Canned beans. Bottles. Bulk items. She had been doing this for thirteen years, since she retired from tribal politics. Part-time work, but she liked the change. The store, her store, was an employee-owned co-op arrangement. "Owner," said the badge on her work shirt. Aurora Davis, in print. Right below that she had written Waubanikway, Dawn Woman, with a black pen that leaked corner tears. She wrote her name because she wrote her Indian name on everything she could, insistent that the chimookomaanag get used to her language as she'd had to theirs.

But the man, the man. Went back to find him inhaling the air over the cantaloupe.

HE LOOKED AT me with his head tucked down and raised his eyebrows. His eyes were a brilliant opaque brown with deep lights of humor. I only glanced at him, I did not meet his stare for long—yet a soft heat of interest stole up inside of me. I stepped toward him and my heart thudded. I could feel it in my shoes, in the soles of my feet, then traveling to my fingertips, a quicker pulse.

"That checker in the line," he addressed me, however. "You know her?"

"My mother," I nodded, not understanding.

He thumped the melon. "That's how I was taught. It's wrong, I guess. And I do like them ripe." All of a sudden, he grinned at me, a nice smile, modest but full of meaning. He put his face to the stem scar of the cantaloupe.

"Ripe," he said again.

"Ripe." His sensuous behavior made me dizzy.

"You're still green," he said, but so gently I felt young.

WALKING WITH MOM across the parking lot, I decide I am a generational anomaly. Some type of odd woman out. You see, my mother was only sixteen years old when she had me. In the historical days, she would have worn down her teeth chewing hides by now. The sun would have fried and refried her skin to sheaves of wrinkles. She would be considered ancient, an elder, past all hope or desire, contented with advising the young and passionate. But now, with her Wild Yam creme, a melon to weigh in each hand, her disposable contact lenses in place, and her hair cut, set, brushed, sprayed, she is antimatter, Ageless. Serene and bitterly competent. However, though she lived through the sexual revolution, she has no seeming interest in men.

"He likes you," I say on the way home, driving.

She swats at the window in irritation, but she is too sharp and disillusioned to play coy.

"I know it. Coming through the line after, with those melons up over his chest. No less, he asked me out."

I can't help it. Jealous pique bites my heart.

"Just like that? Already?"

She lifts up her hands, exasperated and resigned. "He thinks he's so funny, too."

"What did he say?"

"His biological clock was ticking. I told him mine needed new batteries. 'I'd like to charge it,' he replies. Then as I am about to get a good one off in answer to that, of course he hands me his credit card to wipe through the machine."

"Acts all innocent, I suppose. *I'd like to charge it*. Really subtle."

"Pah! He's been around once or twice."

"Twice at least," I agree. "But there's something. He's cute."

"He's a school administrator."

"No shit."

"I told you not to say that kind of thing around your mother."

"I'm forty."

"All the better reason."

"Forty *is* the age of reason," I say, resigned. "That's my problem. Too much reason."

"Too many reasons. Excuses." My mother prods at me. "Why don't you go out with him?"

"He likes them ripe," I say, and then we both start laughing and we can't stop, the two of us, laughing our heads off in the car on the way home where he'll call her and call her until finally she says between the two of us she's tired of fighting the magnetic pull and okay she'll do it. The state fair is on. She'll go if I go too.

END OF AUGUST. Night. The cheese curd stands fry curdled milk. The Australian batter-fried potatoes. Chili con carne bars at war. Dip cones, and beer gardens. Eating something long, snakey, and blue, we watch the show horses practice outside the arena in a sawdust ring. So delicate. So fine. Hooves like sewing machine needless. They do fancy stitchwork up and down the sides of the metal fence. They pass so close we can feel the breath off their velvet noses and smell the warmth of their glossed hides, braided manes, sense the determination of their stiff little riders.

Mom is uncomfortable, even standoffish with Herman—his name—Herman Migwans. Not a Dakota at all, but a Chippewa built like the old-time Indian model of a man. Rangy and lean. Good thing his nose is humped and broken or he'd be almost movie-star attractive. Then again, I think miserably, that nose bump only makes him look street-fighter tough. Maybe my mother is offended that he should pick her instead of me. Maybe my mother is protective. Or it could be that she is locked up in the past. She figures that she is done with, finished, all over with love and those complications. No more. A relief. I understand her and that makes sense. But here is Herman, so kind, his hands pluck-ing cotton candy off a paper cone to hand first to her, then me. And so unassuming. He looks at the prize rabbits of every shape and size, and the bread sculptures and the Elvis faces made of beans and seeds, and he makes no jokes whatsoever about the size of the prize boar's sexual equipment. Nor does he look as though he feels entirely outclassed in that department, like some men, staring back over their shoulders at the pig in envy and fascination. But Herman would be good for her, I think, walking behind the two of them. By rights, since he's just five years younger than she and ten more than me, they are the proper couple, too. I stay evasive, therefore, stand aside, simply follow as they make their way zigzagging to the sizzling zipper lights of the midway. Past the bungee jump, over the Chinese bridge, right before us in a moment the Gravitron rears.

FORTY IS THE fulcrum of society, the sawhorse beneath the seesaw of young and old people. Forty is the balance. What my mother meant by excuses is that I keep saying I'm forty as though that should excuse me from having to make the decisions of either the old or the young. I've never been in the center before, though, of life and of people, and I think as I stand in the drama of light and music and fair noise between Herman and my mother that the center is not as invisible a place as I've wished. I watch the people as they move up like happy zombies to the entrance of the ride, a big crowd. Just over their heads, I see the exit and entrance of a new crowd of people slightly nervous and chattering as bored attendants strap them in. The operator of the ride looks way too young. There are brush strokes of a soft yellow beard, hair in a braid, earring. Vacant. He disappears for a minute under the equipment—to adjust some essential gear, I imagine. Then jumps to his music monitor control panel and begins rattling some strange Wolfman Jack spiel into the microphone.

The Gravitron starts slowly with the purr of a giant motor and a lurch of gears. The deep bass throbs to life, heavy rock beat, a flame of guitars. Strapped in standing, hands at their sides, the riders are hugged by welded bars to the inside of a gigantic pie plate that starts turning now, turning against the night. Green lights in refracting bands. Rippling blue. Pink. A maddened cake stand that swivels on its base! Tipping side to side, it spins faster, faster, gravity a hand flattening the faces of the screamers to one green dimension.

"Looks like fun," says my mother. Her tone is so dry I think she's kidding, but she's actually not. This is how on the next run I find myself watching alone, astounded at Herman and my mother as they walk into the cages that close over them like alien claws. Again the ride comes to life, now, Herman and my mother clinging to the bars and straps, blurring into one unit as the ride commences. Since I've seen it before, I turn away for a moment. Turning back the other way around, I casually catch the eye of the operator, or not his eye so much as his strange fixed grin that he is shooting right through me from the little cage he inhabits next to the gears and motors that run the Gravitron.

He stares at me and I stare back at him until I realize he's not seeing me. Staring through me as though he's disordered, his whole body fixed and frozen, he's a shirt-store dummy.

High, I think in total understanding. Very, very high on some drug that did not exist yet when I was twenty.

"Hey you!" I wave my hands at him, yell. He whips his head away from them, and with a screech of Wolfman Jack laughter only crazier and nastier, he accelerates the ride. Faster. Higher. Cranked up and down with fire shooting from their eyes, the riders scream. The operator starts to blow froth bubbles. Rabies! An overdose! And he's garbled, makes no sense. There's only this overarching manic howl that penetrates the Hendrix Purple Haze lick and funk. I am certain he's hit the far edge. I start forward. Others, concerned, do the same. We surround his lighted booth and start to knock, and then we find that his door's wedged shut. We claw and beat and yammer like horror-show blue-faced undead. He's spouting chilling warbles and declaiming as he revs the inner body of the Gravitron.

What follows from above is frightful, the riders understanding now that something has gone most horrifically wrong and the ride, a killer to begin with, now juiced up to unbearable, is whipping them mercilessly through time and space. They're roaring. Puking. Blurred. They're like those tigers turned to butter. They're all one face of horror smeared across the inner circle of the Gravitron. They'll die. Brain damage, inner organs turned to mush. I'm so terrified I grab a railing and begin, with another desperate and grounded loved one, to wrench the bar from the walkway. We'll use it to batter in the Plexiglas window, flail against the door, somehow stick it into the mechanism. But no, someone there before us. With a tire iron she is beating and beating in the window until it smashes and then there are people at the marked controls and the ride is slowing and each rider, coming into focus, is the very picture of sick and dazzled terror except for one.

My mother. She steps out of her cage, doesn't falter, not a single mis-step. She helps a wobbly, limp, gray-green-faced, sweating Herman off and leads him to a place in the grass where he sits in grateful wonder with his eyes still spinning. She strokes his hand. She steadies his shoul-der, puts her arm around him, and just holds him the way I cannot ever remember her holding on to me. The way she acts is so different, so natural, so real, so warm and naked that I suddenly have this picture of what has just happened to her.

My mother's been scaled. All the scales of convention and ironic dis-tance have been scuffed off her. All the boney armor she affects against the world. She has been stripped by centrifugal force and jumbled up inside. The wrench of gravity has undone all her strings. There is this sense of dawning wonder, this pleasant inner ease, this substance of ten-derness suddenly in her gaze as she looks at Herman.

• • •

ONE WEEK LATER. Many phone calls between them. Lots of late-night whispers. Mom walks into the living room and sits down beside me on the gray couch.

"All right then. I suppose I should have it."

I don't even think of asking whether she means what I assumed she does. Sex. With a man. Herman. I decide to pretend as though her attitude of sacrifice is normal, and I sigh, "What else can you do?"

"It's a fact of life now, isn't it."

I nod. "Yes."

"Not that it wasn't there in the past . . ." Her voice, when she continues, begins to drift. "But we put a different emphasis. Went by certain rules. The book . . ."

"The book?"

"Went by the book."

"There was a book? Which book, Mom?"

"Not a real book. More a so-called book, of accepted ways. How-tos that were, you know, passed down from woman to woman."

"In the family? The tribe?"

"Both." Her voice now is firm. We have switched roles, her from asking to telling. Me from advice giver into seeker.

"So the grandma, she would sit down with the girl something just like this, and she would make it very clear what the girl could and could not do."

"For instance . . ."

"Stepping over streams when you have your period."

"You never said a thing."

"Well, I don't believe in it. Besides that, how can you describe this to a girl growing up in the city? You never had to cross a stream anyway."

"There were cracks in sidewalks, sewer systems, hoses, that sort of thing."

"Now you're fooling with me. These things were sacred, I tell you. We had other women to rely upon, my daughter, and now, look. No medicine women to ask."

"Ask what?"

"If I'm still capable."

"Of sex?"

Her silence tells me.

"Mom, you're capable. Believe me, you are."

She nods, but she still doesn't speak for a while, and then she finally mumbles into the flowery print of her lap that she's made an appointment at the clinic, with a "women's expert." Could I drive her over there for moral support. She hasn't ever had a full exam.

"What? So you never had a . . ."

"No."

"But the doctor. Can't they . . ."

"Force me to get a checkup?"

"I see what you mean. I just thought it was so normal, so inevitable, that there wouldn't be a question. You'd have a full exam. Why?"

"I knew what I knew. I told the doctor it was my business, not his. Grandma helped me when I had you. But now, times are different. I think I should. Not that I have any problem, it's just that I want to know whether I'm . . ."

She hesitates.

"Healthy?"

"Normal."

"Mom, of course you're normal."

"Okay, but I just want to check."

So the morning we drive to the clinic, she spends about an hour in the bathroom, getting ready, scrubbing and showering, worrying. When she finally emerges, she looks the same, not even much cleaner really, and I can't help it but I ask.

"What was that about?"

She doesn't hear me, however, she is too busy trying on and throwing off clothes. I stand back and let her go through her closet. She's so nervous. It's like having a skittish daughter. I offer to go into the office with her, but she grimly sets a purse on her arm and leaves, muttering in apprehension, low, beneath her breath.

Hours pass. The door slams. She is back. Working up a fury. She stamps into the house and throws the keys on the table, sits down. Fumes. I carefully, slowly, put some water into the kettle and boil tea. I don't want to ask. She finally speaks.

"That young doctor was forward with me!"

"How?"

"I was lying there, covered with that sheet, and he came in for the exam. When he lifted that sheet for the exam he said, 'My, aren't we glitzy today!'"

"You're kidding!"

She pouts. "I hate when you say that. Of course I am not kidding. That is the way it was, the phrase of words, *my, aren't we glitzy!* I said nothing, of course. Why in the world do you think he said it?"

"Maybe you're"—I try to think—"unusually better than normal down there!"

The truth is, I don't have a clue either. "Did you wear some fancy underwear or something?"

"I had none on, of course. None on at that time. No, it was simple rudeness."

"Did you wear some perfume, then?"

"That neither. I just, well, I used some of that feminine hygiene spray they advertise. I took it from your side of the bathroom, that's all."

I look at her quizzically.

"I don't have any of that stuff."

"You don't have any."

"No."

"Then . . . well, it looked like a can of what they advertise. Same color."

"Mom!"

"What?"

I go check the bathroom, remembering, and bring back the can stashed from last Halloween's party where I did my hair with a frosting of gold-spray glitter. I pick the can of glitter up and bring it to her.

"Is this what you used?"

She nods.

"Read the label," I say.

She does, then rears back, thoughtfully blinking.

THERE IS THIS problem of where they're going to go to have this sexual thing. Herman's place is shared with a son and his family and Mom's is shared with me. I mean, it's not that they actually say anything direct, but I know I should find a way to really make myself as neutral and unobtrusive as I wish I was.

Afternoon. Sunday. I think of the word matinee. I look at the great outdoors through our second-floor window. Spitting snow. Nevertheless, I get my coat as soon as Herman arrives and I take myself for a very long walk. I catch a movie about a wise dragon and I check out two library books. I purchase baking soda, garlic salt, milk. I look in store windows, contemplate shoes, and finally I walk back slowly, trying not to shiver as the sun has disappeared. I reach the house just as Herman is going out, looking very grave and sad and humbled with the weight of the world.

"So?" I say to Mom as soon as I'm inside.

"So what?" she answers.

"Oh." I gather the earth didn't move.

"Don't 'oh' me. You don't know!"

"What don't I?"

"You never told me!"

She's not been in such a state before, I see all of a sudden. She's jumping up and pacing back and forth. Strewn with a blasted weight of emotion. I can sense waves of feeling, banners with cutting edges, huge sensations ranging from her, all set loose. Dressed, but awkwardly, her collar turned inside, she bats away my hands when I try to fix it. Goes to a corner of the room. And it is here from watching her back and shoulders tremble that I understand it is too big for her, too much. It is pulling at her with inexorable weight. She's falling into it. Gravity. She can't contain her feelings for the first time in her life. And as for me, I am emptied out, hungry and chilled. It is terrible to see your mother in love. His hands, his kiss, his almost frantic desire, his bewilderment, and for the first time a man's gentleness, she says. She can't stop talking. We have these earthly bodies. We don't know what they want. Half the time, we pretend they are under our mental thumb, but that is the illusion of the healthy and the protected. Of sedate lovers. Not my mother. Not me, ever. For the body has emotions it conceives and carries through without concern for anyone or anything but it. Love is one of those. Going back to something very old knit into the brain as we were growing. Hopeless. Scorching. Ordinary. He feels it too or she would certainly go crazy. Already in the other room, the phone is ringing, he is calling her, and my mother as she walks toward the receiver with her hand outstretched seems to shrink and fall into the steady pull.

# History of the Puyats

YOU NO DOUBT have heard of the missionary priest named Father La-Combe, who passed his nights in a coffin to grow comfortable with his mortality, and who was revered by his flock for attracting divine luck to the great and rowdy hunts undertaken for buffalo. Although the history of the Puyats begins well before that time, the central astonishment of their story touches on the hunt. From spring to midsummer, the Plains Ojibwe and Michif people killed the buffalo. Hard as was the killing, those deaths were easy compared with the sheer volume of labor it took to skin the beasts and butcher them, dress the meat, and preserve the extra in the form of pemmican. This long-lasting food was their primary winter and travel sustenance. The beast was deboned, cooked, pulverized, mixed with its own rendered tallow, and returned to its hairless skin. The huge, fleet, brutal-willed animal was concentrated to a form that a woman could carry on her back, if she had to. Mostly the transformed buffalo were loaded in stacked bales onto wooden Red River oxcarts that screamed as they moved across the violently flat plains.

Upon the topmost of these bales, in the partial history I now recount, there rode a young girl in whom the bitterness of seven generations of peasant French and an equal seven of enemy-harassed Ojibwe ancestors was concentrated. Her parents, the mother a crane clan girl of fretful, peaceless energy, and her father, small and arrogant with Montreal-based spleen, positively hated each other. At the same time, they could not abide the frustrations of separation. Their child, created of spilled-over complexity and given the French name Pauline according to the father's wish, seethed in the high noon sun and considered the tedium of their slow and inevitable progress so impossible to bear that she was almost glad, when spotting a party of Bwaanag, a source of mortal hatred, to call out her find from the top of the bale of skins.

The band of Ojibweg and French-Indian Michifs halted in alarm. All who could shoot well were armed and arranged behind cover. The Bwaanag did the same and for hours, without a shot being fired, the two enemy camps exchanged volleys of shouted insults increasing in amazed fury and filth, which of course neither side could understand as they had no language in common, but which did vastly increase the knowledge of the children and their accompanying priest. He, the good priest, whose job it was to bless the hunt, found himself in the middle of an enmity so old that even his holy presence wasn't sufficient to cause the women to contain their contempt. All he could do, then, was to break up his candles and knead the beeswax into plugs, which he stuffed into the children's ears, and his own. Ever after, then, the first Pauline's memory of what followed was a soundless vision.

She saw at one point her enraged mother, pained to madness by the memory of her brothers' loss to the Bwaanag, climb the bales and throw off her skirts. Pointing to her nakedness and flaunting it boldly, she screamed a challenge so foul and instantly understandable that a Bwaan rushed from cover and was nearly killed, one bullet clipping his ear half off and the other bullet shattering a wooden club that flew from his hand so that he sensibly retreated. The two sides returned to shouting, but it was clear, by then, that both parties were returning from successful hunting and were not only low on ammunition but more interested in supplying their home camps with meat than in taking revenge. Still, in retaliation for that bold Anishinaabekwe's affront, a Bwaan woman of equal fury lifted her buckskins and cried a challenge in her own language and in so severe and scathing a manner that one of the men from Pauline's camp leaped forward out of cover and was seriously wounded in the thigh. Pauline's mother threw herself high up the bales and now other women did as well, so that the cacophony of insults exchanged became at once an earsplitting din and the men, seeing their half-naked wives frothing wild, began to think they were by contrast the more restrained and rational. The husband of Pauline's mother in particular was disgusted by his wife's display. In fact, he became at length so crazed with irritation that he raised a white flag, the symbolism of which long had been learned from the protocol of the U.S. Cavalry, and he walked unarmed to the center of the field. Being French, and of French traders, he knew enough of the Bwaan language to make himself understood. When he raised his hands, a curious silence fell. He spoke to both sides.

"We are not war parties! Hear me! We are laden with meat to survive. Both of our caravans would be wise to depart in peace. But since it is our hotheaded women who are looking to shed blood, and as we are French and Ojibwe men who always satisfy our women, let two of the women race to the death. The winner of the race, we all agree, shall have the other's life. After this is accomplished, we will go our separate directions and meet to fight, as men and warriors, another day."

The child heard this speech by her father with an inner sense of glee, as did the others in the camp, for all knew that Pauline's mother was a superb and unbested runner. She had challenged the young men who came to court her to footraces, claiming that she would not stoop to marry a man who could not beat her. She vowed she would marry the one who could. Her boast was the reason she eventually wed the unprepossessing, even ugly, deer-legged, *voyageur* who was her much despised husband. He had embarrassed her by winning, a bad way to start a marriage. Her swiftness had only increased since that day, as had his own. Although, at his speech, her pride rose up instantly, she experienced an inner pang that he, the father of her child, could so arrogantly put up her life. What if there were by chance a better runner among the Bwaan women? Anger beat its wing inside of her. It was as she walked to the race ground to take her place that she decided, then, to lose the race. In pride before his compatriots, her man would have to offer up his life for her own. At last, and how well he deserved it, she would be rid of him!

The enemy camps, having laid down their weapons, ranged to either side of a finish mark. The Bwaan woman who was to race was short of leg but light boned. Both wore dresses of light calico. At the starting point, they divested themselves of what might hamper them—the Bwaan woman wore a long bone breastplate, a clapperless cowbell, a cradle board into which a fat infant was bound. Both women put down their skinning knives—over the razor-edged slender blades of steel their eyes met briefly in opaque agreement. They turned away. Pauline's mother carefully lifted strand after strand of trader's beads over her head—those beads, from Africa and Venice, Bohemia and Quechee, Vermont, she put into her daughter's hands. She unbuckled a wide belt of bull leather studded with brass, but did not remove from her ears the shining cones dripping small tinklers of German silver, so that, when the women began to run, her mother's swift progress began with light music that, as her stride lengthened, silenced in the smooth wind of her movement.

Running, that first Pauline's mother felt a tremendous ease and freedom. The earth purred underneath her makizinan that day. She reached the turn a bit before her desperate opponent, picked up the stick she was to take with one swift movement, and in returning found it very hard to force herself to lose.

When she did, Pauline, though treated by her mother with no kindness, heard as if from outside herself an animal howl that tore her chest. The incredible noise ripped her breath out by the roots. Her lungs shut. She fell upon her mother in a haze of yellow spots and clutched her dress so tightly that her fingers pressed through the soft weave and her knuckles ground against her mother's thighs. It was, then, more the weight of his treasured daughter's horror than love for his merciless wife or even male pride that caused Pauline's father to step forward just as the Bwaan woman raised her skinning knife, and to offer, as his wife had known he would, to substitute his own life for hers.

The Bwaan woman drew back, her eyes roamed over the man with the pelt on his chin and the child, equally ugly, who so obviously belonged to him. She wanted very much to kill the woman of the Ojibwe because of her own losses in the immemorial blood feud between their tribes, and because she had sensed, in running beside her, that the woman withheld her power and could easily have beaten her. Such an ignominy scorched her stone roaster's heart. But then, as the child's grief turned with even more violence upon her father, whom, to be quite frank about it, the girl preferred, the Bwaan woman, recalling the pain of her own loss of her own father at the age of this child, and in a nighttime raid by Ojibwe, decided instantly that if she could balance this girl's grief with her own, like a stick on her finger, she would be solved of her need for revenge.

She stood aside to let the other woman rise.

A gift for clever thought, a certain talent for talking, a swiftness with the language, became a Puyat trait after this quick Frenchman who then spoke to save his life. He spoke clearly, as though suddenly struck with his idea.

"Of course, if any of you big-bellied Bwaan men can beat me in a running race, then each of you can murder half of me. The woman can have my left side to cut my heart out, and eat it too, if there's anything left— after all, my wife has sharpened her teeth on it for years. The man can have my right side because niinag swings there, long and heavy. When I run, I'm forced to tie it up or it will strike my thigh and bruise me. But today, since this may be the last race I'll run, I'll let it gallop free!"

By the time he finished speaking the two sides were laughing and there was no question that the race would occur. The only problem the Bwaanag had was in choosing a runner. There were two, and equally matched. One was a powerful bull-chested hunter with legs that bulged with fabulous muscles, and the other was a woman-man, a graceful sly boy who sighed, poised with grave nuance, combed his hair, and peered into the tortoiseshell hand mirror that hung around his neck by a rawhide thong. The wife of the hunter refused to let her valued husband risk his life in such a ridiculous game, and she yelled, browbeat, pulled her knife on him herself, while the others were lost in a debate. Was the preening boy a man or a woman for the purposes of this race?

Some of the Ojibweg, who judged his catlike stance too threatening, rejected him as a male runner on account of his female spirit. Others were wary of the scowling hunter and argued that as the man-woman would run with legs that grew beneath a penis as unmistakable as his opponent's, he was enough of a male to suit the terms. The hunter's wife finally won, delivering to her husband such a blow with the butt of his own rifle that he fell senseless and gagging. The woman-man narrowed eyes rimmed with smoky black, shrugged off a heavy dress of fine-tanned deerhide, and stood, astonishingly pure and lovely, in nothing but a white woman's lace-trimmed pantalets. At the signal, then, both commenced to race.

They tested each other, pulling a step ahead and dropping a step behind, speeding and slowing to throw the other off pace, and found themselves equally matched. It would be a race of wit as well as strength then. When to spend the ultimate energy and when to conserve, draw ahead to the last reserve of strength early to discourage, or save some for the final kick? The clever Montrealer decided by the time he grasped the stick at halfway that he'd tag a pace behind and wheeze to confuse his opponent and then in his last lengths, sign of the cross, kiss of God, he'd fly past, surprising the Bwaan, and show him the heels of his feet. This would have worked more easily had not his opponent, whose job it was as a woman to study men and whose immediacy of manhood gave him an uncanny understanding, read the mind of the Frenchman and slowed to conserve the ability to finish. They both knew, then, that their strategies came down to a hot finale and they each determined to blister straight through their lungs and guts to cross the line ahead and live.

When it came right down to the end, though, the Frenchman had the stronger kick and the man-woman, losing by a toe, swiped her dress neatly from the grass and simply kept running, across the broad plains, into the hills. Those who wished to start after her were detained now by the priest, who, though slow to understand the outcome of the wager and the sequence of events, launched forth a God-inspired tirade that cowed the French Ojibwe Michifs and brought them to their Catholic senses, so that they did not chase the fleeing Bwaan but grudgingly agreed with the priest's diplomatic statement that the race had been an exact tie. No blood should be spilled.

Yet the Bwaan woman would have satisfaction for her relatives. Lunging forward with one arrowing blur of movement, she slipped her skinning knife beneath the ribs of the Frenchman, Pauline's father, and drew a sickening arc so that he found, quite suddenly, he was kneeling in prayer, his intestines slowly popping into his hands. And then his daughter was before him trying gently to stuff them back in their exact mysterious intricate folds, but failing even as he crumpled. Leaning sideways, he spilled about himself. Dying, he looked into his daughter's face and said to her in the clarity of last vision that she must kill her mother.

IT WAS IMPERISHABLE, the command of the father imposed upon the daughter. And no less the will she had to carry it out. Her intention was forged in the heat of grief and tempered in its freezing aftermath. Though young, the girl now harbored a blade of certainty that waited calmly in her for its chance. Pauline's mother knew. That is why, one day, with no warning and no word but a filthy cry, she dragged the girl to the shit pile and forced her snarling child face-down and said to her in a deadly voice, "This is where you'll be if ever you go against me."

A mistake, on the mother's part, to challenge one so like herself.

Ever after, the stink of waste reminded the girl. Her mother pushed Pauline into the fire next, and so that too became an unforgettable piece of the promise. The burns of hot coals on her skin were memories. As was the soup her mother would not feed her—a bitter absence in her stomach. And the sticks of wood that broke against her legs and over her back. The air that tore open her chest each time she breathed with the broken rib, and bloody snow. The only thing her mother let her eat one winter when the meat was scarce was the bloody snow beneath the death of the animal or its butchering.

Yet the girl survived on that. She grew fast on the blows that didn't land and even faster on the ones that did. She flourished in twisted energy and grew taller than her father and meaner than her mother until one day, as her mother lay weakened by fever in the brush lean-to, on the trapline, the daughter brought a horn of foul boiling stew of bark and diseased rabbit and a mole that an owl must have dropped. Although her mother clawed at her, she held the woman's mouth open and poured the boiling stuff straight down her gullet so that her throat was seared, her mouth severely blistered, and all she could do was gasp, in her agonized delirium, for three days, the name Pauline.

That girl sat as far as possible from her mother, by the fire, surrounded by warm blankets and skins. With satisfaction, she watched the woman who bore her shake and chatter her teeth like a turtle rattle and weep as the fever alternately scorched and froze her. Recovering, the woman lost one side of her face. The nerves destroyed by inner heat, her flesh sagged in a bizarre leer that made her suddenly frightening to men so that, though she could still run, there was no one to catch her.

At the same time Pauline, who had inherited none of her mother's grace and all of her father's squat, exaggerated pop-eyed vigor, suddenly became irresistible to men. She was courted famously by love flute. She tried her lovers out across the tent, while her mother burned in dark nothingness. Men brought Pauline shells, a dress of red calico that reflected fire. They offered her stamped trade silver—owls, turtles, otters twining, bears, and horned frogs. They brought her meat so that she never went hungry. A necklace of brass beads appeared, hung beside her door by a night visitor. A good kettle. Cakes of maple sugar. She wanted for nothing. Men sought her though they were befuddled by their fascination. Was it her slim long waist, tight in the red calico? Maybe it was the way she looked so boldly at a man, then shyly away. It was not her face, or maybe it was, for her childhood ugliness had become something else—a ferocity, a sexual charm partaking of no sweetness, a look that registered and gloated over everything about a man. A hunger.

The young girl's appetite became a famishment and then a ravenous emptiness that she found men, for very short amounts of time, were capable of solving. Still, though she had her pick of them, she was restless, so she took the poison, started drinking the way her mother had started long ago. The terrible fact was this: In creating the emptiness, the mother disallowed her the means to fill her void. Pauline could not love or be loved. She had been robbed of her capacity either to give or receive anything so profoundly good.

Her mother drank until her face sagged and her tongue froze to the roof of her mouth. Her brain locked. She became so helpless that she could not move even when she was invaded by worms. She was thus eaten before her body was put in the ground, removing the burden of her doom from Pauline. Freed, the girl married four times to different Frenchmen. With every marriage she experienced the beginning as a wicked and promising intensity that grew unbearable and then subsided into indifference so profound that, one day, the indifference extended to herself. She collected and drank the juice of catfish spines, which, mixed with raw alcohol, killed her in her sleep.

IF YOU KNOW about the buffalo hunts, you perhaps know that the one I describe, now many generations past, was one of the last. Directly after that hunt, in fact, before which the priest made a great act of contrition and the whirlwind destruction, lasting twenty minutes, left eight hundred animals dead, the rest of the herd did not bolt away but behaved in a chilling fashion.

As many witnesses told it, the surviving buffalo milled at the outskirts of the carnage, not grazing but watching with an insane intensity, as one by one, swiftly and painstakingly, each carcass was dismantled. Even through the night, the buffalo stayed, and were seen by the uneasy hunters and their families the next dawn to have remained standing quietly as though mourning their young and their dead, all their relatives that lay before them more or less unjointed, detongued, legless, headless, skinned. At noon the flies descended. The buzzing was horrendous. The sky went black. It was then, at the sun's zenith, the light shredded by scarves of moving black insects, that the buffalo began to make a sound.

It was a sound never heard before; no buffalo had ever made this sound. No one knew what the sound meant, except that one old toughened hunter sucked his breath in when he heard it and as the sound increased he attempted not to cry out. Tears ran over his cheeks and down his throat, anyway, wetting his shoulders, for the sound gathered power until everyone was lost in the immensity. That sound was heard once and never to be heard again, that sound made the body ache, the mind pinch shut. An unmistakable and violent grief, it was as though the earth itself was sobbing. One cow, then a bull, charged the carcasses. Then there was another sight to add to the sound never heard before. Situated on a slight rise, the camp of hunters watched in mystery as the entire herd, which still numbered thousands, began to move. Slightly at first, then more violently, the buffalo proceeded to trample, gore, even bite their dead, to crush their brothers' bones into the ground with their stone hooves, to toss into the air chunks of murdered flesh, and even, soon, to run down their own calves. The whole time they uttered a sound so terrible that the people were struck to the core and could never speak of what they saw for a long time afterward.

*The buffalo were taking leave of the earth and all they loved,* said the old chiefs and hunters after years had passed and they could tell what split their hearts. *The buffalo went crazy with grief to see the end of things. Like us, they saw the end of things and like many of us, many today, they did not care to live.*

What does that tell you about the great pain of the end of things that lives in every family, here on the reservation? The daughter was, of course, the warped result of all that twisted her mother. She was the hope, the poison, what came next, beyond the end of things. She was the residue of what occurred when some of our grief-mad people trampled their children. And so the history of the Puyats is the history of the end of things. It is bound up in despair and the red beasts lust for self-slaughter, an act the priests call suicide, which our people rarely practiced until now.

# Le Mooz

MARGARET HAD EXHAUSTED three husbands, and Nanapush outlived his six wives. They were old by the time they shacked up out in the deep bush. Besides, as Anishinaabeg in the last century's first decades, having starved and grieved, seen prodigious loss, having endured theft by agents of the government and chimookomaanag farmers, they were tired. You would think, at last, they'd just want simple comfort. A harmless mate. Quiet. Companionship and sleep. But times did not go smoothly. Peace eluded them. For Nanapush and Margaret found a surprising heat in their hearts. Fierce and sudden, it sometimes eclipsed both age and anger in tenderness. Then, they made love with an amazed greed and purity that astounded them. At the same time, this was apt to burn out of control.

When their love heated up, Margaret and Nanapush fought. Stinging flames of words scorched their hearts and blistered their tongues. Silence was worse. Beneath its slow-burning weight, their black looks singed. After a few days their minds shriveled into dead coals. Some speechless nights, they lay together like logs turned completely to ash. They were almost afraid to move, lest they sift into light flakes and disintegrate. It was a young love set blazing in bodies aged and overused, and sometimes it cracked them like too much fire in an old tin stove.

To survive in their marriage, they developed many strategies. For instance, they rarely collaborated on any task. Each hunted, trapped, and fished alone. They could not agree even on so little a thing as how and where to set a net. The gun, which belonged to Nanapush, was never clean when it was needed. Traps rusted. It was up to Margaret to scour the rifle barrel, smoke the steel jaws. Setting snares together was impossible, for in truth they snared themselves time and again in rude opinions and mockery over where a rabbit might jump or how to set the loop. Their avoidance only hardened them in their individual ways, and so when Margaret beached the leaky old boat and jumped ashore desperate for help, there was no chance of agreement.

Margaret sometimes added little Frenchisms to her Ojibwemowin, just the way the fancy-sounding wives of the French *voyageurs* added, like a dash of spice, random *le*'s and *la*'s. So when she banged into the cabin screaming of *le moož*, Nanapush woke, irritated, with reproof on his lips, as he was always pleased to find some tiny fault with his beloved.

*"Le moož! Le moož!"* she shouted into his face. She grabbed him by the shirt so violently that he could hear the flimsy threads part.

"Booni' ishin!" He tried to struggle from her grip, but Margaret rapidly explained to him that she had seen a moose swimming across the lake and here was their winter's provisions, easy! With this moose meat dried and stored, they would survive. "Get up, old man!" She grabbed the gun and dragged him to the boat before he even mentally prepared himself to hunt moose.

Nanapush pushed off with his paddle, sulking. Besides their natural inclination to disagree, it was always the case that if one of them was particularly intrigued and eager about some idea, the other was sure to feel the opposite way just to polarize the situation. If Nanapush asked for maple syrup with his meat, Margaret gave him wild onion. If Margaret relished a certain color of cloth, Nanapush declared that he could not look upon that blue or red—it made him mean and dizzy. When it came to sleeping on the fancy spring bed that Margaret had bought with this year's bark money, Nanapush adored the bounce and she was stingy with it, so as not to use it up. Sometimes he sat on the bed and joggled up and down when she was gone, just to spite her. For her part, once he began craftily to ask for wild onion, she figured he'd developed a taste for it and so bargained for a small jar of maple syrup, thus beginning the obvious next stage of their contradictoriness, which was that each asked the opposite of what they really wanted and so got what they wanted. It was confusing to their old friend Father Damien, but to the two of them it brought serene harmony. So when Margaret displayed such extreme determination in the matter of the moose that morning, not only was Nanapush feeling particularly lazy but he also decided to believe she really meant the opposite of what she cried out, and so he dawdled with his paddle and tried to tell her a joke or two. She, however, was in dead earnest.

"Paddle! Paddle for all you're worth!" she yelled.

"Break your backs, boys, or break wind!" Nanapush mocked her.

Over the summer, as it wasn't the proper time for telling Ojibwe aadizookaanag, Father Damien had tried to convert Nanapush by telling as many big fish tales as he could remember, including the ones about the fish that multiplied, the fish that swallowed Jonah. Soon, Father Damien had had to reach beyond the Bible. Nanapush's favorite was the tale of the vast infernal white fish and the maddened chief who gave chase through the upper and lower regions of the earth.

"Gitimishk!" Margaret nearly choked in frustration, for the moose had slightly changed direction and they were not closing in quickly enough for her liking.

"Aye, aye, Ahabikwe," shouted Nanapush, lighting his pipe as she vented her fury in deep strokes. If the truth be told, he was delighted with her anger, for when she lost control like this during the day she often lost control once the sun went down also, and he was already anticipating their pleasure.

"Use that paddle or my legs are shut to you, lazy fool!" she growled.

At that, he went to work and they quickly drew alongside the moose. Margaret steadied herself, threw a loop of strong rope around its wide, spreading antlers, and then secured the rope tightly to the front of the boat, which was something of an odd canoe, having a flat, tough bottom, a good racing boat but not all that easy to steer.

"Now," she ordered Nanapush, "now, take up the gun and shoot! Shoot!"

But Nanapush did not. He had killed a moose this way once before in his life, and he had nothing to prove. He hefted the gun and made certain it was loaded, but, as he quite enjoyed the free ride they were receiving from the hardworking moose, he decided to wait.

"Let's turn him around, my adorable pigeon," he cried to his lady. "Let him tow us back home. I'll shoot him once he reaches the shallow water just before our cabin."

Margaret knew the dangers, but could not help but agree that this particular plan arrived at by her lazy husband was a good one, and so, by using more rope and hauling on first one antler and then another with all of their strength, they proceeded to turn their beast and head him in the right direction. Nanapush sat back smoking his pipe and relaxed once they were pointed homeward. The sun was out and the air was cool, fresh. All seemed right between the two of them now. Margaret even admonished him about the tangle of fishing tackle all around his seat, and there was affection in her voice.

"You'll poke yourself," she said, "you fool." At that moment, the meat pulling them right up to their doorstep, she did not really even care. "I'll fry the rump steaks tonight with a little maple syrup over them," she said, her mouth watering. "Old man, you're gonna eat good! Oooh"—she almost cried with appreciation—"our moose is so fat!"

"He's a fine moose," Nanapush agreed passionately. "You've got an eye, Mindimooyenh. He's a juicy one, our moose!"

"I'll roast his ribs, cook the fat with our beans, and keep his brains in a bucket to tan that big hide! Oooh, ishte, my husband, the old men are going to envy the makizinan that I will sew for you."

"Beautiful wife!" Nanapush was overcome. "Precious sweetheart!" They looked at one another with great love.

As they gazed, holding the rare moment of mutual agreeableness, the hooves of the moose struck the first sandbar near shore, and Margaret cried out for her husband to lift the gun and shoot.

"Not quite yet, my beloved," said Nanapush confidently, "he can drag us nearer yet!"

"Watch out! Shoot now!"

The moose indeed approached the shallows, but Nanapush planned in his pride to shoot the animal just as he began to pull them from the water, therefore making their task of dressing and hauling mere child's play. He got the moose in his sights and then waited as it gained purchase. The old man's feet, annoyingly, tangled in the fishing tackle he had been too lazy to put away, and he jigged attempting to kick it aside.

"Margaret, duck!" he cried. Just as the moose lunged onto land he let blast, completely missing and totally terrifying the moose, which gave a hopping skip that seemed impossible for a thing so huge, and plunged straight up the bank. Margaret, reaching back to tear the gun from her husband's hands, was bucked completely out of the boat and said later that if only her stubborn no-good man hadn't insisted on holding on to the gun she could have landed, aimed, and killed them both, as she then wished to do most intensely. Instead, as the moose tore off with the boat still securely tied by three ropes to his antlers, she was left behind screaming for the fool to jump. But he did not and within moments, the rampaging moose, with the boat bounding behind, disappeared into the woods.

"My man is stubborn, anyway," she said, dusting off her skirt, checking to make sure that she was still together in a piece, nothing broken or cut. "He will surely kill that moose!" She spoke, in wishful hope but inside she felt stuffed with a combination of such anxiety and rage that she did not know what to do—to try to rescue Nanapush or to chop him into pieces with the hatchet that she found herself sharpening as she listened for the second report of his gun.

"Bloof!"

Yes. There it was. Good thing he hadn't jumped out, she muttered. She began to tramp, with her carrying straps and an extra sharp knife, in the direction of the noise.

In fact, that Nanapush did not jump out of the boat had little to do with his great stubbornness or bravery. When the moose jolted the boat up the lakeshore, the tackle that already wound around his leg flew beneath his seat as he bounced upward and three of his finest fishing hooks stuck deep into his buttocks as he landed, fastening him tight. The fishline tangled him round and round, winding the bench of the boat. He screeched in pain, further horrifying the animal, and struggled, driving the hooks in still deeper, until he could only hold on to the edge of the boat with one hand, gasping in agony, as with the other he attempted to raise the gun to his shoulder and kill the moose.

All the time, of course, the moose was running wildly. Pursued by this strange, heavy, screeching, banging, booming thing, it fled in dull terror through bush and slough. It ran and continued to run. Those who saw Nanapush, as he passed all up and down the reservation, stood a moment in fascinated shock and rubbed their eyes, then went to fetch others, so that soon the predicament of Nanapush was known and reported everywhere. By then, the moose had attained a smooth loping trot, and passed with swift ease through farmsteads and pastures, the boat flying up and then disappearing down behind.

Nanapush again raised his gun, but as there was nothing to aim at but the rump of the huge animal, he stung its hindquarters, at which point, said Nanapush later, the moose began shooting back at him, the pellets whizzing by his nose and brow. Again he shot. This time the moose pellets all hit their target. The boat jumped high in the air and cracked down as the moose sped forward, raising a groan from Nanapush that those who heard it for miles around would always remember for the flat depth of its despair. Many stopped whatever they were doing to gape and yell, and others ran for their rifles, but they were all too late to shoot the moose and free poor Nanapush.

One day passed. In his moose-drawn fishing boat, Nanapush toured every part of the reservation that he'd ever hunted, and saw everyone he'd ever known, and then went to places he hadn't visited since childhood. At one point, a family digging cattail roots were stunned to see the boat, the moose towing it across a slough, and a man slumped over, for by now poor Nanapush had given up and surrendered to the pain, which, at least, he said later, he shared with the beast whose rump he'd stung with bullets. He'd already tried to leave the best part of his butt on the canoe bench, but no matter how he tried he couldn't tear himself free, so he had given up and went to sleep as he always did in times of stress, hoping that he'd wake up with an idea of how to end his tortured ride.

But when he woke up, he realized that the moose was heading for the most remote parts of the reservation, where poor Nanapush was convinced he surely would die. So he began to talk to the moose as they strode along—the words jounced out of him.

"Niiji!" he cried, "my brother, slow down!"

The moose flicked back an ear to catch the sound of the thing's voice, but didn't stop.

"I will kill no more!" declared Nanapush. "I now throw away my gun!" And he cast it aside after kissing the barrel and noting well his surroundings. But as though it sensed and felt only contempt for the man's hypocrisy, the moose snorted and kept moving.

"I apologize to you," cried Nanapush, "and to all of the moose I ever killed and to the spirit of the moose and the boss of the moose and to every moose that has lived or will ever live in the future."

As if slightly placated, the moose slowed to a walk and Nanapush was able, finally, to snatch a few berries from the bushes they passed, to scoop up a mouthful of water from the slough, and to sleep, though by moonlight the moose still browsed and walked, toward some goal, thought Nanapush, delirious with exhaustion and pain. Perhaps the next world. Perhaps this moose had been sent by the all-clever creator to fetch Nanapush along to the spirit life in this novel way. But just as he was imagining or dreaming such a thing, the first light showed and by that ever strengthening radiance he saw that his moose indeed had a direction and intention and that object was a female moose of an uncommonly robust size, just ahead, peering over her shoulder in a way apparently bewitching to male moose, for the animal uttered a squeal of bullish intensity that Nanapush recognized as pure lust.

Nanapush, now wishing that he had aimed for the huge swinging balls of the moose, wept with exasperation.

"Should I be subjected to this? This too? In addition to all that I have suffered?" And Nanapush cursed the moose, cursed himself, cursed the fishhooks, cursed the person who so carefuly and sturdily constructed the boat that would not fall apart. He cursed in English, as there are no true swear words in Ojibwemowin, and so it was Nanapush and not the devil whom Josette Bizhew heard passing by her remote cabin at first light, shouting all manner of unspeakable and innovative imprecations, and it was Nanapush, furthermore, who was heard howling in the deep slough grass, howling though more dead at this point than alive, at the outrageous acts he was forced to witness, there before his nose, as the boat tipped up and his bull moose in the extremity of his passion loved the female moose with ponderous mountings and thrilling thrusts that swung Nanapush from side to side but did not succeed in dislodging him from the terrible grip of the fishhooks.

No, that was not to happen. Nanapush was bound to suffer for one more day before the satisfied moose toppled over to snore and members of the rescue party Margaret had raised crept up and shot the animal stone dead in its sleep.

The moose, Margaret found, for she had followed with her meat hatchet, had lost a distressing amount of fat and its meat was now stringy from the long flight and sour with a combination of fear and spent sex, so that in butchering it she winced and moaned and traveled far in her raging thoughts, imagined sore revenges she would exact upon her husband, one of which, in the acting out, was eventually to kill him.

In the meantime, Father Damien had followed his friend as best he could in the parish touring car. Hearing the gun's report, he stopped on the nearest road, and so he was able to assist those who emerged from the bush. He drove Nanapush, raving, to Sister Hildegarde, who had an adept way with extracting fishhooks. At the school infirmary, Sister Hildegarde was not upset to see the bare buttocks of Nanapush sticking straight up in the air—she swabbed the area with iodine and tested the strength of her pliers.

Father Damien entered the scene of the operation. With great relief for his friend and a certain amount of pity, he spoke to try to make him smile. "Don't be ashamed of your display. Even the Virgin Mary had two asses, one to sit upon and the other ass that bore her to Egypt."

Nanapush only nodded gloomily and gritted his teeth as Sister Hildegarde pushed the hook with the pliers until the barbed tip broke through his tough skin, then clipped the barb off and pulled out the rest of the hook.

"Is there any chance," he weakly croaked once the operation was accomplished, "that this will affect my manhood?"

"Unfortunately not," said Hildegarde.

THE LOVEMAKING SKILLS of Nanapush, whole or damaged, were to remain untested until after his death. For Margaret took a long time punishing her husband. She ignored him, she browbeat him, and worst of all, she cooked for him.

It was the winter of instructional beans, for every time that Margaret boiled up a pot of rock-hard pellets drawn from the fifty-pound sack of beans that were their only sustenance besides the sour strings of meat, she reminded Nanapush of each brainless turning point last fall in which he should have, but failed to, kill the moose.

"And my," she sneered then, "wasn't its meat both tender and sweet before you ran it to rags?"

She never boiled the beans quite soft enough, either, for she could will her own body to process the toughest sinew with no trouble. Nanapush, however, suffered digestive torments of a nature that soon became destructive to both their health and ruined his nightly rest entirely, for that is when the great explosive winds would gather in his body. His boogidiwinan, which had always been manly, but yet meek enough to remain under his control, overwhelmed the power of his ojiid, and there was nothing he could do but surrender to their whims and force. At least it was a form of revenge on Margaret, he thought, exhausted, near dawn. But at the same time he worried that she would leave him. Already, she made him sleep on a pile of skins near the door so as not to pollute her flowered mattress.

"My precious one," he sometimes begged, "can you not spare me? Boil the beans a while longer, and the moose, as well. Have pity!"

She only raised her brow and her glare was a slice of knifelike light.

Maybe she was angriest because she'd softened toward him during that moose ride across the lake, and now she was determined to punish him for her uncharacteristic lapse into tenderness. At any rate, one night she boiled the beans only long enough to soften their skins and the moose itself that she threw in was coated with a green mold she claimed was medicinal, but which, in the case of Nanapush, tied his guts in knots.

"Eat up, old man." She banged the plate down before him. He saw she was implacable, and then he thought back to the way he had got around the impasse of the maple syrup before, and he resolved to do exactly the opposite of what he felt. And so, resigned to sacrifice this night to pain, desperate, he proceeded to loudly enjoy the beans.

"They are excellent, niwiiw, crunchy and fine! Minopogwud!" He wolfed the beans down, eager as a boy, and tore at the moldy moose as though presented with the finest morsels. "Howah! I've never eaten such a fine dish!" He rubbed his belly and smiled in false satisfaction.

"Nindebisinii, my pretty fawn, oh how well I'll sleep." He rolled up in his blankets by the door then, and waited for the gas pains to tear him apart.

They did come. That night was phenomenal. Margaret was sure that the cans of grease rattled on the windowsill, and she saw a glowing stench rise around her husband, saw with her own eyes but chose to plug her ears with wax and turn to the wall, poking an airhole for herself in the mud between logs, and so she fell asleep not knowing that the symphony of sounds that disarranged papers and blew out the door by morning were her husband's last utterances.

Yes, he was dead. She found when she went to shake him awake the next morning that he was utterly lifeless. She gave a shriek then, of abysmal loss, and began to weep with sudden horror at the depth of her unforgiving nature. She kissed his face all over, patted his hands and hair. He did not look as though death had taken him, no, he looked oddly well. Although it would seem that a death of this sort would shrivel him like a spent sack and leave him wrinkled and limp, he was shut tight and swollen, his mouth a firm line and his eyes squeezed shut as though holding something in. And he was stiff as a horn where she used to love him. There was some mistake! Perhaps, thought Margaret, wild in her grief, he was only deeply asleep and she could love him back awake.

She climbed aboard and commenced to ride him until she herself collapsed, exhausted and weeping, on his still breast. It was no use. His manliness still stood straight up and although she could swear the grim smile had deepened on his face, there were no other signs of life—no breath, not the faintest heartbeat could be detected. Margaret fell beside him, senseless, and was found there disheveled and out cold so that at first Father Damien thought that the two had committed a double suicide, as some old people did those hard winters. But Margaret was soon roused. The cabin was aired out. Father Damien, ravaged with the loss, held his old friend Nanapush's hand all day and allowed his own tears to flow down, soaking his black gown.

And so it was. The wake and the funeral were conducted in the old way. Margaret prepared his body. She cleaned him, wrapped him in her best quilt. As there was no disguising his bone-tough hard-on, she let it stand there proudly and she decided not to be ashamed of her old man's prowess. She laid him on the bed that was her pride, and bitterly regretted how she'd forced him to sleep on the floor in the cold wind by the door.

Everyone showed up that night, bringing food and even a bit of wine, but Margaret wanted nothing of their comfort. Sorrow bit deep into her lungs and the pain radiated out like the shooting rays of a star. She lost her breath. A dizzy veil fell over her. She wanted most of all to express to her husband the terrible depth of the love she felt but had been too proud, too stingy, or, she now saw, too afraid to show him while he lived. She had deprived him of such pleasure: that great horn in his pants, she knew guiltily, was there because she had denied him physical satisfaction ever since the boat ride behind the moose.

"Nimanendam. If only he'd come back to me, I'd make him a happy man." She blew her nose on a big white dishcloth and bowed her head. Whom would she scold? Who would lust after her old body? Whom could she deny? Who would suffer for Margaret Kashpaw now? What was she to do? She dropped her face into her hands and wept with un-characteristic abandon. The whole crowd of Nanapush's friends and loved ones, packed into the house, lifted a toast to the old man and made a salute. At last Father Damien spoke, and his speech was so eloquent that in moments the whole room was bathed in tears and sobs.

It was at that moment, in the depth of their sorrow, just at the hour when everyone felt Nanapush's loss most keenly, that a great explosion occurred, a rip of sound. A vicious cloud of stink sent mourners gasping for air. As soon as the door was opened and the fresh winter cold rolled into the room, everyone returned to find Nanapush sitting straight up, still wrapped in Margaret's best quilt.

"I just couldn't hold it in anymore," he said, embarrassed to find such an assembly of people around him. He proceeded, then, to drink a cup of the mourner's wine. He was unwrapped. He stretched his arms. The wine made him voluble.

"Friends," he said, "how it fills my heart to see you here. I did, indeed, visit the spirit world and there I greeted my old companion, Kashpaw. I saw my former wives, now married to other men. Quill was there, and is now making me a pair of makizinan beaded on the soles, to wear when I travel there for good. Friends, do not fear. On the other side of life there is plenty of food and no government agents."

Nanapush then rose from the bed and walked among the people, tendering greetings and messages from their dead loved ones. At last, however, he came to Margaret, who sat in the corner frozen in shock at her husband's resurrection. "Oh, how I missed my old lady!" he cried, and opened his arms to her. But just as she started forward, eager at his forgiveness, he remembered the beans, dropped his arms, and stepped back.

"No matter how I love you," he then said, "I would rather go to the spirit world than stay here and eat your cooking!"

With that, he sank to the floor quite cold and lifeless again. He was carried to the bed and once more wrapped in the quilt, but his body was closely watched for signs of revival. Nobody yet quite believed that he was gone and it took some time—in fact, they feasted far into the night—before everyone, including poor Margaret, addled now with additional rage and shame, felt certain he was gone. Of course, just as everyone accepted the reality of his demise, Nanapush again jerked upright and his eyes flipped open.

"Oh, yai!" exclaimed one of the old ladies, "he lives yet!"

And although everyone well hid their irritation, it was inevitable that there were some who were impatient. "If you're dead, stay dead," someone muttered. Nobody was so heartless as to express this feeling straight out. There was just a slow but certain drifting away of people from the house and it wasn't long, indeed, before even Father Damien left. He was thrilled to have his old friend back, but in his tactful way intuited that Margaret and Nanapush had much to mend between them and needed to be alone to do it.

Once everyone was gone, Nanapush went over to the door and put the bar down. Then he turned to his wife and spoke before she could say a word.

"I returned for one reason only, my wife. When I was gone and far away, I felt how you tried to revive me with the heat of your body. I was happy you tried to do that—my heart was full. This time when I left with harsh words on my lips about your cooking, I got a ways down the road leading to the spirit world and I just couldn't go any farther, my dear woman, because I had wronged you. I wanted to make things smooth between us. I came back to love you good."

Between the confusion and grief, the exhaustion and bewilderment, Margaret hadn't the wit to do anything but go to her husband and allow all of the hidden sweetness of her nature to join the fire he kindled, so that they spent, together, in her spring bed, the finest and most elegantly accomplished hours that perhaps lovers ever spent on earth. When it was over they both fell asleep, and although only Margaret woke up, her heart was at peace.

MARGARET WOULD NOT have Nanapush buried in the ground, but high in a tree, the way her original people did before the priests came. A year later, his bones and the tattered quilt were put into a box and set under a grave house just to the edge of her yard. The grave house was well built, carefully painted a spanking white, and had a small window with a shelf where Margaret always left food. Sometimes, she left Nanapush a plate of ill-cooked beans because she missed his complaints, but more often she cooked his favorites, seasoned his meat with maple syrup, pampered and pitied him the way she hadn't dared in life for fear he'd get the better of her, though she wondered why that ever mattered, now, without him in the simple quiet of her endless life.

# Naked Woman Playing Chopin

THE STREET THAT runs along the Red River follows the curves of a stream that is muddy and shallow, full of brush, silt, and oxbows that throw the whole town off the strict clean grid laid out by railroad plat. The river floods most springs and drags local backyards into its roil, even though its banks are strengthened with riprap and piled high with concrete torn from reconstructed streets and basements. It is a hopelessly complicated river, one that freezes deceptively, breaks rough, drowns one or two every year in its icy run. It is a dead river in some places, one that harbors only carp and bullheads. Wild in others, it lures moose down from Canada into the town limits. At one time, when the land along its banks was newly broken, paddle boats and barges of grain moved grandly from its source to Winnipeg, for the river flows inscrutably north. And, over on the Minnesota side, across from what is now church land and the town park, a farm spreads generously up and down the river and back into wide hot fields.

The bonanza farm belonged to Easterners who had sold a foundry in Vermont and with their money bought the flat vastness that lay along the river. They raised astounding crops when the land was young— rutabagas that weighed sixty pounds, wheat unbearably lush, corn on cobs like truncheons. Then six grasshopper years occurred during which even the handles on the hoes and rakes were eaten and a cavalry soldier, too, partially devoured while he lay drunk in the insects' path. The enterprise suffered losses on a grand scale. The farm was split among four brothers, eventually, who then sold off half each so that by the time Berndt Vogel escaped the trench war of Europe where he'd been chopped mightily but inconclusively in six places by a British cavalry sabre and then kicked by a horse so that his jaw never shut right again, there was just one beautiful and peaceful swatch of land about to go for grabs. In the time it would take him to gather—by forswearing women, drinking low beers only, and working twenty-hour days—the money to retrieve the farm from the local bank, its price had dropped further and further as the earth rose up in a great ship of destruction. Sails of dust carried half of Berndt's lush dirt over the horizon, but enough remained for him to plant and reap six fields.

So Berndt survived. On his land there stood a hangar-like barn with only one small part still in use—housing a cow, chickens, one depressed pig. Berndt kept the rest in decent repair not only because as a good German he must waste nothing that had come his way, but also because he saw in those grand, dust-filled shafts of light something he could worship. It had once housed teams of great, blue Percherons and Belgian draft horses. Only one horse was left, old and made of brutal velvet, but the others still moved in the powerful synchronicity of his dreams. He fussed over the one remaining mammoth and imagined his farm one day entire, vast and teeming, crews of men under his command, a cookhouse, a bunkhouse, equipment, a woman and children sturdily determined to their toil, and a garden in which seeds bearing the scented pinks and sharp red geraniums of his childhood were planted and thrived.

How surprised he was to find, one afternoon, as though sown by the wind and summoned by his dreams, a woman standing barefoot, starved, and frowzy in the doorway of his barn. She was a pale flower, nearly bald and dressed in a rough shift. He blinked stupidly at the vision. Light poured around her like smoke and swirled at her gesture of need. She spoke with a low, gravelly abruptness.

*"Ich habe Hunger."*

By the way she said it, he knew she was a Swabian and therefore— he tried to thrust the thought from his mind—liable to have certain unruly habits in bed. She continued to speak, her voice husky and bossy. He passed his hand across his eyes. Through the gown of nearly transparent muslin he could see that her breasts were, excitingly, bound tight to her chest with strips of cloth. He blinked hard. Looking directly into her eyes, he experienced the vertigo of confronting a female who did not blush or look away but held him with an honest human calm. He thought at first she must be a loose woman, fleeing a brothel—had Fargo got so big? Or escaping an evil marriage, perhaps. He didn't know she was from God.

## SISTER CECELLIA

IN THE CENTER of the town on the other side of the river there stood a convent made of yellow bricks. Hauled halfway across Minnesota from Little Falls by pious drivers, they still held the peculiar sulfurous moth gold of the clay outside that town. The word "Fleisch" was etched in shallow letters on each one: Fleisch Company Brickworks. Donated to the nuns at cost. The word, of course, was covered by mortar each time a brick was laid. However, because she had organized a few discarded bricks behind the convent into the base for a small birdbath, one of the younger nuns knew, as she gazed at the mute order of the convent's wall, that she lived within the secret repetition of that one word.

She had once been Agnes DeWitt and now was Sister Cecellia, shorn, houseled, clothed in black wool, and bound in starched linen of heatless white. She not only taught but lived music, existed for those hours when she could be concentrated in her being—which was half music, half divine light, flesh only to the degree that she could not admit otherwise. At the piano keyboard, absorbed into the notes that rose beneath her hands, she existed in her essence, a manifestation of compelling sound. Her hands were long and thick-veined, very white, startling against her habit. She rubbed them with lard and beeswax nightly to keep them supple. During the day, when she graded papers or used the blackboard her hands twitched and drummed, patterned and repatterned difficult fingerings. She was no trouble to live with and her obedience was absolute. Only, and with increasing concentration, she played Brahms, Beethoven, Debussy, Schubert, and Chopin.

It wasn't that she neglected her other duties; rather, it was the playing itself—distilled of longing—that disturbed her sisters. In her music Sister Cecellia explored profound emotions. She spoke of her faith and doubt, of her passion as the bride of Christ, of her loneliness, shame, ultimate redemption. The Brahms she played was thoughtful, the Schubert confounding. Debussy was all contrived nature and yet gorgeous as a meadowlark. Beethoven contained all messages, but her crescendos lacked conviction. When it came to the Chopin, however, she did not use the flowery ornamentation or the endless trills and insipid floribunda of so many of her day. Her playing was of the utmost sincerity. And Chopin, played simply, devastates the heart. Sometimes a pause between the piercing sorrows of minor notes made a sister scrubbing the floor weep into the bucket where she dipped her rag so that the convent's boards, washed in tears, seemed to creak in a human tongue. The air of the house thickened with sighs.

Sister Cecellia, however, was emptied. Thinned. It was as though her soul were neatly removed by a drinking straw and siphoned into the green pool of quiet that lay beneath the rippling cascade of notes. One day, exquisite agony built and released, built higher, released more forcefully until slow heat spread between her fingers, up her arms, stung at the points of her bound breasts, and then shot straight down.

Her hands flew off the keyboard—she crouched as though she had been shot, saw yellow spots, and experienced a peaceful wave of oneness in which she entered pure communion. She was locked into the music, held there safely, entirely understood. Such was her innocence that she didn't know she was experiencing a sexual climax but believed, rather, that what she felt was the natural outcome of this particular nocturne played to the utmost of her skills—and so it came to be. Chopin's spirit became her lover. His flats caressed her. His whole notes sank through her body like clear pebbles. His atmospheric trills were the flicker of a tongue. His pauses before the downward sweep of notes nearly drove her insane.

The Mother Superior knew something had to be done when she herself woke, her face bathed with sweat and tears, to the insinuating soft largo of the Prelude in E Minor. In those notes she remembered the death of her mother and sank into an endless afternoon of her loss. The Mother Superior then grew, in her heart, a weed of rage against the God who had taken a mother from a seven-year-old child whose world she was, entirely, without question—heart, arms, guidance, soul—until by evening she felt fury steaming from the hot marrow of her bones and stopped herself.

"Oh, God, forgive me," the Superior prayed. She considered homunculation, but then rushed down to the piano room instead, and with all of the strength in her wide old arms gathered and hid from Cecellia every piece of music but the Bach.

After that, for some weeks, there was relief. Sister Cecellia turned to the Two-Part Inventions. Her fingers moved on the keys with the precision of an insect building its nest. She played each as though she were constructing an airtight box. Stealthily, once Cecellia had moved on to Bach's other works, the Mother Superior removed from the music cabinet and destroyed the Goldberg Variations—clearly capable of lifting subterranean complexities into the mind. Life in the convent returned to normal. The cook, to everyone's gratitude, stopped preparing the rancid, goose-fat-laced beet soup of her youth and stuck to overcooked string beans, boiled cabbage, potatoes. The floors stopped groaning and absorbed fresh wax. The doors ceased to fly open for no reason and closed discreetly. The water stopped rushing continually through the pipes as the sisters no longer took advantage of the new plumbing to drown out the sounds of their emotions.

And then one day Sister Cecellia woke with a tightness in her chest. Pains shot through her and the red lump in her rib cage beat like a wild thing caught in a snare of bones. Her throat shut. She wept. Her hands, drawn to the keyboard, floated into a long appoggiatura. Then, crash, she was inside a thrusting mazurka. The music came back to her. There was the scent of faint gardenias—his hothouse boutonnière. The silk of his heavy brown hair. His sensuous drawing-room sweat. His voice—she heard it—avid and light. It was as if the composer himself had entered the room. Who knows? Surely there was no more desperate, earthly, exacting heart than Cecellia's. Surely something, however paltry, lies beyond the grave.

At any rate, she played Chopin. Played him in utter naturalness until the Mother Superior was forced to shut the cover to the keyboard gently and pull the stool away. Cecellia lifted the lid and played upon her knees. The poor scandalized dame dragged her from the keys. Cecellia crawled back. The Mother, at her wits' end, sank down and urged the girl to pray. She herself spoke first in fear and then in certainty, saying that it was the very Devil who had managed to find a way to Cecellia's soul through the flashing doors of sixteenth notes. Her fears were confirmed when, not moments later, the gentle sister raised her arms and fists and struck the keys as though the instrument were stone and from the rock her thirst would be quenched. But only discord emerged.

"My child, my dear child," comforted the Mother, "come away and rest yourself."

The young nun, breathing deeply, refused. Her severe gray eyes were rimmed in a smoky red. Her lips bled purple. She was in torment. "There is no rest," she declared. She unpinned her veil and studiously dismantled her habit, folding each piece with reverence and setting it upon the piano bench. The Mother remonstrated with Cecellia in the most tender and compassionate tones. However, just as in the depth of her playing the virgin had become the woman, so the woman in the habit became a woman to the bone. She stripped down to her shift, but no further.

"He wouldn't want me to go out unprotected," she told her Mother Superior.

"God?" the older woman asked, bewildered.

"Chopin," Cecellia answered.

Kissing her dear Mother's trembling fingers, Cecellia knelt. She made a true genuflection, murmured an act of contrition, and then walked from the convent made of bricks with the secret word pressed between yellow mortar, and from the music, her music, which the

Mother Superior would keep from then on under lock and key as capable of mayhem.

## MISS AGNES DEWITT

SO IT WAS Sister Cecellia, or Agnes DeWitt of rural Wisconsin, who appeared before Berndt Vogel in the cavern of the barn and said in her mother's dialect, for she knew a German when she met one, that she was hungry. She wanted to ask whether he had a piano, but it was clear to her he wouldn't and at any rate she was exhausted.

*"Jetzt muss ich schlafen,"* she said after eating half a plate of scalded oatmeal with new milk.

So he took her to his bed, the only bed there was, in the corner of the otherwise empty room. He went out to the barn he loved, covered himself with hay, and lay awake all night listening to the rustling of mice and sensing the soundless predatory glide of the barn owls and the stiff erratic flutter of bats. By morning, he had determined to marry her if she would have him, just so that he could unpin and then unwind the long strip of cloth that bound her torso. She refused his offer, but she did speak to him of who she was and where from, and in that first summary she gave of her life she concluded that she must never marry again, for not only had she wed herself soul to soul to Christ, but she had already been unfaithful—her phantom lover the Polish composer. She had already lived out too grievous a destiny to become a bride again. In explaining this to Berndt, however, she had merely moved her first pawn in a long game of words and gestures that the two would play over the course of many months. What she didn't know was that she had opened to a dogged and ruthless opponent.

Berndt Vogel's passion engaged him, mind and heart. He prepared himself. Having dragged Army caissons through hip-deep mud after the horses died in torment, having seen his best friend suddenly uncreated into a mass of shrieking pulp, having lived intimately with pouring tumults of eager lice and rats plump with a horrifying food, he was rudimentarily prepared for the suffering he would experience in love. She, however, had also learned her share of discipline. In addition—for the heart of her gender is stretched, pounded, molded, and tempered for its hot task from the age of four—she was a woman.

The two struck up a temporary bargain and set up housekeeping. She still slept in the indoor bed. He stayed in the barn. A month passed. Three. Six. Each morning she lighted the stove and cooked, then heated water in a big tank for laundry and swept the cool linoleum floors. Monday she sewed. She baked all day Tuesday. On Wednesdays she churned and scrubbed. She sold the butter and the eggs Thursdays. Killed a chicken every Friday. Saturdays she walked into town and practiced the piano in the grade school basement. Sunday she played the organ for Mass and then at the close of the day started the next week's work. Berndt paid her. At first she spent her salary on clothing. When with her earnings she had acquired shoes, stockings, a full set of cotton underclothing and then a woolen one, too, and material for two housedresses—one patterned with twisted leaves and tiny blue berries, and the other of an ivy lattice print—and a sweater and, at last, a winter coat, after she had earned a blanket, quilted overalls, a pair of boots, she decided on a piano.

This is where Berndt thought he could maneuver her into marriage, but she proved too cunning for him. It was early in the evening and the yard was pleasant with the sound of grasshoppers. They sat on the porch drinking glasses of sugared lemon water. Every so often, in the ancient six-foot grasses that survived at the margin of the yard, a firefly signaled or a dove cried out its five hollow notes.

"Why do so many bird songs consist of five?" she asked idly.

"Five what?" said Berndt.

They drank slowly, she in the sprigged-berry dress that skimmed her waist. He noted with disappointment that she wore a normal woman's underclothing now, had stopped binding her breasts. Perhaps, he thought, he could persuade her to resume her old ways, at least occasionally, just for him. It was a wan hope. She looked so comfortable, so free. She'd taken on a little weight and lost her anemic pallor. She had a square boy's chin and a sturdy, graceful neck. Her arms were brown, muscular. In the sun, her fine hair, growing out in curls, glinted with green-gold sparks of light and her eyes were deceptively clear.

"I can teach music," she told him. "Piano." She had decided that her suggestion must sound merely practical, a moneymaking ploy. She did not say she could actually play nor did she express any pleasure or zeal, though at the very thought each separate tiny muscle in her hands ached. "It would be a way of bringing in some money."

He was left to absorb this. He might have believed her casual proposition, except that Miss DeWitt's restless fingers gave her away, and he noted their insistent motions. She was playing the Adagio of the "Pathétique" on the arms of her chair, a childhood piece that nervously possessed her from time to time.

"You would need a piano," he told her. She nodded and held his gaze in that aloof and unbearably sexual way that had first skewered him.

"It's the sort of thing a husband gives his wife," he dared.

Her fingers stopped moving. She cast down her eyes in contempt.

"I can walk to town and use the school instrument. I've spoken to the school principal already."

Berndt looked at the moon-shaped bone of her ankle, at her foot in the brown, thick-heeled shoe she'd bought. He ached to hold her foot in his lap, untie her oxford shoe with his teeth, move his hand up her leg covering her calf with kisses, and breathe against the delicate folds of berry cloth.

He offered marriage once again. His heart. His troth. His farm. She spurned the lot. She would simply walk into town. He let her know that he would like to buy the piano, it wasn't that, but there was not a store for many miles where it could be purchased. She knew better and with exasperated heat described the way that she would, if assisted with his money, go about locating and then acquiring the best piano for the best price. She vowed that she would not purchase the instrument in Fargo but in Minneapolis. From there, she could get it hauled cheaper than the freight markup. She would take the train to Minneapolis, make her arrangements in one day, and return by night in order not to spend one extra dime either on food she couldn't carry or on a hotel room. When he resisted to the last, she told him that she was leaving. She would find a small room in town and there she would acquire students, give lessons.

She betrayed her desperation. Some clench of her fingers gave her away, and it was as much Berndt's unconfused love of her and wish that she might be happy as any worry she might leave him that finally caused him to agree. In the six months he'd known Agnes DeWitt she had become someone to reckon with, and even he, who understood desperation and self denial, was finding her proximity most difficult. He worked himself into exhaustion, and his farm prospered. Sleeping in the barn was difficult, but he had set into one wall a bunk room for himself and his hired man and installed a stove that burned red hot on cold nights; only, sometimes, as he looked sleepily into the glowering flanks of iron, he could not help his own fingers moving along the rough mattress in faint imitation of the way he would, if he ever could, touch her hips. He, too, was practicing.

## THE CARAMACCHIONE

THE PIANO MOVED across the table fields of drought-sucked wheat like a shield, a dark upended black thing, an ebony locust. Agnes made friends with a hauler out of Morris and he gave her a slow-wagon price. Both were to accompany into North Dakota the last grand piano made by Caramacchione. It had been shipped to Minneapolis, unsold until Agnes entered with her bean sock of money. She accompanied the instrument back to the farm during the dog days. Hot weather was beloved by this particular piano. It tuned itself on muggy days. And so, as it moved across the flat expanse, Miss Agnes DeWitt mounted the back of the wagon and played to the clouds.

They had to remove one side of the house to get the piano into the front room, and it took four strong men the next day to do the job. By the time the instrument was settled into place by the window, Berndt was persuaded of its necessary presence, and proud. He sent the men away, although the side of the house was still open to swirling light of stars. Dark breezes moved the curtains; he asked her to play for him. She did. The music gripped her, and she did not, could not, stop.

Late that night she turned from the last chord of the simple Nocturne in C Minor into the silence of Berndt's listening presence. Three slow claps from his large hands died in the waiting quiet. His eyes rested upon her and she returned his gaze with a long and mysterious stare of gentle regard. The side of the house admitted a great swatch of moonlight. Spiders built their webs of phosphorescence across black space. Berndt ticked through what he knew—she would not marry him because she had been married and unfaithful, in her mind at least. He was desperate not to throw her off, repel her, damage the mood set by the boom of nighthawks flying in, swooping out, by the rustle of black oak and willow, by the scent of the blasted petals of summer's last wild roses. His courage was at its lowest ebb. Fraught with sheer need and emotion he stood before Agnes, finally, and asked in a low voice, *"Schlaf mit mir. Bitte. Schlaf mit mir."*

Agnes looked into his face, openly at last, showing him the great weight of feeling she carried. As she had for her Mother Superior, she removed her clothing carefully and folded it, only she did not stop undressing at her shift but continued until she slipped off her large tissuey bloomers and seated herself naked at the piano. Her body was a pale blush of silver, and her hands, when they began to move, rose and fell with the simplicity of water.

It became clear to Berndt Vogel, as the music slowly wrapped around him, that he was engaged in something for which he would have had to pay a whore in Fargo—if there really were any whores in Fargo—a great sum to perform. A snake of hair wound down her spine. Her pale buttocks seemed to float off the invisible bench. Her legs moved like a swimmer's, and he thought he heard her moan. He watched her fingers spin like white shadows across the keys, and found that his body was responding as though he lay fully twined with her underneath a quilt of music and stars. His breath came short, shorter, rasping and ragged. Beyond control, he gasped painfully and gave himself into some furtive cleft of halftones and anger that opened beneath the ice of high keys.

Shocked, weak and wet, Berndt rose and slipped through the open side wall. He trod aimless crop lines until he could allow himself to collapse in the low fervor of night wheat. It was true, wasn't it, that the heart was a lying cheat? And as the songs Chopin invented were as much him as his body, so it followed that Berndt had just watched the woman he loved make love to a dead man. Furthermore, in watching, he'd sunk into a strange excitement beyond his will and let his seed onto the floor Agnes had just that afternoon scrubbed and waxed. Now, as he listened to the music, he thought of returning. Imagined the meal of her white shoulders. Shut his eyes and entered the confounding depth between her legs.

## BLESSING

THEN FOLLOWED THEIR best years. Together, they constructed a good life in which the erotic merged into the daily so that every task and small kindness was charged with a sexual humor. Some mornings the two staggered from the bedroom disoriented, still half drunk on the perfume and unlikely eagerness of the other's body. These frenzied periods occurred to them every so often, like spells in the weather. They would be drawn, sink, disappear into their greed, until the cow groaned for milking or the hired man swore and banged on the outside gate. If nothing else intervened, they'd only stop from sheer exhaustion. Then they would look at one another oddly, questingly, as if the other person were a complete stranger, and gradually resume their normal treatment, which was offhand and distracted, but upheld by the assurance of people who thought alike. Even when they fought, it was with impatient dispatch. They were anxious to get to the exciting part of the fight where they lost their tempers and approached one another with a frisson of rage that turned sexual so that they could be slightly cruel and then surrender themselves to tenderness.

Agnes DeWitt was too young to understand what a precious gift she shared with Berndt. She possessed, and so easily, a love most humans never know and those who know about it are quite willing to die or go mad for. And Agnes had done nothing but find her way into the barn of a good man who had a singular gift for everyday affection as well as the deepest tones of human love.

Through fall and winter Agnes DeWitt gave music lessons, and although the two weren't married, even the Catholics and the children came to her. This was because it was well-known that Miss DeWitt's first commitment had been to Christ. It was understandable that she would have no other marriage and also, although she did not take the Holy Eucharist upon her tongue she was there at church each Sunday morning, faithful and devout, to play the organ. And, so, when the priest spoke from the pulpit, his reference was quite clear.

"Jesus insisted that Mary Magdelene be incorporated into the holy body of his church and it is said by some that in her hands there was celestial music. Her heart clearly contained the divine flame—and she was loved and forgiven."

Therefore, every morning Miss Dewitt played the church organ. She of course played Bach with a purity of intent purged of any subterranean feeling, but strictly and for God.

## Arnold "The Actor" Anderson

ONLY A SHORT time into their happiness, the countryside and the small towns were preyed upon by a ring of bank robbers with a fast Overland automobile. This was before small towns even had sheriffs, some of them, let alone a car held in common to chase the precursors of such criminals as Basil "The Owl" Banghart, Ma Barker's Boys, Alvin Karpus, Henry LaFay. The first, and most insidious of these men, was Arnold "The Actor" Anderson.

The Actor and his troupe of thugs plundered the countryside at will, appearing as though from nowhere and descending into the towns with pitiless ease. The car—the color of which was always reported differently—white one time, gray the next, even blue, always pulled idling into the street before the doors of the bank. The passenger who emerged was sometimes an old man, other times a pregnant woman, a crippled youth, someone who inspired others to acts of polite assistance. The Good Samaritan would open doors, and even escort the actor to the teller at which point the object of good works would straighten, throw off his disguise, shout to his gang in a ringing voice and proceed to rob the bank. It would all be over in a trice. Sometimes, of course, there was resistance from a bank official or an intrepid do-gooder in which case a death or two might result, for The Actor, who took on the disguises and masterminded the activities of the gang, was entirely ruthless and cared nothing for human life. It was said that he could be quite charming as he shot people, even funny. Eight people in the past two years had perished laughing.

One clear but muddy spring day Miss DeWitt removed her egg and butter money from the crevice between two stones in the root cellar. She told Berndt that she was walking to town to deposit the money against the mortgage payment. He agreed, absently. Touched her arm. She shoved him off balance, ducked from under his arm, and ran out the door laughing at his awkward hops and shouts. She slowed and picked her way along the ruts of the muddy road. The huge canopy sky threatened gray blue in the northwest, but the weather was far away and the wind desultory, the air watery, clear, the buds split in a faint green haze. The first of her tulip bulbs were pink at the green lips, ready to bloom. Under the tough grama and sideoats, the new shoots of grass were strengthening and gathering their eager power. She thought of Berndt's head tossed back, the cords running taut from the corner of his jaw roping into his chest. The way he nearly wept as he threw his famished weight into her again and again, and the way he glanced sideways, hungrily, after, until they began once again. Her need to touch him moved through her like a wave and she stopped, distractedly, passed a hand over her face, almost put her errand off, but then moved on.

THE BANK WAS a solid square of Nebraska limestone, great windowed with deep blond sills and brass handles on the doors. The high ceiling was of ornate white pressed tin set off by thick crown mouldings and a center medallion of sheaves of wheat. In the summer great fans turned the sluggish air. The velvet roped lanes and spittoons, the pink and gray mica granite countertops and the teller's cages seemed caught in a dim hush of order while outside the noise of the town continued, erratic. The relationship between the getting of money, a scrabbling and disorderly business, contrasted with the storing of money, an enterprise based on the satisfactory premise that human effort, struggle, even time iself, could be quantified, counted, stacked neatly away in a safe.

Outside, on the day Miss DeWitt walked swiftly to town, the streets seemed unusually quiet and orderly. Even the bum sleeping against the side of the young elm had his arms neatly folded, and the one automobile parked, idling, was an elegant car of the sort—well, yes—she thought, oddly, that a bishop would use. Sure enough who but a priest should remove himself from the back seat kicking to the side his black soutane. With a meek and tentative squint at the bank, through tiny rimless eyeglasses, he made his way up the walk and steps. On the way, he bowed to Miss DeWitt, who followed him respectfully. As they walked together up the roped path in the lobby she said to him, loudly and clearly, in an amused tone of voice, "Sir, why this pretense? You are not a priest!"

Whereupon the stooped old man straightened, magically broadened, and waved a hand across his face very much as she herself had, in the road, to erase her thoughts. Only he erased his character. He removed his glasses and from beneath his robe drew a snub-nosed pistol that he pointed straight at Miss DeWitt's forehead.

"Righto," he said.

There was no other perceptible signal, but all of a sudden another male customer held a gun out as well, first at the chin of a florid red-headed woman teller and then at the broad chest of a young dark-haired bristling man. This young former baseball star's heart filled immediately, then swelled. He wanted to be a hero, but was struggling with the how of it. Foolish! Foolish! Miss DeWitt wanted to tell him. But it was clear from the beginning that he had just the right amount of stubborn stuff in him to be killed. Which he was. When he fell down dead behind his cage of iron, mouth open to catch the punch line of a joke, the money was harder to get. A stiff pointy-faced woman was called upon to open his drawer and instructed not to trip the alarm. When she did anyway, the eighteen customers, including Agnes, were all instructed to gather in one corner behind a velvet rope. Exactly, Miss DeWitt thought, like a flock of blank-eyed sheep. There was a shout outside. It was the sheriff, Slow Johnny Mercier, who really was slow and clumsy, and his deputy with him, pistols drawn. They stood just outside the door yelling for the robbers to come out.

It was clear, then, to Miss DeWitt and probably to the others that their sheriff was an amateur and that the professional involved was inside the bank. For The Actor continued gesturing to the pointy-faced woman to add to the bills, add more and add more. Then, in his dull black robe with its giveaway wrinkles, creases which no self-respecting Catholic lay or nun housekeeper would have allowed him to don, and his ridiculous brown Episcopalian shoes, he sprang to the bunched people swift and graceful as a wolf, chose from just behind the rope Miss DeWitt.

He chose her as though choosing a dancing partner. He did everything but bow—walked up to her and took her hand with a polite but peremptory firmness so that it would not have been out of character with his manner for the two of them to step out onto the dance floor and begin a slow waltz. And it was as though they were engaged in some sort of dance as they walked out the door. Only she was held the wrong way. When she stumbled, perhaps purposely, not following his lead, he wrenched her closer. As he pulled her against the door of the car he'd entered, as she balanced on the running board, he called out, "Come after me and I will blow her head off, Mister Sheriff."

Then the ragged bum who had sat with arms neatly crossed at the side of the street accelerated the car with a roar. Slow Johnny the sheriff, solid in his tracks, raised his pistol, sighted carefully along the barrel, pulled the trigger and shot Miss DeWitt. She took the bullet in the hip. So much was happening all at once—more shots fired, mad swerving to avoid an ice truck, two children diving into the roots of a lilac bush, sheer speed—that she felt the impact as a blow that rang her bones, but did not pain her, until the car hit a great freak of earth that nearly threw Miss DeWitt halfway through the open window on the driver's side. Immediately, she was cast into an almost mystical state of agony. The heavens seemed to open. Black stars rang down. She heard the motor and then, later, more gunshots as from a great, muted distance. Thick strains of music looped through her mental hearing, all jumbled and spectacular. Held on the running board by an arm that seemed strung of pitiless wire, proceeding at a dreamlike pace down the smoothly tamped and rolled roadbeds that led out of town, in a state of clarity and focused keenness she told herself,

"I am being kidnapped. I have been shot."

As the auto jounced her along she began to lose certainty. In her pain she imagined herself back at the convent in her tiny closet of a room. She closed the door, crawled dog-like into the wet bush of unconsciousness, lay huddled small and unknowing. From time to time, she experienced a moment of reprieve. She was capable of standing upright. Gravely, she surveyed the country she passed through and found in the faint spring clouds of green a raw sweetness. The robber's arm gripped her waist. She gripped the luggage rack. Her hair, unpinned and flying backward, made a short banner in the wet, fresh wind.

THE ACTOR TOOK the old Patterson road, by which she knew he understood the lay of the land, and by which, too, she knew if he took the turnoff he would pass by one of Berndt's fields, their fields, where Berndt was likely to be working. Her heart pounded in hope. But the driver dressed in rags did not turn and she then thought instantly in great relief that Berndt wouldn't be put in danger now. Just as she thought that, the car sped first past the hired man and then farther on, Berndt, on his big slow horse, plodding. He was dragging along a harrow to be repaired. She tried to hide herself when he came by, but she was still balanced on the running board. So it was, he saw her approach from down the road like a figurehead on the prow of a ship. She stood at grand attention, her one leg a flare of blood. He stopped. His face went slack with uncomprehending shock. She rushed by close enough for their hands to meet and then she was gone, swallowed into the distance.

## BERNDT VOGEL

BERNDT FOLLOWED THE car not because he saw fear in her eyes—there was none, only a dreamy concentration—but because he grasped the whole scenario. He was not afraid for her. Having met her in the first place nearly naked within the smoky radiance of his own barn, he knew she would survive the ordeal. There was always a side to her he could not touch. He felt indeed that she was a woman created of impossibility. Unhitching the harrow, then turning on his horse to follow, he had no precise notion of her danger or any thought of how to rescue her but acted on instinct and absurdity. Although he sent his horse along at a smart pace, the car was soon out of sight. He had to keep an eye on the road to know from their tire marks at each turn off that they had, in fact, stayed on the main road. And they did, moving farther from him at every moment. He moved, following them, wondering in useless desperation the location of Slow Johnny. On the chase? No, not quite. He and the deputy, in trying to commandeer a car, met resistance not so much for the owner's lack of agreement about the need for it, but because Slow Johnny was a notoriously poor driver. Beyond that, the two or three citizens that he approached thought he would do more harm than good chasing down The Actor and probably get Miss De-Witt completely killed, if not himself, the deputy, and any bystander in a stone's throw radius.

Berndt was far ahead, then, of any other form of help. As he traveled along behind The Actor's car, he put his mind to the subject. By the process of recalling certain news items about local robberies, he had pretty well figured out what was happening. His equilibrium failed, and he experienced a wave of terror for Agnes so intense that he whipped the poor horse to a momentary froth. As soon as the Percheron rocked into a huge gallop, Berndt realized that he would kill his horse if he continued. Speed now was useless, and besides, with each mile covered he gained a distinct advantage. The car would eventually run out of gas. The horse, if Berndt was careful to conserve its energy, would last. And then, too, Berndt had the advantage of terrible road conditions. It was spring and it would be surprising if any car could get through the big washout Berndt knew of six miles up the road.

## THE BLUE HORSE

THE ACTOR'S CAR ripped through the silent country until, just as Berndt knew, they hit the washout. The car shimmied to a perplexed stall. The Actor pulled Agnes roughly into the backseat and the driver revved twice without result. With a fabulous jolt the powerful engine caught and they lurched free, only then to slip off the other side of the road into a more serious predicament. There was no moving, not at all, no matter how the three men pushed, roared, swore, kicked. Turning in a circle of frustrated fury, The Actor spied at some distance the horse, the rider.

"Look sharp," he spoke. The men and he changed suddenly to meeker, commoner sorts and began to work with assiduous uselessness on the car's engaged tires. Pulling up beside them, Berndt casually offered his assistance. The words did not strangle his throat. He was calm. He tapped his farmer's brim as he glanced into the backseat. The Actor had spread a blanket over Miss DeWitt's legs, and she looked all right, though pale and dazzled.

Berndt could not tell that The Actor, with an eye to concealing the stolen money, had taken wads of it from the canvas bag. During the ride he had thrust as many bills as he could into his shirt. He had shoved the bag itself under the blanket, next to Miss DeWitt, whom he instructed not to bother getting out of the car. He smiled a genial greeting to Berndt, who nodded at Miss DeWitt, and set to work.

BY EAGERLY HOOKING the good beast to the car's bumper and making an ostentatious show of straining its powers, Berndt made every appearance of helping the gang. Yet by degrees, through prods and signs, he actually caused the horse to mire them ever deeper. Soon they were in a more helpless state than before. The Actor didn't see it at first, but then, he caught some glance between the farmer and the hostage that betrayed their connection. Just as he moved to grab the reins and question this, there appeared at last Slow Johnny, riding in the dead teller's car.

The men of the law stopped close upon the robbers and gingerly stepped toward them, guns drawn.

"You're done for," shouted Slow Johnny.

"Halt, you jackass!"

Crouching so that his body was shielded by the car door and his gun level with the head of Miss DeWitt, The Actor warned off the sheriff.

"Back! Back!" Berndt signaled to Johnny.

"I'll shoot her, yes by damn I will," called The Actor.

At a great distance from herself, Agnes felt her mouth open and words emerge. She spoke to The Actor, who cried out, warningly, again. Slow Johnny, though, was hard of hearing as well as slow and he kept walking forward. Berndt saw the thumb of The Actor lift off the hammer of the gun. He struck him just as the gun went off, so that the last Agnes DeWitt saw of The Actor was his unflinching look at her. The last thought she had about him was amazement—that he did not regard her words or her life as important or even useful at all, or have a moment's hesitation about ending it—ending all of the thousands of hours of tedious intensity of musical practice, ending the rippling music that her hands could bring into being, ending the episodes of greed and wonder in the arms of Berndt, and further back, into the convent where her sisters had already unsewn, pressed, and restitched her habit for another hopeful, none of which was of any consequence, not even the mountains of prayers for the souls so like his or the vivid attempts beseeching Mary to intercede. Nothing mattered. None of that. And beyond that, to her childhood and the tar roofs of the homestead and the alien bread of her mother's cruel visions and her father's terrifying gestures of love and all the precious jumble of her littleness, her thoughts, her creamy baby skin, her howls and burbles, all of this was as nothing to his casual wish to kill her.

This fact smote her as a marvel and a sorrow, and she knew it was because of what she saw, now, straight on, in The Actor that she so fervently loved Chopin. And God. Now, she had to give herself entirely to God's will, whatever that might be. And it was just as she wondered, indeed, if for her to die was that will, that the gun went off, the bullet plowed along her hairline, and blackness stormed behind her eyes.

While Berndt jumped to her side, The Actor neatly grabbed the reins and somehow pulled himself onto the table-broad back of the horse. He dug in his heels, gave a desperate kick to the horse's belly, and they were off, though the horse slowed at once just as soon as they entered the vast horizon-bound treeless wet field of thick gumbo. Berndt, kissing Agnes in a strange roar of grief, then followed The Actor, leaving the other two bank robbers and Slow Johnny and the deputy shouting back and forth and leveling their guns but not knowing whom to shoot. Berndt walked straight on. Just as he had when the car roared past, he understood his advantage lay in the increase of distance. He knew how exhausted his horse was, and he knew, too, that he, Berndt, could bend over from time to time to clean off his feet, but his horse could not. The Actor would either have to dismount, or the horse would eventually slow to a stop, repossessed by the dirt.

And so it was—a low speed chase.

There in that empty landscape they were a cipher of strained pursuit—the man plodding forward on the horse, the other man plodding after. They seemed on that plain and under that spun sky eternal—bound to trudge on no matter what. The clods on the hooves of the horse were soon great rich cakes. Still, on and on, slower, they pressed. Then slower yet so that The Actor kicked in savage indignation until the horse's flanks bled. Slower yet. Berndt kept coming. The Actor screamed straight into the ear of the horse. With a frantic ripple of muscles it attempted to undo itself from the earth. Only sank itself further, deeper. Raging, futile, The Actor saw the horse was stuck, leaped off, and put the pistol to its eye.

The shot echoed out, a crack. Another thinner crack echoed, against the mirage horizon. By the time the echo was lost, the horse was dead.

Berndt saw his horse kneel in the wet cement dirt the way the animals worshipped the Christ. Then, to Berndt's grief and rage, there was added a contemptuous bewilderment which made him capable of what he did next.

The first bullet that The Actor fired struck Berndt in the chest but went through without touching a vital organ. Berndt merely felt a stunning rip of fire. He staggered one step back and then kept moving. When the next bullet struck him mortally, he seemed to absorb it and strengthen. Rising to the next steps, he skipped from the mud. The Actor's face stiffened in green shock and he fired point blank. The empty chamber clicked over just as Berndt clasped The Actor by the shoulders and spoke into his face.

"If you hadn't shot my horse, you wouldn't have to die now," said Berndt, abstractly stating a fact by which he perhaps meant that he would have preferred to deliver The Actor to the terrors of justice, or perhaps that Berndt would have preferred to die in the place of the horse, or yet, that the last bullet would have been his own coup de grâce. As there was life left in him, Berndt set his hands with a dogged weariness upon The Actor's face, put his thumbs to the gangster's eyeballs and pressed, pressed with an inexorable parental dispassion, pressed until it was clear the gangster's aim would be forever spoiled. Then Berndt toppled forward onto the ground, into the nearly liquid gumbo, pinning The Actor full length.

It was hours before anyone got to the scene and in that time Alvin The Actor Anderson could not budge the dead man off of him. Inch by inch, with incremental slowness and tiny sucking noises the earth crept over The Actor and into him, first swallowing his heels, back, elbows, and then stopping up his ears, so his body slowly filled with soupy, rich topsoil. At the last, he could not hear his own scream. Dirt filled his nose and then his tipped up straining mouth. No matter how he spat the earth kept coming and the mud trickled down his throat. Slowly, infinitely slowly, brachia by brachia the earth stopped up each passage of his lungs and packed them tight. The ground absorbed him. When at last the first member of the reluctantly formed posse arrived, he thought at first the robber had escaped, but then saw how only the hands of The

Actor, clutching Berndt's arms and back like a raft, still extended above the level of the horizon.

## FREDERIC CHOPIN

WHEN AGNES CAME to, she was back in the convent, her scalp wound bandaged, her hands still busily patterning grand passages of an unconscious concerto. As Agnes recovered her strength, did she dream of Berndt? Think of him entering her and her receiving him? Long for the curve of his hand on her breast? Yes and no. She thought of music. Chopin. Berndt. Chopin.

He had written a will, in which he declared her his common-law wife and left to her the farm and all upon it.

There, she raised Rosecomb Bantams, Dominikers, Reds. She continued to play with an isolated intensity that absorbed her spirit.

A year or so after Berndt's death, her students noticed that she would stop in the middle of a lesson and smile out the window as though welcoming a long expected visitor. One day the neighbor children went to pick up the usual order of eggs and were most struck to see the white-and-black-flecked Dominikers flapping up in alarm around Miss DeWitt as she stood magnificent upon the green grass.

Tall, slender, legs slightly bowed, breasts jutting a bit to either side, and the flare of hair flicking up the center of her—naked. She looked at the children with remote kindness. Asked, "How many dozen?" Walked off to gather the eggs.

That episode made the gossip-table rounds. People put it off to Berndt's death and a relapse of nerves. She lost only a Lutheran student or two. She continued playing the organ for Mass, and at home, in the black, black nights, Chopin. And if she was asked, by an innocent pupil too young to understand the meaning of discretion, why she sometimes didn't wear clothes, Miss DeWitt would answer that she removed her clothing when she played the music of a particular bare-souled composer. She would nod meditatively and say in her firmest manner that when one enters into such music, one should be naked. And then she would touch the keys.

# Shamengwa

## I

AT THE EDGE of our reservation settlement there lived an old man whose arm was twisted up winglike along his side, and who was for that reason named for a butterfly—Shamengwa. Other than his arm, he was an extremely well-made person. Anyone could see that he had been handsome, and he still cut a graceful figure, slim and of medium height. His head was covered with a startling thick mane of white hair, which he was proud of. Every few weeks, he had it carefully trimmed and styled by his daughter, Geraldine, who traveled in from the bush just to do it.

Shamengwa was a man of refinement, who prepared himself carefully to meet life every day. In the Ojibwe language that is spoken on our reservation, owehzhee is the way men get themselves up—pluck stray hairs, brush each tooth, make a precise part in their hair, and, these days, press a sharp crease down the front of their blue jeans—in order to show that, although the government has tried in every way possible to destroy their manhood, they are undefeatable. Owehzhee. We still look good and we know it. The old man was never seen in disarray, and yet there was more to it.

He played the fiddle. How he played the fiddle! Although his arm was so twisted and disfigured that his shirts had to be carefully altered and pinned to accommodate the gnarled shape, he had agility in that arm, even strength. Ever since he was very young, Shamengwa had, with the aid of a white silk scarf, tied his elbow into a position that allowed the elegant hand and fingers at the end of the damaged arm full play across the fiddle's strings. With his other hand, he drew the bow. When I try to explain the sound he made, I come to some trouble with words. Inside became outside when Shamengwa played music. Yet inside to outside does not half sum it up. The music was more than music—at least, more than what we are used to hearing. The sound connected instantly with something deep and joyous. Those powerful moments of true knowledge which we paper over with daily life. The music tapped our terrors, too. Things we'd lived through and wanted never to repeat. Shredded imaginings, unadmitted longings, fear, and also surprising pleasures. We can't live at that pitch. But every so often something shatters like ice, and we fall into the river of our own existence. We are aware. This realization was in the music, somehow, or in the way Shamengwa played it.

Thus Shamengwa wasn't wanted at every party. The wild joy his jigs and reels brought forth might just as easily send people crashing onto the rocks of their roughest memories and they'd end up stunned and addled or crying in their beer. So it is. People's emotions often turn on them. Geraldine, a dedicated, headstrong woman who six years back had borne a baby, dumped its father, and earned a degree in education, sometimes drove Shamengwa to fiddling contests, where he could perform in more of a concert setting. He even won awards, prizes of the cheap sort given at local musical contests—engraved plaques and small tin cups set on plastic pedestals. These he placed on a triangular scrap of shelf high in one corner of his house. The awards were never dusted, and sometimes, when his grandchild asked him to take them down for her to play with, they came apart. Shamengwa didn't care. He was, however, fanatical about his violin.

He treated this instrument with the reverence we accord our drums, which are considered living beings and require from us food, water, shelter, and love. He fussed over it, stroked it clean with a soft cotton handkerchief, laid it carefully away in the cupboard every night in a leather case that he kept as well polished as his shoes. The case was lined with velvet that had been faded by time from a heavy bloodred to a pallid and streaked violet. I don't know violins, but his was thought to be exceptionally beautiful; it was generally understood to be old and quite valuable, too. So when Geraldine came to trim her father's hair one morning and found him on the floor, his good hand bound behind his back, his ankles tied, she was not surprised to see the lock of the cupboard smashed and the violin gone.

I AM A tribal judge, and things come to me through the grapevine of the court system or the tribal police. Gossip, rumors, scuttlebutt, B.S., or just flawed information. I always tune in, and I even take notes on what I hear around. It's sometimes wrong, or exaggerated, but just as often it contains a germ of useful truth. In this case, for instance, the name Corwin Peace was on people's lips, although there was no direct evidence that he had committed the crime.

Corwin was one of those I see again and again. A bad thing waiting for a worse thing to happen. A mistake, but one that we kept trying to salvage, because he was so young. Some thought he had no redeeming value whatsoever. A sociopath. A clever manipulator, who drugged himself dangerous each weekend. Others pitied him and blamed his behavior on his mother's drinking. F.A.E. F.A.S. A.D.D. He wore those initials after his name the way educated people append their degrees. Still others thought they saw something in him that could be saved— perhaps the most dangerous idea of all. He was a petty dealer with a string of girlfriends. He was, unfortunately, good-looking, with the features of an Edward Curtis subject, though the crack and vodka were beginning to make him puffy.

Drugs now travel the old fur-trade routes, and where once Corwin would have sat high on a bale of buffalo robes and sung traveling songs to the screeching of an oxcart, now he drove a 1991 Impala with hubcaps missing and its back end dragging. He drove it hard and he drove it all cranked up, but he was rarely caught, because he traveled such erratic hours. He drove without a license—it had long ago been taken from him. D.U.I. And he was always looking for money—scamming, betting, shooting pool, even now and then working a job that, horrifyingly, put him on the other side of a counter frying Chinese chicken strips. He was one of those whom I kept track of because I imagined I'd be seeing the full down-arcing shape of his life's trajectory. I wanted to make certain that if I had to put him away I could do it and sleep well that same night. So far, he had confirmed this.

As the days passed, Corwin lay low and picked up his job at the deep fryer. He made one of those rallying attempts that gave heart to so many of his would-be saviors. He straightened out, stayed sober, used his best manners, and when questioned was convincingly hopeful about his prospects and affable about his failures. "I'm a jackass," he admitted, "but I never sank so low as to rip off the old man's fiddle."

Yet he had, of course. And, while we waited for him to make his move, there was the old man, who quickly began to fail. I had not realized how much I loved to hear him play—sometimes out on his scrubby back lawn after dusk, sometimes at those little concerts, and other times just for groups of people who would gather round. After weeks had passed, a dull spot opened and I ached with surprising poignance for Shamengwa's loss, which I honestly shared, so that I had to seek him out and sit with him as if it would help to mourn the absence of his music together. I wanted to know, too, whether, if the violin did not turn up, we could get together and buy him a new, perhaps even better instrument. So I sat in Shamengwa's little front room one afternoon and tried to find an opening.

"Of course," I said, "we think we know who took your fiddle. We've got our eye on him."

Shamengwa swept his hair back with the one graceful hand and said, as he had many times, "I was struck from behind."

Where he'd hit the ground, his cheekbone had split and the white of his eye was an angry red. He moved with a stiff, pained slowness, the rigidity of a very old person. He lowered himself piece by piece into a padded brown rocking chair and gazed at me, or past me, really. I soon understood that although he spoke quietly and answered questions, he was not fully engaged in the conversation. In fact, he was only half present, and somewhat disheveled, irritable as well, neither of which I'd ever seen in him before. His shirt was buttoned wrong, the plaid askew, and he hadn't shaved that morning. His breath was sour, and he didn't seem at all glad that I had come.

We sat together in a challenging silence until Geraldine brought two mugs of hot, strong, sugared tea and got another for herself. Shamengwa's hand shook as he lifted the cup, but he drank. His face cleared a bit as the tea went down, and I decided that there would be no better time to put forth my idea.

"Uncle," I said, "we would like to buy a new fiddle for you."

Shamengwa said nothing, but put down the cup and folded his hands in his lap. He looked past me and frowned in a thoughtful way.

"Wouldn't he like a new violin?" I appealed to Geraldine. She shook her head as if she were both annoyed with me and exasperated with her father. We sat in silence. I didn't know where to go from there. Shamengwa had leaned back in his chair and closed his eyes. I thought he might be trying to get rid of me. But I was stubborn and did not want to go. I wanted to hear Shamengwa's music again.

"Oh, tell him about it, Daddy," Geraldine said at last.

Shamengwa leaned forward and bent his head over his hands as though he were praying.

I relaxed now and understood that I was going to hear something. It was that breathless gathering moment I've known just before composure cracks, the witness breaks, the truth comes out. I am familiar with it, and although this was not exactly a confession, it was, as it turned out, something not generally known on the reservation.

## I I

MY MOTHER LOST a baby boy to diphtheria when I was but four years old, Shamengwa said, and it was that loss that turned my mother to the Church. Before that, I remember my father playing chansons, reels, and jigs on his fiddle, but after the baby's death he put the fiddle down and took the Holy Communion. My mother out of grief became strict with my father, my older sister, and me. Where before we'd had a lively house that people liked to visit, now there was quiet. No wine and no music. We kept our voices down because our noise hurt, my mother said, and there was no laughing or teasing by my father, who had once been a dancing and hilarious man.

I don't believe my mother meant things to change so, but the sorrow she bore was beyond her strength. As though her heart, too, were buried underneath that small white headstone in the Catholic cemetery, she turned cold, turned away from the rest of us. Now that I am old and know the ways of grief, I understand she felt too much, loved too hard, and was afraid to lose us as she had lost my brother. But to a little boy these things are hidden. It only seemed to me that, along with that baby, I had lost her love. Her strong arms, her kisses, the clean soap smell of her face, her voice calming me—all of this was gone. She was like a statue in a church. Every so often we would find her in the kitchen, standing still, staring through the wall. At first we touched her clothes, petted her hands. My father kissed her, spoke gently into her ear, combed her hair into a shawl around her shoulders. Later, after we had given up, we just walked around her as you would a stump. My sister took up the cooking, and gradually we accepted that the lively, loving mother we had known wasn't going to return. We didn't try to coax her out. She spent most of her time at the church, her ivory-and-silver rosary draped over her right fist, her left hand wearing the beads smoother, smaller, until I thought one day for sure they would disappear between her fingers.

We lived right here then, but in those days trees and bush still surrounded us. There were no houses to the west. We pastured our horses where the Dairy Queen now stands. One day, while my family was in town and I was home with a cold, I became restless. I began to poke around, and soon enough I came across the fiddle that my mother had forced my father to stop playing. There it was. I was alone with it. I was only five or six years old, but I could balance a fiddle and I remembered how my father had used the bow. I got sound out of it all right, though nothing pleasing. The noise made my bones shiver. I put the fiddle back carefully, well before my parents came home, and climbed underneath my blankets when they walked into the yard. I pretended to sleep, not because I wanted to keep up the appearance of being sick but because I could not bear to return to the way things had been. Something had changed. Something had disrupted the nature of all that I knew. This deep thing had to do with the fiddle.

After that, I contrived, as often as I could, to stay alone in the house. As soon as everyone was gone I took the fiddle from its hiding place, and I tuned it to my own liking. I learned how to play it one string at a time, and I started to fit these sounds together. The sequence of notes made my brain itch. It became a torment for me to have to put away the fiddle when my family came home. Sometimes, if the wind was right, I sneaked the fiddle from the house and played out in the woods. I was always careful that the wind should carry my music away to the west, where there was no one to hear it. But one day the wind may have shifted. Or perhaps my mother's ears were more sensitive than my sister's and my father's. Because when I came back into the house I found her staring out the window, to the west. She was excited, breathing fast. Did you hear it? she cried out. Did you hear it? Terrified to be discovered, I said no. She was very agitated, and my father had a hard time calming her. After he finally got her to sleep, he sat at the table with his head in his hands. I tiptoed around the house, did the chores. I felt terrible not telling him that my music was what she'd heard. But now, as I look back, I consider my silence the first decision I made as a true musician. An artist. My playing was more important to me than my father's pain. I said nothing, but after that I was all the more sly and twice as secretive.

It was a question of survival, after all. If I had not found the music, I would have died of the silence. There are ways of being abandoned even when your parents are right there.

We had two cows, and I did the milking in the morning and evening. Lucky, because if my parents forgot to cook at least I had the milk.

I can't say I really ever suffered from a stomach kind of hunger, but another kind of human hunger bit me. I was lonely. It was about that time that I received a terrible kick from the cow, an accident, as she was usually mild. A wasp sting, perhaps, caused her to lash out in surprise. She caught my arm and, although I had no way of knowing it, shattered the bone. Painful? Oh, for certain it was, but my parents did not think to take me to a doctor. They did not notice, I suppose. I did tell my father about it, but he only nodded, pretending that he had heard, and went back to whatever he was doing.

The pain in my arm kept me awake, and at night, when I couldn't distract myself, I moaned in my blankets by the stove. But worse was the uselessness of the arm in playing the fiddle. I tried to prop it up, but it fell like a rag doll's arm. I finally hit upon a solution. I started tying up my broken arm, just as I do now. I had, of course, no idea that it would heal that way and that as a result I would be considered a permanent cripple. I only knew that with the arm tied up I could play, and that playing saved my life. So I was, like most artists, deformed by my art. I was shaped.

SCHOOL IS WHERE I got the name I carry now. Shamengwa, the black-and-orange butterfly. It was a joke on my "wing arm." Although a nun told me that a picture of a butterfly in a painting of Our Lady was meant to represent the Holy Spirit, I didn't like the name at first. My bashfulness about the shape of my arm caused me to avoid people even once I was older, and I made no friends. Human friends. My true friend was my fiddle, anyway, the only friend I really needed. And then I lost that friend.

My parents had gone to church, but there was on that winter's day some problem with the stove. Smoke had filled the nave at the start of Mass and everyone was sent straight home. When my mother and father arrived, I was deep into my playing. They listened, standing at the door rooted by the surprise of what they heard, for how long I do not know. I had not heard the door open and, with my eyes shut, had not seen the light thereby admitted. Finally, I noticed the cold breeze that swirled around me, turned, and we stared at one another with a shocked gravity that my father broke at last by asking, "How long?"

I did not answer, although I wanted to. *Seven years. Seven years!*

He led my mother in. They shut the door behind them. Then he said, in a voice of troubled softness, "Keep on."

So I played, and when I stopped he said nothing.

Discovered, I thought the worst was over. But the next morning, waking to a silence where I usually heard my father's noises, hearing a vacancy before I even knew it for sure, I understood that the worst was yet to come. My playing had woken something in him. That was the reason he left. But I don't know why he had to take the violin. When I saw that it was missing, all breath left me, all thought, all feeling. For a while after that I was the same as my mother. In our loss, we were cut off from the true, bright, normal routines of living. I might have stayed that way, joined my mother in the darkness from which she could not return. I might have lived on in that diminished form, if I had not had a dream.

The dream was simple. A voice. *Go to the lake and sit by the southern rock. Wait there. I will come to you.*

I decided to follow these instructions. I took my bedroll, a scrap of jerky, and a loaf of bannock, and sat myself down on the crackling lichen of the southern rock. That plate of stone jutted out into the water, which dropped off from its edges into a green-black depth. From that rock, I could see all that happened on the water. I put tobacco down for the spirits. All day, I sat there waiting. Flies bit me. The wind boomed in my ears. Nothing happened. I curled up when the light left and I slept. Stayed on the next morning. The next day, too. It was the first time that I had ever slept out on the shores, and I began to understand why people said of the lake that there was no end to it, even though it was bounded by rocks. There were rivers flowing in and flowing out, secret currents, six kinds of weather working on its surface and a hidden terrain beneath. Each wave washed in from somewhere unseen and washed out again to somewhere unknown. I saw birds, strange-feathered and unfamiliar, passing through on their way to somewhere else. Listening to the water, I was for the first time comforted by sounds other than my fiddle playing. I let go. I thought I might just stay there forever, staring at the blue thread of the horizon. Nothing mattered. When a small bit of the horizon's thread detached, darkened, proceeded forward slowly, I observed it with only mild interest. The speck seemed to both advance and retreat. It wavered back and forth. I lost sight of it for long stretches, then it popped closer, over a wave.

It was a canoe. But either the paddler was asleep in the bottom or the canoe was drifting. As it came nearer, I decided for sure that it must be adrift, it rode so lightly in the waves, nosing this way, then the other. But always, no matter how hesitantly, it ended up advancing straight toward the southern rock, straight toward me. I watched until I could clearly see there was nobody in it. Then the words of my dream returned. *I will come to you.* I dove in eagerly, swam for the canoe—I had learned, as boys do, to compensate for my arm, and although my stroke was peculiar, I was strong. I thought perhaps the canoe had been badly tied and slipped its mooring, but no rope trailed. Perhaps high waves had coaxed it off a beach where its owner had dragged it up, thinking it safe. I pushed the canoe in to shore, then pulled it up behind me, wedged it in a cleft between two rocks. Only then did I look inside. There, lashed to a crosspiece in the bow, was a black case of womanly shape that fastened on the side with two brass locks.

That is how my fiddle came to me, Shamengwa said, raising his head to look steadily at me. He smiled, shook his fine head, and spoke softly. And that is why no other fiddle will I play.

## III

CORWIN SHUT THE door to his room. It wasn't really his room, but some people were letting him stay in their basement in return for several favors. Standing on a board propped on sawhorses, he pushed his outspread fingers against the panel of the false ceiling. He placed the panel to one side and groped up behind it among wires and underneath a pad of yellow fiberglass insulation, until he located the handle of the case.

He bore it down to the piece of foam rubber that served as his mattress and through which, every night, he felt the hard cold of the concrete floor seep into his legs. He had taken the old man's fiddle because he needed money, but he hadn't thought much about where he would sell it or who would buy it. Then he had an inspiration. One of the women in the house went to Spirit Lake every weekend to stay with her boyfriend's family. He'd put the fiddle in the trunk and hitch along. They'd let him out at Miracle Village Mall, and he'd take the violin there and sell it to a music lover.

Corwin got out of the car and carried the violin into the mall. There are two kinds of people, he thought, the givers and the takers. I'm a taker. Render unto Corwin what is due him. His favorite movie of recent times was about a cop with such a twisted way of looking at the world that you couldn't tell if he was evil or good—you only knew that he could seize your mind with language. Corwin had a thing for language. He inhaled it from movies, rap and rock music, television. It rubbed around inside him, word against word. He thought he was writing poems sometimes in his thoughts, but the poems would not come out. The words stuck in odd configurations and made patterns that raced across the screen of his shut eyes and off the edge, down his temples and into the darkness of his neck. So when he walked through the air-lock doors into the warm cathedral space of the central food court, his brain was a mumble.

Taking a seat, peering at the distracted-looking shoppers, he quickly understood that none of them was likely to buy the fiddle. He walked into a music store and tried to show the instrument to the manager, who said only, "Nah, we don't take used." Corwin walked out again. He tried a few people. They shied away or turned him down flat.

"Gotta regroup," Corwin told himself, and went back to sit on the length of bench he had decided to call his own. That was where he got the idea that became a gold mine. He remembered a scene from a TV show, a clip of a musician in a city street. He was playing a saxophone or something of that sort, and at his feet there was an open instrument case. A woman stopped and smiled and threw a dollar in the case. Corwin took the violin out and laid the open case invitingly at his feet. He took the fiddle in one hand and drew the bow across the strings with the other. It made a terrible, strange sound. The screech echoed in the food court and several people raised their lips from the waxed-paper food wrappers to look at Corwin. He looked back at them, poised and frozen. It was a moment of drama—he had them. An audience. He had to act instantly or lose them. Instinctively, he gave a flowery, low bow, as though he were accepting an ovation. There were a few murmurs of amusement. Someone even applauded. These sounds acted on Corwin Peace at once, more powerfully than any drug he had tried. A surge of unfamiliar zeal filled him, and he took up the instrument again, threw back his hair, and began to play a swift, silent passage of music.

His mimicry was impeccable. Where had he learned it? He didn't know. He didn't touch the bow to the strings, but he played music all the same. Music ricocheted around between his ears. He could hardly keep up with what he heard. His body spilled over with drama. When the music in his head stopped, he dipped low and did the splits, which he'd learned from Prince videos. He held the violin and the bow overhead. Applause broke over him. A skein of dazzling sound.

THEY PICKED UP Corwin Peace pretending to play the fiddle in a Fargo mall, and brought him to me. I have a great deal of latitude in sentencing. In spite of myself, I was intrigued by Corwin's unusual treatment of the instrument, and I decided to set a precedent. First, I cleared my decision with Shamengwa. Then I sentenced Corwin to apprentice himself with the old master. Six days a week, two hours each morning. Three hours of practice after work. He would either learn to play the violin or he would do time. In truth, I didn't know who was being punished, the boy or the old man. But at least now, from Shamengwa's house, we began to hear the violin again.

It was the middle of September on the reservation, the mornings chill, the afternoons warm, the leaves still green and thick in their final sweetness. All the hay was mowed. The wild rice was beaten flat. The radiators in the tribal offices went on at night, but by noon we had to open the windows to cool off. The woodsmoke of parching fires and the spent breeze of diesel entered then, and sometimes the squall of Corwin's music from down the hill. The first weeks were not promising. Then the days turned uniformly cold, we kept the windows shut, and until spring the only news of Corwin's progress came through his probation officer. I didn't expect much. It was not until the first hot afternoon in early May that I opened my window and actually heard Corwin playing.

"Not half bad," I said that night when I visited Shamengwa. "I listened to your student."

"He's clumsy as hell, but he's got the fire," Shamengwa said, touching his chest. I could tell that he was proud of Corwin and allowed myself to consider the possibility that something as idealistic as putting an old man and a hard-core juvenile delinquent together had worked, or hadn't, anyway, ended up a disaster.

The lessons and the relationship outlasted, in fact, the sentence. Fall came, and we closed the windows again. In spring, we opened them, and once or twice heard Corwin playing. Then Shamengwa died.

His was a peaceful death, the sort of death we used to pray to St. Joseph to give us all. He was asleep, his violin next to the bed, covers pulled to his chin. Found in the morning by Geraldine.

There was a large funeral with the usual viewing, at which people filed up to his body and tucked flowers and pipe tobacco and small tokens into Shamengwa's coffin to accompany him into the earth. Geraldine placed a monarch butterfly upon his shoulder. She said that she had found it that morning on the grille of her car. Halfway through the service, she stood up and took the violin from the coffin, where it had been tucked up close to her father.

"A few months ago, Dad told me that when he died I was to give this violin to Corwin Peace," she told everyone. "And so I'm offering it to him now. And I've already asked him to play us one of Dad's favorites today."

Corwin had been sitting in the back and now he walked up to the front, his shoulders hunched, hands shoved in his pockets. The sorrow in his face surprised me. It made me uneasy to see such a direct show of emotion in one who had been so volatile. But Corwin's feelings seemed directed once he took up the fiddle and began to play. He played a chanson everyone knew, a song typical of our people because it began tender and slow, then broke into a wild strangeness that pricked our pulses and strained our breath. Corwin played with passion, if not precision, and there was enough of the old man's energy in his music that by the time he'd finished everybody was in tears.

Then came the shock. Amid the dabbing of eyes and discreet nose-blowing, Corwin stood gazing into the coffin at his teacher, the violin dangling from one hand. Beside the coffin there was an ornate Communion rail. Corwin raised the violin high and smashed it on the rail, once, twice, three times, to do the job right. I was in the front pew, and I jumped from my seat as though I'd been prepared for something like this. I grasped Corwin's arm as he laid the violin carefully back beside Shamengwa, but then I let him go, for I recognized that his gesture was spent. My focus moved from Corwin to the violin itself, because I saw, sticking from its smashed wood, a roll of paper. I drew the paper out. It was old and covered with a stiff, antique flow of writing. The priest, somewhat shaken, began the service again. I put the roll of paper into my jacket pocket and returned to my seat. I didn't exactly forget to read it. There was just so much happening after the funeral, what with the windy burial and then the six-kinds-of-fry-bread supper in the Knights of Columbus Hall, that I didn't get the chance to sit still and concentrate. It was evening and I was at home, comfortable in my chair with a bright lamp turned on behind me, so the radiance fell over my shoulder, before I finally read what had been hidden in the violin for so many years.

# IV

I, BAPTISTE PARENTHEAU, also known as Billy Peace, leave to my brother Edwin this message, being a history of the violin which on this day of Our Lord August 20, 1897, I send out onto the waters to find him.

A recapitulation to begin with: Having read of LaFountaine's mission to the Iroquois, during which that priest avoided having his liver plucked out before his eyes by nimbly playing the flute, our own Father

Jasprine thought it wise to learn to play a musical instrument before he ventured forth into the wastelands past the Lake of the Woods. Therefore, he set off with music as his protection. He studied and brought along his violin, a noble instrument, which he played less than adequately. If the truth were told, he'd have done better not to impose his slight talents on the Ojibwe. Yet, as he died young and left the violin to his altar boy, my father, I should say nothing against good Jasprine. I should, instead, be grateful for the joys his violin afforded my family. I should be happy in the hours that my father spent tuning and then playing the thing, and in the devotion that my brother and I eagerly gave to it. Yet, as things ended so hard between my brother and myself because of the instrument, I find myself imagining that we never knew the violin, that I'd never played its music or understood its voice. For when my father died he left the fiddle to both my brother Edwin and myself, with the stipulation that were we unable to decide who should have it, then we were to race for it as true sons of the great waters, by paddling our canoes.

When my brother and I heard this declaration read, we said nothing. There was nothing to say, for as much as it was true that we loved each other, we both wanted that violin. Each of us had given it years of practice, each of us had whispered into its hollow our sorrows and taken hold of its joys. That violin had soothed our wild hours, courted our wives. But now we were done with the passing of it back and forth. And if it had to belong to one of us two brothers I determined that it would be me.

Two nights before we took our canoes out, I conceived of a sure plan. When the moon slipped behind clouds and the world was dark, I went out to the shore with a pannikin of heated pitch. I had decided to interfere with Edwin's balance. Our canoes were so carefully constructed that each side matched ounce for ounce. By thickening the seams on one side with a heavy application of pitch, I'd throw off Edwin's paddle stroke enough, I was sure, to give me a telling advantage.

Ours is a wide lake and full of islands. It is haunted by birds who utter sarcastic or sorrowful cries. One loses sight of others easily, and sound travels skewed, bouncing off the rock cliffs. There are flying skeletons, floating bogs, caves containing the spirits of little children, and black moods of weather. We love it well, and we know its secrets—in some part, at least. Not all. And not the secret that I put in motion.

We were to set off on the far northern end of the lake and arrive at the south, where our uncles had lit fires and brought the violin, wrapped in red cloth, in its fancy case. We started out together, joking. Edwin, you remember how we paddled through the first two narrows, laughing as we exaggerated our efforts, and how I said, as what I'd done with the soft pitch weighed on me, "Maybe we should share the damn thing after all."

You laughed and said that our uncles would be disappointed, waiting there, and that when you won the contest things would be as they were before, except all would know that Edwin was the faster paddler. I promised you the same. Then you swerved behind a skim of rock and took your secret shortcut. As I paddled, I had to stop occasionally and bail. At first I thought that I had sprung a slow leak, but in time I understood. While I was painting on extra pitch, you were piercing the bottom of my canoe. I was not, in fact, in any danger, and when the wind shifted all of a sudden and it began to storm—no thunder or lightning, just a buffet of cold rain—I laughed and thanked you. For the water I took on actually helped to steady me. I rode lower, and stayed on course. But you foundered. It was worse to be set off balance. You must have overturned.

THE BONFIRES DIE to coals on the south shore. I curl in blankets but I do not sleep. I am keeping watch. At first when you are waiting for someone, every shadow is an arrival. Then the shadows become the very substance of dread. We hunt for you, call your name until our voices are worn to whispers. No answer. In one old man's dream everything goes around the other way, the not-sun-way, counterclockwise, which means that the dream is of the spirit world. And then he sees you there in his dream, going the wrong way, too.

The uncles have returned to their houses, pastures, children, wives. I am alone on the shore. As the night goes black, I sing for you. As the sun comes up, I call across the water. White gulls answer. As the time goes on, I begin to accept what I have done. I begin to know the truth of things.

They have left the violin here with me. Each night I play for you, brother, and when I can play no more I'll lash our fiddle into the canoe and send it out to you, to find you wherever you are. I won't have to pierce the bottom so it will travel the bed of the lake. Your holes will do the trick, brother, as my trick did for you.

## V

OF COURSE, THE canoe did not sink to the bottom of the lake. Nor did it stray. The canoe and its violin eventually found a different Peace, through the person of Shamengwa. The fiddle had searched long, I had no doubt of that. For what stuck in my mind, what woke me in the middle of the night, was the date on the letter: 1897. The violin had spoken to Shamengwa and called him out onto the lake more than twenty years later.

"How about that?" I said to Geraldine. "Can you explain such a thing?"

She looked at me steadily.

"We know nothing" is what she said.

I was to marry her. We took in Corwin. The violin lies buried in the arms of the man it saved, while the boy it also saved plays for money now and prospers here on the surface of the earth. I do my work. I do my best to make the small decisions well, and I try not to hunger for the greater things, for the deeper explanations. For I am sentenced to keep watch over this little patch of earth, to judge its miseries and tell its stories. That's who I am. Mii'sago iw.

# The Shawl

AMONG THE ANISHINAABEG on the road where I live, it is told how a woman loved a man other than her husband and went off into the bush and bore his child. Her name was Aanakwad, which means cloud, and like a cloud she was changeable. She was moody and sullen one moment, her lower lip jutting and her eyes flashing, filled with storms. The next, she would shake her hair over her face and blow it straight out in front of her to make her children scream with laughter. For she also had two children by her husband, one a yearning boy of five years and the other a capable daughter of nine.

When Aanakwad brought the new baby out of the trees that autumn, the older girl was like a second mother, even waking in the night to clean the baby and nudge it to her mother's breast. Aanakwad slept through its cries, hardly woke. It wasn't that she didn't love her baby, no, it was the opposite—she loved it too much, the way she loved its father, and not her husband. This passion ate away at her, and her feelings were unbearable. If she could have thrown off that wronghearted love, she would have, but the thought of the other man, who lived across the lake, was with her always. She became a gray sky, stared monotonously at the walls, sometimes wept into her hands for hours at a time. Soon, she couldn't rise to cook or keep the cabin neat, and it was too much for the girl, who curled up each night exhausted in her red-and-brown plaid shawl, and slept and slept, until the husband had to wake her to awaken her mother, for he was afraid of his wife's bad temper, and it was he who roused Aanakwad into anger by the sheer fact that he was himself and not the other.

At last, even though he loved Aanakwad, the husband had to admit that their life together was no good anymore. And it was he who sent for the other man's uncle. In those days, our people lived widely scattered, along the shores and in the islands, even out on the plains. There were no roads then, just trails, though we had horses and wagons and, for the winter, sleds. When the uncle came around to fetch Aanakwad, in his wagon fitted out with sled runners, it was very hard, for she and her husband had argued right up to the last about the children, argued fiercely until the husband had finally given in. He turned his face to the wall, and did not move to see the daughter, whom he treasured, sit down beside her mother, wrapped in her plaid robe in the wagon bed. They left right away, with their bundles and sacks, not bothering to heat up the stones to warm their feet. The father had stopped his ears, so he did not hear his son cry out when he suddenly understood that he would be left behind.

As the uncle slapped the reins and the horse lurched forward, the boy tried to jump into the wagon, but his mother pried his hands off the boards, crying, *Gego, gego,* and he fell down hard. But there was something in him that would not let her leave. He jumped up and, although he was wearing only light clothing, he ran behind the wagon over the packed drifts. The horses picked up speed. His chest was scorched with pain, and yet he pushed himself on. He'd never run so fast, so hard and furiously, but he was determined, and he refused to believe that the increasing distance between him and the wagon was real. He kept going until his throat closed, he saw red, and in the ice of the air his lungs shut. Then, as he fell onto the board-hard snow, he raised his head. He watched the back of the wagon and the tiny figures of his mother and sister disappear, and something failed in him. Something broke. At that moment he truly did not care if he was alive or dead. So when he saw the gray shapes, the shadows, bounding lightly from the trees to either side of the trail, far ahead, he was not afraid.

•  •  •

THE NEXT THE boy knew, his father had him wrapped in a blanket and was carrying him home. His father's chest was broad and, although he already spat the tubercular blood that would write the end of his story, he was still a strong man. It would take him many years to die. In those years, the father would tell the boy, who had forgotten this part entirely, that at first when he talked about the shadows the father thought he'd been visited by manidoog. But then, as the boy described the shapes, his father had understood that they were not spirits. Uneasy, he had decided to take his gun back along the trail. He built up the fire in the cabin, and settled his boy near it, and went back out into the snow. Perhaps the story spread through our settlements because the father had to tell what he saw, again and again, in order to get rid of it. Perhaps as with all frightful dreams, amaaniso, he had to talk about it to destroy its power—though in this case nothing could stop the dream from being real.

The shadows' tracks were the tracks of wolves, and in those days, when our guns had taken all their food for furs and hides to sell, the wolves were bold and had abandoned the old agreement between them and the first humans. For a time, until we understood and let the game increase, the wolves hunted us. The father bounded forward when he saw the tracks. He could see where the pack, desperate, had tried to slash the tendons of the horses' legs. Next, where they'd leaped for the back of the wagon. He hurried on to where the trail gave out at the broad empty ice of the lake. There, he saw what he saw, scattered, and the ravens, attending to the bitter small leavings of the wolves.

For a time, the boy had no understanding of what had happened. His father kept what he knew to himself, at least that first year, and when his son asked about his sister's torn plaid shawl, and why it was kept in the house, his father said nothing. But he wept when the boy asked if his sister was cold. It was only after his father had been weakened by the disease that he began to tell the story, far too often and always the same way: he told how when the wolves closed in, Aanakwad had thrown her daughter to them.

When his father said those words, the boy went still. What had his sister felt? What had thrust through her heart? Had something broken inside her, too, as it had in him? Even then, he knew that this broken place inside him would not be mended, except by some terrible means. For he kept seeing his mother put the baby down and grip his sister around the waist. He saw Aanakwad swing the girl lightly out over the side of the wagon. He saw the brown shawl with its red lines flying open. He saw the shadows, the wolves, rush together, quick and avid, as the wagon with sled runners disappeared into the distance—forever, for neither he nor his father saw Aanakwad again.

WHEN I WAS little, my own father terrified us with his drinking. This was after we lost our mother, because before that the only time I was aware that he touched the ishkodewaaboo was on an occasional week-end when they got home late, or sometimes during berry-picking gatherings when we went out to the bush and camped with others. Not until she died did he start the heavy sort of drinking, the continuous drinking, where we were left alone in the house for days. The kind where, when he came home, we'd jump out the window and hide in the woods while he barged around, shouting for us. We'd go back only after he had fallen dead asleep.

There were three of us: me, the oldest at ten, and my little sister and brother, twins, and only six years old. I was surprisingly good at taking care of them, I think, and because we learned to survive together during those drinking years we have always been close. Their names are Doris and Raymond, and they married a brother and sister. When we get together, which is often, for we live on the same road, there come times in the talking and card playing, and maybe even in the light beer now and then, when we will bring up those days. Most people understand how it was. Our story isn't uncommon. But for us it helps to compare our points of view.

How else would I know, for instance, that Raymond saw me the first time I hid my father's belt? I pulled it from around his waist while he was passed out, and then I buried it in the woods. I kept doing it after that. Our father couldn't understand why his belt was always stolen when he went to town drinking. He even accused his shkwebii buddies of the theft. But I had good reasons. Not only was he embarrassed, afterward, to go out with his pants held up by rope, but he couldn't snake his belt out in anger and snap the hooked buckle end in the air. He couldn't hit us with it. Of course, being resourceful, he used other things. There was a board. A willow wand. And there was himself—his hands and fists and boots—and things he could throw. But eventually it became easy, to evade him, and after a while we rarely suffered a bruise or a scratch. We had our own place in the woods, even a little campfire for the cold nights. And we'd take money from him every chance we got, slip it from his shoe, where he thought it well hidden. He became, for us, a thing to be avoided, outsmarted, and exploited. We survived off him as if he were a capricious and dangerous line of work. I suppose we stopped thinking of him as a human being, certainly as a father.

I got my growth earlier than some boys, and, one night when I was thirteen and Doris and Raymond and I were sitting around wishing for something besides the oatmeal and commodity canned milk I'd stashed so he couldn't sell them, I heard him coming down the road. He was shouting and making noise all the way to the house, and Doris and Raymond looked at me and headed for the back window. When they saw that I wasn't coming, they stopped. C'mon, get with it—they tried to pull me along. I shook them off and told them to get out quickly—I was staying. I think I can take him now is what I said.

He was big; he hadn't yet wasted away from the alcohol. His nose had been pushed to one side in a fight, then slammed back to the other side, so now it was straight. His teeth were half gone, and he smelled the way he had to smell, being five days drunk. When he came in the door, he paused for a moment, his eyes red and swollen, tiny slits. Then he saw that I was waiting for him, and he smiled in a bad way. My first punch surprised him. I had been practicing on a hay-stuffed bag, then on a padded board, toughening my fists, and I'd got so quick I flickered like fire. I still wasn't as strong as he was, and he had a good twenty pounds on me. Yet I'd do some damage, I was sure of it. I'd teach him not to mess with me. What I didn't foresee was how the fight itself would get right into me.

There is something terrible about fighting your father. It came on suddenly, with the second blow—a frightful kind of joy. A power surged up from the center of me, and I danced at him, light and giddy, full of a heady rightness. Here is the thing: I wanted to waste him, waste him good. I wanted to smack the living shit out of him. Kill him, if I must. A punch for Doris, a kick for Raymond. And all the while I was silent, then screaming, then silent again, in this rage of happiness that filled me with a simultaneous despair so that, I guess you could say, I stood apart from myself.

He came at me, crashed over a chair that was already broken, then threw the pieces. I grabbed one of the legs and whacked him on the ear so that his head spun and turned back to me, bloody. I watched myself striking him again and again. I knew what I was doing, but not really, not in the ordinary sense. It was as if I were standing calm, against the wall with my arms folded, pitying us both. I saw the boy, the chair leg, the man fold and fall, his hands held up in begging fashion. Then I also saw that, for a while now, the bigger man had not even bothered to fight back.

Suddenly, he was my father again. And when I knelt down next to him, I was his son. I reached for the closest rag, and picked up this piece of blanket that my father always kept with him for some reason. And as I picked it up and wiped the blood off his face, I said to him, Your nose is crooked again. He looked at me, steady and quizzical, as though he had never had a drink in his life, and I wiped his face again with that frayed piece of blanket. Well, it was a shawl, really, a kind of old-fashioned woman's blanket-shawl. Once, maybe, it had been plaid. You could still see lines, some red, the background a faded brown. He watched intently as my hand brought the rag to his face. I was pretty sure, then, that I'd clocked him too hard, that he'd really lost it now. Gently, though, he clasped one hand around my wrist. With the other hand he took the shawl. He crumpled it and held it to the middle of his forehead. It was as if he were praying, as if he were having thoughts he wanted to collect in that piece of cloth. For a while he lay like that, and I, crouched over, let him be, hardly breathing. Something told me to sit there, still. And then at last he said to me, in the sober new voice I would hear from then on, *Did you know I had a sister once?*

THERE WAS A time when the government moved everybody off the farthest reaches of the reservation, onto roads, into towns, into housing. It looked good at first, and then it all went sour. Shortly afterward, it seemed that anyone who was someone was either drunk, killed, near suicide, or had just dusted himself. None of the old sort were left, it seemed—the old kind of people, the Gete-anishinaabeg, who are kind beyond kindness and would do anything for others. It was during that time that my mother died and my father hurt us, as I have said.

Now, gradually, that term of despair has lifted somewhat and yielded up its survivors. But we still have sorrows that are passed to us from early generations, sorrows to handle in addition to our own, and cruelties lodged where we cannot forget them. We have the need to forget. We are always walking on oblivion's edge.

Some get away, like my brother and sister, married now and living quietly down the road. And me, to some degree, though I prefer to live alone. And even my father, who recently found a woman. Once, when he brought up the old days, and we went over the story again, I told him at last the two things I had been thinking.

First, I told him that keeping his sister's shawl was wrong, because we never keep the clothing of the dead. Now's the time to burn it, I said. Send it off to cloak her spirit. And he agreed.

The other thing I said to him was in the form of a question. Have you ever considered, I asked him, given how tenderhearted your sister was, and how brave, that she looked at the whole situation? She saw that the wolves were only hungry. She knew that their need was only need. She knew that you were back there, alone in the snow. She understood that the baby she loved would not live without a mother, and that only the uncle knew the way. She saw clearly that one person on the

wagon had to be offered up, or they all would die. And in that moment
of knowledge, don't you think, being who she was, of the old sort of
Anishinaabeg, who thinks of the good of the people first, she jumped,
my father, indede, brother to that little girl? Don't you think she lifted
her shawl and flew?

# The Butcher's Wife

HERE'S AN ODD and paradoxical truth: a man's experience of happiness can later kill him. Though he appeared to be no more than an everyday drunk, Delphine Watzka's father, Roy, was more. He was a dangerous romantic. In his life, he had loved deeply, even selflessly, with all the profound gratitude of a surprised Pole. But the woman he had loved and married, Minnie Watzka, née Kust, now existed only in the person of her daughter, Delphine, and in photographs. Minnie had died when Delphine was very young, and afterward Roy indulged in a worship of those photographs. Some nights, he lit a line of votive candles on the dresser and drank steadily and spoke to Minnie until, from deep in his cups, she answered.

During the first years after Minnie's death, Roy bounced in and out of drink with the resilience of a man with a healthy liver. He remained remarkably sloshed even through Prohibition by becoming ecumenical. Hair tonic, orange-flower water, cough syrups of all types, even women's monthly elixirs fueled his grieving rituals. Gradually, he destroyed the organ he'd mistaken for his heart. By the time Delphine reached her twelfth year, her father's need to drink was produced less by her mother's memory than by the drink itself. After that, she knew her father mainly as a pickled wreck. Home was chaos. Now Delphine was a grown woman and he was completely failing. In the spring of 1936, she quit secretarial school and moved back from the Twin Cities to their Minnesota farm to care for him.

As Delphine walked into town for supplies, she thought of her mother. She possessed only one tiny locket photo of Minnie, and while she was away she had found herself missing the other photographs. It was in that fit of longing to see her mother's face that Delphine entered Waldvogel's Meats, and met Eva Waldvogel.

THE FIRST TRUE meeting of their minds was over lard.

"I'll take half a pound," Delphine said. She was mentally worn out by her father's insistence that since he was dying anyway he might as well kill himself more pleasurably with schnapps.

All day long he'd been drunk underneath the mulberry trees, laughing to himself and trying to catch the fruit in his mouth. He was now stained purple with the juice.

"There's lard and there is lard." Eva reached into the glass case that was cooled by an electric fan. "My husband was trained back in Germany as a master butcher, and he uses a secret process to render his fat. Taste," she commanded, holding out a small pan. Delphine swiped a bit with the tip of her finger.

"Pure as butter!"

"We don't salt it much," Eva whispered, as though this were not for just anyone to overhear. "But it won't keep unless you have an icebox."

"I don't have one," Delphine admitted. "Well, I did, but my dad sold it while I was away."

"Who is he, may I ask?"

Delphine liked Eva's direct but polite manners and admired her thick bun of bronze-red hair stuck through with two yellow lead pencils. Eva's eyes were a very pale, washed-out blue with flecks of green. There was, in one eye, an odd golden streak that would turn black when the life finally left her body, like a light going out behind the crack in a door.

"Roy Watzka," Delphine said slowly.

Eva nodded. The name seemed to tell her all that she needed to know. "Come back here." Eva swept her arm around the counter. "I'll teach you to make a mincemeat pie better than you've ever eaten. It's all in the goddamn suet."

Delphine went behind the counter, past an office cascading with papers and bills, past little cupboards full of clean aprons and rags, and a knickknack shelf displaying figures made of German porcelain. She and Eva entered the kitchen, which was full of light from big windows set into the thick walls. Here, for Delphine, all time stopped. As she took in the room, she experienced a profound and fabulous expansion of being.

There was a shelf for big clay bread bowls and a pull-out bin containing flour. Wooden cupboards painted an astounding green matched the floor's linoleum. A heavy, polished meat grinder was bolted to the counter. The round table was covered with a piece of oilcloth with squares. In each red-trimmed square was printed a bunch of blue grapes or a fat pink-gold peach, an apple or a delicate green pear. On the windowsills, pots of geraniums bloomed, scarlet and ferociously cheerful.

Suddenly extremely happy, Delphine sat in a solid, square-backed chair while Eva spooned roasted coffee beans into a grinder and then began to grind them. A wonderful fragrance emerged. Delphine took a huge breath. Eva, her hands quick and certain, dumped the thin wooden drawer full of fresh grounds into a pale-blue speckled enamel coffeepot. She got water from a faucet in her sink, instead of from a pump, and then she put the coffee on the stove and lit the burner of a stunning white gas range with chrome trim swirled into the words "Magic Chef."

"My God," Delphine breathed. She couldn't speak. But that was fine, for Eva had already whipped one of the pencils out of her hair and taken up a pad of paper to set down the mincemeat recipe. Eva spoke English very well but her writing was of the old, ornate German style, and she wasn't a good speller. Delphine was grateful for this tiny flaw, for Eva appeared so fantastically skilled a being, so assured—she was also the mother of two sturdy and intelligent sons—that she would have been an unapproachable paragon to Delphine otherwise. Delphine— who had never really had a mother, much less a sister, who cleaned up shameful things in her father's house, who had been toughened by cold and hunger and was regarded as beneath notice by the town's best society, and yet could spell—stole confidence from the misspelled recipe.

• • •

THE NEXT TIME Delphine visited the Waldvogels' store, she noted the jangle of a cheerful shop bell. She imagined that it was only the first of many times that she would ring the bell as she entered the shop. This did not prove to be the case. By the next time Delphine came to the shop, she had already attained a status so familiar that she entered by the back door.

Delphine placed her order, as before, and, as before, Eva asked her to come in and sit down for a coffee. There was no cleanser on Eva's shelf that would be strong enough for the work Delphine had to do to make Roy's place habitable again, and Eva wanted to concoct something of her own.

"First off, a good vinegar-and-water washdown. Then I should order the industrial-strength ammonia for you, only be careful with the fumes. Maybe, if that doesn't work, raw lye."

Delphine shook her head. She was smitten with shame, and could not tell Eva that she was afraid her father might try to drink the stuff. Eva sipped her coffee. Today, her hair was bound back in a singular knot, in the shape of a figure eight, which Delphine knew was the ancient sign for eternity. Eva rose and turned away, walked across the green squares of linoleum to punch down the risen dough. As Delphine watched, a strange notion popped into her head, the idea that perhaps the most strongly experienced moments—such as this one, when Eva turned, and the sun met her hair, and for that one instant the symbol blazed out—those particular moments were eternal. They actually went somewhere—into a file of moments that existed beyond time's range and could not be pilfered by God.

Well, it *was* God, wasn't it, Delphine went on stubbornly, who had made time and thereby created the end of everything? Tell me this, Delphine wanted to say to her new friend, why are we given the curse of imagining eternity when we can't experience it, when we ourselves are so finite? She wanted to say it, but suddenly grew shy, and it was in that state of concentrated inattention that she first met Eva's husband, Fidelis Waldvogel, Master Butcher.

Before she actually met him, she sensed him, like a surge of electric power in the air when the clouds are low. Then she felt a heaviness. A field of gravity moved through her body. She was trying to rise, to shake the feeling, when he suddenly filled the doorway.

It was not his size. He was not extraordinarily tall or broad. But he shed power, as though there were a bigger man crammed into him. One thick hand hung down at his side like a hook; the other balanced on his shoulder a slab of meat. That cow's haunch weighed perhaps a hundred pounds or double that. He held it lightly, although the veins in his neck throbbed, heavy-blooded as a bull's. He looked at Delphine, and his eyes were white-blue. Their stares locked. Delphine's cheeks went fever red, and she looked down first. Clouds moved across the sun, and the red mouths of the geraniums on the windowsill yawned. The shock of his gaze caused her to pick up one of Eva's cigarettes. To light it. He looked away from her and conversed with his wife. Then he left without asking to be introduced.

That abruptness, though rude, was more than fine with Delphine. Already, she didn't want to know him. She hoped that she could avoid him. It didn't matter, so long as she could still be friends with Eva, and hold the job that she soon was offered, waiting on customers.

So it was. From then on, Delphine used the back door, which led past the furnace and the washtubs, the shelves of tools, the bleached aprons slowly drying on racks and hooks. She walked down the hallway cluttered with papers and equipment and lifted from a hook by the shop door the apron Eva had given her, blue with tiny white flowers. From then on, she heard the customer bell ring from the other side of the counter.

Within a week, Delphine had met most of the regular customers. Then she met Tante Marie-Christine, who was not a customer but Fidelis's sister. One afternoon, Tante swept in with just one clang of the bell, as though the bell itself had been muted by her elegance. She went right around to the case that held the sausage, wrenched it open, fished out a ring of the best baloney, and put it in her purse. Delphine stood back and watched—actually, she stood back and envied the woman's shoes. They were made of a thin, flexible Italian leather and were cleverly buttoned. They fit Tante's rather long, narrow feet with a winsome precision. She might not have had a captivating face—for she resembled her brother, replicated his powerful neck and too stern chin, and the eyes that on him were commanding on her were a ghostly blue that gave Delphine the shivers—but her feet were slim and pretty. She was vain about them, and all her shoes were made of the most expensive leather.

"Who are you?" Tante asked, rearing her head back and then swirling off in her fur coat without deigning to accept an answer. The question hung in the air long after Tante had gone back to invade Eva's kitchen. "Who are you?" is a question with a long answer or a short answer. When Tante dropped it in the air like that, Delphine was left to consider its larger meaning as she scrubbed down the meat counters and prepared to mop the floor.

*Who are you*, Delphine Watzka, you drunkard's child, you dropout secretary, you creature with a belly of steel and a heart that longs for a mother? Who are you, *what* are you—born a dirty Pole in a Polack's dirt? You with a cellar full of empty bottles and a stewed father lying on the floor? What makes you think you belong anywhere near this house, this shop, and especially my brother Fidelis, who is the master of all that he does?

When Tante swept back out with a loaf of her sister-in-law's fresh bread under her arm, and grabbed a bottle of milk, Delphine wrote it all down on a slip: "Tante took a bottle of milk, a ring of number-one baloney and a loaf of bread." And she left it at that. When Tante found out that Delphine had written the items down, she was furious. Tante didn't take things. By her reckoning, she was owed things. She had once given her brother five hundred dollars to purchase equipment, and although he had paid her back she continued to take the interest out in ways that were intended to remind him of her dutiful generosity.

Eva's two boys, Franz and Louis, did not like Tante. Delphine could see that. Not that she knew all that much about children. She had not been around them often. But, as these boys belonged to Eva, she was interested in who they were.

At fourteen, Franz was strong and athletic, with one of those proud, easygoing American temperaments that are simultaneously transparent and opaque. His inner thoughts and feelings were either nonevident or nonexistent; she couldn't tell which. He always smiled at her and said hello, with only the faintest of German accents. He played football and was, in fact, a local hero. The second boy was more reclusive. Louis had a philosophical bent and a monkish nature, though he'd play with tough abandon when he could. His grades were perfect for one year, and abysmal the next, according to his interests. He had inherited his mother's long hands, her floss of red-gold hair, her thin cheeks, and eyes that looked out sometimes with a sad curiosity and amusement, as if to say, What an idiotic spectacle. Louis was polite, though more restrained than his brother. He anxiously accomplished errands for his father, but he clearly doted on his mother. Eva often stroked his hair, so like her own, with its curls clipped. When she held him close and kissed him, he pulled away, as boys had to, but did it gently, to show that he didn't want to hurt her feelings.

NINETEEN THIRTY-SIX WAS a year of extremes. That winter, Minnesota had endured a bout of intense cold. Now it sucked in its breath and wilted in a brutal heat. As the heat wave wore on, cleaning became more difficult. Eva Waldvogel, who prided herself on triumphing over anything that circumstance brought her way, could not keep the shop functioning with the efficiency she usually demanded. Now that Delphine was around Eva from the early morning on, she could see how her friend suffered. Eva's face was pale with the daily effort and sometimes she announced that she had to lie down, just for a minute, and rest. When Delphine checked on her, she often found Eva in such a sunken dead shock of slumber that she didn't have the heart to wake her. After an hour or two, Eva woke anyway, in a frenzy of energy, and pushed herself again.

They mopped down the floors of the slaughter room with bleach every single day. Otherwise, the smell of raw blood curdled and was sickening. The meat cases were run on full cold, yet they were lukewarm and the meat within had to be checked constantly for rot. They bought only the smallest amount of milk to sell because it often soured during the drive to the store. They kept little butter or lard. The heat kept getting worse. The boys slept outside on the roof in just their undershorts. Eva dragged a mattress and sheets up there, too, and slept with them while Fidelis stayed downstairs, near his gun, for fear of a break-in.

When Delphine walked to work, just an hour after sunrise, the air was already stiff and metallic. If it broke, it would break violently, Fidelis said, to no one in particular. As he systematically sharpened the blades of his knives and saws, his back turned, he started singing, and Delphine realized, with a strange shock, that his voice was very beautiful. The heat made her flustered, and his voice dismayed her, so pure in a room that was slippery with blood. Sharply, she banged a ham down on the metal counter, and he went silent. It was a relief not to have to listen.

The sky went dark, the leaves turned brown, and nothing happened. Rain hung painfully nearby in an iron-gray sheet that stretched across the sky, but nothing moved. No breeze. No air. Delphine washed her face and donned the limp apron by the door. Late in the day, she stripped the wax off the linoleum in order to apply a new coat. The floor was already dry when she flipped the cardboard sign in the entry window from OPEN to CLOSED. Now, in a special bucket, she mixed the wax and with a long brush painted the floor, back to front, in perfect swipes. She painted herself right up to the counter, put a box in the doorway so that the boys would not ruin the drying surface. She retreated. Hung up her apron, said a quick good-bye, and went home to swelter. Early the next morning, before the store opened, she'd return and apply another coat. Let it dry while she drank her morning coffee with Eva. Then, between customers, she'd polish that linoleum to a mighty finish with a buffing rag and elbow grease. That's what she had planned, anyway, and all that she had planned did occur, but over weeks and under radically different circumstances.

The next morning, while Delphine sat in the kitchen, the heat pushed at the walls. The strong black coffee sent her into a sweat. She drank from a pitcher of water that Eva had set on the table.

"Listen." Eva had been awake most of the night, doing her weekly baking in the thread of cool air. "I don't feel so good."

She said this in such an offhand way that Delphine hardly registered the words, but then she repeated herself as though she did not remember having said it. "I don't feel so good," Eva whispered. She put her elbows on the table and her hands curled around her china cup.

"What do you mean you don't feel so good?"

"It's my stomach. I get pains. I'm all lumped up." Beads of sweat trembled on her upper lip. "They come and go." Eva drew a deep breath and held it, then let it out. *There.* She pressed a dish towel to her face, blotted away the sweat. "Like a cramp, but I'm never quite over the monthly. . . . That comes and goes, too."

"Maybe you're just stopping early?"

"I think so," Eva said. "My mother . . ."

But then she shook her head and smiled, spoke in a high, thin voice. "Don't you hate a whiner?"

She jumped up awkwardly, banging herself against the counter, but then she bustled to the oven, moved swiftly through the kitchen, as though motion would cure whatever it was that had gripped her. Within moments, she seemed to have turned back into the unworried, capable Eva.

"I'm going out front to start polishing the floor," Delphine said. "By now, in this heat, it's surely dry."

"That's good," Eva said, but as Delphine passed her to put her coffee cup in the gray soapstone sink, the butcher's wife took one of Delphine's hands in hers. Lightly, her voice a shade too careless, she said the words that even in the heat chilled her friend.

"Take me to the doctor."

Then she smiled as though this were a great joke, lay down on the floor, closed her eyes, and did not move.

FIDELIS HAD LEFT early on a delivery, and he could not be found. He wasn't home, either, when Delphine returned from the doctor's. By then, she had Eva drugged with morphine in the backseat, and a sheaf of instructions telling her whom to seek. What could possibly be done. Old Dr. Heech was telephoning the clinic to tell a surgeon he knew there to prepare for a patient named Eva Waldvogel.

Delphine found Louis and gave him a note for Fidelis. Louis dropped it, picked it up, his lithe boy's fingers for once clumsy with fright. He ran straight out to the car and climbed into the backseat, which was where Delphine found him, holding Eva as she sighed in the fervent relief of the drug. She was so serene that Louis was reassured and Delphine was able to lead him carefully away, terrified that Eva would suddenly wake, in front of the boy, and recognize her pain. From what Delphine had gathered so far, Eva must have been suffering for many months now. Her illness was remarkably advanced, and Heech in his alarm, as well as his fondness for Eva, scolded her with the violent despair of a doctor who knows he is helpless.

As Delphine led Louis back to the house, she tried to stroke his hair. He jerked away in terror at the unfamiliar tenderness. It was, of course, a sign to him that something was really wrong with Eva.

"Fidelis," Delphine had written in the note, "I have taken Eva to the clinic to the south called the Mayo, where Heech says emergency help will be found. She passed out this morning. It is a cancer. You can talk to Heech."

It was on the drive down to the Mayo Clinic that Delphine first really listened to the butcher's singing; only this time it was in her mind. She replayed it like a comforting record on a phonograph as she kept her foot calmly on the gas pedal of Dr. Heech's DeSoto and the speedometer hovered near eighty miles an hour. The world blurred. Fields fumed like spoked wheels. She caught the flash of houses, cows, horses, barns. Then there was the long stop-and-go of the city. All through the drive, she replayed the song that Fidelis had sung just the morning before, in the concrete of the slaughter room, when she had been too crushed by the heat to marvel at the buoyant mildness of his tenor. *"Die Gedanken sind frei,"* he had sung, and the walls had spun each note higher, as if he were singing beneath the dome of a beautiful church. Who would think that a slaughterhouse would have the acoustics of a cathedral?

The song wheeled in her thoughts as she drove, and using what ragtag German she knew, Delphine made out the words: *"Die Gedanken sind frei, / Wer kann sie erraten, / Sie fliehen vorbei, / Wie nächtliche Schatten"*—"Thoughts are free . . . they fly around like shadows of the night." The dead crops turned, row by row, in the fields, the vent blew the hot air hotter, and the wind boomed into the open windows. Even when it finally started to rain, Delphine did not roll the windows back up. The car was moving so fast that the drops stung like BBs on the side of her face and kept her alert. Occasionally, behind her, Eva made sounds. Perhaps the morphine, as well as dulling her pain, had loosened her self-control, for in the wet crackle of the wind Delphine heard a moan that could have come from Eva. A growling, as though her pain were an animal she had wrestled to earth.

THE FIRST TREATMENT after Eva's surgery consisted of inserting into her uterus several hollow metal bombs, cast of German silver, containing radium. During the weeks that Eva spent in the hospital, the tubes were taken out, refilled, and reinserted several times. By the time she was sent home, she smelled like a blackened pot roast.

"I smell burned," she said, "like bad cooking. Get some lilac at the drugstore." Delphine bought a great purple bottle of flower water to wash her with, but it didn't help. For weeks, Eva passed charcoal and blood, and the smell lingered. The cancer spread. Next, Dr. Heech gave her monthly treatments of radium via long twenty-four-karat-gold needles, tipped with iridium, that he pushed into the new tumor with forceps so as not to burn his fingers. She took those treatments in his office, strapped to a table, dosed with ether for the insertion, then, after she woke, with a hypodermic of morphine. Delphine sat with her, for the needles had to stay in place for six hours.

"I'M A DAMN pincushion now," Eva said once, rousing slightly. Then she dropped back into her restless dream. Delphine tried to read, but shooting pains stabbed her own stomach when the needles went in; she even had a sympathetic morphine sweat. But she kept on going, and as she approached the house each day she said the prayer to God that she'd selected as the most appropriate to the situation: "Spit in your eye." The curse wasn't much, it didn't register the depth of her feeling, but at least she was not a hypocrite. Why should she even pretend to pray? That was Tante's field.

Tante had mustered a host of pious Lutheran ladies, and they came around every few afternoons to try to convert Eva, who was Catholic. Once Eva became too weak to chase them off, Delphine did whatever she could think of to keep them from crowding around the bed like a flock of turkey vultures in a gloating prayer circle. Feeding them was her best strategy, for they filed out quickly enough when they knew that there was grub in the kitchen. After they'd gorged on Eva's pain and her signature Linzer torte, the recipe for which she'd given to Delphine, Tante would lead them away one small step at a time.

Delphine bleached the bloody aprons. She scrubbed the grimy socks. The boys' stained drawers and their one-strap overalls. She took their good suits out of mothballs and aired and pressed them. She sprinkled Fidelis's thick white cotton shirts with starch and every morning she ironed one for him, just as Eva had done. She took on the sheets, the sweat, the shit, and the blood, always blood. The towels and the tablecloths. Doing this laundry was a kind of good-bye gift. For once Eva left, Delphine would be leaving, too. Fidelis had others to help him. Tante, Delphine was sure, would find stepping in to care for the boys and her brother a perfect showcase for her pieties.

FOR ALL THAT he was a truly unbearable souse, no one in town disliked Roy Watzka. There were several reasons for this. First, his gross slide into abandon had been triggered by loss. That he had loved to the point of self-destruction fed a certain reflex feature in many a female heart, and he got handouts easily when strapped. Women made him sandwiches of pork or cold beans, and wrapped them carefully for him to eat when coming off a binge. Another reason was that Roy Watzka, during those short, rare times when he was sober, had a capacity for intense bouts of hard labor. He could work phenomenally. Plus, he told a good tale. He was not a mean drunk or a rampager, and it was well-known that, although she certainly put up with more than a daughter should ever have to, he did love Delphine.

Eva liked him, or felt sorry for him, anyway, and she was one of those who had always given him a meal. Now that she was in trouble, Roy showed up for a different purpose. He came to the shop almost every afternoon, sometimes stinking of schnapps. But, once there, he'd do anything. He'd move the outhouse, shovel guts. Before he left, he'd sit with Eva and tell her crazy stories about the things that had happened to him as a young man: the pet hog he'd trained to read, how to extract the venom from a rattlesnake, the actual wolf man he'd once known who taught him words in the Lycanthropian language, or the Latin names of flowers and where they came from. Listening sometimes, Delphine was both glad of Roy's adept distractions and resentful. Where had he learned these things? In bars, he said. She'd cleaned up after him all her life and never had he talked to her like this.

DELPHINE AND EVA sat together on broken chairs in Eva's garden, each with a bottle of Fidelis's earth-dark home-brewed beer held tight between their feet. They were protected from the mosquitoes by citronella burning in a bucket, and sprigs of basil which Eva snapped off and thrust into their hair. Delphine wore a wash dress and an apron and a pair of low green pumps. Eva wore a nightgown and a light woolen shawl, with her feet bare in Japanese thongs. The slugs were naked. Antlered and feeble, they lived in the thickness of hay and the shredded newspapers that Eva had put down for mulch. They had already eaten many of the new seedlings from the topmost leaves down to the ground, and Eva had vowed to destroy them.

"Their last feast," she said, gesturing at her bean plants as she poured a little beer into a pie plate. "Now they are doomed."

The beer was chilled from the glass refrigerator case in the store, newly installed. It seemed a shame to waste it on slugs. The two women sipped it slowly as the sun slanted through the margins of the stock pens.

"Maybe we should simply have shriveled them with salt," Delphine said. But then she had a thought: We are close to Eva's own death, and can afford to make death easy on the helpless. She said nothing.

Eva's garden, Delphine had decided, reflected the dark underside of her organizational genius. It was everything raw and wild that Eva was not. It had grown rich on junk. Pot scrapings, tea leaves, and cucumber peelings all went into the dirt buried haphazardly, sometimes just piled. Everything rotted down beneath the blistering Minnesota sun. Eva's method was to have no method. Give nature its head. She had apple trees that grew from cores. Rosebushes, bristling near the runner that collected steers' blood, were covered with blooms so fat and hearty that they looked sinister. The boys' dog dug up old bones that some former dog had buried and refused to rebury them. It would be awful in the spring, Delphine thought, when the snow melted away, to see the litter of femurs and clavicles, the knobs and knuckles. As if the scattered dead, rising to meet the Judgment, had had to change and swap their parts to fit.

Delphine had always had a tendency to think about fate, but she did so more often now that Eva's sickness put her constantly in mind of mortality, and also made her marvel at how anyone managed to live at all. Life was a precious feat of daring, she saw, improbable, as strange as a feast of slugs.

Eva bent over, flipped out a small pocket of earth with her trowel, and tamped in her quarter-full beer bottle as a trap. "Die happy," she encouraged. Delphine handed over her own three-quarters-drunk bottle, too. This one Eva planted by a hill of squash that would overpower the rest of the garden by fall, though she would not be there to see it. She settled back against the crisscrossed canvas webbing of her chair and forked open another bottle. It was a good day, a very good day for her.

"I'm going," Delphine said, but she continued to sit with Eva through sunset and on into the rising dark. It was as if they knew that no moment of the weeks to come would be this peaceful and that they would both, in fearful nights, remember these hours. How the air turned blue around them and the moths came out, invisible and sightless, flapping against the shuttered lamp at the other end of the yard.

Delphine shut her eyes, and her mind grew alert. All around her, she felt how quickly things formed and were consumed. It was going on beyond the wall of her sight, out of her control. She felt as though she could drift away like a boat of skin, never to return, leaving only her crumpled dress and worn green shoes.

She heard Eva's voice.

"I wish it were true, what I read—that the mind stays intact. The brain. The eyes to read with."

Delphine had sometimes thought that her friend didn't care if she became an animal or a plant, if all this thinking and figuring and selling of pork and blood meal were wasted effort. She treated her death with scorn or ridicule. But with that statement Eva revealed a certain fear she'd never shown before. Or a wistfulness.

"Your mind stays itself," Delphine said, as lightly as she could. "There you'll be, strumming on your harp, looking down on all the foolish crap people do."

"I could never play the harp," Eva said. "I think they'll give me a kazoo."

"Save me a cloud and I'll play a tune with you," Delphine said.

It wasn't very funny, so they laughed all the harder, laughed until tears started in their eyes, then they gasped and fell utterly silent.

"THE BOYS ARE playing in the orchard. The men are already half lit," Delphine reported. It was the first weekend in September, a holiday. Eva struggled and Delphine helped her to sit up and look out the window of the little room off the kitchen where Fidelis had set up her bed. Eva smiled faintly, then fell back, nodding at the sight.

"Men are such fools," she whispered. "They think they're so smart hiding the Everclear in the gooseberry bush."

There was no saving her. They were well beyond that now. But even though the last few days were nightmarish, Eva refused to die in a morbid way. She sometimes laughed freakishly at pain and made fun of her condition, more so now when the end was close.

They'd closed the shop at noon. Now everyone in town was celebrating. Fidelis had the old chairs and table out in the yard and on the table he had a summer sausage and a beer sausage, a watermelon, bowls of crackers, and beer in a tub of ice underneath the tomato plants, to wash down the high-proof alcohol that Eva knew he was hiding. Over and over the men sneaked their arms into the gooseberry fronds. With a furtive look at the house, they'd tip the bottle to their lips. Even Fidelis, normally so powerful and purposeful, acted like a guilty boy.

The men's voices rose and fell, rumbling with laughter at the tall tales they told; stern with argument at the outrages committed by the government, and sometimes they even fell silent and gazed stuporously into the tangled foliage. Roy was out there, trying to nurse along a beer, not gulp. As always, Fidelis was at the center of the gathering, prodding ever bolder stories out of the men or challenging them to feats of strength.

In the kitchen, Delphine cut cold butter into flour for a pastry. She had decided to make pies for the holiday supper—the men would need them to counteract the booze. The potatoes were boiling now, and she had a crock of beans laced with hot mustard, brown sugar, and blackstrap molasses. There were, of course, sausages. Delphine added a pinch of salt, rolled her dough in waxed paper, and set it in the icebox. Then she started on the fruit, slicing thin moons from the crate of peaches, peeling out the brownest bits of rosy flesh. It's nearly time, she thought, nearly time. She was thinking of Eva's pain. Delphine's sense of time passing had to do only with the duration of a dose of opium wine, flavored with cloves and cinnamon, or of the morphine that Dr. Heech had taught her to administer, though he warned her not to give too much, lest by the end even the morphine lose its effect.

Hearing Eva stir, Delphine set aside her pie makings. She put some water on to boil, to sterilize the hypodermic needle. Last night, she'd prepared a vial and set it in the icebox, the 1:30 solution, which Heech had told her she was better than any nurse at giving to Eva. Delphine was proud of this. The more so because she secretly hated needles, abhorred them, grew sickly hollow when she filled the syringe, and felt the prick in her own flesh when she gave the dose to Eva.

Now she knew, when she checked on Eva, not so much by the time elapsed as by the lucid shock of agony in Eva's stare, her mouth half open, her brows clenched, that she would need the relief very soon, as soon as the water had boiled. Delphine thought to divert her friend by massaging her sore hands.

Eva groaned as Delphine worked the dips between her knuckles, and then her forehead smoothed, her translucent eyelids closed over, she began to breathe more peacefully and said, softly, "How are the damn fools?"

Delphine glanced out the window and observed that they were in an uproar. Sheriff Hock had now joined them, and Fidelis was standing, gesturing, laughing at the big man's belly. Then they were all comparing their bellies. In the lengthening afternoon light, Fidelis's face was slightly fuzzy with the unaccustomed drink, and with the fellowship of other men, too, for lately he had been isolated in Eva's struggle to die.

"They're showing off their big guts to each other," Delphine said.

"At least not the thing below," Eva croaked.

"Oh, for shame!" Delphine laughed. "No, they've kept their peckers in. But something's going on. Here, I'm going to prop you up. They're better than burlesque."

She took down extra pillows from the shelves, shoved the bed up to the window, and propped Eva where she would see the doings in the yard. Now it looked like they were making and taking bets. Bills were waved. The men weren't stumbling drunk, but loud drunk. Roaring with jokes. All of a sudden, with a clatter, the men cleared the glasses and bottles, the crackers and the sticks of sausage, the bits of cheddar, and the plates off the table. And then the sheriff, a former actor who'd played large characters in local productions, lay down upon it on his back. He was longer than the table, and he balanced there, like a boat in dry dock, his booted feet sticking absurdly straight up and his head extended off the other end. His stomach made a mound. Now on the other side of the table, directly beneath Eva's window, stood Fidelis. He'd unbuttoned the top buttons of his white shirt and rolled his sleeves up over his solid forearms.

Suddenly, Fidelis bent over Sheriff Hock in a weight lifter's crouch and threw his arms fiercely out to either side. Delicately, firmly, he grasped in his jaws a loop that the women now saw had been specially created for this purpose in Sheriff Hock's thick belt.

There was a moment in which everything went still. Nothing happened. Then, a huge thing happened. Fidelis gathered his power. It was as if the ground itself flowed up through him, and flexed. His jaws flared bone-white around the belt loop, his arms tightened in the air, his neck and shoulders swelled impossibly, and he lifted Sheriff Hock off the table. With the belt loop in his teeth, he moved the town's Falstaff. Just a fraction of an inch. Then Fidelis paused. His whole being surged with a blind, suffusing ease. He jerked the sheriff higher, balancing now, half out of the crouch.

In that moment of tremendous effort, Delphine saw the butcher's true face—his animal face, his ears flaming with heat, his neck cords popping—and then his deranged eye, straining out of its socket, rolled up to the window to see if Eva was watching. That's when Delphine felt a thud of awful sympathy. He was doing this for Eva. He was trying to distract her, and Delphine suddenly understood that Fidelis loved Eva with a helpless and fierce canine devotion, which made him do things that seemed foolish. Lift a grown man by the belt with his teeth. A stupid thing. Showing clearly that all his strength was nothing. Against her sickness, he was weak as a child.

Once Fidelis had dropped the sheriff, to roars of laughter, Delphine went back into the kitchen to fetch the medicine. She opened the door of the icebox. Looked once, then rummaged with a searching hand. The morphine that Fidelis had labored with vicious self-disregard to pay for and which Delphine had guarded jealously was gone. The vial, the powder, the other syringe. She couldn't believe it. Searched once again, and then again. It wasn't there, and already Eva was restless in the next room.

Delphine rushed out and beckoned Fidelis away from the men. He was wiping down his face and neck, the sweat still pouring off him.

"Eva's medicine is gone."

"Gone?"

He was not as drunk as she'd imagined, or maybe the effort of lifting the Sheriff had sobered him.

"Gone. Nowhere. I've looked. Someone stole it."

*"Heiligeskreuz Donnerwetter . . . ,"* he began, whirling around. That was just the beginning of what he had to say, but Delphine left before he got any further. She went back to Eva and gave her the rest of the opium wine. Spoon by spoon it went down; in a flash it came back up. "What a mess," Eva said. "I'm worse than a puking baby." She tried to laugh, but it came out a surprised, hushed groan. And then she was gasping, taking the shallow panting breaths she used to keep herself from shrieking.

*"Bitte . . ."* Her eyes rolled back and she arched off the bed. She gestured for a rolled-up washcloth to set between her teeth. It was coming. It was coming like a mighty storm in her. No one could stop it from breaking. It would take hours for Delphine to get another prescription from Dr. Heech, wherever he happened to be celebrating the holiday, and then to find the pharmacist. Delphine yelled out the garden door to Fidelis, and then sped out the other way. As she ran, a thought came into her mind. She decided to act on it. Instead of steering straight for Heech she gunned the shop's truck and stopped short at Tante's little closet of a house, two blocks from the Lutheran church, where Tante prayed every Sunday that the deplorable Catholic her brother had married desist from idolatry—saint worship—before her two nephews were confirmed.

*"Was wollen Sie?"*

When Tante opened the door to Delphine, her face had all the knowledge in it and Delphine knew she'd guessed right. Delphine had remembered her clucking over the dose of the drug with her prayer friends in whispered consultation as they pressed up crumbs of lemon pound cake with their fingers.

*"Wo ist die Medicin?"* Delphine said, first in a normal tone of voice.

Tante affected Hochdeutsch around Delphine and made great pretense of having trouble understanding her. When Tante gave only a cold twist of a smile, Delphine screamed: "Where is Eva's medicine?"

Delphine stepped in the door, shoved past Tante, and dashed to the refrigerator. On the way there, with an outraged Tante trailing, she passed a table with a long slim object wrapped in a handkerchief. Delphine grabbed for it on instinct, unrolled it, and nearly dropped the missing hypodermic.

"Where is it?" Delphine's voice was deadly. She turned, jabbing the needle at Tante, and then found herself as in a stage play advancing with an air of threat. The feeling of being in a dramatic production gave her leave to speak the lines she wished had been written for the moment.

"Come on, you rough old bitch, you don't fool me. So you're a habitual fiend on the sly!"

Delphine didn't really think that, but she wanted to make Tante so indignant that she would tell her where the morphine was. But when Tante gaped and couldn't rally her wits to answer, Delphine, disgusted, went to the little icebox, rooted frantically through it. With a savage permission, she tossed out all of Tante's food, even the eggs, and then she turned and confronted Tante. Her brain was swimming with desperation.

"Please, you've got to tell me. Where is it?"

Now Tante had gained control. She even spoke English.

"You will owe me for those eggs."

"All right," Delphine said, "Just tell me." But Tante, with the upper hand, enjoyed her moment.

"They are saying that she is addicted. This cannot be. The wife of my brother? It is a great shame on us."

Delphine now saw that she had been stupid to antagonize the only person who could provide morphine quickly. She'd blown her cover and now she regretted her self-indulgence, grew meek.

"Oh, Tante," she sighed, "you know the truth, don't you? Tante, our Eva will probably not make it, and she is suffering terribly. You see her only when she's comfortable, so of course how can you possibly know how the agony builds? Tante, have mercy on your brother's wife. There is no shame in keeping her comfortable—the doctor has said so."

"I think," Tante said, her black figure precise, "the doctor doesn't really know. He feels too sorry for her, and she is addicted, that is for sure, my good friend Mrs. Orlen Sorven can tell this."

"Tante, Tante, for the love of God . . ." Delphine begged from her heart. She thought of falling on her knees. Tante's frozen little mouth twitched.

"It doesn't matter, anyway. I have thrown it down the sinkhole."

Delphine turned and saw that on the edge of Tante's porcelain sink a clean-washed vial and the bottle that had held the powder were drying in the glow of sun. And when she saw this, she lost all control and didn't quite know what she was doing. She was strong, suddenly phenomenally strong, and when she grabbed Tante by the bodice, jerked her forward, and said, into her face, "Okay. You come and nurse her through this. You'll see." Tante found herself unable to resist, her struggles feeble against Delphine's surging force as she dragged her to the car, stuffed her inside, then roared off and dumped her at the house.

"I don't have time to go in there. You help her. You stay with her. You," she shrieked, roaring the engine. Then she was gone and Tante, with the smug grimness of a woman who has at last been allowed to take charge, entered the back door.

IT DID TAKE hours, and in those hours, Delphine did pray. She prayed as though she meant what she said. She prayed her heart out, cussed and swore, implored the devil, made bargains, came to tears at the thwarted junctures where she was directed to one place and ended up at another. It proved impossible to track down either Heech or the pharmacist. She was returning empty-handed, driving back to the house, weeping angrily, when she saw her father stumbling along the road, his pants sagging, his loose shirt flopping off his hunched, skinny shoulders. As she drew near, she looked around to see if anyone else was watching, for an all-seeing rage had boiled up in her and she suddenly wanted to run him over. She put the truck in low gear and followed him, thinking how simple it would be. He was drunk again and wouldn't even notice. Then her life would be that much easier. But as she drew alongside him, she was surprised to meet his eyes, and see that they were clear. He shuffled anxiously around to the side door, she saw that he had a purpose: out snaking himself booze at a time like this. Only the bottle in his hand was not the usual schnapps but a brown square-shouldered medicine bottle labeled "Sulphate of Morphia," for which he'd broken into the drugstore and sawed through the lock of the cabinet where the pharmacist kept the drugs he had to secure by law.

As Delphine slammed on the brakes, jumped from the truck, and ran to the house, she heard it from outside, the high-pitched keen of advanced agony, a white-silver whine. She rushed in, skidded across a litter of canning smashed down off the shelves, and entered the kitchen. There was Tante, white and sick with shock, slumped useless in the corner of the kitchen, on the floor. Louis and Franz, weeping and holding on to their mother as she rummaged in the drawer for a knife. The whole of her being was concentrated on the necessity. Even young, strong Franz couldn't hold her back.

"Yes, yes," Delphine said, entering the scene. She'd come upon so many scenes of mayhem in her own house that now a cold flood of competence descended on her. With a swift step, she stood before Eva. "My friend," she said, plucking the knife away, "not now. Soon enough. I've got the medicine. Don't leave your boys like this."

Then Eva, still swooning and grunting as the waves of pain hit and twisted in her, allowed herself to be lowered to the floor.

"Get a blanket and a pillow," Delphine said, kindly, to Franz. "And you," she said to Louis, "hold her hand while I make this up and keep saying to her, 'Mama, she's making the medicine now. It will be soon. It will be soon.'"

# Revival Road

FROM THE AIR, our road must look like a length of rope flung down haphazardly, a thing of inscrutable loops and half-finished question marks. But there is a design to Revival Road. The beginning of the road is paved, though with a material inferior to that of the main highway, which snakes south from our college town into the villages and factory cities of New Hampshire. When the town has the money, the road is also coated with light gravel. Over the course of a summer, those bits of stone are pressed into the softened tar, making a smooth surface on which the cars pick up speed. By midwinter, though, the frost has crept beneath the road and flexed, creating heaves that force the cars to slow again. I'm glad when that happens, for children walk down this road to the bus stop below. They walk past our house with their dogs, wearing puffy jackets of saturated brilliance—hot pink, hot yellow, hot blue. They change shape and grow before my eyes, becoming the young drivers of fast cars that barely miss the smaller children, who, in their turn, grow up and drive away from here.

One day in the dead of winter, one of these young drivers appeared at our door, knocking so frantically that my mother called to me in alarm. I came rushing from the basement laundry room to see him standing behind the glass of the back storm door, jacketless and shivering. I saw that he was missing a finger from the hand he raised, and recognized him as the Eyke boy, now grown, years past fooling with his father's chain saw. But not his father's new credit-bought car.

Davan Eyke had sneaked his father's automobile out for an illicit spin and lost control as he came down the hill beside our house. The car had slid toward a steep gully lined with birch and, by lucky chance, had come to rest pinned precisely between two trunks. The trees now held the expensive and unpaid-for white car in a perfect vise. Not one dent. Not one silvery scratch. Not yet. It was Davan's hope that if I hooked a chain to my Subaru and backed up the hill I would be able to pull his car gently free.

My chain snapped. So did many others over the course of the afternoon. At the bottom of the road, a collection of cars, trucks, equipment, and people gathered. As the car was unwedged, as it was rocked, yanked, pushed, and released, as other ideas were tried and discarded, and as the newness of the machine wore off, Davan saw that his plan had failed and he began to despair. With empty eyes, he watched a dump truck winch his father's vehicle half free, then slam it flat on its side and drag it shrieking up a lick of gravel that the town's road agent had laid down for traction.

OVER THE YEARS our town, famous for the softness and drama of its natural light, has drawn artists from the large cities of the eastern seaboard. Most of them have had some success in the marketplace, and since New Hampshire does not tax income—preferring a thousand other less effective ways to raise revenue—they find themselves wealthier here, albeit slightly bored. For company, they are forced to rely on locals such as myself—a former schoolteacher, fired for insubordination, a semi-educated art lover. Down at the end of our road, in a large brick Cape attached to a white clapboard carriage house (now a studio), there lives such an artist.

Kurt Heissman is a striking man, formerly much celebrated for his assemblages of stone, but now mainly ignored. He hasn't produced a major piece in years. His works often incorporate massive pieces of native slate or granite, and he occasionally hires young local men to help with their execution. His assistants live on the grounds—there is a small cottage sheltered by an old white pine—and are required to be available for work at any time of the day or night. There is no telling when the inspiration to fit one stone in a certain position upon another may finally strike.

Heissman favors the heavy plaid woolens sold by mail, and his movements are ponderous and considered. His gray hair is cut in a brushy crew cut, the same 'do that Uncle Sam once gave him. Though he complains about his loss of energy, he is in remarkable health at fifty. His hands are oddly, surprisingly, delicate and small. His feet are almost girlish in their neatly tied boots, a contrast to the rest of him, so boldly cut and rugged. I have heard that the size of a man's hands and feet is an accurate predictor of the size of his sex, but with Kurt Heissman this does not prove to be the case. If this statement is crude, that is of no concern to me—I am citing a fact. I love the way this man is made.

The stones that he gathers for possible use intrigue me. I think I know, sometimes, what it is about them that draws him. He says that the Japanese have a word for the essence apparent in a rock, and I suppose that I love him for his ability to see that essence. Only, I wish sometimes that I were stone. Then he would see me as I am: peach-colored granite with flecks of angry mica. My balance is slightly off. I am leaning toward him, farther, farther. Should I try to right myself? This is not an aesthetic choice.

WHEN DAVAN EYKE was forced to leave home after the accident, he did not go far, just up to Kurt Heissman's little guest cottage beneath the boughs of the beautiful, enfolding pine. The tree has an unusually powerful shape, and Heissman and I have speculated often on its age. We are both quite certain that it was small, a mere sapling, too tender to bother with, when the agents of the English king first marked the tallest and straightest trees in the forests of New England as destined for the shipyards of the Royal Navy, where they would become masts from which to hang great sails. Any large pine growing now was a seedling when the pine canopy, so huge and dense that no light shone onto the centuries of bronze needles below, was axed down. This tree splits, halfway up its trunk, into three parts that form an enormous crown. In that crotch there is a raven's nest, which is unusual, since ravens are shy of northeasterners, having a long collective memory for the guns, nets, and poisons with which they were once almost eradicated.

The ravens watched when Davan Eyke moved in, but they watch everything. They are humorous, highly intelligent birds, and knew immediately that Davan Eyke would be trouble. Therefore they disturbed his sleep by dropping twigs and pinecones on the painted tin roof of his cottage; they shat on the lintel, stole small things he left in the yard—pencils, coins, his watch—and hid them. They also laughed. The laughter of a raven is a sound unendurably human. You may know it, if you have heard it in your own throat, as the noise of that peculiarly German word *Schadenfreude*. Perhaps the raven's laughter, its low rasp, reminds us of the depth of our own human darkness. Of course, there is nothing human about it and its source is unknowable, as are the hearts of all things wild. Davan Eyke was bothered, though, enough so that he complained to Heissman about the birds.

"Get used to them" was all the artist said to Davan Eyke.

Heissman tells me this one day as I bring him the mail, a thing I do often when he feels close to tossing himself into the throes of some ambitious piece. At those times, he cannot or will not break the thread of his concentration by making a trip to the post office. There is too much at stake. This could be the day that his talent will resurrect itself painfully from the grief into which it has been plunged.

"I have in mind a perception of balance, although the whole thing must be brutally off the mark and highly dysphoric." He speaks like this—pompous, amused at his own pronouncements, his eyes brightening beneath their heavy gray brows.

"Awkward," I say, to deflate him. "Maybe even ugly."

In his self-satisfaction there is more than a hint of the repressed Kansas farm boy he was when he first left home for New York City. That boy is buried under many layers now—there is a veneer of faked European ennui, an aggressive macho crackle, an edge of judgmental Lutheranism, and a stratum of terrible sadness over the not so recent loss of his second wife, who was killed in a car accident out West.

"Do you know," Heissman said once, "that a stone can be wedged just so into the undercarriage of a car so that, when you press the gas pedal, it sticks and shoots the car forward at an amazing speed?" That was the gist of the fluke occurrence that had killed his wife. A high school prank in Montana, near Flathead Lake. Stones on the highway. As she pressed on the brakes, Heissman says, her speed increased. Not a beautiful woman, in her pictures, but forceful, intelligent, athletic. She is resembled by their daughter, Freda, a girl who seems to have committed herself to dressing in nothing but black and purple since she entered Sarah Lawrence. When Heissman speaks of Freda's coming home for a weekend, his voice is tender, almost dreamy. At those times, it has a kind of yearning that I would do anything to hear directed toward me. I'm jealous. That is just the way it is. I tell myself that he sees Freda not as his actual self-absorbed and petulant daughter but as the incarnation of his lost wife. But I don't like Freda and she doesn't like me.

"HE'S NOT WORKING out," Heissman says now, of Davan Eyke. "I shouldn't hire locals."

I shrug off his use of the word "local." After all, I am one, although I qualify in Heissman's mind as both local and of the larger world, since I spent several years in London, living in fearful solitude on the edge of Soho and failing my degree.

"You wouldn't have to hire anybody if you used smaller rocks," I answer, my voice falsely dismissive.

Our friendship is based, partly, on the pretense that I do not take his work, or his failure to work, seriously, and do not mind whether we are sexual or not, when in fact we both know that I value his work and am quietly, desperately, with no hope of satisfaction, in love with him. He believes that I am invulnerable. I protect myself with every trick I know.

"This guy's a brainless punk," Heissman continues.

"I thought you knew that when you hired him."

"I suppose I could have told by looking at him, but I didn't really look."

"The only job he's ever had was cutting grass, and half the time he broke the lawn mower. He broke so many on this road that people stopped hiring him. Still," I tell Heissman, "he's not a bad person, not even close to bad. He's just . . ." I try to get at the thing about Eyke. "He doesn't care about anything." My defense is lame, and my lover does not buy it.

"I was desperate. I was working on *Construction Number Twenty.*"

*Number Twenty* is the working title of a piece commissioned many, many years ago by a large Minneapolis cereal company for its corporate grounds. It is still not finished.

Davan Eyke appears, and I stay and watch the two men wrestle steel and stone. Eyke looks slight next to his boss. Together, though, they haul stones from the woods, drag and lever blocks of pale marble delivered from the Rutland quarries. If Davan were artistic, this would be an ideal job, a chance to live close to and learn from a master. As it is, Davan's enthusiasm quickly gives way to the resentment he transfers from his father to his boss.

MY MOTHER SIGHS and makes a face when I tell her that Freda Heissman is visiting her father, and that he has invited us to dinner. Heissman often invites us to dinners that do not happen once Freda becomes involved. She rails against me; I suspect that she has prevailed upon her father more than once to break off our friendship. There is a low energy to Freda, a fantastic kind of drama, a way of doing ordinary things with immense conviction. When I first met her, it was hard to believe that the dots she splashed on paper, the $C^+$ science projects she displayed with such bravura were only adequate. Looking at her through the lens of her dead mother's image, however, Heissman is convinced that she is extraordinary.

I shouldn't be so hard on Freda, I suppose. But is it proper for the young to be so disappointing? And Heissman—why can't he see? I have dearly wished that she'd find a boyfriend for herself, and yet our sense of class distinction in this country is so ingrained that neither of us had considered Davan Eyke, either to dismiss or encourage such a match. There he was, sullenly enduring his surroundings, winging pebbles at the tormenting birds, but since he was not of the intelligentsia (such as we are) who live on Revival Road, he didn't occur to us.

This is the sort of family he is from: the Eykes. His father is a tinkering, sporadically employed mechanic. His mother drives the local gas truck. In their packed-earth yard, a dog was tied for many years, a lovely thing, part German shepherd and part husky, one eye brown and one blue. The dog was never taken off a short chain that bound it to the trunk of a tree. It lived in that tiny radius through all weathers, lived patiently, enduring each dull moment of its life, showing no hint of going mean.

I suppose I am no better than the Eykes. I called the Humane Society once, but when no one came and the dog still wound the chain one way and then the other, around and around the tree, I did nothing more. Rather than confronting the Eykes—which seemed unthinkable to me, since Mr. Eyke not only hauled away our trash but mowed our field and kept the trees in good condition by plucking away the tall grasses at their trunks—I was silent. From time to time, I brought the dog a bone when I passed, and felt a certain degree of contempt for the Eykes, as one does for people who mistreat an animal.

That is one failure I regret having to do with the Eykes. The other is my shortsightedness regarding Davan and Freda.

A TURBULENT FLOW of hormones runs up and down this road. On my walks, I've seen adolescence bolt each neighbor child upward like a sun-drunk plant. Most of the houses on the road are surrounded by dark trees and a tangle of undergrowth. No two are within shouting distance. Yet you *know*, merely by waving to the parents whose haunted eyes bore through the windshields of their cars. You hear, as new trail bikes and motorbikes rip the quiet, as boom boxes blare from their perches on newly muscled shoulders. The family cars, once so predictable in their routes, buck and raise dust as they race up and down the hill. This is a painful time, and you avert your eyes from the houses that contain it. The very foundations of those homes seem less secure. Love falters and blows. Steam rises from the ditches, and sensible neighbors ask no questions.

Davan hit like that, a compact freckled boy who suddenly grew long-jawed and reckless. Mother says that she knew it was the end when he started breaking lawn mowers, slamming them onto the grass and stones so savagely that the blades bent. She quietly had our mower fixed and did not hire him again. His brown hair grew until it reached his shoulders, and a new beard came in across his chin like streaks of dirt. Frighteningly, Davan walked the road from time to time, dressed in camouflage, hugging his father's crossbow and arrows, with which he transfixed woodchucks. That phase passed, and then he lapsed into a stupor of anger that lasted for years and culminated in the damage he did to his father's new car by driving it into the trees. It was the most expensive thing his family had ever bought, and since he left home soon after that, it was clear he was not forgiven.

Freda Heissman, on the other hand, had resolved her adolescence beautifully. After a few stormy junior high school years following her mother's death, she settled into a pattern of achieving small things with great flair, for, as I mentioned, she had no talents and was at most a mediocre student. She gave the impression that she was going places, though, and so she did go places. Still, her acceptance into a prestigious college was a mystery to all who knew her. Her teachers, including me, were stymied. Perhaps it was the interview, one woman told my mother.

LATER, IN THE seething, watery spring darkness, Heissman enters our house via the back-porch screen door, to which he has the key. It is the only door of the house that unlocks with that key, and I keep things that way for the following reason: should I tire, should I have the enlightenment or the self-discipline or the good sense to stop Heissman from coming to me in the night, it will be a simple matter. One locksmith's fee. One tossed key. No explanation owed. Though my mother must sense, must conjecture, must know without ever saying so that Heissman's night visits occur, we do not speak of it and never have. Her room is at the other end of the house. We live privately, in many respects, and although this is how we prefer to live, there are times when I nearly spill over with the need to confide my feelings.

For when he steps into my room it is as though I am waking on some strange and unlikely margin. As though the ocean has been set suddenly before me. Landlocked, you forget. Then, suddenly, you are wading hip high into the surge of waves. There is so much meaning, so much hunger in our mouths and skin. This is happiness, I think every time! I've had lovers, several, and what I like best is the curious unfolding confessional quality of sex. I seek it, demand it of Heissman, and for a matter of hours he is bare to me, all candor and desire. He begs things of me. *Put your mouth here.* In nakedness we are the reverse of our day selves.

RAVENS ARE THE birds I'll miss most when I die. If only the darkness into which we must look were composed of the black light of their limber intelligence. If only we did not have to die at all and instead became ravens. I've watched these birds so hard that I feel their black feathers split out of my skin. To fly from one tree to another, the raven hangs itself, hawklike, on the air. I hang myself that same way in sleep, between one day and the next. When we're young, we think we are the only species worth knowing. But the more I come to know people, the better I like ravens. In this house, open to a wide back field and pond, I am living within their territory. A few years ago, there were eight or more of them in Heissman's white pine. Now just four live there, and six live somewhere in the heavy fringe of woods beyond my field. Two made their nest in the pine. Three hatchlings were reared. The other raven was killed by Davan Eyke.

You may wonder how on earth an undisciplined, highly unpleasant, not particularly coordinated youth could catch and kill a raven. They are infernally cautious birds. For instance, having long experience with poisoned carcasses, they will not take the first taste of dead food but let the opportunistic blue jays eat their fill. Only when they see that the bold, greedy jays have survived do the ravens drive them off and settle in to feed. Davan had to use his father's crossbow to kill a raven. One day when Heissman was gone, he sat on the front stoop of his little cottage and waited for the birds to gather in the usual circle of derision. As they laughed at him among themselves, stepping through the branches, he slowly raised the crossbow. They would have vanished at the sight of a gun. But they were unfamiliar with other instruments. They did not know the purpose or the range of the bow. One strayed down too far, and Davan's arrow pierced it completely. Heissman drove into the yard and saw Davan standing over the bird. Amazingly, it wasn't dead. With some fascination, Davan was watching it struggle on the shaft of the arrow, the point of which was driven into the earth. Heissman walked over, snapped the arrow off, and drew it tenderly, terribly, from the bird's body. For a moment the raven sprawled, limp, on the ground, and then it gathered itself, walked away, and entered the woods to die. Overhead and out of range, the other birds wheeled. For once, they were silent.

"Let me see the bow," Heissman said conversationally. Davan handed it to him, prepared to point out its marvelous and lethal features. "And the arrows." Davan handed those over, too. "I'll be right back," Heissman said.

Davan waited. Heissman walked across the yard to his woodpile, turned, and fitted an arrow into the groove. Then he raised the bow. Davan stepped aside, looked around for the target, looked uneasily back at Heissman, then touched his own breast as the sculptor lifted the shoulder piece. *Shot.* Davan leapt to the other side of the white pine and vaulted off into the brush. The arrow stuck in the tree, just behind his shoulder. Then Heissman laid the bow on the block he used to split his firewood. He axed the weapon neatly in half. He laid the arrows down next, like a bunch of scallions, and chopped them into short lengths. He walked into his house and phoned me. "If you see that boy running past your house," he said, "here's why."

"You shot at him?"

"Not to hit him."

"But still, my God."

Heissman, embarrassed, did not speak of this again.

• • •

DAVAN HAD SAVED enough money, from Heissman's pay (or so we thought), to buy himself an old Toyota, dusty red with a splash of dark rust on the door where a dent had raised metal through the paint. The car now spewed grit and smoke on the road as he drove it back and forth to town. He had returned to his room in his parents' house and he resumed his chore of feeding the dog every day, though he never untied it from the tree.

The dog's maple grew great patches of liver-colored moss and dropped dead limbs. Shit-poisoned, soaked with urine at the base, and nearly girdled by the continual sawing and wearing of the chain, the tree had, for years, yellowed and then blazed orange, unhealthily, the first of all the trees on the road. Then, one day that spring, it fell over, and the dog walked off calmly, like the raven, into the woods, dragging a three-foot length of chain. Only the dog didn't die. Perhaps it had been completely mad all along, or perhaps it was that moment after the tree went down when, unwrapping itself nervously, the dog took one step beyond the radius of packed dirt within which it had lived since it was a fat puppy. Perhaps that step, the paw meeting grass, rang along the spine of the dog, fed such new light into its brain that it could not contain the barrage of information. At any rate, the outcome of that moment wasn't to be seen for several weeks, by which time Davan had successfully raised dust near Freda on illicit visits, and had secretly taken her out with him to local parties, where at first she enjoyed her status as a college-goer and the small sensation caused by her New York clothing styles. Then, at some point, something awakened in her, some sense of pity or conscience. Before that, I'd seen nothing remarkable about Heissman's daughter, other than her clothes. Her unkindness, her laziness, her feeling of enormous self-worth—all were typical of women her age. Then, suddenly, she had this urge to care for and rescue Davan Eyke, an abrupt unblocking of compassion which made her come clean with her father, a humanity that thoroughly terrified Heissman.

I STEP OUT of the car with the mail and see Heissman standing, block-like, in front of Davan, who slouches before the older man with obdurate weariness. Locked in their man-space, they do not acknowledge me. Heissman is, of course, telling Davan Eyke that he doesn't want him to see Freda. He probably calls Davan some name, or makes some threat, for Davan steps back and stares at him alertly, hands up, as though ready to block a punch, which never comes. Heissman kicks him over, instead, with a rageful ease that astonishes Davan Eyke. From the ground, he shakes his head in puzzlement at Heissman's feet. When Heissman draws his leg back to kick again, I move forward. The kick stops midway. Davan rises. The two stare at each other with spinning hatred—I can almost see the black web between them.

"Pay me," Davan says, backing away.

"Say you won't see her first."

Davan starts to laugh, raucous, crackling, a raven's laugh. I can still hear it through the car window when he revs and peels out.

I don't understand why Heissman detests the boy so much; it is as though he has tapped some awful gusher in the artist and now, in a welter of frustrated energy, Heissman starts working. He finishes *Number Twenty*. He produces, hardly sleeps. Hardly sees me.

IT IS DIFFICULT for a woman to admit that she gets along with her own mother. Somehow, it seems a form of betrayal. So few do. To join in the company of women, to be adults, we go through a period of proudly boasting of having survived our mothers' indifference, anger, overpowering love, the burden of their pain, their tendency to drink or teetotal, their warmth or coldness, praise or criticism, sexual confusion or embarrassing clarity. It isn't enough that our mothers sweated, labored, bore their daughters nobly or under total anesthesia or both. No. They must be responsible for our psychic weaknesses for the rest of their lives. It is all right to forgive our fathers. We all know that. But our mothers are held to a standard so exacting that it has no principles. They simply must be to blame.

I reject that, as my mother sits before me here. She has just had an operation to restore her vision. Her eyes are closed beneath small plastic cups and gauze bandages. When I change the gauze and put in the drops twice a day, it strikes me that there is something in the nakedness of her face and shut eyes that is like that of a newborn animal. Her skin has always been extremely clean and fine. Often, she has smelled to me of soap, but now she has added a light perfume, which enables her in her blindness to retrace her steps through the house with confidence, by smell.

That is how I know that she knows he has been here. Last night, he came down off the manic high in which he had hung between one uninspired month and the next. It is morning. Even to me, the house smells different after Heissman has made love to me in the night, more alive, alert with a fresh exquisite maleness. Still, for me to openly become Heissman's lover would upset the balance of our lives. My deadlocked secret love and unsecret contempt are the only hold I have over him, my only power. So things remain as they are. My mother and I maintain a calm life together. I do not dread, as others might, her increasing dependence. It is only that I have the strange, unadult wish that if she must pass into death, that rough mountain, she take me with her. Not leave me scratching at the shut seam of stone.

SPRING ON THIS road commences with a rush of dark rain, slick mud, and then dry warmth, which is bad for our wells and ponds but wonderful to see in the woods. New sounds, the rapturous trilling of peepers, that electric sexual whine, the caterwauling of the barred owls, startling us from sleep, raising bubbles of tension in my blood. I cannot imagine myself changing the lock. Without a word, without a sound, I circle Heissman, dragging my chain.

All of March, there is no sign of the dog that slipped free of the dead maple, and Mother and I can only assume that it has been taken in somewhere as a stray or, perhaps, shot from a farmer's back porch for running deer. That is how it probably survives—if it does—squeezing through a hole in the game-park fence, living on hand-raised pheasants and winter-killed carcasses.

The dog reappears in the full blush of April. During that week, leaves shoot from buds and the air films over with a bitter and intangible green that sweetens and darkens in so short a time. One balmy night, my neighbors up the road, the ones who clear-cut fifty acres of standing timber in four shocking days, have their cocker spaniel eaten. They leave the dog out all night on its wire run, and the next morning, from the back door, Ann Flaud in her nightgown pulls the dog's lead toward her. It rattles across the ground. At the end of it hangs an empty collar, half gnawed through.

There is little else to find. Just a patch of blood and the two long, mitteny brown ears. Coydogs are blamed—those mythical creatures invoked for every loss—then Satanists. I know it is the dog. I have seen her at the edge of our field, loping on long springy wolf legs. She does not look starved. She is alive—fat, glossy, huge.

She takes a veal calf for supper one night, pulled from its standup torture pen at the one working farm on the road that survived the eighties. She steals suet out of people's bird feeders, eats garbage, meadow voles, and frogs. A few cats disappear. She is now seen regularly, never caught. People build stout fences around their chicken pens. It is not until she meets the school bus, though, mouth open, the sad eye of liquid brown and the hungry eye of crystal blue trained on the doors as they swish open, that the state police become involved.

A DRAGNET OF shotgun-armed volunteers and local police fans through the woods. Parked on this road, an officer with a vague memory of a car theft in Concord runs a check on Davan Eyke's red car as it flashes past. Eyke is on his way up to Heissman's, where Freda, less boldly attired than usual and biting black lacquer from her nails, waits to counsel him. They go for a walk in the woods, leaving the car in the driveway, in full view of Heissman's studio. They return, and then, despite Heissman's express, uncompromising, direct orders, Freda does exactly what young people sometimes do—the opposite. The human heart is every bit as tangled as our road. She gets into the car with Eyke.

On the police check, the car turns up stolen, and as it speeds back down from Heissman's an hour later the police officer puts on his siren and spins out in pursuit. There ensues a dangerous game of tag that the newspapers will call a high-speed chase. On our narrow roads, filled with hairpin turns, sudden drops, and abrupt hills, speed is a harrowing prospect. Davan Eyke tears down the highway, hangs a sharp left on Tapper Road, and jumps the car onto a narrow gravel path used mainly for walking horses. He winds up and down the hill like a slingshot, joins the wider road, then continues toward Windsor, over the country's longest covered bridge, into Vermont, where, at the first stoplight, he screeches between two cars in a sudden left-hand turn against the red. On blacktop now, the car is clocked at over a hundred miles per hour. There isn't much the police can do but follow as fast as they dare.

Another left, and it seems that Davan is intent on fleeing back toward Claremont, on the New Hampshire side. The police car radios ahead as he swings around a curve on two wheels and makes for the bridge that crosses the wide, calm Connecticut, which serves as a boundary between New Hampshire and Vermont. It is a cold, wet, late-spring afternoon, and, according to the sign that blurs before Davan's eyes, the bridge is liable to freeze before the road. It has. The car hits ice at perhaps a hundred and twenty and soars straight over the low guardrail. A woman in the oncoming lane says later that the red car was traveling at such a velocity that it seemed to gain purchase in the air and hang above the river. She also swears that she saw, before the car flew over, the white flower of a face pressing toward the window. No one sees a thing after that, although the fisherman pulling his boat onto shore below the bridge is suddenly aware of a great shadow behind him, as though a cloud has fallen out of the sky or a bird has touched his back lightly with its wing. He turns too slowly, even in his panic, to see anything but the river in its timeless run. The impact of the small car on the water is so tremendous that there is no ripple to mark its passage from a state of movement to complete arrest. It is as though the car and its passengers are simply atomized, reduced instantaneously to their elements.

WITHIN FIFTEEN MINUTES of the radio call, all the pickups and cars on our road gather their passengers and firearms and sweep away from the dog posse to the scene of greater drama at the bridge. Although the wreckage isn't found for days and requires four wet-suited divers to locate and gather, the police make a visit to Heissman's, on the strength of the woman witness's story. Believing that Freda has gone over the bridge as well, they take me along to break the news to my friend.

I wait on the edge of the field for Heissman, my hand on the stump of an old pine's first limb. I hear the ravens, deep in the brush, the grating haw-haw of their announcement, and it occurs to me that he might just show up with Freda. But he doesn't, only shambles toward me alone at my call. I feel for the first time in our mutual life that I am invested with startling height, even power, perhaps more intelligence than I am used to admitting I possess. I feel a sickening omnipotence.

He starts at my naked expression, asks, "What?"

"Davan's car," I report, "went over the bridge."

I don't know what I expect, then, from Heissman. Anything but his offhand, strangely shuttered nonreaction. He apparently has no idea that Freda could be in the car. Unable to go on, I fall silent. For all his sullen gravity, Davan had experienced and expressed only a shy love for Heissman's daughter. It was an emotion he was capable of feeling, as was the fear that made him press the gas pedal. *The gas pedal*, I think. *The gas pedal and the wedged-in stone.*

I stare at Heissman. My heart creaks shut. I turn away from him and walk into the woods. At first, I think I'm going off to suffer like the raven, but as I walk on and on I know that I will be fine and I will be loyal, pathologically faithful. The realization grounds me. I feel more alive. The grass cracks beneath each step I take and the sweet dry dust of it stirs around my ankles. In a long, low swale of a field that runs into a dense pressure of trees, I stop and breathe carefully.

Whenever you leave cleared land, when you step from some place carved out, plowed, or traced by a human and pass into the woods, you must leave something of yourself behind. It is that sudden loss, I think, even more than the difficulty of walking through undergrowth, that keeps people firmly fixed to paths. In the woods, there is no right way to go, of course, no trail to follow but the law of growth. You must leave behind the notion that things are right. Just look around you. Here is the way things are. Twisted, fallen, split at the root. What grows best does so at the expense of what's beneath. A white birch feeds on the pulp of an old hemlock and supports the grapevine that will slowly throttle it. In the dead wood of another tree grow fungi black as devil's hooves. Overhead the canopy, tall pines that whistle and shudder and choke off light from their own lower branches.

The dog is not seen and never returns to Revival Road, never kills another spaniel or chicken, never appears again near the house where her nature devolved, never howls in the park, and never harms a child. Yet at night, in bed, my door unlocked, as I wait I imagine that she pauses at the edge of my field, suspicious of the open space, then lopes off with her length of chain striking sparks from the exposed ledge and boulders. I have the greatest wish to stare into her eyes, but if I should meet her face-to-face, breathless and heavy muzzled, shining with blood, would the brown eye see me or the blue eye? Which would set me free?

He has weakened, Heissman, he needs me these days. My mother says, out of nowhere, *He's not who you think he is.* I touch her shoulders, reassuringly. She shrugs me off because she senses with disappointment that I actually do know him. Shame, pleasure, ugliness, loss: they are the heat in the night that tempers the links. And then there is forgiveness when a person is unforgivable, and a man weeping like a child, and the dark house soaking up the hollow cries.

# The Painted Drum

I WAS CALLED upon to handle the estate of John Jewett Tatro just after his Presbyterian funeral. I went to make my appraisal of the contents of the house on an overcast morning in spring. The sky was a threatful gray, yet the willows blazed in tender bud, and drifts of wild-apple blossoms floated in the cavern pines. I kept the windows slightly open as I drove the back roads to the Tatro house, and breathed in the watery air. The Tatros had always been too cheap to keep up their road, and the final quarter mile was partly washed out, the gnarled bedrock exposed. Overgrown swamps and ponds lapped close to either side. As I bounced along, the frogs quieted momentarily, so that I seemed to be continuously pushing against a wall of sound. Once I stopped, the frogs began trilling again. Making my way up the flagstone walkway to where the Tatros' grandniece waited, I stopped a moment, caught in the vehemence. Spring in New Hampshire can be disorienting—virginal and loudly sexual all at once.

The Tatro house was not grand anymore. The original nineteenth-century homestead had been renovated and enlarged so many times that its style was obscured. Here a cornice, there a ledge. The building was now a great clapboard mishmash, with aluminum-clad storm windows bolted over the old rippled glass and a screen porch tacked darkly across its front. The siding was painted the brown-red color of old blood. The overall appearance of the house was ramshackle and sad, but the woman who greeted me was cheerful enough, and the interior was comfortable, though dim. We began my first, casual viewing. The rooms were filled with an odor I have grown used to in my work. It is an indefinable scent, really, made up of mothballs and citrus oil, of dust and cracked leather. The smell of old things. I noted that an inordinate number of closets seemed to have been added to the house during some period of expansion, even on the ground floor.

The niece, whose name was Sarah, was a pleasant, square-jawed woman, with light-brown hair and blue eyes. She was in her midthirties, perhaps ten years younger than I am, and the sort of woman who volunteers to supervise recess or construct grade school art projects. I knew the type. I had attempted to *be* the type. So had my mother. But our fascination with the stuff of life, or, more precisely with the afterlife of stuff, had always set us apart. Mother had started the business, and we had run it jointly now for nearly two decades. We are fair, discreet, honest, and knowledgeable. We are well-known in our part of New Hampshire, and well respected, I think. There is a certain advantage to our gender. More often than not, it is the women of the family who get stuck dealing with the physical estate, the possessions, and we are also women. We understand what it is like to face a mountain of petty decisions when in grief. As I sat down with Sarah, to formalize things over a cup of coffee, I felt the comfortable and immediate sense of solidarity that I often feel with other women at times like this—there is sympathy, of course, but also some relief. Finally, to get on with things! There is even some excitement at the idea of the task ahead. Cleaning out a house can numb you to the bone, but there are always discoveries along the way. Some are valuable—an original Shaker table under a coat of milk paint, a fabulous porcelain or saccharine but valuable old Hummels amid chipped salt-and-pepper shakers. Once, an old bucket forgotten in a pantry corner turned out to be a hand-painted Leder, worth thousands. First editions turn up, too: a signed Mark Twain, a Wharton, maybe a pristine Salinger—you never know what will surface from even the most unpromising pile. And then some discoveries are revelatory—diaries, packets of love letters, a case of antique pornography featuring trained ponies, certificates listing surprising causes of death or unknown births. The contents of a house can trigger all sorts of revisions to a family history.

Behind my eagerness to take on the Tatro estate, there was also a thread of connection that reached back several generations. My mother and I specialize in Native American antiquities. In *The History of Stiles and Stokes*, a book published on subscription by our local historical society, there is an entire chapter devoted to the Tatro family, and within that chapter a paragraph about the great-grandfather of the most recently deceased Tatro. Jewett Parker Tatro had been an Indian agent on the Ojibwe reservation in North Dakota, where my own grandmother was born and where she lived until the age of six, at which time she was taken east and enrolled at the Carlisle Indian School, in Pennsylvania. There she had learned to sew intricately, to add and subtract, to do laundry, to scrub a floor clean, to read, write, and recite Bible passages, Shakespeare sonnets, Keats odes, and the Declaration of Independence. The Carlisle school was also where she fell in love.

My grandmother had stayed in the East with the young teacher she married shortly after graduating, though she returned for visits and bore my mother on her own allotment land. But we have never really been Easterners. The connection between Tatro and the reservation was of interest to us because it wasn't uncommon for Indian agents back then to amass extensive collections of artifacts, and of course we had always wondered whether the Tatro house held such a trove. Although we'd had little indication while the last two Tatro brothers were alive (they died within two months of each other), and at first I saw nothing that would lead me to think that those closets held anything more exotic than magazines and clothing and phonograph records, there had been rumors. And to our knowledge a large-scale Tatro collection had never been donated to any local, state, or college museum. There were those many closets and the thick walls of the downstairs rooms. Also, there was the Tatros' character—there was certainly that—to consider.

They were sharp, they were shrewd, they were flinty, calm cheaters, and secret hoarders. They haunted tag sales. Bought food in bulk. Hitchhiked when gas was expensive, though they were not poor. Saved the rubber bands off broccoli and bananas, when they bought such lux-uries. They boiled the sap from their trees and stole the corn from their neighbors' fields. They picked fiddleheads, tore fruit off stunted trees, shot and roasted raccoons. Each fall they bought and salted down a pig, devouring it from snout to hock over the course of a year. To my mind, the Tatros were the sort of cheap old Yankee bachelors who would keep a valuable collection of artifacts just because it had never occurred to them to part with anything. They would simply have hung on to their stuff—moldering, mothballed, packed away with cedar blocks—until Judgment Day.

Curiously, perhaps, the house I live in with my mother is not clut-tered. It's not that our vocation has made us snobbish. Rather, it is the constant reminder of our own mortality that reins us in. To strive to own anything of extraordinary value generally strikes us as absurd, given our biodegradability. Still, there are a few objects we've found irresistible. Their nature probably reveals that we are more captive to our background than we admit: a lustrous double-throated Maria Martinez wedding vase; an Ojibwe cradle board, with a wrap of intri-cately beaded velvet; three very fine Navajo rugs; a bandolier bag that was probably carried by the last Ojibwe war leader, Buganogiizhig himself; a few seed pots; several shaved-quill boxes; and some heavy old turquoise that must be continually polished. Yes, we'd like to leave our path to heaven clear, to travel a spare, true road. Yet we're human enough.

Sarah Tatro did not intend to let the house and its contents trap her. Over the cup of coffee—one of those thick diner-style white mugs, surely swiped from a local café by one of the uncles—she told me that she was anxious to clear the place out and put it on the market. I found her forthrightness appealing and, at the same time, the idea that the Tatro house would pass from Tatro ownership after nearly two centu-ries infected me with a faint melancholy. It is unusual for one place to remain so long in the same family—I was, surprisingly, tempted to try to dissuade her from breaking with the past and carrying on with, of all things, her own life. I controlled myself. I took out my notebook and began to make a rough list of the contents of the house. Later, I would be joined by two assistants, but I prefer to work alone at first, as does my mother. I like to get a feel for the things in a house, a sense of the outlook of the person who, though safely in the next world, still lingers in the arrangement and treatment of his goods. I like to make peace with the dead.

I asked Sarah if her great-uncle had had any particular interest or collection that might require special handling or appraisal. "Oh, I don't know, there's just so much of everything." She waved her hands. "So many old sets of dishes. And he owned a number of guns. Some of those are old. And then the closets on the ground floor go way back behind the walls. They're stuffed. So, really, it's anybody's guess."

I WAS ON my own, and soon I was immersed in the pleasures of my job. The sorrows of strangers are part of my business, and, were I to examine my motives for choosing this line of work, I might find that from their losses I extract some bit of comfort—as though my constant proximity to death protects me and those I love. The furniture in the first two rooms on the ground floor was in adequate repair and quite good, though there were no "finds." Predictably, the Tatros hadn't been bibliophiles, nor was there much in the way of decorative touches—lamps, vases, figurines. Yet the walls were hung with six nice paintings by local artists, and there was one oil sketch, a sort of pre-painting drawing, by Maxfield Parrish. That discovery alone would have made my day at any other time. In this case, it also indicated the Tatro tendency to hold on to things, as Parrish was well-known and the work could easily have been sold. I tried not to get my hopes up, but when I opened the door to the first closet my fingers were clumsy with excitement. Quickly, I went through what I could see. The usual boxes of magazines. Piles of curtains and old and faded linen. A great many boots of all styles, reaching back for decades. Mothballed coats made of everything from wool to skunk fur. The closet went on and on, but soon enough I decided to leave it to my assistants. The next closet was stuffed with records. Mostly 78 rpm, swing or big band. I was beginning to worry that the rumors were just that, when, upon embarking on a wide bank of shelves built into a wall, I found the first indication of, it seems curious to say, life.

Some estates come to life and others don't. Some holdings have little personality, others much. There is a moment I think of still, one I nearly missed. Years ago, I opened a small wooden chest containing what appeared to be handkerchiefs wrapped in tissue paper, just handkerchiefs, bearing the owner's initials: L.M.B. I was about to empty the box and scatter its contents among the linens, when I noticed a label. Pinned to each cotton, lawn, lace-trimmed, or embroidered handkerchief, I realized, was a carefully cut label with a date inked in ladylike script. A name, or names, were written. And occasions: "Teddy's Christening." "Venetta and John Howard's Wedding." "Teddy's Funeral." "Brother Adamantine's Wake." "First Opera, 'La Traviata.' " "Broken Arm." And far down at the bottom, perhaps the handkerchief that started the collection, a child's small square of fabric clumsily labeled "My Mother's Funeral." I remember sitting with the handkerchiefs of L.M.B. as the rest of the work of pricing and sorting swirled around me. Here was a box containing a woman's lifetime of tears. I passed through several stages of emotion. The first was elation at the novelty of such an idea, and I felt the urge to show the box to my assistants. Next, I was swept through with irritation. I almost never think of non-Indians as "white"; after all, my own skin is pale. But I experienced a sudden jolt of prejudice that surprised me. *Just like a white lady—so stingy with her tears she kept them*, I thought. Then I recovered myself and sat a little longer, holding the box, which was very light, old varnished pine, and turning over one handkerchief after another. "Theodor's Precious Birth." "Aunt Lilac's Deathbed Supper." What was a deathbed supper? "Cousin Franklin's Wedding to Mildred Vost." More funerals. The other workers left to tackle the next room, and it was then, sitting with L.M.B.'s sorrows and joys, that my own eyes filled with tears. There weren't many. I am not the crying sort anymore. But when I did feel that swell of sadness I reached immediately for one of the handkerchiefs, dabbed my eyes, and added my own tears to the box. Then I closed the box. I knew that what had happened was exactly right. "Tears Shed for L.M.B.," I might have written on a scrap of paper. I'd have to buy the box myself now, but that seemed the proper close to the collection. I'd heard that the owner had become a ferocious bore in her old age, critical, churchy, and prone to making complaint calls to the parents of young boys who cut across her front lawn or spoiled her tulips. But that's what I mean by coming to life.

THE ESTATE OF John Jewett Tatro came into a similar focus when I made the acquaintance of a doll with a face of fawnskin and eyes of jet. I knew that the doll was something special the moment I put my hands on it. It was wrapped in faded red trade cloth and placed inside a shoe box. The shoe box had been mistakenly stored on a shelf of shoes, and when I opened it I caught an unmistakable whiff of smoked hide—a smell that could only have accumulated, molecule by molecule, over the course of years. As I removed the doll from its wrapping, the fugitive taste of smoke vanished and there was the doll herself, exquisite. The perfectly cured hide that was her skin had somehow retained its softness, though from the faintly smudged darknesses on her arms and skirt I saw that she had been loved as a toy. Her red quill lips were stitched into a calm, amused smile, and her bead eyes were set at a lively angle. Her coarse black hair had been plucked from a horse's mane and divided into braids. Her dress was also made of tanned hide, decorated with bits of shell and the old antique beads called "greasy yellow" and "ruby-red whiteheart" and "German blue." Her waist was belted with a woven sash. Attached to it, she wore a scabbard that secured a tiny skinning knife. Her moccasins were sewn with flowers, and a ring of trade silver made a bracelet on her arm. From her pierced fawnskin ears dangled miniature earbobs, hawk's bells so unusually small that they could have hung from the throats of warblers. She carried a thimble-size basket woven so cleverly that I laughed in pleasure. I brought the doll out at once, and showed her to Sarah.

"Oh, there she is!" She took the doll from its wrapping and handled it with familiar tenderness, smoothing the coarse hair down and caressing the slender horsehair brows embroidered above the glittering eyes. "My uncles used to let me play with her if I was very good."

"*She's* very good, you know. Valuable, I mean. We should have a museum curator look at her."

"Yeah?" Sarah was surprised, but not particularly pleased. I think she felt the same way I did about the doll. It was personal—the delight of owning the doll had nothing to do with its worth.

"Were there other things—American Indian, I mean—of that era?" I asked. "Did your uncles keep them all together somewhere? In a cabinet? Trunks?"

"Oh, God, yes, I'd forgotten all about it. One of the Tatros way back lived with the Indians," she said. "There was a lot of old beadwork and stuff. Come on upstairs, I'll show you."

On the way up the stairs, I tried to breathe slowly. There was an attic room, of course—a long, unfinished tar-papered hall lined with simple board shelves and stuffed with old suitcases. Most of the artifacts were kept in these suitcases, Sarah told me. There were also some larger things, wrapped in old bedspreads and horse blankets. We unveiled these at once—a cradle board not as good as mine, large birchbark winnowing baskets, a beadworked footstool, a drum. The suitcases held some precious examples of late-nineteenth- and early-twentieth-century bead-and-cloth appliqué work. There were moccasins, leggings, beaded ceremonial breech clouts, a vest, and two bandolier bags (in extraordinary condition, worth a great deal). There were also a number of lesser items—small purses of the sort once sold to tourists, a band for a headdress from which all the feathers had been removed, tobacco pouches, woven carrying straps, and reed mats. We laid things out, unwrapped, on the tops of suitcases, draped off the edges of drawers and shelves, but stopped eventually. The collection went on and on.

"Congratulations," I said, and there must have been some degree of feeling in my voice. Sarah Tatro looked startled.

"Congratulations for what?"

"You can probably retire," I said. "Or at least take a long vacation. No more early-morning wakeup calls."

"You think all this is valuable?"

"Very."

Sarah dropped to a trunk and put her head in her hands. "You mean they were sitting on this all along?"

I said nothing, and after a time she shook her head and laughed shortly, without humor. "They were so cheap they ate oatmeal for dinner. And they spread Crisco on their bread instead of butter. The taxes on this place had gone sky-high, of course, and they wanted to keep it. So they lived on nothing. But in the end"—her voice lifted—"I have to say I think they enjoyed their stinginess." And then she laughed with more ease. "They probably even enjoyed what they had here. You can see they went through these things. Checked them for mildew or bugs, I guess, rewrapped them. Set mousetraps. Look." She showed me the date on a newspaper that had been used to cushion a little sweet-grass basket. "Last year's."

"That's fortunate," I said. "The acid in the newspaper could have ruined that basket." I moved closer to look at the little coiled and sewn basket, and that is when I stepped near the drum.

I'm not a sentimental person. How could I be? I have seen the most intimate objects proceed to other hands, indifferent to the love once bestowed on them. Some people believe that things absorb their owners' essence. I stay clear of that. And yet when I stepped near the drum I swear it sounded. One deep, low, resonant note. I stopped dead, staring at the drum. I heard it, I know I heard it, and yet Sarah Tatro did not.

"I'm getting out of here," she said. "Too dusty. I'll be back later on this afternoon. I've got some errands in town."

And so I was left with Tatro's loot. I continued to stare at the drum, or what I could see, since it was mostly swaddled in a faded quilt. I'm not subject to imaginative fits, and I don't just hear things. There had to be an explanation. Something shifting to strike the skin. A change in air pressure. The quilt wasn't anything special, a simple collection of squares, machine-stitched and yarn-tied. I went over to the drum and pulled the fabric entirely away. The light in the attic came from two bare bulbs with pull chains, which cast harsh shadows. The head of the drum glared out, huge, three feet across at least. The moose that was skinned to make it must have been a giant. Yet there was something delicate about the drum, for it was intricately decorated, with a beaded belt and skirt, hung with tassels of pulled red yarn and sewn tightly all around with small tin cones, or tinklers. Four broad tabs were spaced equally around the top. Into their indigo tongues, four crosses were set, woven with brass beads. On the face of the drum, at the very center, a small bird was painted, in lighter blue. That was all. But the bird detail, the red-flowered skirts, the tinklers, combined with the size of the drum, gave it an unusual sense of both power and sweetness.

I drew a folding chair close, sat, and jotted down the details. My hand dragged across the page. This was the sort of find that should have thrilled me, but I was uneasy, anxious. I looked around. I set my hand on the drum and then I felt, pulling through me like a nerve, a clear conviction. It was visceral. Not a thought but an instinct. I covered the drum again and went out to make sure that Sarah had gone. When I saw that the garage was empty and I was alone, I propped open the back door and went straight to the attic. I bundled the quilt more tightly around the drum, and then I carried it out of the house, slid it into the trunk of my car, and hid it by pulling down the theft-deterring blind I always use when parking at big auctions.

I worked the rest of the afternoon without thinking about what I'd done. When my thoughts flickered toward the drum, I veered away from any further examination. What I'd just done, or was about to do, was probably a felony and could ruin our business. The ease with which I had done it bewildered me. For a person who had not stolen so much as a candy bar all her life to walk coolly out of a client's house with such a valuable object might signal insanity. The beginning of a nervous breakdown. But I didn't feel that way. I felt quite lucid. And I wondered whether others who committed irrational and criminal acts felt this calm acceptance of a previously unknown part of themselves.

DUSK WAS FORMING, blue and cold, by the time I arrived home. I left the drum in the car, wrapped in the quilt, underneath its stretched plastic curtain. I didn't want it in the house yet. I had to think—not about whether what I'd done was right. By then I had decided that I wouldn't have done it unless it was, on some level, *right*. And yet the explanation of this rightness swirled beyond my reach. My real concerns were whether I could keep the drum hidden and whether I'd get caught. I was pretty sure that Sarah Tatro hadn't noticed the drum; in fact, she'd seemed indifferent to all her uncle's objects, save the doll she had played with as a child. I was also fairly certain that she was the only person who would have any knowledge of her uncle's collection. And even she had forgotten that it existed. I'd had to take the drum that afternoon, if I was to take it at all. I knew that, once I had cataloged the objects and had them appraised, the drum would have priced itself out of the reach of all but the wealthiest collectors or a museum. Yet I didn't want the drum. What would I do with such a thing? Where would I keep it? No, I hadn't taken the drum for myself. I reassured myself of this as I sat down to dinner with my mother.

"You have an odd look on your face," she said. "So, how was it?"

I took the salad bowl from her hands and began forking leaves onto my plate.

"Well, it was all there," I told her.

"Oh!" She put her fork down.

I'd taken a mouthful of spinach, but suddenly I felt too tired to even chew. I slumped down in my chair. Then I threw my head back, stretched my arms. "I've been crouched over the notebook all afternoon. It's a real haul. Old—I mean old *old*—Tatro walked away with everything. Dolls, beadwork, cradle boards. You name it."

"So he got away with the good stuff. He had an eye."

We sat there with our food between us. My mother's hair, sleek and pulled back in a knot, was very white. She bore me late in age, when she had given up on getting pregnant. I was a gift. It's nice to be told, all your life, that you are a gift to someone. We were very happy right then, although I don't know exactly why. Perhaps it was just because our secret expectations had been met.

"There was a drum," I said to her.

She pushed her plate away and leaned toward me, her elbows on the table. Her eyes were narrow and slightly upturned at the corners. The irises, dark brown, had the milky blue ring of age, but her gaze was still sharp. She was waiting for me to describe the drum.

"One of the big drums," I said. Her fingers flickered on the table.

"Was it dressed?"

"What?"

"Decorated."

"Yes."

"How?"

I told her about the crosses.

"Not crosses, not Christian. Those are stars. Was it painted?"

"There was a bird. A little blue bird."

She closed her eyes, pressed two fingers to the space between her eyebrows. I watched her carefully, because she does this when she is trying to form a thought. Finally, she spoke. She talked a long time, and I can only sum up what she said: The drum is the universe. The people who take their place at each side represent the spirits who sit at the four directions. A painted drum, especially, is considered a living thing and must be fed as the spirits are fed—with tobacco and a glass of water set nearby, sometimes a plate of food. A drum is never to be placed on the ground, or left alone, and it is always to be covered with a blanket or quilt. Drums are known to cure and known to kill. They become one with their keeper. They are made for serious reasons by people who dream the details of their construction. No two are alike, but every drum is related to every other drum. They speak to one another and they give their songs to humans. I should be careful around the drum, she said. She was bothered by its presence in the collection.

"It's more alive than a set of human bones," she finished.

After she went to bed, I cleared off a low table in the corner of my bedroom and then I brought the drum inside and balanced it carefully on the table. I shoved two chairs up against each side. Whenever I touched the drum, even to set it down, it made a sound. A high, hollow note. Or a low, uncertain tone, like a question. A slight tap on its edge set up reverberations. It was exquisitely sensitive for so powerful an instrument, and I wondered what it sounded like when struck with force, by many and in unison. I turned off the light and got into bed. I leave my windows open just a crack at night, even in winter. The darkness seethed with spring music, and from time to time, deep in the woods, a barred owl screamed like a woman in pain. I thought I might have dreams—as pragmatic as I consider myself, it had been a long, strange day. The realization that I'd stolen the drum outright surfaced and sank in my consciousness. No matter how justified by history I felt, I promised myself that I would not evade my guilt or rationalize my conduct.

Which was not the same as even considering that I might do the proper thing and return the drum to Sarah Tatro.

ALL I HAVE is other people's lives. What I do belongs to them and to my mother—her business, her legacy, her blood. Even the box of tears in my closet belongs to another woman, L.M.B. But now I've stolen the drum. And it seems to me, as I lie in the dark of my room, that my instinctive theft signifies something so essential that it might be called survival. I have stepped out of rules and laws and am breathing thin, new air. My theft is but the first of many I'll accomplish—though not of objects. There are other things I need and will have to have, other things I'll take. Thoughts, plans, private rages, and even joys, now secret to myself.

I am usually a sound sleeper, but tonight, all night, it seems, I am listening. Thinking. So many ideas float in half formed, and then veer off.

Our old house ticks. Not regularly, like a clock, but softly all through itself as the slats in the walls change temperature or the plaster tightens or the earth shifts underneath the granite-slab foundation. From time to time, the little sounds that the house makes reverberate inside the drum. My breath does, too. I hear a rising, then a falling. In and out. A greatness, a lightness. I grow heavier, and then so inert that my body seems without life. Between breaths, I lose feeling. And then my chest fills, a resurrection.

There is another thing that this house does in the deep of night. I have heard it before and now I wait for it to happen. The house releases the day's footsteps. All day we press down minutely on the wide old floorboards, moving about on regular errands, from room to room. It takes hours for the boards to readjust, to squeak back up the nails, for the old fibers of the pinewood to recover their give. As they do so, they reproduce the sound of the footsteps. In the night our maze of pathways is audibly retraced. I am used to it, as is Mother, but sometimes a wakeful guest is frightened. I can understand this. For now, as I rise and stand in half darkness in the doorway of my bedroom, I hear the distinct creak of footsteps proceeding toward me, then past me, over to my bed. I feel the breath of my own passage, as though my dead self and my living self briefly met in that doorway to sleep.

# Hasta Namaste, Baby

EACH DAY WHEN I finish work—I sell industrial lighting fixtures—I cleanse myself with a little prayer, although I have no specific religion. I close my eyes as I remove my jacket from its hook or shut down my computer, and I let myself visit the secret thought of nothingness. This practice was taught to me by Sonia, my wife. My attempt is usually effective in erasing the petty cares and slipping numbers that might worry me, so that I can enjoy my nightly walk home. Though my company is located in a great mall vast with product, there is right behind the store dumpsters a bicycle path that leads to within a block of my suburban condominium. While on the walk, if I have done a good job on feeling nothingness, I can actually sense the presence and then the loss of each new moment as it passes by. I can watch the leaves shake, note the trill or wire-whine of crickets and cicadas. The chuck of nuthatches. The outrage of crows. Or this time of year, November, the stark beauty of leafless trees. By the time I am home I am usually at peace enough to help my wife in her quest to conceive a child.

Sonia is a yoga instructor at a suburban health spa called The Forest. Oddly, The Forest removed a real forest of old oaks and hornbeam in order to situate itself properly near the highway. It is now surrounded by curved plantings of spindly birch. On her own, Sonia practices a very disciplined form of yoga called Iyengar. But for the spa-goers she conducts a more lenient relaxation class. Although she conducts evening classes, Sonia usually takes an early supper break to have sex.

We eat quickly, whatever dinner one or the other of us has thrown together, and then we go into the bedroom. She pulls back the green comforter and puts a pillow underneath her hips to tip her pelvis into the optimal position. I enter her and move until I come. She lies with her hips up for forty-five minutes to an hour. Sometimes I touch her while she is lying there. Sometimes we talk our day over and we plan things—where we'll move to when we have more money, the people we might invite over if we ever entertain. We laugh about family, wonder whether we'll get a dog.

This attempt to conceive began eight months ago. Ever since the quest began I've felt an enormous sense of guilt over this knowledge I have, which I find impossible to share. I am sterile, and I know it because I had my sperm tested when I entered a scientific trial in college—it was the sort of thing that sounds like a good idea to drinking buddies who want to finance a fishing trip. Anyway, I did not qualify for the experiment. And although Sonia and I have been together since our junior year in high school, I have never told her, or anyone.

Sonia has got a very lovely, strong, supple body, shaped of course by her work, and it isn't difficult for me to have sex with her nearly every day. But also, I am in love with her in an ordinary yet attached way that occasionally gets a little crazy—we take a trip, the weather changes, we look at each other funny, and the whole crush starts over, just like in high school. However, since we started on this effort I feel that I'm lying every time we touch. I've been looking forward to the times in her cycle when her body is infertile or unreceptive, because I am reminded that I can't bear to tell her the truth.

Heading home tonight, breathing the cool, sweet air, I resolve that the moment I walk in I will simply tell her, blurt it out, say what has to be said. Then we can start over, dealing with the consequences.

So when I walk up the stairs around six P.M. I am ready with the words on my lips, but Sonia opens the door and begins to dance up and down with the plastic wand from a test kit in her hand.

"Positive," she cries. "Positive! I'm positive!"

When I grasp this, I am literally knocked to the floor. I kneel there, before her in the entryway, holding her legs. She is pleased by my reaction, or the way she interprets it, and she strokes my hair, excitedly murmuring. Later, she wants to make love. Her skin has a golden undertone and her feathery blond-tipped haircut makes her head into a little sun. A special beauty is shining out of her brown eyes, so warm, inviting. I tell her that I am afraid to disturb the embryo and I walk out back across the sodded lawn and gravel of the landscaping, to where the city stops. Beyond us is wild marsh some developer is getting permits to drain. I am a farmer's second son, the one who moves to the Cities, gets a job in construction, in sales, or becomes a teacher. I am sick to death. I have to grab the gentle reeds to hold myself up.

ALL THAT NIGHT, I am awake. My thoughts ascend and fall with every breath. Each time Sonia moves beside me in the sheet, I feel us winding tighter in the twisted cloth.

THE WEEKLY YOGA class that she says she attends to refresh her skill level meets the next morning in uptown Minneapolis in an old storefront next to a record shop. I wait across the street drinking a $4.25 cappuccino until I see her enter the place. I pay, walk across the street, and stand before the plate glass window. I am there because of the way she speaks of her instructor—a bit too offhand. Ambivalent information: he's harsh, he's gentle. He's amazing, or he's so-so. Now I see her approach a man, the instructor I suppose, for he turns to her from a little desk where papers and T-shirts are stacked. There is a small lockbox and a desk calendar. The man gets up and walks around the desk. He is wearing an orange sleeveless T-shirt with *Namaste* written on the front in ornate script. His running shorts are short. Very short and silky. He looks ridiculous. As you might expect, he's limber, but he's got some muscle on him, too.

She's telling him, I think, telling him!

This is the revealing moment. But although she is talking and gesturing in an excited way, he is so far keeping his distance. He nods and listens. His smile is a white gleam, just a flash. There are a few other students in stretchy clothes doing what must be warm-up exercises in the corner. Sonia stops talking and is about to move away, when he grabs her arm. It is not a casual grab. It is an all-revealing grab. What tells me he's the one is this: just as he reaches for her he also does a quick scan of the students to make sure nobody is watching. Holding on to her arm he then stands just a bit too near, in her space, and as he speaks he stares into her eyes.

That's enough for me. Hasta namaste, baby. There is no question now. I walk away, get into my car, start driving. Pretty soon I am on I–94 heading west and I think, what the hell. I'll go visit my parents. So I drive to North Dakota. The four hours pass like nothing. Because it is nothing—I am caught in a swoon of that moment I search out every day. That nothing moment. I am almost at my hometown, Mooreton, driving through a bigger town, when to one side I see a store called Lock 'n Load. Actually, what was an empty storefront last time I drove through now has a huge piece of white tag board in the window and the sign is written with Magic Marker, black letters carefully outlined. I stop the car and get out. The apostrophe before the 'n is a little cowboy pistol, drawn by a child.

A buzzer sounds when I walk in and a short man with a thick brown crew cut asks what he can do for me. He's soft and pale in his black T-shirt, though at one time he might have lifted weights. He has that stocky high school football player look but his neck and shoulder muscles are sliding down, collecting on his gut. I tell him that I need a gun. He gets a wise and intimate look on his face, and he says he will be glad to help me.

I rub my chin and walk around the little square room. There are shotguns and hunting rifles propped in glass cases, handguns and handgun equipment under the glass counter. Ammunition on shelves behind the counter. A display of hunting knives in a circular flower of blades.

"Target practice?"

"No. I have to kill a yoga dude."

"Something to defend the home, then."

I nod.

"I'd suggest a safe box you could lock and keep bedside. You could secure this inside."

He reaches under the counter and takes out a black Rossi, a .38 special, sets it on the glass.

"Are you a gun owner at present?"

"No."

"Welcome. Where are you from?"

"Minneapolis, but I grew up around here."

I pick up the Rossi and he shows me how to pull back the action, how to load it. He tells me about the practice range nearby and recommends that I take a gun safety course. He also says that to carry this weapon concealed, in Minneapolis, I will have to apply for a permit. I ask about the guns in the case.

"Those you can just take home," he says.

"Over state lines?"

"Provided you check out."

I put down the Rossi and hand him my driver's license. While he does something at the computer I heft the shotguns, one after another. There is something sad, comforting, stubborn, slow, or too personal about each one of them. I put them back until I come to a sleek pump-action 12-gauge shotgun. I remember the old battered 12-gauge my father once owned.

"All clear," says the gun-shop owner. "Not even an unpaid parking ticket."

I pick up the new version of the shotgun.

"That's a good choice. There's no deterrent like the sound of that pump action."

I buy it. He sells me the Rossi, too, and ammunition. A box of deer slugs for the shotgun. I take everything out, put it in the trunk of my car, then drive to Mooreton. My parents live on the edge of the town where the farm butts up to the last street to the west. My brother took the farm over when they retired. Behind their house there is a small strip of yard and then a half mile of sunflowers. The dead black heads hang heavy on the hollow stalks, staring down at the earth.

● · ●

MY MOTHER STANDS on the front steps. She is wearing a floppy pink checkered dress and a tight cardigan. Her ankles run straight down into her shoes.

"Oh for Pete's sake! Gene, get out here. It's Dave!"

I get out of the car. The smell of November dust off the fields is familiar, cold and clear. I put my arms around my mother's shoulders and we walk into the house together. My father is emerging from the bathroom. He's stooped, and faded, but when he sees me his whole face re-forms around a giant smile that people say that I have inherited. He brushes his teeth with whitening toothpaste because he's proud of every one of his teeth. His face has shrunken a little, and I can see for the first time the outline of his skull.

"You've dropped weight, Dad."

"You nearly caught me with my pants around my ankles. I been sick with the flu. The runs. But I'm okay now. I just had a solid one, Betts."

"Oh, good, Pop. You hungry, Dave?"

My sister gives my parents grief about how they talk about their bowels, but I don't care. I sit down and visit, as we always do, getting caught up with things, sorting things over, ironing things out. Cookies, coffee, coffee cake. My brother Glen comes over, but leaves to pick up a daughter from debate club in town. Soup comes out. German spaetzle noodles. Butter beans. More coffee. It is getting toward late afternoon.

"Well, I gotta go now."

"Back to the Cities? You won't get in until way after dark."

I tell them that I took the day off, but have to be in again at 8 A.M. tomorrow morning. Big staff meeting.

They are used to this. My mother throws her hands up and shakes her head. My father nods. As I'm leaning forward to hug him, he suddenly puts his hands out and catches my shoulders, holds me at arm's length, and squints into my face. There is a shrewd look on his face.

"There's something else, I'll bet."

"I think so, too, Gene," says Mom. When I say nothing, her face shuts too. "But let him alone. He'll tell us when he is good and ready, like he always does." She pats my arm. "Won't you, Dave."

I PULL OUT of Mooreton and am driving back east when all of a sudden I take a turnoff. The road narrows and then winds around to a gravel pit—the place where Sonia and I used to go and park when we were in high school. I'd take the car out on weekends. Pick her up in town, but we wouldn't party, or we'd leave early. We'd make out until the windows steamed, then we'd open the windows a crack until we got too cold. She held out for two months, which seemed like forever. After we started having sex, we could not stop and did not even pretend to go to parties or movies. We just headed right out of town every chance we could and came to this gravel pit.

Nobody digs gravel there any longer, and it is just a hole filled with cold, black water. Trees surround it. A woods has grown up. Just past the pit there are tall fields of corn stubble. As soon as I park the car, I understand it all—why I stopped and bought the guns and visited my folks and came out here. Only which gun I will use, I don't know. I get out and open the trunk, then lift each out very carefully and in the fading light I load them. My hands shake, so I rub them together, to take the chill off. I carry the Rossi into the strip of woods, but then I go back and get the shotgun. I can't decide. I am standing there in the woods weighing one in my hand, cradling the other, when across the cornfield I hear gunshots, quick, boom, boom, boom. I haven't forgotten hunting season, or remembered it, either. But now I am momentarily spooked because I'm wearing brown. Then I laugh at the irony of being bothered at all considering that I'm walking toward the gravel pits with both of the guns, one of which, the Rossi, I periodically lift to my head.

With the Rossi in place, I am staring at the brown grass, the faintly crushed tracks, a rusted Pabst can. I am listening to myself breathe, as if from far away, when there is a sudden crash. I put the gun down and drop to my knees. Deer, four or five or maybe six of them, flying from the hunters, spring through the air. They float up and around and over me. Deep-eyed, precise, serene. There is no sound. There is the scent of grass, the tang of musk. Then behind me their hooves strike down.

After a while, I stand up and turn around. We are specks flicked across the face of the earth. I take the guns back to the car, unload them, and put them in the trunk again. Then I drive to Glen's house. He is still in town picking up his daughter, so I put the guns on a high shelf in his garage with all the ammo and drive off.

LATE THAT NIGHT, Sonia and I crawl into bed. We spent the hour after I returned in the same room, on the same couch, music playing, us not talking. Now that we are lying side by side in the dark, I let it out.

I tell her that I know about her yoga instructor.

"You can never go back there," I say.

She denies it at first, but my certainty breaks her down. I have a sense of power and a sense of peace. I am not angry, I am not foolish, I am not suicidal. None of these things am I. I sleep soundly and do not dream. When I wake, I hear her in the kitchen. I decide that I will not speak to her all morning, not even to answer her when she says good-bye. But she does not say good-bye. She just walks out the door. At work, I take a moment to put away all of the pictures of Sonia that I keep on my desk. Sonia laughing. Sonia's profile. Sonia and the cat she rescued. Me and Sonia. Behind us, the waters of a lake.

Several times, I have to say it: none of these things am I. Yet that afternoon, instead of my nothingness moment, I think about the yoga dude's T-shirt. My blood drums in my ears. I drive back to the uptown storefront and park in the spot behind marked RESERVED. I stand next to the car, and when he drives up I wait until he stops gesturing from behind the wheel and gets out of the car. He is wearing gray sweat pants and a hoodie, and he leaves his car running.

"Please move. This is my parking spot," he says.

"I'm Sonia's husband," I say.

I move toward him with my arms out and smash him into the side of the car, but I'm not a fighter and don't know exactly what to do next except use my high school wrestler's moves and try to grapple him to the ground. I can't do it. Once I get him halfway down he springs up, rubbery and embarrassed, and he tries to talk like a reasonable person. Eventually, I throw a punch and graze his teeth with my knuckles. His eyes get very big. His eyes are brown, like hers, and his face has severe, handsome features, which is good for the baby, I think. I begin to batter him with my knuckles, my elbows, even my head. I am a ridiculous machine. He is bleeding from the mouth, soon, from the ears, from the nose, gagging, calling for help, and suddenly all sorts of people are in the alley with us, yoga students, clawing at me with their skinny arms and kicking at me with their sticky yoga shoes.

That night Sonia is mystified.

"Why did you do that?" she keeps saying. "Why?"

"Go to him if you want," I say, "but I am telling you, what begins in deceit will end in deceit."

She wants to stay with me and says she loves me, but as the weeks go by I find I cannot be near her. She touches me one night and I push her hand off—just with that, I think, it is over inside of me. We lie in silence with our arms at our sides like mummies and it seems like we are buried in the air, in the brown dark, and I am so heavy with grief I know I'll break.

"This won't work," I finally say. "You'll have to go back to him."

"But I don't love him," she says, sounding reasonable like him.

"Then why did you poison us?"

She can't answer. But then, I can't tell her the truth about me either. I have decided that I will not, she can never know, about the college experiment.

"I'm sure it's not his! The baby is yours. I'm positive," she cries suddenly.

I am quiet with knowing that this is what I was waiting to hear.

She begins to tell me more and I say, "No, shut the fuck up. I do not want to know."

But now the sorrow is grinding itself out of my bones. I yank her toward me and she opens her legs around me.

"All right," I tell her, my voice brutal and cracking, "I am claiming this child. This child is mine. You are mine."

My face smashes against hers and I realize what I am doing comes from the crazy place where I was before the deer passed over me and I was darkly blessed.

"The baby is yours, and I am yours," she says.

Then in a sadder, softer, furious voice, she tells me that she would rather die than ever do what she did again. That she is not that person. I listen to all that she says. But I know she is that person. People are their actions. They do not change. There is a weak spot, some rotted place, a hidden board in a beautiful floor. And I know even as I kiss her and sink into her that she will do it again. There will come a time. I will again know this derangement of all I thought I understood. My world will turn over. I will puke out my guts behind some plumbing store or developed marsh or yoga studio. But I also know that a fair amount of time will go by before the abjection and shame and gratitude fades from her heart and again she is bored. Afterward, I touch where the baby is and imagine the shifting swirl. The deer float over us. I am sure. The years before it happens will be wonderful years

# Future Home of the Living God

WALKING DOWN THE long sage-green corridor at Fairview Riverside Hospital in Minneapolis, on my way to a Class 2 Diagnostic Ultrasound, I promise you this: I'll be a good mother even though I've fucked up everything so far. I've been keeping track of you in my secondhand edition of the *Mayo Clinic Guide to a Healthy Pregnancy*, and so I am prepared. You will be ugly, but recognizably human. You've gone from tadpole to vaguely humanoid and lost your embryonic tail. Absorbed the webs between your toes and fingers and developed eyelids, ears, a tiny skeleton. Grown a 250,000-neuron-per-minute brain. I have paged past Spina Bifida, Down Syndrome, Trisomy 13. I know you're fine. You can already squint, frown, smile, hiccup, and perhaps are doing so as I slide my hand along the banisters that line the wall.

"GOD, THEY SHOULD call the uterus, just . . . *God*," I tell the slender nurse, who has the body of a ballet dancer and is probably Vietnamese. "Then they could say her *God* was filled with a baby, or her *God* had fibroids, or they had to do a *Goderectomy* on her—don't you think?"

"Excuse me, what did you say?"

"Don't you *think*?"

"Oh, you bet."

The perfect Minnesota Nice accent is surprising, coming from such an exotic and elegant person. She leans over the form with me. There are questions upon questions, all dealing with inherited conditions of the heart and liver, cancers, even addictive behaviors.

"I'm adopted," I say.

"Do ya know your biological parents?"

"My biological mother wrote me a letter about a year ago."

The exquisite nurse waits.

"We correspond," I say faintly, which is a minor fib, though I do still have a letter from her. One page, never answered.

"Wull, I guess you could ask her, anyways," she approves. "This information could really help your baby." She cradles my elbow. "Your name is beautiful. Cedar Hawk Songmaker. Where'd you get that, your tribe?"

Most people notice my name. "Songmaker is an old British name."

"What about the Cedar? What about the Hawk?"

"My Indian name is Mary Potts," I tell her. She looks down at the sheet of paper again, musingly; her face has a permanent mysterious smile.

As Mary, I was removed from my Potts mother because of our mutual addiction to a substance she loved more than me. As Cedar, I am the adopted child of Minneapolis liberals, whom I disappoint. As for the letter from my Potts mother, I opened the envelope, read what it contained, said, *Fuck that*, crumpled it up, and threw it, then retrieved it. I know exactly where the letter is—at home.

"I will, I *will* ask her," I say forcefully as the nurse steers me into a darkened room.

"You got nice hair, anyways." She smooths it down my back.

After she helps me up onto the high tablelike bed from a portable stool, I feel exposed and shaky. Other women bring friends, maybe even a husband. But my friends are dead, or in jail. My parents are alienated from me and they don't even know, yet, that I am pregnant. I'm about to lose the job I've faked my credentials to get. Also, five months ago, I forgot to get the name of your father—a man I knew for one night.

I tuck my shirt up underneath my breasts. The doctor, tall and businesslike, unsmiling, shakes my hand. His palm is hard and dry. He sits on a stool next to the swivel chair just at my right thigh, where a technician, a sinewy blond woman, touches a keyboard and adjusts a computer screen.

"Let's get going," says the doctor.

The technician puts a dollop of clear gel on my skin and holds the probe like a fat pencil. I've read all about this thing and know the probe contains traducers that produce and receive sound. The machine is already producing sound waves at frequencies of 1 to 20 million cycles per second. Impossible of course to hear. Propped on my elbows, I watch as the computer interprets the signals bouncing off you.

"This will be cold," says the technician, and she pats my leg. I crane toward the screen. The technician moves the wand carefully, stopping twice. "There you are," she says as she discovers you. She rotates the traducer to one side of my stomach and keeps moving it. At first there is only the gray uterine blur, and then suddenly the screen goes charcoal and out of the murk your hand wavers. It is detailed, three dimensional, and I glimpse tiny wrinkles in your palm and wrinkle bracelets around your wrist before your hand disappears into the screen's fuzz. There is something about your hand, and I am upset for a moment. I want to get off the table. I want to say, *Enough, no more*, but at the same time I want to see you again.

"Can you tell the gender?" I ask. "Can you see?"

But nobody in the room is listening to me, nobody hears. I see the arch of your spine, a tiny white snake, and again your hand flips open, pressing at the darkness. The technician touches out knee bones, an elbow. Then she goes in through the thicket of your ribs. The heart, she says. I see the hollows of the chambers, gray mist, then the valves of your heart slapping up and down like a little man playing a drum. Your whole heart is on the screen and then the technician does something with the machine so that your blood is made of light moving in and out of your heart. The outflow is golden fire and the inflow is blue fire. I see the fire of life flickering all through your body.

I whisper, or sigh, and I want to cry out. The room yawns open. I have the sensation time has shifted, that we are in a directionless flow, as if this one room in the hospital has suddenly opened out onto the universe.

"Can you do that again," I murmur, but the doctor is very intent now, pointing and nodding. There, he says, and the technician clicks something.

"Can you tell if I have a boy or a girl?" I ask, louder. But neither one answers. The technician is intent, focused utterly on what she sees. They are inside of your head now, peering up from beneath your jaw and then over into the structure of your brain, which I see as an icy swirl of motion held in a perfect circle of white ash. It looks to me as though your thoughts are arranging and rearranging already, and as I imagine this I also know that there is something wrong, something off. The atmosphere has changed; the doctor is silent. The picture is fixed. They are looking at it, and looking. They will not stop looking.

"Boy or girl?" My throat is suddenly scratchy and dry. I see nothing on the screen, now, just white marks. Then tiny black crosses. Still, they couldn't seem to take their eyes away until I cry out.

*"What the fuck do I have?"*

They both turn and I see that they are trying to think of what to say to me.

"We can't tell," says the doctor in a very careful voice. His eyes are wide and staring.

A crack opens deep inside, a dark place, and fear seeps into my heart. I am suddenly extremely calm.

"It's Down syndrome."

"No, no, I don't think so. Do you know your genetic . . ."

"She's adopted," says the nurse.

"What's wrong?" I ask them.

The doctor takes the hand of the frozen-looking technician and gently draws the wand away from my body. He is a kind man, I see now, an ordinary-looking man about my Songmaker father's age, with a square, worn face and gray eyes lighted in the screen's glow.

"I'm not sure," he says gently. "Do you know your biological parents? Can we get some information?"

I JUMP UP while they are consulting, throw my shirt on and reel out of the hospital, wanting in the very worst way to get drunk, pop back a couple Ativans, chill. And when I wake up not be pregnant. My hands shake, rattling the car keys. Before I can even start the car, I have to open the door and barf. *That did not go well,* I say, pulling away from the hospital. *That did not go very well at all.* I suppose it is panic, tears stinging up behind my eyes, the feeling that I am a child again caught in giant trouble. I suppose it is these things that make me grip the wheel and decide I should answer that letter or, first, make that phone call.

My adoptive parents are Sera and Alan Songmaker. We are church mice in a wealthy neighborhood. My parents inherited money, but they made extravagant gestures for causes now defunct, choices they still laugh about over dinner, toasting the large, lost amounts with cheap bag wine. They are, the two of them, descended of those legendary robber barons who scalped the Minnesota earth of ancient forests, who scooped the copper out of Red Cliff mines, ravaged the iron range, and built rails and railroads that still trace the Dakotas like great Frankensteinian stitches. All of that accumulation petered out in Alan and Sera Song-maker. There is nothing left but the carriage house I grew up in, which was divided off from the great, old family mansion. That "perfectly proportioned Georgian beauty"—I've heard about it ad nauseam— was torn down and replaced by a tan brick sixteen-unit apartment building.

Alan's still bitter. When he sold the mansion to the city, it was to become a museum. But the administration changed and that new city government resold the building during the blighted 1970s, when everyone was moving to the suburbs. They stayed on to live near a wide green lake which has of late been invaded by exotic weeds and purple loosestrife and, in 1988, adopted me. During one of Sera's many self-invented ceremonies, which she put together from her eclectic readings on indigenous culture and Rudolf Steiner, we placed sacred tobacco all around our house and then smudged white candles with sage and stuck them in the ground and lighted them too. We ate bread, Jarlsberg cheese, I drank ginger beer, and my parents drank wine. In the shadow of the apartment complex, we curled on blankets in the grass and sang peace march songs until we fell asleep. That was before I fell from grace, before I made them unhappy, before I grew up. It is one of the best memories of my life.

I stop the car in the driveway, and my eyes blur again. Panic tears.

It is a mistake to come here, and I know it. As I walk in the back door, I mean to tell my parents about you right away. But they are not home. I use the key they do not know I possess and I go into the kitchen, pour a glass of milk because I am supposed to drink milk. I drink it looking out the back window. In the backyard, Sera has planted the bursts of zinnias, daisies, lythrum, and digitalis. It is an unusually warm September, and a sweet breeze stirs the heavy weight of leaves in the hundred-year-old trees that line our alley.

I drag myself upstairs to my old room, open the suitcase into which I casually threw the letter. There it is, still crumpled in a shoe pocket.

*I would like to meet her if possible . . . I have never forgot . . . the old lady is still living . . . me and my daughter Mary own the Superpumper now . . . hoping to hear*

I smooth it out and bring it down to the kitchen. There is a phone number at the bottom, which I dial.

"Boozhoo?"

God, I think, they speak French.

"Bon jour," I say.

"H' lo?"

"Hello."

"Who's this?"

"I'm, ah, Mary Potts, originally. I got this letter from Mary Potts Senior about a year ago; she contacted me about the fact that she is my biological mother. Is this? I mean, you don't sound like Mary Potts Senior, but are you maybe—"

"Whatthefuck?"

"No, I mean, I've got a little sister—"

"MAAAAAHM! Some INSANE BITCH is on the phone who says you're her mom and wrote her last year."

Mumbling. A voice. *Gimme that.* A crackling thump as someone drops the receiver. A quavery voice saying *Who's that, Sweetie?* Woman's voice. *Nobody!* First voice again. *Getthefuckawayfromme.* A raging scream that fades and ends abruptly in a crash—slamming door?

"Mary Potts Senior?" I ask the hollow breath on the other end.

"Speaking." A whisper. A croak as she clears her throat. "Yeah, it's me. The one that wrote you."

And I suddenly want to cry, my chest hurts, I can't breathe, I'm breaking. The only thing that could possibly overcome what I feel in right that moment is a simultaneous mad crazy anger that bubbles up in me and freezes my voice solid.

"By any chance, will you be in tomorrow?"

"In?"

"Home."

"I'm not doin' nothing."

"I am coming up there. I am going to visit you. I have to speak to you."

"Awright."

*Who's that, Sweetie?* Old lady voice. *Nobody!* she says again.

I ignore the awful prickling in my throat, the reaction to the second time that she has said *nobody.*

"Who's calling you sweetie?" I say.

"That's my name," says Mary Potts Senior. "They call me Sweetie."

"Oh."

Her voice is so humble, so hushed, so astonished, so afraid. I feel a sweep of something, maybe more rage, that makes me shaky, but it just comes out in cold, weirdly complicated, grammar.

"Well that's very fitting, I am sure, Sweetie. However, I think that I will just call you Mary Potts Senior, if that's all right."

"I'm not senior though. I'm almost senior, not quite. Grandma's still alive."

"Okay, Mary Potts Almost Senior. Now, might I ask for directions to your house?"

"Sure you might," says Mary Potts, or Sweetie, but then she doesn't say anything.

"Well?" I say, icy voice.

Sweetie gets a little sly now.

"You said you *might* ask. You asking?"

Now I feel a stab of what is probably instant hatred, because she is the one who wrote me and she is the one who asked me to contact her and she is the one who originally bore me from her body and then dumped me. But I can handle her petty manipulations.

"Just tell me," I say in a cool, neutral voice. "I'll be coming up from Minneapolis."

LATER, I AM about to leave the house, but then, my childhood training takes over. Always tell us where you're going to go! I leave a note for my parents. *Dear Sera and Alan, a.k.a. Mom and Dad. I am pregnant. I am driving up to see my biological mother because I need information. Your erstwhile daughter, Cedar.*

I get into my vintage Chevy Cavalier, the car that will not die. It is a dark, classic red with matching red squares set into the centers of the hubcaps. I love my car although it has no airbags and the shoulder belt is a weird rig that would probably strangle me if I stopped too fast. I pull onto the highway, which bears only slightly less traffic than usual, and travel north to my Potts reservation home. Always, on four-lane highways, I have this peculiar sensation, as though I am going backwards and forwards at the same time. The future could be pouring into the past, and it would be like this, my car the connecting bottleneck.

It comforts me to see things pass too swiftly to absorb. Just surface impressions linger. Pines, maples, roadside malls, insurance companies, and tattoo joints. Ditch weeds and the people entering or leaving their houses. Church billboards. ENDTIME AT LAST! GET READY TO RAPTURE! In one enormous, empty field stretching to the sky a sign is planted that reads FUTURE HOME OF THE LIVING GOD.

It's just a bare field, fallow and weedy, stretching to the pale horizon.

MY HEAD CLEARS, and a few hours later I am on the reservation. I pass the Potts Superpumper without stopping, though I do slow up a little. *Well, there it is,* I think as it goes by, *my ancestral holding*—a lighted canopy.

I cross a bridge with a trickle of water underneath—qualifies just barely as a river. But no turn for a while. The left turn I do take leads past six houses. Five are neat and tidy, trimmed out and gardened, birdhoused, decorated with black plywood bears and moose or bent-over lady-butts with dotted bloomers. One yard is filled with amazing junk—three upended kid swimming pools of brilliant blue and pink plastic, a wild trampoline sprouting foam noodles, dead cars, stove-in boats getting patched I guess, heaped-up lawn mowers, and little rusted-out lawn tractors and barbecue grills. Dogs pop from the ditches here and there, at random, and pump themselves after the car, snapping harrowingly at the wheels. Finally, I come to a bridge and a big river. A real river. At last, one with moving water. And a left-hand turnoff right after with a promising road I know will end in a yellow house.

And there it is. I turn into the gravel drive out front of my birth family's yellow house—fairly new, three or four bedrooms. There is the inverted bathtub with a plastic statue of the Blessed Virgin, a wheelchair ramp and doghouse out front, the broken-down black van with purple detailing to one side, a brand-new pickup to the other side and the bent wooden, willow frame that must be the sweat lodge. And there, about the appropriate age, Mary Potts Almost Senior. She wields a garden hose, an unattached garden hose, and she is beating the crap out of a dusty couch cushion. She grins a sly, lopsided smile as I drive up, and gives the cushion a few finishing whacks.

Here is the woman who gave me life.

"Holeee . . . ," she puts her arms out and comes over to the car. She is wearing a tight, black muscle shirt that shows pink bra straps, and a pair of flared black capris. Her shapely, bearlike body is all muscular fat, and she has a pretty face with neat features. She's so much prettier, and younger than I imagined. She has all of her teeth and shifty little merry black eyes. Her dark brown hair with red highlights painted in is fastened on top of her head in one of those plastic claw clips, a blue one, and she wears pearl earrings. They look like real pearls. I get out of the car.

We stand facing each other, completely awkward. This is not a hugging moment for me, and I don't know what to do about the tears filling the eyes of my birth mother.

"Pretty," I say, touching my ears. "Pretty earrings."

She sniffs and looks away, blinking.

I notice that she is chewing on a shoelace. She notices that I notice and says that she does that when she's trying to quit smoking. Then she starts smiling at me, a little, but with the shoelace in her mouth this is very strange.

"You look like . . . ," she says.

"Who?"

"Never mind."

"Who? Really?"

"Well, me."

"I do not," I say instantly, without thinking, just a gut reaction. She looks down at her feet. Then she turns with a little shake of her topknot and walks away, which makes me notice that although she is built sort of thickly up and down, she has the perfectly flat hard butt of a much younger woman. As it is packed tightly into those black capri jeans I can't help but wish, for a moment, I'd inherited her ass. I'm so soft and round all over. When I do not follow my birth mother—I am actually just watching her ass move, as lots of people probably do—she looks over her shoulder, jerks her head at the house. I walk behind her, up the wheelchair ramp, through the little porch, in the front door. The house is thickly carpeted inside and smells of wild stuff—bark, maybe, or birdseed, or boiling berries—and cigarette smoke.

"You wanna smoke," she says, "I got a coffee can of sand outside for butts. I don't smoke in here, though."

Well, somebody does, I think.

I put my backpack and my laptop by the door and sit down at the table—speckled Formica. I watch while in silence she makes a strong pot of tea. She gives me a mug of the tea, sugared, and sits down across from me.

"You turned out nice," she says right off, then yells into the next room. "She turned out nice!"

"Who's in there?"

"Oh, your grandma. She's old, she had me when she was fifty-three, no lie, remember that. Use condoms until you're sixty, ha!"

"Hundred and a half," says a reedy little voice from around the corner. A tiny, brown, hunched-up little lady then wheels herself incrementally—she's wheeling herself on carpet—around the corner.

"Here," says my birth mother, "Mary Potts the Very Senior."

"Pleazzzzzz," the little woman actually buzzes, or hisses, inching closer. I jump up and push her to the table.

"Mary Ignatia," says the grandma, nodding wisely as I park her. "Hundred and one."

"Everybody's driving me crazy," says my birth mother, to nobody. "And her"—she gestures at me—"she calls me Mary Potts Almost Senior. She thinks that's funny."

"I don't think it's funny," I say, "I just don't know what to call you. You're not Sweetie to me."

"Hehhehheh." The ancient grandma laughs, waving forward a cup of tea that Mary Almost Senior is pushing carefully across the table. I can't bear this and decide to get it over with. I lean forward and address my birth mother.

"Two things. First, why did you give me up? Second thing. I want to know about genetic illnesses."

Both of the women are quiet now, sipping tea and looking at the top of the table. My birth mother studies the freckles in the Formica like she is divining the future from their pattern. At last, she gives one of her sighs—I'm getting to know her sighs—and then she starts to cough. She's getting wound up to speak. After several false starts, she begins.

"It wasn't because I was that young," she says, "obviously." Big sigh again. Restart. "It was because . . . it was because . . . I was stupid. Not one day has gone by since then where I haven't thought. Have not thought about how stupid I was."

She just looks at me.

"Stupid," she says again, and nods. She curls and uncurls her fingers from the handle of the cup. "Took drugs. Not while I was pregnant.

After. Fucked every jackass in sight. Just dumbass stupid," she whispers. "Not one day has gone by, though, when I have not thought about you."

Not one day? How about not one hour? I think. *I wanted you. I wanted you.*

"Well, you thought about me more than I thought about you," I say, shrugging.

Nobody talks after that. We're kind of deadlocked. Her tears dry up and we sit there in silence.

"You got a good family, yeah, rich as hell," she says, shaking herself up straight. "They sent me pictures for two years. Then I wrote and said no more, I can't take it."

"You couldn't take it?" I feel my eyes narrow, and this thing builds up in me, this thing I know well and which I say mantras and breathe deeply to avoid, this anger. It fizzes up like shook pop. "*You couldn't take it?*"

"I lost . . . ," she begins.

"Lost what?"

But there is the sound of a motor roaring off outside and footsteps, fast clunking footsteps. The door behind me slams and I turn around to witness the dramatic entry of the Princess of the Damned—Little Mary.

"She's a Mary, too?" I can't believe it. "What? Have you no originality?"

I sound exactly like my father, Alan, but I don't care. Mary Potts Almost Senior shrugs at me, her face sad, as her non-adopted-out daughter stalks into the room on three-inch-heeled black boots, in ripped fishnets, too many piercings to list, and long hair with clipped pieces spiked purple. The spikes are comically drooping from the humidity, not bristling except for a wisp of bangs. Her eyes are surrounded neatly with red paint—Magic Marker? Sharpie? The pupils are black and luminous. She sways in the doorway, obviously high.

"Soooo," she says.

"This is your sister," says my birth mother, nodding at me. Her look is gentle. "The one I told you about last night."

"Oh, *nobody*?" Little Mary smiles at us, dreamily vicious. Her teeth look sharpened, could they be? Her incisors are a bit longer than her front cuspids, and very white against the black lipstick, like elegant fangs. She's pretty, like her mom, prettier than me, I think, instantly doing that thing girls do. Who's prettier. I suppose sisters compare all of the time and right at this minute I am glad I didn't have a sister, ever before, in my life. I'm glad I didn't have this mother and this family, except maybe the grandma. I think of Alan and Sera and all that we share, and tears now do come into my eyes. I turn to my birth mother and I reach over. I take her fingers off the handle of her tea mug. I hold her fingers and then warmly grasp her whole hand in mine.

"It's all right, Sweetie. Really, it's all right," I say, with absolute sincerity. "Just looking at Little Mary I can tell what a good mother you would have been."

MY SISTER MARY is sixteen and it turns out, after Mary leaves, and we really start to talk, it turns out that my Potts parent believes that, although she isn't doing very well in school, Little Mary has no drug habit—she does not abuse alcohol nor does she smoke. Sweetie actually shakes her head, marveling, and takes her shoelace out of her teeth.

"I know you meant your comment as sarcastic, you know, ironic, what have you. Good mom. I know I'm not the best mom. I know that. But Little Mary's really doing good. She's the only girl who doesn't fuck and do drugs in her whole class. She says that she's about to crack, though."

"And who can blame her." I swallow the urge to fall down on the floor and laugh.

After a while, Sweetie walks into the bathroom. All is silent. She does not come out. Then I hear her quietly talking, as if on a cell phone. Little Mary is sitting in front of the television and she does not acknowledge me. There is an odd smell emanating from her—more than that something wild I smelled the first time I entered the house. This time, it's a powerful feet smell, plus something slowly going rotten. Behind her, I notice, the door to her room is open. Through that doorway, I can see it—the sort of spectacle you can't help gawking at, like a car accident. Only this is a stupefying dump. I stand there a moment, gaping at the mess, and then see that Grandma's wheelchair is drawn up to the table and she's snoozing upright. I walk past Little Mary and sit down to wait for Grandma to surface.

While she's sleeping, I watch her. I've never seen anybody this old. Grandma Mary Ignatia has the softest skin, silkier than a baby's, and her hands are little delicate curled claws. Her eyes are covered with thin membranes of skin. I think perhaps she can see right through her lids, they're so transparent. I do know, from before, that she can stare a long time at you without blinking. She has not allowed anyone to cut her hair, I see, not for a very long time. Maybe an entire hundred years. It is braided into one thin white plait and wound into a bun. Her ears stick out a little as her hair is so thin. A pair of white shell earrings hang off her earlobes, which are delicate and soft as flower petals. Most remarkably, I notice when she happens to yawn, she still seems to have most of her own teeth. Though they are darkened by time, her teeth are still strong.

Suddenly, she's looking at me, those bright eyes tack-sharp. Grandma Mary Ignatia laughs, soft and breathy, when she sees she's startled me. She has a very sweet, ancient type of laughter that comes out in panting gusts. We laugh together and I ask about her teeth. She tells me that she had a full French grandfather who counseled her on the importance of scrubbing her teeth with a peeled willow twig. She takes a cracker from the table and shows me how she chews and bites with the vigor of a young person. The strength of her teeth, she says, is the key to her longevity.

"I am pregnant." I tell her quietly, so my newfound sister will not hear. "Are there illnesses in the family? Genetic anomalies? Anything my baby might inherit?"

At first, her expression does not change. I think perhaps my identity, our place in time, the muddy river of reality, all of this is bundled in shadow. But then she puts out her withered little paw and says, "We lose some."

"You lose some? What do you mean?"

Grandma Ignatia drops her head and sinks into a motionless and rigid sleep. I wheel her into her room and help stand her up beside the little single bed, then lower her slowly onto the mattress and lift her legs over and set them gently down. Her little tan moccasins stick straight up. Her arms are plucked brown chicken wings, soft and limp. I cover her with a bright quilt made of all different versions of yellow calico—a golden cloud.

When I come back out, my little sister is again sitting in the TV glow. She has on so much black eyeliner that her eyes smolder demonically into the changing screen. I count her piercings—her ears have six or seven each—her earrings look like twisted nails and screws. She has sprayed her bangs straight up into a black woodpecker's crest. The rest of her long, thin hair—permanented and bleached and colored with those purple highlights or bleached again and again—hangs down her back in a dead and crinkled curtain. She's made some changes to her outfit, though, added a pink bow to her hair. She's wearing an incongruously sexy baby-doll nightie, ankle socks, and white Mary Janes. The cuteness/evil contrast has an effect even creepier than when she was dressed in full Goth. She's sort of a nightmare kitten.

"Hey." I sit down next to her.

She maintains her stony pose.

"Hey," I say again, "what's up with you?"

"What's it look like?"

"I mean in general, what are you up to in a general way?"

She looks at me with black contempt, her eyes sizzle from their deep mask. Her lips part in a snarl and the pink bow in her hair bobs up and down like a sinister butterfly. She nods as she speaks, agreeing with herself.

"You're just a stinking slut. You suck, you impostor. You're not my sister, you're an STD. You're a piece of syphilis."

Her outfit keeps throwing me—cutie-pie vampire. But her hatred is simple. Predictable. I tear my gaze away and try to hold my own.

"You're suffering from misplaced self-disgust," I tell her. "Your feelings have nothing to do with me. I've never hurt you."

"And I heard you tell Grandma you're pregnant, but I can see it any-way," she sneers. "You're such a whore."

"Oh, really. How do you think my being pregnant makes me a whore?"

My heart is surging but I keep my voice calm. I've always found that the best way to deflect hostility is to ask questions. But Little Mary is like a politician, adept at not answering the question asked but sticking hard to her own agenda. She stays on the attack. There's a frilly white garter on her leg.

"You got adopted out and grew up rich and think you're smart as hell, but you had unprotected sex! Ooh!" She opens her painted eyes wide and screws up her mouth like a wooden doll's.

"You're possessed," I tell her and, embarrassingly, my voice squeaks. "Your brain's all cooked on meth."

"Oh yeah!" She cocks her fists. "Oh yeah! Let's go!"

But then she slumps down and in a typical display of sick emotional lability begins to cry. Fat tears swell from her eyes.

"Don't tell Daddy, don't tell Mom, okay?"

"I think they know. They live around you. They smell your room. I can smell it from here."

"Will you help me clean it, huh?"

I stare at her and my mouth drops open. It is so bizarre that I might be charmed, in a weird way, were it not for the room itself. That un-natural disaster. Still, I stand up and follow her as she makes her way to the open door.

Little Mary's room has the odor of rank socks, dried blood, spoiled cheese, girl sweat, and Secret. The room is knee deep in dirty clothes she's packed down and walked on—sort of a new conglomerate floor-ing. Within the stratified layers of clothing I can see potato and corn chip bags, cans of pop she hasn't even drunk dry. A tiny haze of baby flies circles one orange Sunkist. Stuff is balled up, pasted together with sparkle glue, thrown on the wall, smearing the windows. Spray-can confetti hangs off the fancy fanlight fixture, and thongs are every place I look. Pink glitter thongs, black ones, gold lamé, sequined, lace spiderweb, and zipper thongs, thongs with little devils on them. She's undressed by kicking them up onto the blades of the ceiling fan. The curtains are balled up around the cock-eyed rods and there's broken glass sifted over one entire corner.

"It's your mother's job to make you clean this," I say, feebly.

"Yeah, maybe," says Little Mary. "She read in a parenting magazine that it is best to pick your battles with teenagers and that a teen's room is her own personal space. But I'm"—her chin trembles and her painted mouth sags—"just don't know how . . . it's too much."

"I can't face your room," I tell her now, but I try to be kind. Obviously, she's suffering from some heritable mental instability and it's all come out in the feral state of this room. Thongs. Darkness. Chaos. While I'm thinking apocalyptic thoughts, Little Mary takes a deep, sobbing breath, and edges past me, into that ninth circle. I step back as the door to her room gently closes and I reel away and sit down on the couch. I move off the warm spot she's just vacated, thinking of an unseen thong. After a while, watching the nothingness go by on some teen TV channel, where there is a dating show sadly rerunning, I decide that I will leave a note for Sweetie. I get up, lift my bag, take out a pen, and find a scrap of paper on which to compose it. As I am writing the words *It was such a pleasure to finally meet you,* Sweetie comes out of the bathroom with her cell phone pressed up to her ear. She looks out the window and I follow her gaze. I see a vintage Volvo just like Alan and Sera's. Then, astounded, I see my adoptive parents get out of the Volvo. First Alan, then Sera. Without a word to me, Sweetie goes outside to meet them. They approach my birth mother, both with a hand out to shake.

They must have worried about me. They must have always known Sweetie, or been in touch. The explanation doesn't really matter right then, though, just the fact that they are *here.*

From the picture window of the house, I can see them in the driveway, all together now, gesturing and talking, a phantasmagoria of parents—I don't understand it, but it's happening. Now they are actually walking toward the house together. I am at the center of some sort of vortex. I go dizzy. I hold the strap of my backpack in one hand, and now I lift my laptop in the other, and I slowly walk backwards, navigating through the living room, somehow, by subterranean memory, not bumping into anything, retreating. I put my hand behind me and there is a doorknob. I turn it, and I back into the room, Little Mary's room. I close the door and stare at it.

The reverse side of the door is pasted over with hand-drawn green Magic Marker hearts, a tragic-eyed Siouxsie and the Banshees poster, an Alien Sex Fiend T-shirt, a thong with actual little silver spikes in it, held up by a tack, many German beer coasters, and what all else. Frills, those too. Bucketloads of frills—lots of candy-pink flounces and bows. I turn around. Little Mary is sitting on the mammoth pile of clothing that is probably her bed. We look at each other. Her eyeliner has run down her face in two tracks like the tears of a tragic clown. When she opens her mouth, I think that she might scream, or belt out a high C, anything but use a normal voice and speak to me as a normal person for the first time.

"You changed your mind? Oh, wow! I know it's a lot to ask," she says. "But this is, like, a big statement. Really nice of you. Thanks."

I look down. At my feet there is a box of black Hefty steel sacks, no doubt placed there by Sweetie as a subtle hint. I bend over, put my pack and computer where I hope I'll find them again, and pull the first plastic bag from the box.

Slowly, I stand up straight again. Outside the door, I hear the other door open, shuffling feet, voices.

"Let's put all of the colored dirty clothes in this one," I say, holding up the bag. "And the ones we need to bleach, the white stuff, in this one." I hand Little Mary a second black trash bag. Her pink bow bobs and sways again, sweet and strangely demure.

"Your look's kind of shocking, I like it," I tell her.

"Gothlolita, " she says.

"Lolita? You read the book?"

"Wha . . . it's a look I got off a Web site."

"Huh."

She takes the bag and looks at me with something like grateful awe. I don't have to bend over yet. I can pick up one limp black piece of clothing, another, another, off piles at waist height, off hooks on the wall. I pray that as I do excavate ever deeper there are no used condoms or old puke or large insects in the pile that I see that I will have to peel up from the floor, layer by layer.

I hear them in the kitchen now, the two sets of parents clinking mugs and making tea, together, talking.

At my feet there is a powdering of Asian twelve-spotted lady beetles from last fall's infestation, but they are dead, and crumbled to dust. There are thongs like aggregate rock, glued into patterned bricks. I just heave those into the bag.

"So," says Little Mary, shaking out the quarter-moon cups of a 36A, "you got the name yet?"

"There's something wrong with my baby," I tell her. "They saw it on the ultrasound."

"Yeah?"

I'm all of a sudden light and dizzy. My vision is narrowing. Blackness and shadow are welling all around me.

"Mom lost two babies before she had me," says Little Mary. "That's why I'm spoiled. She told me last night that she thought losing the babies was punishment for giving you up."

"Is there a name for what they had?"

"It has a 'thirteen' in it. Bad luck. She said that she promised to name me Mary, after you, if I lived."

"That makes sense." Nothing makes sense, and I sit down in the thickest litter, sensing the numb edge of the beginning of a feeling so powerful it has no name.

"Hey! You're not going to call your baby Mary, are you?"

I am slumping over the stuff on my lap.

"You got the name yet? Say if it's a girl?"

I hold up a swatch of red boy-leg lace and read the label.

"Victoria."

"Wow," says my little sister, "that's beautiful."

She leans over and puts her arms around me. As she holds me, we begin to sway back and forth. My sister is rocking me in her Gothlolita, boy-smelling, strangely comforting live-wire arms. She is wearing tattered gloves with the fingers cut off and frayed. Green chipped fingernail polish on her fingers. The scent of a harrowing musk—sulfurous, sweet, distantly volcanic, a perfume that consoles and irritates me all at once so that I begin to cry, not with pity for myself, but with a sense that I have accidentally tampered with and entered some huge place. I do not know what giant lives in this vast and future home. I don't know whether the door opens in or opens out. I hold on to my sister just waiting for the hinge to creak.

# *Beauty Stolen from Another World*

WHILE BROWSING THROUGH the library stacks at University College in London, I was approached by a handsome Eurasian doctor who pretended to be interested in the book I was skimming, *The Milk of Paradise*, by M.H. Abrams. The year was 1979 and I was on a college exchange program. The doctor said that he would like to make me an omelet. For some reason, perhaps the novelty of the omelet pickup line, I allowed him to lead me down the street and then, after some hesitation, in which he assured me that his roommate was home, I got into his car, a brown Mercedes-Benz. As we drove to his place I realized that I'd done something foolish and dangerous and, if not bizarre, at least very unlike my Midwestern upbringing. The more so when we got to his flat and his roommate turned out to live in the next apartment. There was a sturdy wall between the two, surely impenetrable to screams, and I made the doctor introduce me to the neighbor so that if I "disappeared into night London," as the provost of the college had darkly warned during our orientation, there would at least be someone who could identify my face from pictures on the news. Then I did go into the apartment with the doctor, who actually seemed quite harmless.

We entered the kitchen. He broke the eggs expertly against the pan, one-handed, and he did not chop up onions or peppers with a big chef's knife, as I feared, but merely added some cheese, which he grated from a block with a little aluminum mill. I ate, and as I did so, I thought that perhaps he really had just taken me across the city to feed me an omelet.

But when I was done he asked if I would like to take a bath while he answered some telephone calls, and again I knew I'd done something foolish and that I should turn back. He grew charming and persuasive. As though humoring a skittish horse he gently drew me toward his very masculine bath—all tiled in black and white—with a magnificent soaking tub. The door had a sturdy lock.

It was the bathtub that seduced me into staying. I lived in the cheapest student housing, a building that reeked of disinfectant. The moldy showers wept so slowly over your body that it took half an hour to get the soap off. I hadn't had a real bath in months, which may have been apparent to the doctor, now that I think of it, and I instantly longed to get into the tub. I stayed there for an hour and would not come out. Nor, empowered by my cleansing soak, would I consent to have sex with him although he cajoled me and showed me his stash of what he called pessaries, a thing I'd never seen. The absurd-looking little bullets of jelly completely dampened my interest.

I slept on his couch and was very happy to be dropped off, back at the library. I didn't want him to know where I lived. But I had made the mistake of telling him my name, and somehow he got into the college records and showed up at my hall. He was perhaps in his late twenties— as I said he was a very young doctor—but I had just turned nineteen and to me he seemed old. I did show him up to my room, which had a very good view of the post office tower, but I actually did have a real roommate and I lived in a room that was half the size of his bathroom. She was there, studying, responded to a signal we had developed between us, and did not leave.

I found soon afterward that I had committed a theft, and it shames me to say that I was never able to rectify it. This is the only thing that I have ever stolen in my life. When I was picked up by the doctor, I kept the book I'd been skimming—that small paperback book called *The Milk of Paradise*. I held it among my other books, and was aware of it when I left the library. I could have returned it, simply slipped it back into its slot on the shelf, but I forgot all about it. Then a few days later during a lecture on Samuel Taylor Coleridge, before about a hundred of us, the professor took off his glasses and looked us over singly and thoroughly and then announced, "one of you is a thief." And he expounded so energetically upon the selfishness and immorality of stealing a book, the very one I'd taken, and certainly meant to return, that I was very much impressed, for who would have thought one book, and so small a book, would be instantly missed from the library, and furthermore, deserve a half-hour lecture?

Only now, of course, I could not find the book. Then I realized I'd carried it with me to the doctor's apartment, and so I called him. When I asked him to mail it back to me, instead of returning it in person, he sounded miffed. The book never showed up in the mail. I never called again. Anyway as there was no book drop, I'd have had to either sneak it in, or to place it in a librarian's hands, and I probably couldn't have done it for fear of being discovered. Yet, *The Milk of Paradise* now resides on a top bookshelf among other mass-market-size books. That I have it back now is the basis of my story.

As I said, it was a small book, which began in fact as an M.H. Abrams's essay for a survey course in English literature at Harvard, and was expanded to a thesis and published in 1934. My version of the book, republished with an author's preface in 1969, has a cover very much of its day—there sits a blank-eyed Coleridge with his forehead sprouting rainbows and psychedelic green devils with golden beards. He holds a little white pipe, though in fact he did not smoke opium but took laudanum, which came in liquid form and was administered drop by drop.

Although I became a doctor and left Coleridge behind somewhat regretfully, I remained connected to *The Milk of Paradise* in several ways. The title refers to a line from "Kubla Khan" and describes the milk of the opium poppy, source of the laudanum much employed by Coleridge, at first to dull rheumatic pain, and later to try to ease the mental sufferings of his addiction. As it turns out, I have become interested in certain kinds of brain chemistry relating to addiction, and have written a number of articles on how various addictive substances, opium derivatives especially, interact with the brain on a molecular level, which is how, as it turns out, I once again entered the presence of the omelet-making doctor who had kept the book—his name was Walter Ing.

THIS TIME I was in a town suburban to Paris, attending a conference with many plainly dressed doctors whose interests adjoined mine. I am always surprised at the timidity, even mousiness, of our dress and manner, as if we feel we must compensate for the notoriety, however slight, of our chosen field. There is an old castle in that town where Mata Hari was killed. But although I wanted to see the castle very much, we were tightly scheduled and it also happened that each time I got to the entrance I met other conference attendees and became immersed in conversations that always ended up with someone suggesting lunch or dinner. As I live alone and am always hungry for well-cooked food, I always joined the group. That is how I ended up sitting at a long, narrow table across from the man in whose tub I had soaked twenty-five years before.

Our dance of recognition was comical. He shook his head, ventured, "It's odd . . ." I sat back in my chair, murmuring, "I'm sure . . ." I could not place him and it took us most of an exquisite lunch—I had an eggplant-and-salmon salad prepared like nothing I'd ever tasted—before we'd rifled through our respective pasts, still dogged by something familiar about the other person, and hit on London. We'd both had a little wine. I said, "Omelet" and started laughing. He was still confused until I described our meeting in the library. Then he dropped his fork and clapped his hand to his forehead. He kept it there as though stanching a blood wound and cried out, "You are the girl, the one with the room overlooking the post office tower!" He began to apologize immediately for trying to seduce me. He had thought I was a faculty member, he said, which was a laughable excuse and I told him so. He then insisted he had only come by the dormitory to apologize, and I told him again that wasn't true, either, and that he still had my book. He said he didn't remember it, and when I told him that I didn't really care, anyway, about the book or about what his intentions had been, he looked relieved and sat back in his chair.

Walter Ing had a slight Australian accent. He'd grown up there, he said, though his parents had moved to London and were deceased. He now lived in New York, as it turned out, and furthermore, he was soon to take part in a yearlong study at the Mayo Clinic, which is an hour and a half south of Minneapolis, where I teach at the university and do my research. The welter of coincidence intimidated me at first, but after a time I grew used to the state of things and agreed to guide Dr. Walter Ing around the area when he visited, which would be soon.

ONE MONTH LATER, I had a date to accompany Dr. Ing. Perhaps since meeting in France we had both shrunk at the same rate. I am used to thinking of myself as tall and so I thought Walter Ing was tall, too, since I didn't recall that he was any shorter than me. But when I looked out the window of my town house and saw him emerge from a tan sedan, carrying a craft-paper triangle of flowers, he looked somewhat diminutive. He was dressed with the same formality as I'd remembered—a camel's-hair topcoat, a soft gray men's scarf, even gloves. I had reverted to my Minnesota casual look, a sweater, skirt, soft boots. I decided at once that I wouldn't sleep with him. He dropped a glove and bent over to pick it up. I had that sensation of pity one has watching a man when he doesn't know that he's being observed and judged, but then I was surprised by Walter Ing. He straightened with the glove in his hand, and looked not at the door but at the window, where I stood. He looked precisely into my eyes. We exchanged the same sort of thoughtful gaze as over the table at our conference. It was just on the verge of becoming an uncomfortable and maybe confrontational stare, when he suddenly broke into a smile and waved the package at me in such a cheerful and comforting way that I smiled back at him and was laughing a little when I opened the door to exclaim over the flowers and draw him in.

We decided to take his car, which was new and austere, a reliable sort of car with a cloth interior. It turned out that he had leased the car for the year that he would keep the job. We drove through Dinkytown, parked, toured the appropriate buildings, and then walked through the Weissman Museum, the outside of which looks like supple, bending, shiny cans. We ate dinner at a downtown dinner spot decorated with small tiles that resembled the backs of iridescent beetles. I liked the way Walter's face had aged so symmetrically, the lines around his smile strict as parentheses, the perfect rays of laugh lines, an unworried forehead. His gray hair was a little too long and floppy and touched his collar, but research doctors can get away with that. He had a neat mouth, polished skin, surprisingly hard hands. To relax, he made furniture. He showed me pictures of some pieces—Biedermeier copies. There were some other photos in the little envelope he'd drawn out—were they of his children, wife, girlfriend? He hesitated, I thought he was going to show me, but then he folded the envelope and put it back into his suit pocket.

"Well," I said, as we were finished eating, "should we go?"

"I would like to see you again," said Walter.

I nodded at the place he'd hidden the photographs. "But perhaps you are attached," I said.

He smiled and drew the envelope out. They were pictures of a neat, imperious blue Abyssinian cat.

"I thought you might think me strange," he said. He drew out his wallet and showed the high school graduation pictures of two children—both sweet, freckled All-American 1950s faces. They were finishing college and graduate school, both in Massachusetts. He'd divorced six years ago and there was no other woman in his life at present. "And while I'm at it, not that I expected to, but here." He gave me a piece of paper. I squinted to read, by the low light of the table's candle, a set of test results for all of the usual sexually transmitted diseases with checkmarks in all of the negative boxes. I started to laugh.

"I'm sorry," I said, handing it back, "I don't have one of these papers. I haven't even had sex since some of these diseases became commonly tested for."

Perhaps there appeared on my face a faint shadow of sadness, or longing. He touched my hand gently and said, "Do you have a bathtub?"

I AM A shy person, physically, and socially. I never did lose my small-town awkwardness after all. I've had very few lovers. Some bitter experiences early on were enough. I've never cared to throw myself in harm's way again. So when I allowed Walter to undress me it was partly because I hadn't slept with anyone for such a long time that I wondered, frankly, if I was still functional. If I could even respond to a man. Things did not go badly, though I was sure Walter was only pretending to be thrilled by everything about me. But then, unexpectedly, after it all seemed to have concluded, he pulled me to him and looked into my eyes in much the same way he had when he gazed through the window. And when he did that, I felt something rise in me to meet him. It was as though there was some recognition that had nothing to do with the two selves we were in our daily jobs and with our families—it was a different sort of knowing.

A thick silence flowered in us. These two beings, not us, but living in our skins, had realized something in the other. I have tried to understand what it was, or is. I have no words for it or the words sound weak and silly. It was a speechless negotiation conducted between two interior shadows. What, I wonder now, accounts for this in all of my favorite studies? What was decided? Was it, in the truest sense, chemistry? Were those poetic inner beings actually composed of interactions of compounds that signaled back and forth in ways too complex for consciousness to understand? Is this what it means to bless unaware?

In the middle of this dramatic tension, Walter and I began to laugh and smile. We kept looking at each other. Then I watched the smile leave his face like breath from a mirror. He kissed me, deeply, and so the night went on. We dozed and woke every hour or two. We didn't stop discovering each other and although my body was awkward, unused to touch, and he kept getting cold, I piled on more blankets and at last we woke in daylight and did not start our usual day at all.

WALTER AND I have been together now for almost a year, commuting back and forth between Minneapolis and Rochester. He has come to Arizona to meet my parents, who, like so many Minnesotans, have retired into the piercing heat. His children never come to visit, but he tells me news of their busy lives. I spend at least one weekend every month at his place, a Rochester sublet. His cat stayed with his ex-wife and we adopted one who goes back and forth with us. Sometimes as we are lying naked, spent, after making love, the cat walks across our bodies with the disdain of an emperor, then curls between Walter's legs and purrs.

One day, Walter asks me if I have read any of the studies on the brain chemistry of romantic love, and I look at him and laugh. We both know that the ventral tegmental area and the caudate nucleus are stimulated when a person is in love. The caudate nucleus possesses a dense spread of receptors for dopamine, a crucial neurotransmitter that lets us live for a while on overdrive and enhances the moments we are around the object of our love. He says, quite casually, that if we could cure addictions we could also treat love. Romantic love will be more treatable than a virus. Those desperate, unrequited, could swallow a pill of release. I think about this a few weeks later, when Walter leaves me.

He goes back to New York City, intending to get his things sent out here, and to arrange a transfer. But he's gone what seems a long time, about two weeks, and during that time I find that the ability I once had, to live alone happily and find security within a daily routine, has been destroyed. I am agitated, and find it difficult to concentrate. I dwell on Walter's phone calls, hidden meanings in his words, a tremor in his voice. I take long, hot baths every night, for comfort, and also because the bathroom is a small place and I won't wander about aimlessly. I am taking care of the cat and as I absently brush its fur tears fill my eyes. I don't know what to do with myself. I eat all one thing for dinner—six oranges or a bag of pretzels. Carrot cake. An entire melon. When Walter calls and says that he will need another week at least, I decide that he is trying to soften the blow and doesn't know how to say that he is not going to return. I hang up and sit numbly, staring at the telephone. He calls back and says he's booked me a cheap ticket online. Can I come for the weekend?

I ask if I should bring the cat.

"No," he says, "can you get someone to look in on him?"

I draw a suddenly deep quiet breath. I am amazed to realize that I imagined, for a moment, that he was flying me out only to deliver the cat.

WALTER DOES NOT believe there will ever be a perfect anti-addiction medication because addiction itself is so complex and involves learned behaviors, experience, feelings, and memories, as well as a specific genetic vulnerability. His research is material and involves DNA testing in order to isolate and study certain inherited enzymes that process drugs either with unusual avidity or with passive indifference. He imagines a world where babies are tested for addictive vulnerabilities and treated in utero.

As we are working along, day after day, month after month, we develop a comforting routine. Evenings, music. Reading. A little fire. Bed. Mornings, tea with cream and honey. We like ours brewed hot, thick and swampy. The way we had it in London. We like plain steel cut oats for oatmeal, whatever fruit is in season. Sweet red grapefruit in the winter. Raspberries in midsummer. Over time, if the relationship is good, a substance called oxytocin becomes implicated in warm feelings of attachment. We both agree that, technically speaking, we are addicted to each other. It is a good addiction, in our case, both reciprocated and probably conducive to a longer, happier life. But after the New York absence, I also realize how afraid I am of losing Walter. Afraid in the way a heroin addict is afraid. I could never go back to my life pre-Walter without feeling at every moment Walter's absence. Sometimes it gnaws at me. I urge Walter to drive carefully, avoid butter, update his tetanus shot. Sometimes, when I am looking at him, I imagine him dead and tears fill my eyes. I've worked on cadavers, of course, and I can easily imagine the lifeless absence of Walter in Walter's body, the rigid, deeply cold limbs and gray skin.

I HAVE BEEN working with CART peptide receptors. CART peptide is a chemical that occurs naturally within the human brain and shows some promise, or implication, in the development of what could be the perfect medication to counter and cure addiction to cocaine. I've had dreams where I manage to find an antidote to addiction—one more effective than the best pharmaceutical model we have now: methadone or buprenorphine for opiate withdrawals—and with fewer side effects than the opiate blocker naltrexone.

In my dreams, people do not die of desire or become affixed in a cycle of desperate need. They are able to use drugs without lasting physical or mental harm. Sometimes, I am in a vast crowd of people I have saved, and I am overcome by excitement. Satisfaction rolls through me. I am surrounded by freed minds. Thousands of smoothly running brains. I feel the buzz of thought. The hum of neural energy. Intricate signals passing back and forth. Sometimes I actually faint in my sleep—from joy. Sometimes I wake myself up by dreaming I have fainted this way, and I'm very happy until I realize that I haven't cured anything at all.

ONE DAY, IT happens that we both fall ill. It is a common influenza virus and we must have been exposed at the same time because our symptoms begin practically at the same hour and are identical. First the dreadful joint aches, sore throat, malaise, then the fever and the horrid nausea, which is where mine stops after roughly thirty-six hours. But Walter doesn't get well when I do—he remains sick for nearly two weeks. During that time, he asks me to look on the top shelf of his bookcase, where I spot *The Milk of Paradise*.

"I did have it all along," he says, "I stole it from you."

He kept it as a memento of our meeting, and now wants to give it back to me. I look inside the book and see that he used, as a marker, a torn margin of brittled newspaper that bears my full name.

The sight of my name, written in his hand so long ago, upsets me. I am uneasy with it, remembering how he went to the college and tracked me down. 49 Grafton Way is where I lived, within walking distance of Pollock's Toy Museum. I found the toy museum, with its tiny passages and opaque-eyed ancient dolls, irresistibly sinister. I went there time after time. I have kept some of the beautiful cutouts of reproduction jesters, court clowns, and paper stage sets for miniature plays. Thinking of the toy museum and my attraction to it, I am startled to think that my impulse to get into Walter's car was somehow connected to the avid passivity of those dolls. For the first time, I try to question Walter about his life in London. He professes not to remember much. It was a time of turbulence, he only says. Looking at the torn newspaper, I wonder at his impulse to commit the little theft.

He sees me looking. "Yes," he says, "I must have known that one day you would mean everything to me. I went out with many women. Why else would I have written down your name and kept it?"

I swallow the sudden jolt of anger. So, he saw many women? I know the pinpricks around my heart are unreasonable and I keep my voice calm.

"Perhaps you wrote down my name because I was the only one who wouldn't have sex."

Walter smiles in a way that strikes me as a little smug.

"That might have made me a bit more curious, yes."

"Did you have an inkling that we would be so attracted?"

"I'm sure I did. And now, I don't know what I'd do without you, I really don't know."

He takes a short breath and it seems to stick in his chest. There is something much more desperate about his voice than this annoying illness warrants.

"Being sick is tedious," I say, taking his hand.

He doesn't answer, but grips my fingers so hard that I have to smile as I gently shake his hand away.

When ill, Walter behaves much differently than I do. I like to be left alone, he doesn't. I have never really taken care of a sick person, not someone I love, not in my house. So I am surprised, the next day, when as I am about to leave the room having brought him a glass of water, Walter tells me that he is lonely, and asks me to sit and talk to him. I have to force myself to turn back, sit down next to the bed. But I'm late for work and eager to get back—I am pleased about something I'm doing. I don't like being drawn back into the sick room. I think he feels my absence as I talk to him, but is also comforted by the fact that I am there even though I do not want to be there.

His face is droopy, gray, and sprouting white stubble in tiny patches. Age has freckled his temples, his hair sticks out on one side. His nose is bone pale. He is breathing rather quickly, but says that he feels better. As I sit with him, it occurs to me that he probably is hungry, and I tell him that I am leaving just to make him something to eat. He smiles, but his hand oddly clutches at mine. I smile at him and stroke his hand. I tell him not to worry, and then I walk out into the kitchen. I make him an omelet. I have often teased him about his strange pickup line, and I think he will laugh when I present this plate to him. He calls out to me. I am decorating the plate with clipped basil and I call back to him that I am coming. But it is two or three minutes longer before I walk into the room. He is looking at me silently with his hand on his heart. He isn't dead yet. That will take the rest of the day, and a night.

I AM BESIDE his bed, at the hospital, in one of those uncomfortable fold-back plastic armchairs. Walter's children have not arrived yet— they are driving down from the Minneapolis airport tomorrow morning. I am not really supposed to be in this room overnight, but I've pulled a doctor's privilege. I won't leave his side, though I've found out that Walter is not who he said he was, exactly. Oh, he is the omelet doctor, to be sure. But Walter was not conducting research, he was being treated here for obliterative cardiomyopathy, a rare heart condition. He'd told no one about this; his children had no idea. In effect, he had come here to die and perhaps had formed the plan even as he sat across from me at that conference in Paris. I have brought *The Milk of Paradise* to read as I sit here, and am struck by the last lines, where Abrams speaks of Coleridge's poems as oases in our dusty lives and says: There is nothing frightening in their rich strangeness. Rather, they are to be the more dearly cherished because of the fearful toll exacted for beauty stolen from another world.

The dragging ache of withdrawal has already begun. Perhaps out of pity, Walter started it by returning the book, and perhaps his mention of other women was a way to throw the grit of some reality into whatever I would think of him. I'm grateful for that because, as I sit with him, I recognize that instead of dreading his impending loss, a fury inhabits me. He made me love him. It is as though he has knowingly infected me with some dangerous disease and then plans to desert me. Liar, I think, and I see those dolls waiting to be held. Still, looking into his face I still feel the mysterious affinity which we are helpless to fully define.

There is the humming, sighing, breathy flutter, the static stutter, the tiny bleeps of machines registering the presence of life in Walter. I watch the screens intently, the levels of oxygen in his blood, the erratic wiggle of his heart, the creak of the ossified heart walls and valves. Sometimes I nearly doze off, but then I startle awake and sit up. I touch Walter, his wrist, his leg covered by a sheet. His skin already bears the waxy indifference of cadavers, though blood flows underneath, and his thready pulse endures.

Waking before dawn, I hate him for showing me how close it is, that other universe. But then he opens his eyes and stares fully into mine, and I am shocked to find myself in two worlds at once. His gaze says that I need not be frightened of such proximity, and then something peaceful and electric flows toward me, from Walter. He offers this ineffable thing and I accept it. When the nurses hurry into the room they stop short.

I tell them that he is gone.

It was agreed that it would be so. Nothing extraordinary. I close his eyes with a brush of my hand, and tell the nurses that I need to be alone with Walter. My eyes are drooping, my brain is full of drowsy fuzz. I have the greatest need to crawl into bed beside him and sleep. The nurses unhook Walter from the machine. They make notes in hushed murmurs, and at last go, closing the curtain, shutting the door with a soft click, padding down the hall.

# Acknowledgments

THE AUTHOR GRATEFULLY acknowledges the publications in which these stories originally appeared:

"The Red Convertible" in *The Mississippi Valley Review*, 1981.

"Scales" in *The North American Review*, March 1982, and *Best American Short Stories, 1983*.

"The World's Greatest Fisherman" in *Chicago* magazine, October 1982.

"Saint Marie" in *Atlantic Monthly*, March 1984, and *O. Henry Prize Stories, 1985*.

"The Plunge of the Brave" in *New England Review*, Fall 1984.

"The Blue Velvet Box" as "The Beet Queen" in *The Paris Review*, Spring 1985.

"Pounding the Dog" in *The Kenyon Review*, Fall 1985.

"Knives" in *Granta*, June 1986.

"Destiny" in *Atlantic Monthly*, January 1985.

"The Little Book" in *Formations*, Spring 1985.

"Snares" in *Harper's* Magazine, May 1987, and *Best American Short Stories*, 1988.

"The Dress" in *Mother Jones*, July/August 1990.

"Fleur" in *Esquire*, August 1986, and *O. Henry Prize Stories, 1987*.

"A Wedge of Shade" in *The New Yorker*, March 6, 1989.

"The Fat Man's Race" in *The New Yorker*, November 3, 2008.

"The Leap" in *Harper's*, March 1990.

"The Bingo Van" in *The New Yorker*, February 19, 1990.

"Best Western" in *Vogue*, May 1990.

"Tales of Burning Love" in *Cosmopolitan*, March 1996.

"Le Mooz" in *The New Yorker*, January 24, 2000.

"Naked Woman Playing Chopin" in *The New Yorker*, June 27, 1998.

"Shamengwa" in *The New Yorker*, December 2, 2002, and *Best American Short Stories*, 2003.

"The Shawl" in *The New Yorker*, March 5, 2001.

"The Butcher's Wife" in *The New Yorker*, April 17, 2000, and *O. Henry Prize Stories*, 2002.

"Revival Road" in *The New Yorker*, April 17, 2000, and *O. Henry Prize Stories*, 2001.

"The Painted Drum" in *The New Yorker*, March 3, 2003.

GRATEFUL ACKNOWLEDGEMENT IS made to Henry Holt, for permission to print stories that later appeared in *Love Medicine*, *The Beet Queen*, and *Tracks* in slightly different form:

From *Love Medicine* (Holt, Rinehart and Winston, 1984): "The Red Convertible," "Scales," "The World's Greatest Fisherman," "Saint Marie," and "The Plunge of the Brave."

From *The Beet Queen* (Henry Holt, 1986): "The Beet Queen," "Pounding the Dog," "Knives," "Destiny," and "The Little Book."

From *Tracks* (Henry Holt, 1988): "Snares" and "Fleur."